Praise for

PATRICIA POTTER'S
bestselling novels

Cold Target

"Potter weaves suspense and emotional drama in rare form in this fascinating novel of corrupt power on a collision course with family honor."   —*BookPage*

"Potter spins a complex web of buried secrets into a gripping tale of betrayal, lust, love, and conspiracy. The way she weaves all the threads together is nothing short of brilliant."   —*Rendezvous*

Twisted Shadows

"With three fully developed characters, a number of likable minor ones, and a slew of villains, not to mention an edge-of-the-seat plot, it is nearly impossible to put *Twisted Shadows* down, once started. There is nothing better than a novel that is equally character-driven and plot-driven, and Patricia Potter excels in them . . . She knows how to entertain readers . . . For a story of love that grows amidst lies and betrayals, be sure to block out sufficient time to thoroughly enjoy this riveting, highly recommended novel."   —*Romance Reviews Today*

"Ms. Potter delivers with this thrilling drama. The characters are great and the tension is kept at a high level through the whole book."   —*Rendezvous*

continued . . .

"Potter's recent foray into the contemporary arena has been a dazzling success. With romantic flair and emotional intensity that is classic Potter, *Twisted Shadows* ensures that her success is likely to continue." —*Library Journal*

"Fraught with danger at every turn, this read grips you with its suspense and holds your attention with the sizzling romance." —*The Best Reviews*

Broken Honor

"Palms will sweat and hearts will race . . . This well-written crossover novel will thrill lovers of the suspense genre as well as those who enjoy a good romance." —*Booklist*

"Although Potter is better known for her historical romances, this bracing romantic thriller proves that she's just as comfortable writing in the contemporary arena." —*Publishers Weekly*

The Perfect Family

"The reader loses all sense of time as they become entangled in a web of mystery Ms. Potter spins in *The Perfect Family* . . . Flawless characterizations . . . You are holding a work of art when you pick up a book by Patricia Potter." —*Rendezvous*

"This is a novel that will long be remembered by those who read it." —*Midwest Book Review*

PATRICIA POTTER . . .

". . . will thrill lovers of the suspense genre
as well as those who enjoy a good romance."
—*Booklist*

". . . proves herself a gifted writer as artisan,
creating a rich fabric of strong characters
whose wit and intellect will enthrall
even as their adventures entertain."
—*BookPage*

". . . has a special gift for giving an audience
a first-class romantic story line."
—*Affaire de Coeur*

"The Potter treatment . . . is pure action and
excitement, and the characters are wonderful."
—*Midwest Book Review*

"One of the best."
—*BookBrowser*

Tangle of Lies

Patricia Potter

BERKLEY SENSATION, NEW YORK

THE BERKLEY PUBLISHING GROUP
Published by the Penguin Group
Penguin Group (USA) Inc.
375 Hudson Street, New York, New York 10014, USA
Penguin Group (Canada), 10 Alcorn Avenue, Toronto, Ontario M4V 3B2, Canada
(a division of Pearson Penguin Canada Inc.)
Penguin Books Ltd., 80 Strand, London WC2R 0RL, England
Penguin Group Ireland, 25 St. Stephen's Green, Dublin 2, Ireland (a division of Penguin Books Ltd.)
Penguin Group (Australia), 250 Camberwell Road, Camberwell, Victoria 3124, Australia
(a division of Pearson Australia Group Pty. Ltd.)
Penguin Books India Pvt. Ltd., 11 Community Centre, Panchsheel Park, New Delhi—110 017, India
Penguin Group (NZ), Cnr. Airborne and Rosedale Roads, Albany, Auckland 1310, New Zealand
(a division of Pearson New Zealand Ltd.)
Penguin Books (South Africa) (Pty.) Ltd., 24 Sturdee Avenue, Rosebank, Johannesburg 2196,
South Africa

Penguin Books Ltd., Registered Offices: 80 Strand, London WC2R 0RL, England

This is a work of fiction. Names, characters, places, and incidents either are the product of the author's imagination or are used fictitiously, and any resemblance to actual persons, living or dead, business establishments, events, or locales is entirely coincidental.

TANGLE OF LIES

A Berkley Sensation Book / published by arrangement with the author

PRINTING HISTORY
Berkley Sensation edition / June 2005

Copyright © 2005 by Patricia Potter.
Cover design by Brad Springer.

ISBN: 0-425-20394-8

BERKLEY® SENSATION
Berkley Sensation Books are published by The Berkley Publishing Group,
a division of Penguin Group (USA) Inc.,
375 Hudson Street, New York, New York 10014.
BERKLEY SENSATION and the "B" design are trademarks belonging to Penguin Group (USA) Inc.

PRINTED IN THE UNITED STATES OF AMERICA

10 9 8 7 6 5 4 3 2 1

chapter one

SANTA FE, NEW MEXICO
JUNE 2004

Missing!

Her father's panicked voice raised the hackles on Liz Connor's spine.

Don't jump to conclusions.

"Dad, slow down. Tell me again." Her hand clutched the receiver tightly.

"I came home to pick up your mother to meet you," he said, a raw edge in his voice. "I had an early meeting with the school superintendent. When I arrived home, the front door was unlocked. Daisy was outside."

"Maybe one of Sue's kids had an emergency," she said, although her father's panic was beginning to affect her. Even if her sister, Sue, had an emergency, her mother would never, ever leave the dog outside nor the door unlocked. "When did you get home?"

"At noon. There's something else," he continued. "The computers are gone."

The first cold tentacles of fear crawled up her back as her father's words sank in. Her mother had called early this morning, clearly excited about Liz's closing on a business she'd been seeking for several years, a business that was intended to involve them all. The celebratory luncheon had been her mother's idea, another step toward conciliation in a rocky path that had stretched from childhood.

They were coming together as a family. Finally.

"Computers?" she asked, still trying to understand.

"Both are gone. Neither is worth the trouble of dragging them out," her father continued in a ragged voice. "But I'd hoped she might be there with you or had tried to call you, or . . ." His voice trailed off.

"No," she said. "I've been here at the law offices for an hour, but my cell phone is on. What about Sue? Has she heard anything?"

"I called you first. I thought . . . well, since we were to meet you . . . that Betty would call if anything had delayed her."

Liz sought some kind of logical explanation, but her mother was probably the most dependable, conscientious person in Santa Fe. "Is anything else missing from the house?"

"Not that I could tell."

"She's probably out running an errand," Liz said with more conviction than she really had. "Maybe there was a problem with the computers, or she took them over for the kids, or . . ." Her mother doted on Sue, who'd always been the perfect daughter and was now the perfect mother of two very nice children.

It sounded weak even to her. There were two things her mother never did: leave the dog outside and leave the door unlocked.

Nor would she miss this lunch. She and her mother had fought for twenty years. Liz had always been her father's daughter, and she had a streak of independence that had confused and alarmed an overly protective mother who then had set stronger rules. As a result, Liz had rebelled over and over again. There had been a tremendous explosion when she'd set off with several friends on a bicycle trek halfway around the country after finishing high school, and the damage had lasted twelve years. It was only recently that they'd made their peace, that each had come to appreciate the other.

Today—Monday—was to have been a culmination of

that reconciliation. A celebration after Liz signed the papers making her owner of Santa Fe Adventures and her recent appointment to the Santa Fe City Council.

Her mother and father should have been at her attorney's office an hour ago.

It had been unlike them to be late, but she hadn't really been worried. She attributed it to traffic in the tourist-clogged streets of summer.

She jiggled the phone in her hand as she tried to reassure both her father and herself. "Perhaps she decided to come alone and meet you here and is just running late. The traffic . . ."

Her voice trailed off. Then, "We're jumping to conclusions," she said, trying desperately to tamp down the growing sense of disquiet. "There's a simple explanation, and we'll all laugh about it when she gets here."

But what about the missing computers?

Thieves wouldn't have taken two almost obsolete computers. Not unless they'd been interrupted. But still, wouldn't they have grabbed something else?

Though her parents weren't wealthy, they did own some wonderful pieces of western art and silver Native American jewelry her father had bought for her mother.

"That's probably it," her father said, but his voice was laced with the doubt—even the touch of the panic—she felt. Her mother and father had always been very close, sometimes so close they seemed to be the only two people in the world. Liz had once resented that. Now she appreciated it.

"Have you called the sheriff's department?"

"I thought I would call you first and make sure we hadn't gotten our signals mixed in some way."

"Call Sue," she said. "If she hasn't heard anything, then call Roy Barrett. I'll wait here."

Her heart thudding, she went into the attorney's office. She told herself there was no reason to panic. There must be a reasonable explanation. Yet her mother certainly would have left a note.

She's at Sue's. There must be an emergency. One of the kids had an accident, or . . .

Her hands shook, and she didn't quite know why.

Perhaps it had been the fear in her father's voice. A high school principal, he was the steadiest and most balanced man she knew. Yet Liz had felt his terror over the line. And he did not frighten easily.

Did he know something he wasn't telling her?

No, not her father. He'd always stressed openness. Truth. Justice. The American way. For a moment she had to smile, because it was so darn corny.

She swallowed hard as the receptionist stared at her. "Is there anything I can do for you, Ms. Connor?" she asked.

"May I stay here a few moments?" Liz asked. "I'm waiting for a phone call."

"Of course," the woman said. "Stay as long as you like."

Liz prayed it would be a very short stay.

She glanced over the papers in the yellow envelope and tried to think of the contents.

Hers. She'd finally been able to buy the business that had employed her these past eight years. Now she could do things her way. Her father would serve as a teacher guide during the summer months when his school was closed. No one knew more about the Pueblos—and the area's Native American heritage—than he did. Nor loved them more. Her mother, who was an amazing cook, would prepare food for rafting and trail trips, and Sue would be the book-keeper.

Liz had high hopes for the plan. Her mother had been a homemaker and, as far as Liz knew, had not worked since her marriage. Now she'd seemed eager to join in the business and contribute what she did best.

Liz thought about calling hospitals, but then she might miss her father's call. So she sat, staring at the door, willing it to open and admit her mother. She thought about possibilities. There had been a number of burglaries, and one had resulted in the death of a prominent Santa Fe resident. But her parents' home was not in the same class as those burglarized. Theirs was a fairly modest ranch, more valuable now that property prices were spiraling but certainly nothing in the class of recent burglaries.

The phone rang again, and she answered it before the first ring ended.

"Dad?"

"Susan hasn't heard anything from her," he said. "I called the sheriff's department, but they said they couldn't do anything unless she was missing twenty-four hours. I told them some items were missing, that there was reason to suspect something had happened." He paused. "There was something odd about the response, almost as if—"

"As if what?"

"I'm not sure. The duty officer sounded almost . . . re-hearsed. I know it probably sounds paranoid, but he didn't pause to check with anyone."

"He probably gets these calls every day," she said.

"I called Roy Barrett, but his secretary said he was out and couldn't be reached. Dammit, we're friends."

Roy was the county sheriff and a frequent visitor to their home. "You said the computers were gone. Anything else?"

"I haven't had a chance to check everything, but your mom's address book isn't where she always keeps it. I thought I would call some of her friends, but it's gone."

"We'll find her," she said. "Perhaps she cut herself and went to the hospital, or a friend needed her."

"She would have called. She knows I have my cell phone with me all the time."

That's what bothered Liz as well. "Maybe she can't get to a phone," Liz said. Her mother had never liked cell phones, had never remembered to keep hers charged.

"I'll call the hospital," her father said.

"Call me if you hear anything. I'll do the same."

"I will," he said and clicked off.

Liz flipped the cell phone shut. *There's a reasonable explanation.* She kept repeating that mantra.

Roland Mathis, the attorney who had just guided her through the paperwork, entered the room and regarded her with concerned eyes. "Is anything wrong?"

"We've lost my mother," she said lightly, but a heaviness pressed hard against her heart. Her mother would never have left Daisy outside, no matter what the emergency. She protected that dog like it was her third born, particularly because the mutt didn't have the sense of a coconut. She was adorable but not very smart.

"Is there anything I can do?" Roland asked.

"I'm going to do a little searching. If she arrives, just tell her to call my dad or me immediately."

"I'll do that."

She left the office and headed for her car parked in the lot outside.

The sheriff's office said they couldn't do anything now.

Damn, but she would do something about that.

Computers gone.

That didn't make sense. Her mother had her own computer she used mostly to store recipes, chat with her grandchildren, and sometimes play solitaire. Her father's computer was used almost entirely for school business and research, and to accommodate his almost insatiable appetite for history.

No one would be interested in their content, and if thieves wanted the computers to sell, then there were more valuable things in her parents' home, particularly their paintings.

She looked down at the cell phone still clutched in her hand. She tried Susan, but the line was busy.

Finally, she dialed Robert Ames, the district attorney. If nothing else, he should be able to get the sheriff's department out to the house or at least alert them to look for her mother.

Like the sheriff, Robert was a close family friend. She'd even dated him for a brief period before he'd met and married her best friend. There had been no regrets, and all three remained close friends. They'd also worked together on several community boards before she'd been appointed to the Santa Fe City Council.

His secretary answered. "Sylvia, it's Liz Connor. Can I speak to Robert?"

There was a long pause. *Odd.* Sylvia was always bubbly and friendly, though often protective of her boss.

"I'll see if he's in," Sylvia finally said.

That was even more unusual. Sylvia would know whether Robert was in.

But she waited. A moment went by, then another, and tension tightened inside her. Something was very, very wrong.

Robert came on the line. "Liz. You should get down to my office."

Apprehension changed to terror. "Has something happened to my mother?"

"I can't talk about it on the phone."

"Is she . . . ?" She heard the quake in the words. *Oh God, please . . .*

"No, she's unharmed, but I would suggest you come down here." There was a discordant note in his voice. A measured objectivity, even wariness.

"Should I call my father? He reported her missing, and the sheriff's department wouldn't come."

"I think you should come alone." Still another oddity. *Why alone?*

"I'll call and tell him she's safe," she said, waiting for an answer that would tell her more.

"I wish you wouldn't," he said. "It's complicated." He hesitated, then added, "When will you be here?"

She stopped in front of her car and reached for her keys. "I'm eight blocks away. I should be there in no more than ten minutes."

The phone went dead before she could ask another question. Another puzzlement. Robert was never rude.

She thought about trying her father, but Robert was a friend to all the family. Surely he had a reason when he suggested she shouldn't. Had he lied about her mother being unharmed? She decided to wait before calling.

Walk or drive? It would probably take less time to walk than trying to move through the slow traffic and then find a parking place. She started walking, every step seeming to echo in the hot summer air.

Something was desperately wrong. Her steps became faster, then she moved into a jog as her heart pounded. She was a runner, but her heart seemed ready to burst when she reached the county building. She didn't wait for an elevator but took the steps two at a time. She knew she must look bedraggled when she entered Robert's outer office. Perspiration trickled down her back.

Sylvia's eyes didn't meet hers. Instead, she buzzed her boss. The door opened, and Robert Ames appeared at the door of his office.

Robert's normally pleasant face was cautious, and he didn't give her the affectionate hug she knew so well. Instead, he took her hand in greeting, then steered her toward his office. She glanced at his face. Nothing about it comforted her. He usually had an open, friendly expression, which worked well in a courtroom; opponents tended to underestimate him, and juries liked him. Behind those amiable brown eyes was a razor-sharp mind.

As they entered the office, she saw two men and a woman, all of them standing.

She studied them. The men wore suits with color-coordinated ties, the woman a dark pants suit. Despite the difference in genders, they had the same look about them. With a sickening feeling, she instinctively recognized them as enemies.

Her gaze returned to Robert who, for the first time since she'd known him, looked desperately uncomfortable.

He turned to the impeccably dressed men. "This is Liz Connor. Her mother is"—he hesitated, then added as if uncertain—"Betty Connor. Liz is a member of the city council."

She ignored the introduction and stared, instead, at Robert. "What is it?" she asked. "Where's my mother?"

One of the strangers stepped forward. He looked at Robert for a moment before saying something, obviously warning him off. Then he took a step toward her. "I'm Special Agent Robert Monroe with the FBI. The other agents are Sam Harris and Lou Mahoud."

She waited, steeling herself.

"Your mother has been arrested for first-degree murder."

chapter two

Murder? The beginning laughter choked in Liz's throat. A mistake. A hoax. A bad joke. Her mother was the most law-abiding, squeaky-clean, return-the-penny-mistakenly-given-to-her person in the universe.

But there was no amusement on any other face. They all looked carved from stone.

Her heartbeat went into overdrive. Her legs nearly buckled under her. She turned to Robert. "That's the most ridiculous thing I've ever heard," she said. "You know it. You know my mother. She can't bring herself to kill a flea."

His silence was like a dagger in her stomach.

"It's a joke," she said. "Something to do with the city council appointment, isn't it? Dad's in on it." She heard the plea in her words, even though she knew her father would never participate in anything so cruel.

"I'm sorry, Liz," Robert said. "It's no joke. Federal marshals arrested your mother a few hours ago on a fugitive warrant."

"I don't understand," she said.

"Her name is, or was, Sarah Jane Maynard," Robert said.

All four of them looked at her closely as if to see whether she would react. She didn't. The name meant nothing to her. But her heart sank as she saw their faces. They were convinced, even if she wasn't.

"What was this . . . this Sarah Jane Maynard supposed to have done?" she asked. "Specifically?"

The three agents exchanged glances, then Monroe shrugged. "She shot two armored car guards thirty-four years ago. They were killed in cold blood. One had a young son, the other five children."

Nothing could have shocked Liz more. "Where was all this supposed to have taken place?" ·

"Boston."

"Now I know you're wrong. She grew up in the Midwest."

"Are you sure? Have you met any of her relatives?"

That stopped her for a moment. "Her parents died. She was an only child."

"Convenient," one of the agents said.

"There'll be a press conference in two hours," Robert interrupted. "The FBI wanted to withhold the news until then. But when you called, I asked permission to tell you."

She stared at him with disbelieving eyes. "Permission?" Her eyes went to the three strangers, then back to Robert. "You weren't going to tell me, tell my father? You were going to let us hear through the media?"

"He wasn't available," Robert said. "If he'd been there when the arrest took place . . ."

"You could have contacted *me*. Tracy can always find me."

He glanced at the FBI agents, then his eyes shifted to the floor before returning to hers and met them squarely. "I couldn't, Liz."

"Oh, God, how long have you known?"

For the first time his eyes looked anguished. "I was sworn to silence," he said. "There's an ongoing investigation. Other . . . subjects of interest are involved."

"Other subjects of interest?" She knew her voice was rising. She didn't care. She couldn't believe what she was hearing.

"She had accomplices who are still at large," the FBI agent named Monroe said. "And there is a matter of a great deal of money that was never recovered. We hoped she would give us some names and locations before the news got out, but we've already been contacted by someone in the Washington media. We decided to move up the press conference."

Murder. Accomplices. She could not equate the words with her mother. Liz stared at the agents with disbelief. A chill seized her, though the room was warm. "Now I know you're wrong," she said. "We've never had 'a great deal of money,' and what do you mean by 'accomplices'?"

A mistake. She kept coming back to that. It must be a mistake. No one in Santa Fe was more respected than her parents. Her father was an educator, her mother a devoted homemaker who tutored poor students, worked quietly with the women's shelter, and made cookies and cakes to raise money for her other favorite endless causes.

Murder. It was absurd. More than absurd. *Impossible.*

The woman agent looked at her curiously, then tried to look sympathetic. "We know this must come as a shock, but surely you must have had some indications, some clues. We'll need the names of all her friends, contacts, acquaintances."

The address book and computers. Now *that,* at least, made sense. Except these people didn't know her mother.

She focused a glare at the female agent. "It's not shock. It's disbelief. Anyone who knows my mother will swear she couldn't hurt a fly."

"Perhaps not today," Agent Monroe interrupted with what Liz felt was false empathy. "But what about thirty-four years ago?"

She ignored his question. "Have you actually filed charges yet? Don't you need a grand jury?"

"There'll be an extradition hearing later this week," Monroe said.

She glared at him. "And you're holding a press conference first? Before you know whether you have the right person?"

"We know," Monroe said simply.

"Has she admitted it?"

"I haven't talked to her."

"Where is she?"

"I'm not sure where they've taken her," Monroe said evasively.

Liz suddenly understood why her father hadn't been told. They'd probably wanted her alone to ask their questions. Her father would have immediately gotten her an attorney. She turned to Robert. "She has a right to legal representation."

"Only if she requests for an attorney," Monroe said.

Fear was turning into anger, a cold fury. "I want to see her."

"She hasn't asked to see anyone."

"How do you know if you haven't seen her?"

He shrugged. "That's what I'm told."

"She's innocent, damn it." She whirled on Robert. "You know her. Tell him he's wrong."

Robert looked at her with pain on his face. When they had dated, the two of them had frequently been invited for supper at her parents' house. Her mother had doted on him. A very respectable husband for her wayward daughter. And she knew that Robert, like everyone, had liked her mother.

"They have proof, Liz."

"There's no doubt, Ms. Connor," Monroe said. "She's not denied it. She's being held as a fugitive."

"You're wrong," Liz insisted again. "My mother can't be the person you want."

Robert's gaze met hers. "I didn't believe it, either, but . . ." He glanced toward the agent who had addressed her, and the man nodded.

"Your mother was at the home of Gay Gardner six weeks ago," Robert continued.

"I was there, too," Liz said. "Half of Santa Fe was. It was a fund-raiser for the local theater."

"But *your* fingerprints didn't bring up anything."

"What do you mean?" she asked.

"The home was burglarized after the party. Because there has been a rash of burglaries and one of the owners was killed, the police collected fingerprints and sent them to AFIS. Several of the thefts had taken place after a party, and they thought the killer might be someone hired for the event. As luck would have it, a very big catch turned up in the database. One of the prints was identified as belonging to Sarah Jane Maynard. We matched her old photo to photos of those who attended the party, and yesterday we were able to get your mother's fingerprints from a water glass in a restaurant. They matched."

"I've heard about FBI mistakes," Liz said, "and I understand fingerprints are no longer considered error-free."

Monroe's pale skin turned red. "I don't know what you've heard, but fingerprints don't lie. The prints lifted from the Gardners' home came from our fugitive. We systematically eliminated everyone at the party but your mother."

She was startled. How long had they sifted through fingerprints and profiles without anyone knowing?

She seized on another question. "Why is the FBI involved?"

"She was a member of a particularly violent group of antiwar protestors. They attacked an armored car carrying worn money from banks to the Federal Reserve. That makes it federal. So does crossing state lines with federal property." He allowed time for the words to make an impact. "It always seemed perverse to me that some people kill to promote a message that killing is bad." He said the last as rather a philosophical observation.

Liz could barely contain her fury. Her mother was not an observation. The good Lord knew she'd had her disagreements with her mother, but only because she thought her mother had been far too protective and couldn't, or wouldn't, understand why Liz had always followed her own drummer. There was no questioning her mother's decency. Now, though, she knew her mother needed an attorney. Fast.

She looked at Robert for help. She tried to think when last she saw him. Had he known then of FBI suspicions? "How long have you known?" she demanded. "Why—"

"There are three other fugitives," Monroe broke in before Robert could answer. "We didn't want to alert them. We hoped to get information from her first."

"But a press conference . . . ?" She turned back to Robert.

"Word leaked out. Damn if I know how, but it did. It was only a matter of hours before the news would be everywhere."

"And you want to claim the credit," she said bitterly. "To hell with reputations and friendships."

Robert had the grace to flush. The others in the room stared at her with blank expressions.

The coward. He dove to the bottom rung of her regard. "She has the right to see an attorney," Liz insisted.

"She told the marshals she did not want one," Monroe replied. "As long as she doesn't ask for an attorney, our people can continue questioning her."

The fear deepened inside her. "I don't believe you."

"Nonetheless, it's true."

The first seed of doubt pricked at her, and she searched for explanations. "She must be confused. Understandably so," Liz said. "Where is she?"

He hesitated, debating about answering, then said, "She'll be held at the Metropolitan Detention Center in Albuquerque."

Liz felt she had landed in another universe. Or in Wonderland. Nothing was as it should be. How could her mother not want an attorney?

The sickness in the pit of her stomach worsened. Something was not right. This was not a minor mistake to be instantly corrected.

"I want to see her," she repeated. "I have a right."

The FBI agent appeared to be considering the request. "We'll want interviews with you and other members of your family."

"Not until we see Mom," she said.

"Cooperate with us, and we'll cooperate with you," he said.

She doubted it. "I want an attorney first. I won't discuss my mother with you until I know more." She turned toward the door. "And I *will* see my mother. But now I have to talk to my father. He's been terrified for her. He came home—" She stopped. "Did you take computers from their home?"

"We had a search warrant."

She was rigid with anger now. "My father is looking everywhere for her. He found the door to the house open, the dog outside, and computers missing. No note, no one waiting there to tell him."

"Marshals picked her up," Monroe said. "They also took the computers. They wanted to get her to Albuquerque—" He stopped suddenly as if wondering why he was explaining himself.

Why the rush? Unless they feared a backlash from this community?

Was that why they were planning a press conference, to get their story out first? She had to get to her father. "You're going to look very silly—and inept—when you have to acknowledge you have the wrong person, but then it will be too late for my parents. Don't you care that you will destroy both my mother and father's reputations?"

"It won't if, as you say, she's innocent," Monroe said.

"You can never remove the stain," Liz said. "You know that. Must you hold a press conference, for God's sake? Even before you know for sure—"

"We know for sure," Monroe said.

"Damn you," she said. She turned toward Robert. "And you." She knew enough about publicity to know what this would do to her mother, to her father's position as principal. *Dear God.*

She had to leave before tears of pure rage and frustration betrayed her.

She gave Robert a long, hard look, then turned and took the few steps toward the door. She thought they might stop her, but they didn't.

She turned back to them as she opened the door. "I'll be in Albuquerque with an attorney within two hours," she repeated. "I expect to see her."

Monroe's expression did not change. "You'll have to wait for visiting hours."

Visiting hours. Another shock. Liz knew then she'd not accepted what was happening as real. They'd been talking about someone else. Not her mother. Hearing the words now was like a splash of freezing water.

"Won't you even consider the possibility that you're wrong and postpone the press conference?" Liz asked, hearing the hopeless plea in her words and hating it.

A fleeting second of empathy raced across Monroe's eyes before they went blank. "I'm sorry, Ms. Connor." He didn't sound sorry at all. He sounded like a man who had just landed a big fish and now wanted to brag about it to everyone.

"My mother is Betty Connor," Liz insisted, though a tiny seed of doubt snaked through her. There was an assurance about the man, and discomfort in Robert. The air was fused with tension. She *knew* they thought they had the right person.

They were wrong.

They *had* to be wrong. Her mother was apolitical. Her father was interested in politics but because of his position kept his opinions to himself except within the family circle. There he'd often encouraged discussions over the dinner table. He'd asked questions and sought answers.

But now she remembered that her mother never gave many. She'd seldom expressed opinions, letting her husband prod conversations. Yet she'd always encouraged her children to read and keep an open mind. "Children must think for themselves," her mother had said. "You must honor values, fight for them."

But Liz also remembered now how her mother tensed when certain subjects were mentioned.

She left Robert's office without another word. She passed Sylvie and went into the hall where she leaned against a wall for a moment. Her heart raced. She could barely breathe.

She had to reach her father, and together they had to find an attorney. Immediately.

Together, as a family, they could prove the charges a lie. Or a terrible mistake that could be corrected.

Still, she couldn't control the fear that numbed her. She knew the power of the federal government. It could turn lives upside down, then leave without regret.

But she and her father were not without influence and friends. And she would not hesitate to call on each and every one of them.

But why had her mother refused an attorney? Or was that a lie? If not, then why?

The why screamed at her as she called her father. He was at home waiting, and she explained briefly what had happened. "It's a case of mistaken identity," she assured him.

She heard his sigh of relief over the line. His wife was alive!

"I'll be there soon and explain everything," she said.

Then she called her sister. Sue answered immediately. She'd obviously been sitting right next to the phone.

"Sue, ask David to find a good criminal attorney. Immediately."

"It has something to do with Mom," Sue said, her panic evident. "Dad said she was missing."

"It's just a mistake. The FBI has her confused with someone else, that's all. But we need an attorney in Albuquerque."

"David's a civil attorney," Sue pointed out.

"I know, but he's active in the bar association. He should know someone."

A pause. Despite being an attorney, Sue's husband hated controversy, hated discord, hated even the hint of scandal.

"I'll call him," Sue said. "Where is Mom now?"

"All I know is they're taking her, or have taken her, to Albuquerque. She's being held on charges of being a fugitive." Liz hesitated, then knew she had to continue. Sue shouldn't hear it on television.

"The FBI is planning to hold a press conference in about two hours," she said. "They're going to say Mom . . . Mom killed someone more than thirty years ago and has been on their most wanted list all these years."

"Mom?" Her own disbelief several minutes earlier was reflected in Sue's voice. "That's crazy."

"You and I know it, but the FBI doesn't. I'm sure a good attorney can sort it out."

"Does Dad know?"

"Some of it. I'm going to pick him up at home and drive to Albuquerque."

A pause. "I wish I could go, but the kids . . ."

"I know. You stay here and take care of things. The phone will be ringing, and you'll probably be mobbed by reporters. Why don't you take the kids over to David's sister's and stay there a few days?"

"I want to tell them they're wrong."

"Anything you say might hurt Mom," Liz said. "Just stay away from the press until we know more."

A silence, then reluctantly, "All right."

"Leave as soon as you can."

"Don't leave me out."

"I won't. I promise. Tell David to call me on my cell phone." Liz hung up and started the walk back to her jeep.

She'd been so happy when she'd driven into the parking lot just three hours earlier—or was it a lifetime ago?

Wrong. Wrong. Wrong. They are wrong.

She unlocked the jeep and stepped into an oven. She turned on the air-conditioning, then called Tracy, the office manager at Adventures.

"Hi, boss," came her cheery greeting.

"Tracy," she said. "I won't be back this afternoon and perhaps tomorrow. Can you handle everything?"

"Of course. Big celebration?"

"Some family business," Liz said, as she left the parking lot and turned onto East Marcy Street. "I have to go, Trace, but thanks. I'll keep in touch. Call the cell phone if you need anything."

"Will do. And congratulations."

The word echoed in the interior of the jeep.

Congratulations.

She took a deep breath. Her heart pounded. Ached.

She had to force herself to drive, to breathe.

Murder.

Robbery.

No matter what anyone said, she knew her mother. Despite their heated arguments over the years, she knew Betty

Connor was incapable of physically hurting another human being.

Still, she shivered in the heat as fear and uncertainty seeped through her body and lingered. Something dark and shadowy was gathering around those she loved.

chapter three

The shadows lingered as she fought the traffic.

She turned on the radio, flipping from station to station to see whether there was even a hint of the coming media hurricane. Nothing.

Then as she turned to another station, she heard a bulletin:

"The FBI has announced it will hold a press conference at three p.m. today at the district attorney's office. No details were disclosed. Keep tuned to this station for a live broadcast."

It was starting. And she knew it would impact her family as nothing else ever could. Even when her mother was cleared, as Liz knew she would be, her family could well be destroyed. Their reputation certainly would be. People remembered only the headlines.

She swallowed the lump in her throat even as she realized none of that was important at the moment. Her mother's life was.

She turned at the next intersection. Her parents lived just five miles outside the city. As she pulled into the driveway, she saw her father on the porch. Daisy sat at his feet, huddling as close to him as possible. The dog obviously sensed something was wrong, but then she had been left out alone this morning, and she hated to be outside. She was a timid soul who always wanted to be around her people.

Liz stepped out of the bright red jeep with Santa Fe Adventures written on both sides.

"Tell me everything," her father said, his eyes boring into hers.

She did. She told him everything the agents had said and watched as her father's ruddy face paled and his hands clenched into fists.

"I know it must be some kind of mistake," she said. "David is looking for an attorney now. I asked him to have someone meet us in Albuquerque."

"You said she didn't want an attorney," her father said. "She has to request one."

"She will. She must be confused and devastated and humiliated," Liz said. "You know how she always wants to save money. She probably thought the mistake could be cleared up without one." She had held on to that thought, dismissing the first traitorous explanation.

Her father looked as if he had aged dramatically. He'd always looked younger than his years with his fit body, full head of hair, and tanned skin. He loved the outdoors as she did, a common interest that had created a special bond between them. Now his eyes were red-rimmed, and worry etched trails in his face.

Liz suddenly realized that her explanation hadn't been so much a surprise as a dreaded confirmation.

"You know something," she said.

He shook his head. "I know something has always haunted your mother, that she seemed worried that someone might find her. You know how careful she has always been about locks, about your safety, and your sister's. I thought it might have been an abusive boyfriend or father. Even a former husband. I thought someday she would tell me, and then years went by, and whenever something came up, or I pressed, she would get a look in her eyes that scared me. I finally stopped probing. I thought someday . . ."

Startled, she could only look at him, wondering about her own lack of observation. She was only too familiar with her mother's overprotectiveness. It had driven a huge wedge between them because Liz by nature was adventuresome and independent. But she'd never seen the fear behind it, not the kind that her father was explaining. How could she have missed it?

"But you never thought she could be involved in anything like theft, much less murder?"

"Of course not," he said. "But she would have been young then, and you know she always wants to save the world. Maybe she was led into something . . ."

"Not murder."

"No," he agreed. "Not Betty."

She looked at him for a long time, wondering about the relationship her parents had. She'd always thought it was perfect. She'd never felt the undercurrents. Never. She remembered a conversation with a friend about a teacher who had been cheating on his wife with one of his students.

"Every family has secrets," her friend said.

"Not mine," Liz had replied with confidence.

She closed her eyes for a moment. *This isn't happening. It can't be happening.*

Then she realized they had no time to waste. Once the press conference was held, they would be surrounded by both print and electronic press.

"There'll be a press conference soon. Reporters will be crawling all over us. We need to go."

"What about Daisy?" The question was another jolt. Steve Connor was a decisive man who made instant decisions. But now he stood in front of her like a man lost.

"Your neighbors will take her in until we get back."

He closed his eyes, then nodded.

"You might want to get a change of clothes and your shaving gear," she said. "We'll probably stay overnight."

He nodded and walked inside. The usual decisiveness in his stride was gone, and he moved like an old man. She went in with him and fetched a bag of Daisy's food and her leash. Daisy followed nervously, whining her confusion and apprehension. Liz leaned down and rubbed her rump, Daisy's favorite place, and the dog wriggled with gratitude. Daisy was another of her mother's causes, a pound dog who had obviously been abused. She had to be forced out of her own yard when her dad wanted to take a walk and usually hid when strangers came. However, her parents' neighbors, the Stewarts, were frequent visitors and had often fed the dog and even had kept her on several occasions. They were the only people Daisy tolerated other than her family.

She put Daisy in the backseat of the jeep and waited.

Minutes later, her father returned, an overnighter in hand. It reminded her she hadn't packed anything, but she wasn't going to waste time by returning to her house. She could buy what she needed.

She was grateful she'd dressed informally for the closing. She'd worn a simple, wash-and-wear short-sleeved blouse, a leather vest, and tailored slacks, her usual uniform at work.

Every moment was important now. Each minute was sixty seconds longer before she reached her mother. Something very wrong was happening, and she suspected things were going to get worse before they got better.

Her father came over to the driver's side and looked in. "I can take my car."

"Let's go together," she said. "I need you." She also suspected he needed *her*.

His hand on the door was trembling slightly. He simply nodded and went around to the passenger's side.

After Liz backed out of the driveway, she reached over and touched his hand. "Everything will be all right," she said. "No one will believe she could do what they're saying. Everyone loves her."

"They do, don't they?" he said. "I don't think there's a cause in Santa Fe she hasn't been involved in." He paused, then added, "But never as an officer, never as a leader despite all the pleas. Hell, it took me years to get her out of the house." He slammed his fist against the dashboard. "Damn, why didn't I ask more questions?"

"She probably wouldn't have answered them," she said, even as the question nagged her as well. Why hadn't she asked more questions as a child? Why hadn't she questioned more why they had no extended family? Her father had been orphaned at a young age. She'd understood that her mother's parents were dead as well. She'd always thought that fact had brought her parents together.

She wanted to probe further. But looking at his face, she knew now was not the time to ask. She also wasn't sure of the legalities involved. He was protected by spousal protection laws. He couldn't be forced to testify against his wife. Liz didn't think she had that same protection.

Was it going to be important?

For the first time in her life, she started to think of the federal authorities as her enemies. "Maybe you shouldn't tell me anything more until you talk to Mom."

"Why?"

"You have spousal privilege, Dad. I don't. Anything we say, well, it might be hearsay, but I don't know all the legalities."

He stared at her with anguish in his eyes, yet she saw a dawning understanding there as well.

They stopped at the Stewarts' house, which was called next door but was actually a quarter mile away. Beth Stewart was there and said she would happily keep Daisy for a few days when Liz explained there was a family emergency. Liz hurried back to her jeep.

What would Beth think when she learned the nature of the "emergency"?

Liz hoped it wouldn't matter. She prayed that it wouldn't.

Sickened by her thoughts, she turned onto the road that would take them to the interstate. Albuquerque was sixty miles away, a fifty-minute drive on the interstate.

She took it rather than the scenic trail she usually preferred. She kept the gas pedal down and tried to concentrate on the road ahead. It was a perfect New Mexico afternoon. The copper-colored sun looked as if it were burning its way through a breathlessly pristine blue sky. Yet it was the most imperfect day Liz could remember.

She darted a look at her father. He sat stiff and silent beside her. She wanted to reach out to him, but he looked frozen and unapproachable, drawn up into himself.

Her cell phone rang.

She usually didn't answer it on the road, but today she

did and heard Sue's stressed voice. "David found an attorney. He should be going to the jail now," she said. "Colton Montgomery. David says he's one of the best criminal attorneys in New Mexico."

Relief flooded Liz. "Good."

"You'll let me know what Mom says? What the attorney says?"

"Of course. As soon as I can."

"They're beginning a press conference on televison. Dear God, Liz, I can't believe this."

"Have you left the house?"

"Yes."

"Stay away and don't answer the phone. Don't talk to anyone until you hear from me and the attorney."

"But someone should defend her."

"Someone who's qualified," Liz said. "We can't have anything come back and haunt us."

A silence. "*You* surely don't think there's anything to this? Not Mom. Anyone but Mom."

"Of course I don't, but we have to be cautious. Just don't say anything at all now," she pleaded.

"David is trying to find out what he can. He'll be vice president of the bar association next year. Oh damn, you don't think . . ." Liz had never heard her sister use even a mild profanity before.

"I don't think anything now," she said.

"Is Daddy there?"

"Yes. Here he is."

Liz handed the phone to her father. His voice didn't brighten as it usually did when he spoke to his children.

"It'll be okay," he said. "I know. I'll ask her to call you. She might even come home with us tonight."

Liz inwardly wept at the faint hope in his voice. Betty Connor would not be coming home tonight, not with the kind of charges she faced, not with a press conference heralding her capture as a fugitive for more than three decades.

Her father finished, folded the phone, and handed it back to her.

They drove the rest of the way in silence, but the fear was shared, and palpable.

SANGRE DE CRISTO MOUNTAINS, NEW MEXICO

Garrett Caleb Adams ignored the incessant ringing of the phone inside his cabin and took another sip of whiskey.

He was doing what he did every afternoon. He started after the sun dropped over the yardarm. But some days he would get a jump on it. After all, somewhere in the universe the sun had dropped over the yardarm.

First there was that pleasant glow as the whiskey hit his system. The sunset would glow a little brighter, the colors would become more intense. He would watch as veins of gold streaked down the face of the mountains, then as the shadows gradually shrouded them.

The loneliness would hit then. The fact that he was watching alone, that his wife and son were gone. And the glow turned into a mindless rush toward oblivion.

He knew the pattern, but he had neither the will nor the desire to change it. It was self-destructive and self-pitying, but he didn't care. He didn't care about a damn thing any longer.

The phone continued to ring. It would stop, then start again.

Resentment filled him. He had cut off contact with everyone. He didn't want friendships. Buddies. Even acquaintances. He wanted to be left alone, except in those rare instances he needed money for the cabin or taxes; then he would contact a few attorneys he knew to let them know he was available again as an investigator.

It didn't happen often, and recently, even less.

That was probably the call. Someone wanted his services. No one else called.

They are persistent.

Tramp emitted a low growl beside him. Even the stray dog who'd adopted him was irritated by the constant ringing.

Reluctantly, he rose, thinking he would take the phone off the hook. But it seldom rang like that. Most people just gave up.

He limped inside, refilled his glass, and glared at the phone. It stopped ringing.

An intimidated phone. He liked that thought.

He started for the door again. It was a cool summer evening, the kind Maryann—his Annie—had relished. The whisper of the breezes through the trees, the haunting cry of an owl, even the occasional howl of coyotes reminded him of the sunsets they'd shared. She'd loved these mountains long before he had come to appreciate them.

The phone started ringing again.

What the hell, he might as well answer it.

"What is it?" he snapped after returning to the phone and picking up the receiver.

"Caleb? Don't you ever answer your phone?"

"Not if I can help it. You were driving my dog nuts."

A chuckle he didn't appreciate.

"What do you want?"

"No hello? How's Ellen? Have I died?"

"If you died, you wouldn't be bothering me."

Another chuckle, then, "I have news you would be interested in," Cam Douglas said. "Knowing your hermit ways, I thought you may not have heard." Cam had been his partner years ago in the Boston Police Department. The two Cs, the others had called them. Not only were their names similar, but they both had blond hair and green eyes. Twins separated by birth was the much too common joke. Even their wives had similar coloring and personalities.

But though friends, they had far different personalities. Caleb, until his marriage, had always been a loner, and Cam was gregarious. Caleb had wanted nothing more than to be home with his family. Cam loved to be with the other cops. They respected each other and were friends, but Cam's sympathy after the death of his wife and son had been difficult to accept. Caleb's wounds had been too deep, his guilt too strong. And Cam's wife was alive and well, and too often neglected.

Caleb waited for Cam to continue.

"No television yet?"

"No."

"Computer?"

"Cam, just tell me."

"The Feds arrested one of the group that robbed the armored car back in the early seventies, the case that so obsessed you. Right down the road from you. We were notified because it's our jurisdiction, or at least it is unless the Feds try to keep it in the federal system."

Caleb stiffened, all the effects of the booze draining from his system. He'd become a cop because of his father's murder. His father had always wanted to be an officer but had never passed the physical because of a bad knee sustained when playing high school football. Other fathers had wanted their kids to be doctors and lawyers. Sam Murphy had wanted his son to be a cop.

Caleb had adored his father, who had played baseball and football with him, attended every game he could, and had given him unconditional love. Then one day Caleb came home and found his mother sobbing. His father had been killed in a robbery. Caleb had made it his life's goal then to track down the killers.

His mother eventually remarried—a life insurance salesman who'd promised security. For her, Caleb had allowed his stepfather to legally adopt him, before they both discovered that the man was abusive both physically and emotionally. When Caleb was thirteen, he'd been big enough and strong enough to confront Charles Adams and tell him to get out of the house or he'd kill him.

His stepfather believed it. But it meant the next thing to poverty, and he'd watched his mother age in front of him and die, as much from heartbreak as illness, when he was eighteen.

Caleb had thought often about casting aside the name, but he didn't because even then he'd known what he was going to do. He was going to find the people who killed his father and destroyed his mother.

"Caleb?"

He wondered how many seconds had passed. Or minutes.

"What do you mean, 'down the road'?"

"The Feds announced the arrest of Sarah Jane Maynard.

She's been going by the name of Betty Connor. And get this, she's the wife of a high school principal in Santa Fe."

Shock rocked him again. He recognized the name of Sarah Jane Maynard. He'd memorized the names of every one of the suspects in the robbery. He'd spent years looking for them. And now, she was fifty miles away. He couldn't believe the irony.

He lived in the Sangre de Cristo Mountains, fifty miles north of Santa Fe, but he seldom went there. He preferred the smaller, less Anglicized communities to do what little shopping he did. Would he have recognized her from old photos if he'd seen her on the rare occasions he'd gone to Santa Fe?

"What about the others?" he said.

"Nothing yet, but they hope the Maynard woman will lead them to the others."

Caleb's throat dried. His heart beat rapidly.

He hadn't thought he was capable of that kind of emotion any longer. But he was. God, but he was. After all these years . . .

"Thanks, Cam," he managed to say.

He thought he heard Cam's surprise across the miles. Caleb knew he had not been kind to his partner after the explosion. He'd retreated from any and every expression of sorrow, concern. He'd simply hurt too much. He was like a wounded animal who'd only wanted to wander off and die alone. The place he came to had been New Mexico, because his wife had once lived in Taos and loved it. They'd vacationed here the year before his wife and son died.

He'd thought that a part of her might still be there.

If so, he hadn't found it.

But the stark landscape had appealed to him, as had the fact that he could be entirely alone.

"I'll keep you posted," Cam said.

"Thanks," Caleb said again, now anxious to get rid of him. He didn't have a televison, but he did have a computer. He didn't use it often, but he hadn't been able to completely sever the cord between himself and civilization, and it was necessary for what investigative work he did.

He hung up without any more words and went back outside, thinking about the arrest, his mind filling with purpose for the first time in years.

Now perhaps he could find a measure of justice. He hadn't found it when searching for his father's killers. Nor had he found it when his wife and son died. But perhaps he could close one of those wounds.

He looked down at the glass of whiskey, then threw it onto the ground. He went inside to his computer. He would find out everything he could about the woman. Then he would attend the first hearing.

He wanted to see the woman who had killed his father.

BOSTON

Win Maynard was unhappy about the interruption. He was engaged in promising negotiations to take over a steel company he'd coveted for years. The company was awash in debt, but it would give Win a needed tax break, and he saw eventual promise in the firm.

His secretary buzzed again when he ignored it the first time.

He knew her well enough to realize she would not incur his wrath unless the call was of the utmost importance.

"What is it, Bess?" he asked impatiently.

"It's a Mr. Cutter from Washington. He said you would want this call."

Win stiffened. There was only one reason Jess Cutter would call. "Thank you. Tell him I'll call him back immediately."

Win rose and looked at the other three men in the room: Roger Mason, president of the steel company, Mason's attorney, and Michael Gallagher, Maynard's attorney.

"A family emergency," he said. "I'll be back immediately. In the meantime, Michael speaks for me."

He walked out of the office he loved. It was spacious and comfortable and often startled people who expected something ornate. He enjoyed surprising people.

He went into a small study adjoining his office and took out a cell phone. He wanted no record of this particular conversation.

"Jess, what's up?"

"The Feds have found Sarah Jane. She's been arrested."

Win's heart paused for a moment, or at least he felt as if it had. After thirty-four years, he'd started to relax. If she was still alive, she'd disappeared so deep he had come to believe she would never surface.

"Children?"

"Two daughters. And a husband who is a school principal. A very respectable family. Pillars of the community."

Win took a deep breath.

"Have they found any of the others?"

"Not yet, but they hope to get them now."

"Thanks, Jess. I owe you."

"Yes, you do," Cutter said.

Win hung up the phone. The steel deal meant nothing now. He mentally envisioned his empire collapsing upon itself.

He went into the next room. "Where are we?" he asked abruptly.

"Roger still has some reservations," Michael said.

Win speared Roger Mason with his gaze. "You have two days to consider it, and then the offer's off the table. You'll go bankrupt and end up with a fraction of what we're offering. Thank you both for coming." Without effort he had Roger Mason and his attorney on their feet and out the door.

When it closed, he turned to Michael, who raised an eyebrow. "Not the smoothest kick in the rear."

"I have more urgent business," Win said.

"I thought Mason Steel was urgent."

"That was before I found out my cousin has just been found."

Michael's brows flew up, but he remained quiet. Waiting.

Win knew Michael was well aware of the scandal in the family, that Sarah Jane Maynard, Win's cousin, had disappeared after a deadly armed robbery three decades ago.

She had also been the only child of the founder and

chairman of Maynard Industries. Win had been the son of the chairman's brother.

Win wouldn't have much faith in Michael had he not realized the attorney had researched his family. Win had wanted a barracuda as his personal and corporate attorney. But he also was aware that a barracuda could turn on its benefactor. He paid Michael enough to make sure that wouldn't happen.

Still, he had few illusions. Michael would know about the old man, the founder of Maynard Industries, about Sarah Jane, and about Sarah Jane's mother, who reportedly committed suicide. Her father had lived on, a shadow of the man he'd once been, until he died ten years ago, but years earlier he'd turned everything over to Win, his nephew and the only blood relative. But he'd never given up hope of finding his daughter and had left half his fortune in a trust for her.

Now the capture of Win's niece would renew the bad publicity that had haunted the family over the decades. Not only that, Win saw the future of Maynard Industries slipping away from him.

The news could not have come at a worse time. Win had finally decided it was safe to run for a Senate seat after years of financing the campaigns of others. He'd planned to announce his candidacy at the end of the month.

"How soon can you retain an attorney in Albuquerque?" he asked Michael.

"A matter of hours."

"I want the very best. I don't give a damn what it costs. I want her out on bail."

"That's not going to happen," Michael said, "not when she's been a fugitive all these years."

"See what you can do. I want to know where they are holding her. I want to reach out to her family. Hell, Michael, I want you on the next plane to New Mexico."

"Family loyalty?" Michael said with only the slightest sarcasm.

"Of course," Win said. "She's my cousin. We were close as children. I'll pay all the legal bills."

"What should I tell the family?"

"I want to meet with them, help them any way I can."

"Sentiment, Win?"

"She's my blood," Win said.

"And it'll help you to publicly stand by her rather than abandoning her," Michael said.

The boy knew him too well. "I want to hear from you within an hour about an attorney."

Michael nodded.

Win gave him a rare smile of approval. Michael had turned out to be more useful than he'd ever hoped. There was nothing like taking a poor kid and giving him opportunity. Hunger was a great motivator. Not hunger for food but hunger for a better future.

He quieted the reminder that he had done that once before. And he was still feeling the consequences.

But Michael was not Tony.

He tried to convince himself of that as Michael turned and disappeared down the hall.

chapter four

Liz drove directly to the Metropolitan Detention Center and parked.

She and her father went to the reception area, waited in line to speak to a clerk, and asked for Betty Connor.

There was no such person in the computer, according to the bored clerk.

"Try Sarah Jane Maynard," she said.

The woman checked the computer again, then shook her head. "Still nothing."

"The FBI said she was here."

"Well, the computer says otherwise. Next."

Liz exchanged a glance with her father and stepped away from the counter. She took out her cell phone and dialed Robert Ames. Sylvie answered.

"Sylvie, this is Liz. Can I talk to Robert?"

"There are reporters in with him," she said.

Liz privately condemned him as a traitor and opportunist. "I don't care," she said.

"I'm sorry. He said he couldn't be disturbed."

"Can you tell me how to reach the agents who were with him?"

"They're still in there with him."

"Will you at least ask him to call me as soon as he can?" Her fingers tightened around the phone until they hurt. She wanted to say something else, but she'd long ago learned anger accomplished little.

"Of course."

A side door opened, and Liz turned to watch a dapper man in his fifties or early sixties walk in. His piercing brown eyes moved around the room as if he was looking for someone, then settled on her. He walked quickly to her. "Ms. Connor?"

She nodded.

"I'm Colton Montgomery. Your brother-in-law asked me to meet you here. Is this your father?"

She took a harder inventory. Montgomery wore an obviously expensive Western-style suit and cowboy boots, and he made no attempt to dye his graying thick brown hair.

She nodded, and both she and her father shook hands with him. She was comforted only slightly by the firm clasp. He was probably practiced in being comforting. "We were told that my mother had been brought here, but the clerk says she's not in the computer."

"It's an old trick, moving a suspect from location to location so an attorney can't catch up with them. I'm sure she's destined for here, but they'll take their time delivering her."

"How can they do that?"

"They can, if she doesn't demand access to an attorney."

"What can *you* do?"

"Put the heat on. I have an associate trying to chase her down now."

"But why are they moving her?"

"They want information. They'll try to keep her away from attorneys until they get what they want or decide she doesn't have what they need."

"She'll be terrified."

"We'll find out where she is, then I'll complain to a judge. It's something we can use later." He paused, then added, "I heard part of the press conference on television after David called me. Hell, it's all everyone is talking about. We'll ask for a gag order immediately."

"You'll take the case then?"

"I have to talk to Mrs. Connor first. She'll have to agree to my representation."

"She will," Liz assured him. And her mother would, if Liz had to get down on her hands and knees and beg.

"I'm expensive."

"Whatever it takes," she said, glancing at her father. She had just bought a business. She could sell it. Her parents had a home that could be mortgaged. They would find the money.

The attorney turned to her father. "Mr. Connor?"

It suddenly struck Liz that her father had been silent. He was usually a take-charge person, but he'd allowed her to do what he normally would do.

"Yes, of course," he said.

"I'll require a retainer," he said. "It'll be returned if she decides against retaining me, but we need it to establish client-attorney privilege."

"How much?" her father asked.

"Five thousand dollars to start. We bill three hundred dollars an hour."

She quickly multiplied that sum in her head and inwardly winced.

Without a word, her father took his wallet from a pocket and quickly wrote a check.

Montgomery took it, then said, "Excuse me for a moment. I'll make some calls." He moved away, pulled a cell phone from his belt, and made several calls before he rejoined them.

"My people found her in the FBI offices here. They went there from the U.S. attorney's office. They're still questioning her. I told them I'd be right there, and they shouldn't question her until then."

"Will they?"

"Depends on what she says. But they know they have to be careful now."

"We'll go with you."

"You should stay here. They might very well bring her here now that they think I'm on the way." He paused. "Do either of you know any reason she'd decline representation?"

She shook her head. "Confused. Afraid of the expense. She might think she can straighten it out herself."

"Always a big mistake," he said. "How can I reach you?"

They exchanged cell phone numbers. Her father gave the attorney his as well.

"If she's brought in here, call me," Montgomery ordered. "Tell her not to say anything."

"It can't be true, Mr. Montgomery," Liz said. "My mother couldn't hurt anyone. It just isn't in her."

He simply nodded. "We'll be talking." He walked away.

Liz and her father looked at each other. She reached out a hand to him. "He must be good if David recommended him. He'll straighten everything out."

"I wish we'd heard the press conference," he said. "At least we would know where we stand."

"I'll get a copy of it from the television station," she said. A knot as big as a boulder formed in her chest. She had to hear what everyone else had heard.

She went to the clerk again. "Where do they bring . . . suspects in?" she asked. She could not use the word prisoners. It was alien to all she knew.

"The back," she said. "But you can't get through the gate."

"Will you know when they bring Mrs. Connor in?"

"Not until the arresting officers complete the paperwork."

Liz wanted to scream. Instead, she and her father left the reception area and sat on a bench outside.

Her fingers tightened around his. More for her sake than his. "It really will be all right."

"She has always been afraid of something," he said in a wrenching voice. "When I first met her . . . she was so wounded, so vulnerable. I knew something terrible had happened to her. She never felt safe, not until a few years ago. I could feel her fear every time the doorbell rang."

"I didn't."

"You weren't looking for it. I did, because I saw it when it was raw and bleeding."

Raw and bleeding.

"You don't think . . ."

"Betty guilty of murder? Hell, no. Never. But I've always known that she feared someone. Or something. She's had nightmares for years. Even now . . ."

Something else she had not known. How could she have not? Did anyone ever know their parents? She thought she had. Now she was discovering any number of secrets and undercurrents.

Her cell phone rang.

"Oh God, Liz," her sister said. "It's horrible. The press conference. They said there was no doubt she killed two men in cold blood. They're charging her with first-degree murder and said they're taking her back to Boston. David's been deluged with phone calls from reporters all over the country."

"He isn't saying anything?"

"He's an attorney, Liz. Of course he isn't saying anything. He stopped answering all but his cell phone. Only a few people have that number." She paused. "How's Daddy?"

Liz glanced over at him. "As well as could be expected."

"Call me when you see her."

"Of course."

She called Colton Montgomery, and he answered immediately. She asked about the extradition.

"It should take a few days, even with her permission. Even the federal government can't whisk someone off without paperwork, particularly when I've made it clear I've been retained by the family."

Feeling lost in the federal juggernaut, Liz hung up the telephone. She'd always had great respect for law and order and the federal government. She'd never believed in the conspiracy theories.

But now . . .

How far would they go to solve a decades-old case?

She looked at her father and saw the same despair she felt. How do you fight all the resources of the government?

KANSAS CITY

Jeff Baker was working his magic on an automotive engine when he heard the news segment on the black-and-white television in the garage bay. He always kept it on when he worked alone. It was usually company, but this time the words chilled him to the bone.

"A fugitive from a Vietnam-era armored car robbery and murder has been apprehended in New Mexico. Betty Connor, identified by federal officials as Sarah Jane Maynard, was arrested today for two murders dating back three decades in Boston. Federal authorities say she will be charged with the murder of two armored car guards in a robbery connected with a radical anti-Vietnam War group. She is currently married to Steven Connor, a high school principal in Santa Fe."

The hackles on his spine rose. His throat went dry. He swore to himself.

After all these years, he was finally beginning to feel safe.

Foolish thought.

She would never say anything.

He knew that, as well as he knew his wife. But his wife didn't know *him*. At least, she didn't know the secret he'd harbored all these years.

He closed his eyes. He couldn't bear the thought of Margaret and the boys discovering the truth. The publicity would destroy his wife, perhaps ruin his son's chances for a scholarship, and mentally maim his sensitive younger son.

He forced himself to finish his work on the '57 Chevy. He'd always been good with cars and motors, a God-given talent that had merely amused him until that fateful day in March. Then it had become his only means of survival. Garages and service stations were so desperate for mechanics he'd managed to evade reference checks and eventually build a new identity.

But now . . .

His first impulse was to pack up his family and run to Mexico.

He forced himself to breathe deeply and focus on the car. He'd promised it first thing in the morning and had stayed after his employees left.

Now it might not matter. The hunt would be on, and he was not sure Sarah Jane Maynard was strong enough to keep their secrets. He stared at the wrench in his hand and sighed. It was no use. The car would have to wait. He turned out the light in the bay, went into his office, and collapsed into a chair.

Would their plan work now? Or was there a trail that would lead to each of them?

He buried his head in his hands. He'd known this day would come. Still, he'd hoped . . .

NEW ORLEANS

Greg Tanner read the news on the Internet. A freelance programmer, he practically lived on the computer. When he wasn't working, he was searching through online editions of newspapers: Miami, Houston, San Francisco, New York, Washington, Phoenix, Denver, Minnesota, Atlanta.

And Chicago.

He always varied his searches, unwilling to give even the slightest hint to anyone that might check his paths. He was simply another news hound who surfed his life away.

He had little else. He'd married once, but his secretive ways had brought it to a quick end. Now he limited himself to one-night stands with ladies who had no curiosity.

Nor did he permit himself anything but casual friendships. Close friends asked questions he couldn't answer. He had only a cat that wandered through his back door one day and refused to leave. The animal was as aloof as he, coming to him only for food, then hiding in some safe place.

Greg identified with that cat.

His heart stopped for a moment as he stared at the news flash on the Internet. "Woman charged in Vietnam-era armored car murder."

He clicked on the headline and went to the news story.

"Federal authorities today announced the arrest of a

woman identified as Sarah Jane Maynard for an armored car robbery—and the murder of two guards—in 1970 in Boston."

The article continued to say that extradition proceedings had already been started, but there was confusion over who should have jurisdiction: the state where the murders occurred, or the federal government.

Two dogs fighting over a bone.

That was it. There would be more later, Greg was sure of it. Newspapers throughout the country would carry the story. Questions would be raised about the other three fugitives. New manhunts would begin.

Would Sarah Jane reveal what she knew to get a reduced sentence?

He read on.

She had a family now. She had done what he'd been too afraid to do.

His stomach churned. The four of them had made a pact in the aftermath of disaster. They had gone separate ways and pledged never to reveal any details that would lead to the others.

He had prepared for this day. He had passports, overseas accounts. Not much, but in some countries he could live quite well. If only he could get to the money. If only . . .

Fifty-four years old, and he felt seventy and tired as hell. He really didn't want to live in Mexico. He didn't speak the language, nor did he wish to trust his fate with France where other fugitives had fled over the years. He did not have one damn worthwhile thing in his life. His own commitment to peace had been shelved. He could not, in any way, be active in any peace movements for fear of drawing the attention of federal authorities.

He had survived. That would be one hell of an epitaph.

But a worse one would be "convicted felon."

GREAT EXUMA, BAHAMAS

Evan Burke was engaged in a sexual adventure of the most intense kind when he heard the news.

He hadn't intended it. In fact, he'd been warding off advances from the wife of his client since the two had boarded the yacht he captained five days earlier. He hadn't needed that kind of trouble. He didn't want complaints.

But when he returned to the yacht from Great Exuma with supplies for the run back to Nassau, he'd found Brittany Carpenter naked in his bed. She was watching the satellite television.

"Robert's gone into town," she said. "I expect him to be gone all evening. We had a fight."

He hoped to hell it wasn't about him and the way her eyes followed him.

He rarely indulged in mixing business with pleasure. Bedding a client's wife was not the best way of promoting his business. But she was a tall redhead with green eyes and legs that would make a Rockette go green with envy. For days, she'd been parading in a bikini that was little more than scraps of cloth and took every opportunity to rub against him.

She'd given him an invitation, and hell, he'd finally accepted. They were reaching a climax together, their bodies heated and sweating and eager, when he'd heard that damn name in the background. Nothing else had registered until then, but that name . . .

He stopped suddenly, then hearing her complaint, resumed what he had started. But one sentence echoed in his head. He tried to make the appropriate responses as she demanded more. Lust became performance. But his mind worked feverishly. *They found Sarah Jane.*

He knew when she climaxed, and he rolled off her. He saw the disappointment in her eyes, but he didn't care.

He had to learn more about Sarah Jane.

Thirty-four damned years. He'd become a boat bum in the Florida Keys, acting as captain for a private owner who leased the sailboat for private charters. He hadn't dared apply with a large charter company for fear of background checks. He'd never earned enough to buy his own boat, though he yearned to do that.

Now he was in his fifties, though he knew he looked younger. He took pride in keeping his body in great shape, because that was part of the role he played. And though some thought the sun and sea and sail a great life, he wearied of catering to the whims of the wealthy when it should have been him being catered to.

He often thought about the charmed childhood he'd had, and how he'd blown it. What a damned fool he'd been to be roped in by Tony. Tony had played on his resentment against a conservative family he'd detested and had, in effect, destroyed his life. Evan had been running ever since.

Now he was little more than a hired hand and gigolo.

He kissed the empty-headed beauty. "You had better leave before your husband returns," he said.

"I don't care."

"I do," he said. "I could lose my job."

She pouted but reluctantly pulled on the scraps of cloth. "I'm bored," she said.

He was frantic now to get her out of the cabin. "I have some work to do," he said. "Tell you what. There's a great shop in town. Why don't you go shopping, and I'll meet you in the inn's bar in an hour."

She brightened. They were docked at the Peace and Plenty Hotel in Georgetown, and it had a great little bar. Brittany loved both shopping and bars. She hurried away.

He closed and locked the door, then turned on his computer. He went directly to national news and quickly found an article on the arrest of Sarah Jane Maynard.

The four of them had escaped detection longer than any one of them had expected. He remembered the night they had split up. The shooting had shocked them all, Sarah Jane in particular. They had nearly two million dollars, but they suspected that could be traced. It was agreed—he was in a minority—that they would take only what they needed to start new lives, and the rest would be hidden away in case one of them needed help, or as a lever if one of them was ever caught. The money now rested in safe-deposit boxes in three banks, each under the assumed name of one of the three men. They had taken precautions, though, that none of them alone could access the boxes. They were false names, but then the small banks they'd chosen had not demanded more than drivers' licenses, and those had been forged. But the boxes could not be opened without the keys, and those were placed in Sarah Jane's hands. She was the only one they trusted.

They'd opened accounts in each bank with $5,000 and made arrangements for the box rent to be paid yearly from that account. That yearly transaction kept the accounts active.

He knew the assumed last names of the other three, but that was all. But they had made arrangements to meet if any one of them was ever caught. Then he'd headed for the Florida Keys. He figured he could always make a run for the Bahamas if necessary. Still, a determined federal government was a formidable foe.

Now he and the others might well need funds to assume new identities and disappear again. That would take money. It wasn't as easy as it was years before sophisticated computers.

And Sarah Jane was the only link.

He knew how weak she'd been years ago. She had been putty in Tony's hands. Evan, then Jacob Terrell Jr., had watched him manipulate the girl like a snake charmer worked a reptile. He'd felt sorry for Sarah Jane until he realized that he, too, had been caught in Tony's net.

The wife of a high school principal. How droll.

He wondered whether the husband had known.

What had she told him? What would she tell him now?

He was about to pick up the phone when he heard footsteps on the deck above and heard his name called out.

Robert Carpenter had returned.

Evan steeled himself to contain his dislike of the overbearing client who found fault with everything from the food to the liquor cabinet.

Only four more days, and he would be free of the Carpenters. But he couldn't wait four days now. A small problem with the engine, and he could leave the ship here for a few days for repairs while he flew to the States.

If all went well, he would have enough money never to worry about people like the Carpenters again.

BOSTON

Tony Woodall's hand tightened around the television remote as he watched the late news.

After so many years he'd never thought this day would come.

Familiar anger boiled inside. He owed all four of his companions from three decades ago. They had run with the money and left him to be captured. The fact that he'd miraculously escaped detection and that he'd planned to betray them all did not mitigate their crime against him.

That nearly two million would have been more like four million today. Even more. He was smart enough to have invested wisely. Instead, he'd had to run like a rat until he was sure the other four had really disappeared and could not be traced back to him. He'd kept that small cell separate and private from his more public activities.

Unlike the others, he had not come from a wealthy family. He had scrounged for everything he'd ever had, including the scholarship to Harvard. He'd always been the odd man out until hc'd seen the antiwar movement as a way to ingratiate himself into the lives of his moneyed classmates. He'd enjoyed the manipulation, and then he'd discovered something more important: the promise of riches.

But the plan didn't work because his companions spooked and ran. And his public flirtation with the antiwar movement ruined any chance he had with big law firms. After a few struggling years, he navigated toward the Boston Mafia, all the time looking for the four and, through them, the money. He'd almost given up when one suddenly appeared, blackmailed him, and told him the money was still intact. Before Tony could find out more, Jacob had slipped away again. And despite his mob connections, he'd never been able to find Jacob nor the other three, despite the fact he'd been the one who had taught them how to disappear. They'd been far better students than he'd realized.

What if Sarah Jane Maynard revealed everything that

had happened that March morning? He had to make sure she didn't.

He picked up a phone. He had friends who would know someone who was immediately available in the Southwest. Someone who could search. Who could bribe.

Who could kill.

chapter five

Liz and her father waited for five hours before being told her mother had arrived at the detention center, but it was after visiting hours. The room, which had been crowded earlier, had thinned out.

Just as she started to use her cell phone to call the attorney, it rang.

She turned it on.

"She's been at the FBI offices, but was moved before I arrived," Montgomery said without preamble. "They claim she says she doesn't want representation, and I tend to believe them. This is too high-profile a case for them to lie."

"You didn't see her?"

"No."

"She just arrived here," Liz said, "but they won't let us see her. Past visiting hours."

"It was probably planned that way," he said. "And I can't do anything unless she requests me," he said. "You might as well leave and try again in the morning."

"There's no way to get us in tonight?"

"No. Not after visiting hours. Believe me, the Feds are working to keep her away from you and from an attorney. And until she requests one, they don't have to let me see her."

"We still want you," Liz said. "Once we talk to her . . ."

"Keep me posted," he said. "And know they will be coming after you now."

"Who?"

"The FBI and prosecutors. They'll want to know everything your father and you might know. Friends. Acquaintances, everything. Every trip she has taken, every relative."

"There aren't any," she blurted out.

"What do you mean?"

"She has no family."

"None?"

She shook her head, realizing how damning the statement must seem.

"Do we have to talk to the FBI?"

"Not if you don't want to. And I definitely wouldn't talk to them without an attorney."

"Will you represent *us?*" she asked.

"Unless—or until—it presents a conflict," he said. "Call me when they contact you. I, or a member of my firm, will be there."

"Thank you," she said as she closed her cell phone and turned to her father. "She hasn't asked for an attorney; the FBI won't let him see her until she does."

Her father looked stunned. She could almost read his mind. Why wouldn't she request an attorney? She certainly was aware that an attorney was the first thing she needed.

"A letter," her father said. "If she knew . . ."

She went to the clerk. "Can we leave a letter for her?"

"It will be read by deputies."

She nodded.

"Leave it with me, and I'll send it through channels."

It was the best she was going to get, and she knew it.

Her father and Liz conferred over the note as he wrote it. Nothing threatening. Nothing demanding. Just love and support. "We'll see you in the morning. We all love you so much. We believe in you."

"We might as well leave," Liz said.

"I'm going to stay here in Albuquerque," he replied, his face agonized. "She might change her mind and ask to see the attorney. Or us."

Liz nodded. She didn't want to return to Santa Fe

tonight and answer questions from the press. She had no
answers.

But as they started to leave, two men entered. Harris
and Monroe, two of the agents from Robert's office.

Monroe spoke first. "Ms. Connor," he acknowledged.
He looked at her father. "And Mr. Connor? I'm Agent
Monroe, and this is Agent Harris."

Her father stiffened.

"I was just talking about you," Liz told the two men.

Monroe raised an eyebrow.

"To our attorney. He advised us not to talk to you without his being present."

"I just want to ask a few questions."

"Sorry," her father broke in, and she heard the anger in
his voice. He was always slow to anger, but she'd learned
that he could be fierce when aroused. He had that fire in his
eyes now, and she felt relieved. His "sorry" was no sorry
at all, and the four of them knew it.

She felt a moment of satisfaction. If the FBI had come
to them prior to the news conference, she might have felt
different. But by holding the press conference, it was obvious the FBI didn't care about hearing anything contrary
to their theories. She was not going to help them destroy
her family.

Monroe sighed. "It could be helpful."

"To whom?"

"Cooperation will help her case."

"Has she told you anything?" her father asked.

"I'm not privy to that information."

Her father glowered at him. "That means she hasn't."

The door to the office opened, and a tall, lean man with
a slight limp entered and walked to the counter. She saw
Monroe's eyes narrow as he watched the newcomer approach the desk and wait for a clerk to acknowledge him.

"Adams?" Monroe said with a question in his voice.

The newcomer turned around, and his face was all contempt as he obviously recognized the agent. "Agent Monroe," he acknowledged, his voice dripping with dislike.

Monroe frowned. "What are you doing here?"

"It's none of your business." The newcomer's eyes

were green ice, and Liz felt they could cool a wildfire. His body seemed totally relaxed in tight jeans that hugged his hips and a brown shirt with the sleeves rolled up to just below his elbow. Both shirt and jeans looked well-worn. His sandy-colored hair looked as if fingers had—unsuccessfully—tried to tame it.

His eyes darted over to her and studied her face for a moment as if wondering why she was with the agent he regarded with disdain, then his gaze slid away and back to the clerk who looked as if she'd been struck by lightning. It was a deliberate dismissal of the FBI agent.

"Sarah Jane Maynard? Or Betty Connor?" he asked the clerk in a slightly louder voice. "Is she here?"

"Yes, but visiting hours are over."

"Do you know when the extradition hearing is scheduled?" The curtness was gone from his voice, and it was all intimate charm. Liz thought if she were sitting in that chair, she would surely be tempted to forget a rule. It was like watching Mr. Hyde turn into Dr. Jekyll, she thought. And if any name other than her mother's had been mentioned, she would have been amused.

Why did he want to know about her mother? She took a step forward to ask him, but then hesitated. He was probably a reporter who had wormed his way inside, just ahead of the pack.

Monroe shook his head at the woman behind the desk.

"I'm sorry," she said. "I don't have that information."

The newcomer nodded as if not surprised.

Monroe stepped closer to him, every step aggressive. "Don't mess this up, or I'll see that you lose your license this time," Monroe said.

"Better men than you have tried," the man named Adams said. His gaze went around the room and settled on Liz, then on her father.

"Who are your friends?" he asked Monroe, and Liz realized his gaze had taken in everything when he'd entered the room.

"None of your business," Monroe said with a stiff smile.

"Are *you* on the Maynard case?" the stranger asked. "Been rehabilitated by the bureau?"

Monroe's face turned a bright red, and he turned away.

Liz stared at the stranger. Though he looked at ease, she saw the muscles bunched in his neck. These two men disliked each other. Not only disliked. Detested.

Monroe turned away from him and strode back to Liz and her father and held out a card. "I'll be in contact," he said. "You can set up something with your attorney."

The two agents left the room, and Liz found the stranger's eyes on her, then her father. Rehabilitate? What was there to rehabilitate about Monroe? Something that could help her mother?

Curious now, she approached him. "I . . . you seem interested in Sarah Jane Maynard. Can I ask you why?"

Standing closer to him, she smelled whiskey or some other alcohol, but his eyes were as clear as a piece of green glass. His lips were curved in a small half smile that was oddly attractive.

"Why are you asking?" he countered, and then she noticed the half smile was no smile at all but a permanent part of his face, probably the result of a small nearly invisible scar that ran from his lip up his cheek. It did nothing to detract from the rugged appeal of his angular face.

"Betty Connor is my mother."

His expression didn't change. It was almost as if he'd expected it.

"Caleb Adams," he identified himself. "I was a detective in Boston."

"That doesn't explain why you're asking about her."

"It's a legendary case. I worked on it in Boston."

"But you no longer do?"

"No."

"Just curiosity then?" she asked, not even attempting to curb the asperity in her voice. She was not in sympathy with curiosity where her family was concerned. She started to turn away, then reconsidered. Perhaps he would know something about the case that could help her.

"I'm writing a book about the robbery. The case has always intrigued me. I always felt there was more to it than was publicized."

A book? That was worse than curiosity. She could not bear the thought of her family being picked apart. Still, his statement piqued her interest.

"What do you mean?"

"Has your mother ever mentioned what happened?"

"Why should she? She isn't this Sarah Jane Maynard."

"This is all a surprise?"

She glared at him. "Of course it is. It's a case of mistaken identity."

"Then you need help, because the Feds are convinced they have the right person. Look, Ms. Connor," he persisted, "I know a great deal about the robbery. It was an open case in Boston, and I worked on it on and off for several years. I'll make you a deal. I'll help you if you help me. I promise you can read anything I write before I submit it anywhere."

"And why should we trust you?" her father said suddenly. He had been silent, listening.

Caleb Adams turned toward him, his expression unchanging. "A good question. I can give you some references. I do some private investigative work around here. People will tell you that when I give my word, I keep it."

Liz studied him, trying to get a take on him. Though she placed his age in the late thirties or early forties, his face had the life lines of an older man. His eyes were enigmatic, and there was a restless energy about his movements. She had the impression of a caged cougar, angry and frustrated. There was something else, too. An air of isolation, of aloneness that caught at her.

She decided to probe further. "You don't like Monroe?"

His green eyes narrowed and hardened. "No."

"Why?"

"He doesn't observe the rules. Sometimes I didn't either, but it wasn't because of ambition," he added.

"Why doesn't he like you?"

"As I told you, I do private investigations now and then. The last one revealed a few mistakes made by Monroe and his friends. He didn't appreciate it. He was, in fact, reprimanded by the judge, and the case was dismissed."

She studied him. A private investigator who was trying to write a book. Probably not that unusual. But what would that book do to her family? To her mother's case? A book was the last thing they needed now. And it didn't explain that intensity she sensed in him.

He was eyeing her speculatively, and she felt a little like a fly under the eyes of a spider. She had no intention of taking that former role.

"I would like to interview you and your family," he said.

"No."

"It could help your mother."

"That's what Monroe said as well," she said. "Somehow I don't believe either of you."

For the first time, his quizzical smile seemed real. "A blunt woman," he said.

She saw her father weighing him. He'd always been a great judge of character.

"I'm sorry," he said, "but our attorney told us not to talk to anyone." It was that "I'm sorry" that surprised her. It was that he had used the word at all. He had not been that polite to the FBI.

"I think we should go," she said to her father, ignoring Adams.

"I would go out the back way," he said. "Reporters are gathering in front. Deputies are keeping them outside, but you'll be mobbed when you leave."

She looked at her father, then back at him. "Thank you."

"I'll show you the way," he offered.

For some reason, she didn't think he was so helpful most of the time. Despite his cordial manner, something about him warned her. She could feel the anger inside him, no matter how hard he was trying to keep it under control. What she didn't know was where it was aimed. And why.

"You don't have to do that. We can find it." It was dismissal again, and she saw a wry amusement in his eyes.

She thought he probably wasn't turned down often. Not by women.

He shrugged. "I'll be around," he said. He dug around in his jeans, took out a pen and a scrap of paper, and jotted a number on it, then handed the paper to her. "My cell number. Call anytime."

She looked down at it. A gas receipt. Their fingers touched for a moment, and she felt an unexpected warmth. Their gazes met briefly, a sudden awareness sparking between them. She stepped back.

He gave her a searching look, then stepped back as well, his mouth curved into something like wry amusement. "Sorry, no business cards."

She felt like a fool standing there and staring at him. He was not a handsome man, but he had a rugged appeal that attracted her far more than conventional good looks. Pain was carved in the lines of his face, giving it character and strength. But the smell of alcohol that lingered on him diminished that image.

She turned. "Let's go," she told her father.

Liz and her father shopped for a few necessities, then found a motel near the detention facility. They booked two adjoining rooms.

Neither of them was hungry, but Liz called room service for hamburgers. They needed food despite the sickening bewilderment she felt and the stark fear she knew her father must be experiencing. As they waited for the food, she turned on the television. They found themselves staring at photos of Sarah Jane Maynard as a high school student. As a debutante. As a college student at Wellesley. A solemn anchor recited her history. She was the daughter of the late chairman of the board of Maynard Shipping, which later became Maynard Industries. Sarah Jane's mother committed suicide soon after her daughter's disappearance.

A chilled silence surrounded them. Liz wanted to turn off the television, but it was like looking at a car wreck. For a moment, she couldn't take her eyes away from it.

Then she turned and looked at her father. The color had drained from his face. There was little doubt that Sarah Jane Maynard *was* Betty Connor. Or was one of those doubles people talked about.

Could doubles have the same quiet, shy smile?

As she listened, Liz had difficulty in believing the rest of the story. Her mother a debutante? The daughter of wealth and privilege who turned murderess?

Nothing seemed more unlikely. Her mother was money conscious and often shopped at discount stores and outlets. Her parents were able to afford the house they owned only because they had bought it twenty-five years ago when prices were modest. They never would have been able to afford today's real estate prices.

The FBI had mentioned that nearly two million dollars were missing. If nothing else, Liz knew it had not gone to her family.

She turned to her father. "You must know something, sensed something, if what . . ."

She couldn't finish the sentence. She realized she was still in a stage of denial. But part of her *had* to know.

Her father met her gaze. They had always been close. She was far more her father's daughter than her mother's.

"I know what you know," he said in a ragged voice. "I just knew something had gone terribly wrong in her life. There were nightmares. An unexplained absence of any family. She avoided any conversation about where she came from."

"Didn't that tell you something?" she asked with sudden anger.

"I always wanted to protect her," he said. "Whenever I would ask anything, her eyes would get this bleak, terrified look and I . . . Goddamn it," he exploded. "I was a coward. I didn't want anything to interfere with what was perfect."

But it wasn't perfect.

That truth lay revealed between them like a raw, ugly wound. If it were perfect, she would have told him what frightened her. He would have asked.

They didn't say anything more to each other. Liz was

trying to reconcile those photos on television with what she knew of her mother.

Then the news program featured a short profile of the other three implicated. Terrence Colby. Stuart Marshall. Jacob Terrell. One was a studious-looking youth, the second looked uncomfortable in a family photo, the third wore a cocky smile as he posed next to a sailboat. She searched their faces and knew her father was doing the same. Had she ever seen them? Any of them?

Then shame swept through her for her disloyalty. Her doubts. She was twisted in knots.

When the news show ended, her father stood. "I'm going to bed." He seemed years older, his eyes bright with something that looked like tears. He went into the adjoining room and closed the door.

She turned off the televison and stared at the blank screen, going over everything that had happened, every word that had been said, every comment she'd heard uttered today.

Liz had been born in 1972, just as the Vietnam War was winding down. She'd always been interested in history and was keenly aware of the war and the social upheaval it had created. She knew she couldn't begin to understand the emotions of the time.

But an armored car robbery? Murder?

She shivered. If there were only a sliver of truth involved, her mother must have lived through years of guilt and regret.

She went to the window and looked out. What was her mother feeling now? Was she silent out of shame? Remorse? Or was it something more visceral? Something like fear?

Then her thoughts went to Caleb Adams and the contradicting emotions he'd aroused in her. Just the thought of his prying into her family sent cold shivers through her, and yet . . . yet there had been something compelling about the barely concealed intensity.

Her cell phone rang. She looked at the clock. Two in the morning.

She looked at the number showing on its display. It was

her neighbor, an insurance executive. He was one of the few people who had her cell number. They had exchanged cell phone numbers in the event of an emergency of some kind.

She flicked the phone open. "Garry?"

"Where are you?"

"Albuquerque."

There was a silence.

"Garry?" she asked again.

"Liz . . . there's been a fire. Your house was damaged."

It took her a moment to understand, to comprehend, then, "How bad is it?"

"A lot of smoke and water damage. I got up to go to the bathroom, looked out the window, and saw the smoke. The fire department got here fast. The walls and roof are intact. Thank God for the adobe. Your car wasn't there . . ." His voice trailed off. He would have heard the news about her mother.

Then she heard him talk to someone else in muffled tones before returning to her. "The fire investigators want to talk to you."

She tried to stand, but her legs seemed boneless. Her heart had stopped when he first started talking, and now that comprehension slowly sifted through her.

Her house. Her beautiful old adobe house. It wasn't hers, but she had leased it these past five years and had loved every foot of it. It was filled with western art she'd found in local galleries, and Native American rugs. Her books. Her clothes. Her computer. Her life.

Fire.

She realized she was still holding the phone. "Tell them I'll be back tomorrow afternoon," she said. "And Garry, thanks." She tried to keep her voice steady. She felt as if someone had knocked her in the knees with two-by-fours, then stomped on her.

"I have a number of meetings tomorrow," Garry said, "but I'll be home late tomorrow night. Let me know if I can do anything."

"Have there been reporters there?"

"Hell, yes. They're crawling all over the place. I shut the door on them. So have your other neighbors."

She felt tears coming to her eyes. "Thank you," she whispered into the phone.

"Stay with me if you need a place," he said.

"I'll remember that," she said. She found herself talking by rote as her brain feverishly tried to take in what she'd been told. *Fire.* Her home. Too much was happening too quickly. There was a certain numbness. But she knew the impact would really hit her later. Just as her mother's arrest would.

She turned off the phone.

Earlier today she'd been embarking on a great new adventure, a business of her own, which she could operate to her own values. No more sending tourists on trips she knew they would not enjoy. She wanted everyone to enjoy New Mexico as she did, not end up terrified because a rafting trip was far more dangerous than they expected, or physically disabled for days because they chose a five-day riding trip when they'd never sat a horse before.

She'd watched her boss do exactly that and had long wanted to run the business in a far different way. She wanted to go after corporate accounts for "adventure" meetings to bring executives together. She wanted to offer educational opportunities above the usual tourist fare. Her father was a historian and amateur archaeologist as well as principal, and he had a way of telling history that enthralled young and old.

She'd been so hopeful hours earlier.

Now she found herself in what seemed to be a never-ending nightmare.

No matter what happened now, the story would follow her parents for the rest of their lives. It could destroy her father's career, take years off her mother's life.

She remembered now how she'd chafed against her mother's protectiveness, had scoffed at her insistence in keeping their house locked when other neighbors left theirs open. How she had been humiliated when her mother insisted on walking her to school.

Had it been fear not of the present but the past? Fear of authorities? Of being discovered?

And now the fire in her home? Coincidence? She closed her eyes. She could feel the heat. See the hungry flames destroy everything she'd built on her own.

She forced herself to turn off the lights and go to bed. She knew she needed every bit of strength she had to get through the next day. She willed sleep to come.

But for the first time in her life she feared it.

chapter six

Liz's sleep was haunted by images. An armored car. Dead guards. Her home in flames. Her mother in a jail cell. Even Caleb Adams, who hovered over them all like a dark angel.

The images didn't leave her when she jerked awake. Light streamed through the curtains. She looked at the clock. A little after six. She'd dozed on and off for about three hours.

Why had Caleb Adams intruded in the midst of chaos? Both in real life and in her thoughts? He was someone to avoid. A writer seeking to profit from her family's troubles.

And at least she had a few friends. She suspected she and her family would discover exactly how many they really did have in the coming weeks. But she knew she could depend on Tracy and Garry. Thank God for both of them.

She heard her father moving around. She debated whether to tell him about her house. He would find out soon enough. The news media would jump on the story.

As if summoned by her thoughts, her father knocked at the door.

She slipped on her slacks and opened the door between their rooms.

Her father was dressed in the same clothes he'd worn yesterday. He'd shaved, though, and his face had more color than last night. The shock was wearing off, and he was ready to protect what was his.

He peered at her. "Is something else wrong?"

"I had a call last night," she said. "There was a fire at my house."

His head jerked up. "Oh, Sport, how bad?"

"Garry called. He got up in the night and saw smoke coming out a window. He called the fire department. He said that there's a lot of smoke and water damage throughout the house."

He put an arm on her shoulder. "Do they have any idea how it started?"

"The fire department wants to talk to me."

"They'll find out what happened," he said.

She certainly hoped so. She went over all her actions yesterday. She'd had a quick cup of coffee, and the coffeemaker turned itself off. She hadn't used any other appliances.

"You should go back."

"I will, after we see Mom."

He held out his arms, and she went into them, feeling the comfort she had years earlier whenever small catastrophes struck. He was the father again, and that meant she could have a few moments of pure, unashamed self-pity. Even now, however, she realized she was still in shock, her mind muddled by events she still didn't fully comprehend. And all she could do now was to set priorities. Her mother was the first priority. She backed away.

"I have insurance," she said. "Most everything can be replaced." But she knew, and knew he knew, that wasn't entirely true. Her life was in that house.

Someone knocked, and they looked at each other. Had a reporter found them?

Her father opened the door slightly and glanced outside.

Through the crack in the door, she saw a tall, well-dressed man.

"Mr. Connor? Ms. Connor?" he asked in a deep, pleasant, eastern-accented voice.

"What do you want?" her father asked abruptly. It was

so unlike his usual friendly, often gregarious self, a shock ran through her.

"I'm Michael Gallagher. I'm an attorney with Maynard Industries in Boston. Your wife's cousin is CEO of the company. He and your wife were once very close. He sent me here to see whether I can help in any way."

Her father hesitated for a moment.

"May I come inside? Only for a moment."

Her father stood aside, and Liz moved to his side as the attorney entered. She'd not even thought of a family in Boston. Another jolt.

Her father wore an equally shocked expression.

"How do we know you are who you say you are?" Liz asked.

He took out a business card along with a bar association card and handed them to her.

"Anyone could print one of these," she said.

He grinned then. "Yes, they can. This is real, however. You can call the company. Or Win Maynard in Boston." He wrote a number on the back of his card. "That's his cell phone. He'll answer it."

"That wouldn't mean anything to me. I don't know him, or his voice."

The area around his eyes crinkled with amusement, even approval. "Cautious. Good. I like that. But try calling, and you'll know it's him."

Liz studied him. He was powerfully built, like a man who worked out or played physical sports. His hair was dark, almost black, and cut in a crisp haircut. His eyes were a dark brown, and lively, though a bit bloodshot. His clothes looked expensive.

"I'm still not quite sure why you're here," she said.

"Your cousin wants to help. He'll pay for an attorney, and I'll help you find one."

"That's quite unnecessary," her father cut in. "We have an attorney. I can manage the fees."

"I'm sure you can," Michael Gallagher said. "There was no disrespect meant, only an offer to help. I'm not a criminal attorney myself, but I do know some of the pitfalls of the system. We can hire the best."

"My sister's husband is an attorney, thank you," Liz said. "And we've already retained Colton Montgomery."

"I've heard of him. He's good. In fact, he's on the list I prepared for you."

"I'm pleased you approve," her father said wryly. "But I still don't see why . . . the Maynard family wants to become involved." She noticed he avoided identifying it as "Betty's family."

"Frankly, neither do I," Gallagher said with a self-depreciatory smile. "But I seldom ask Mr. Maynard why. I only do, and hopefully not die."

She suspected he did a great deal more than just take orders. He had a self-assurance that came with power and confidence.

"You can tell Maynard that we don't need his help," her father said firmly.

"Shouldn't your wife be consulted on that?" Gallagher asked in a mild tone.

"My wife has not seen fit to ask for help, nor has she even mentioned the Maynard family. I hardly expect she wishes to do so now. However, I'll pass the message on to her."

Michael Gallagher hesitated, then asked, "Has she said anything since her arrest?"

Alarm bells went off in Liz's mind. Why would he care what had or had not been said?

"I think that's between my mother and us," she said. She was loath to say they really didn't know. Another internal voice argued that two attorneys together might be more powerful in her mother's defense.

But not until she knew more about his motives. And Mr. Maynard's motives. "How did you get here so fast? And how did you find us?"

"The news is everywhere, including Boston. Mr. Maynard asked me to fly down immediately. I went to the detention center. The clerk said you'd been there. I thought you'd be staying somewhere nearby. You weren't difficult to find."

"We asked the clerk not to tell anyone we were here."

He didn't reply, leaving her to wonder exactly how he

discovered where she and her father were. She was pretty sure he wasn't going to tell them. She wondered if he wouldn't have similar success in extracting other information. She didn't trust him, but perhaps they could use him.

She wanted to check with Colton Montgomery first, though. She wanted to know everything there was to know about the confident Mr. Gallagher before entrusting anything with him.

"I'll talk to Mr. Montgomery about your offer," she said.

"As I said, he was on a list I compiled. I'm impressed by your taste."

"We don't want, or need, your money," her father interrupted.

"You've made that quite clear. But it's available if you need it," he said, then turned to her. "And Mr. Maynard may have contacts in Washington who can help."

"I don't understand."

"He's been active in politics a long time. He knows people in the Justice Department and people who know people in Justice. He also knows nearly everyone in Boston."

"I'll remember that," her father said, but his eyes were cold.

Liz realized Michael Gallagher's offer of help had been met with precious little courtesy. "Thank you," she said.

Her father, though, looked stubbornly aloof. She sensed he distrusted Gallagher. She had the same doubts. His appearance was a little too quick, his words a bit too facile.

She suddenly wanted him gone. She wanted to talk to her father. "I should dress," she said, realizing how she must look—braless in a T-shirt and a pair of wrinkled slacks.

"You look charming," he said.

Liz disliked flattery. She'd always been suspicious of people who used it as easily as he just did. Another mark against him.

Her expression must have said as much, because he gave her another one of those wry smiles. His gaze flicked to her father. "Mr. Connor. Ms. Connor."

Gallagher backed out the door, and she and her father stared at each other.

"I don't trust him," her father said bluntly. "Nor how quickly he turned up."

"We can use his help," she ventured.

"We don't know why he's giving it," he replied.

"Mom never said anything about Boston? About the Maynard family?"

"No," he said.

They exchanged glances. How many more secrets were awaiting them?

Liz went into the bathroom and looked at herself in the mirror. Charming? Now she knew he was a liar. Shadows ringed small bloodshot eyes. Her hair stuck out in all directions. Liz rinsed her face with cold water and tried desperately to bring some sanity back to her life. It didn't work.

She slipped on her bra and the blouse she'd left in the bathroom last night after taking a shower. The slacks she'd slipped into earlier would have to do another day.

Or longer, she thought with a pang of regret. Would any of her clothes at home be salvageable? She closed her eyes and leaned against the wall, overwhelmed by everything that had happened. Bewildered by the way her comfortable life had changed, at how order had descended into chaos.

She had to call Tracy and make sure her business was still there. It was all she had now. It might be all any of them would have.

Her father's position could well be in jeopardy. A principal had to be above suspicion. If he was accused of knowing about his wife's past and had concealed it . . .

Water splashed her hand, and she realized it was still running in the basin. The sound brought her back to reality. No more wishing for something that was gone.

She turned the faucets off and stared at her reflection. Her eyes looked a little better, but the strain was still in her face. She left the bathroom and found the sleeping room empty. Her father had evidently returned to his own room.

She heard him talking to someone on the phone. His voice penetrated the thin wall. He was probably talking to

Sue. The conversation ended, and a moment later he appeared at the door.

She raised an eyebrow in question.

"It was Sue," he confirmed. "She said the fire at your house was featured on television. David seems to think we should hire off-duty police to guard our houses."

"He thinks someone might try to burn your house? Or his?" She was stunned by the idea. She had taken the fire as a terrible coincidence and only fleetingly considered anything else. Deliberately set? She could imagine nothing more visceral. But why her? Unless someone was angry at her mother and couldn't get to her parents' house for the number of reporters there.

"Right now I imagine there's so much press attention that they're safe," she said. The news report last night showed the exterior of her parents' house and the numerous news vans outside.

He nodded. She knew he was probably thinking of the money again. They would need all they had for her mother's legal fees.

"David said his house is swamped by the news media as well, especially since the news of your fire. Sue and the kids have moved to his sister's. The media couldn't find you or me, so they're pursuing them."

"Too bad they weren't at my house."

"I imagine they gave up on you last night."

It was almost amusing, needing the press to protect your property. "You're going to stay here?" she asked.

"For now. Until I know more. Thank God school doesn't start for two more months."

Liz picked up her cell phone and dialed Montgomery's number.

The attorney picked it up instantaneously. "Montgomery."

"This is Liz Connor. Any more news?"

"No. I hope you got some sleep last night."

"A neighbor called to tell me there was a fire in my home."

A pause. Then, "Have you heard what caused it?"

"My neighbor doesn't know."

"Could it have been arson?" he asked. "Any enemies that would take advantage of this situation?"

"I can't think of anyone."

"You're on the city council. Any political enemies, someone who might want the job?"

"Not any who would do something like that."

"I don't believe in coincidences," he said.

"Neither do I," she said. "But they do happen. Which reminds me. Someone appeared at my door this morning. He says he's an attorney for the Maynard family in Boston. Offered to pay the legal bills, but my dad and I will pay them. He plans to get in touch with you."

"What's his name?"

"Gallagher. Michael Gallagher."

"He's from Boston?"

"Yes."

"I'll check him out." A pause. "Do you want to use him?"

"No," she said. "We retained you. He suggested, though, that he has Washington contacts that might help."

"Ms. Connor?"

"Yes?"

"I think you and your father should be careful."

The words were like ice cubes tumbling down her spine. "Why?"

"There are three other people still on the run," he said. "A fortune is missing as well. That's why the government kept the investigation so quiet. They were hoping to find a clue to the others. And the money."

"That was over thirty years ago. Wouldn't it be gone?"

"Only a few serial numbers ever turned up."

Money and safety. Two powerful motives for someone not to want her mother to say anything. But of course her mother would work with the government. She could plea bargain, or . . .

But suddenly she realized she no longer knew what her mother would or would not do. Or why.

"You think my house . . ."

"I don't know. I'm just cautioning you."

"Thank you. When will you try to see her?"

"This morning. I have a hearing at nine, then I'll go over to the detention center. I'll also talk to the federal attorneys handling the case."

"Thank you. We plan to be at the detention center at visiting hours."

"I'll do what I can."

He hung up.

She stood there holding the phone. Could it be possible that she was in jeopardy? And if she was, what about her father and her sister's family?

She turned to her father. "He believes we should be careful," she said.

"It couldn't have anything to do with your mother. No one could work that quickly."

"They could," she said, "if they knew in advance about the arrest." Even as she said the words, she really didn't believe them. That would mean the bad guys had connections to the federal prosecutors. It sounded like a B-movie.

But then neither in her wildest nightmares would she ever have suspected her mother was a fugitive. Those ice cubes she'd felt earlier returned and lodged in her spine. Maybe someone *was* acting swiftly to prevent her mother from speaking. Someone her mother knew from a lifetime ago.

Perhaps even a member of the Maynard family or someone in its employ.

She saw the same realization in her father's eyes.

They didn't say anything more as they went down to breakfast.

To her surprise, Michael Gallagher was at a table, a cup of coffee in his hand and a half-eaten roll on his plate. He looked elegant and comfortable, yet she couldn't escape the idea there was an outlaw behind the smooth exterior.

He rose. "Will you join me?"

Her father started to say no, but she interrupted. "We will." She wanted to know more about him. And Maynard.

The motel offered a free continental breakfast for its patrons, and she noticed Gallagher had helped himself. She raised an eyebrow.

"I took a room here this morning," he said, as if reading her mind.

"I would have thought you liked something more elegant."

"Are you a reverse snob, Ms. Connor?"

Her face heated, knowing she had prejudged him and he knew it. But now everything sent her senses on alert. Besides, his appearance was just too convenient.

Liz went to a coffee machine service counter and poured a cup of coffee, then returned to the table.

"I asked Colton Montgomery about you," she said.

"I would expect you to do exactly that." He flashed her the engaging grin she'd noticed earlier. "I'm not your enemy. I only want to help."

"What flight did you come in on?" she asked.

"A puddle jumper from Dallas." He mentioned the airline, and she knew it well.

"I'll ask Mr. Montgomery to check that as well."

The slight smile remained as he waited for her to continue.

"There was a fire at my house this morning," she said suddenly, watching for any change in his expression.

His expression tightened, and he leaned forward. "When?"

"Early this morning. I don't know much more."

"And you're wondering when I arrived?"

"The thought crossed my mind."

"Early this morning," he said. "I have the ticket, if you would like to see it."

He didn't seem to take offense at her questions.

"You could have hired someone."

"I could, but I didn't. I understand your suspicion. You don't know me, you don't know Win Maynard. I'm not asking you to take me on trust."

She looked at her father and noted that he was listening.

"You're staying?" she asked.

"Mr. Maynard asked me to help in any way I can. I'll be here until I feel I'm not helpful."

She stood, and so did her father.

"We'll remember that," she said and noticed from his expression that he caught the nuance.

"Thanks for hearing me out. You have my card. And my services are not only available for your mother. If I can help you with anything to do with the case, or even your home, let me know."

She merely nodded, then she and her father left. They went to the lobby, and she used her cell phone to call the fire department.

She gave her name and was referred to someone named Calhoun, who had a very preliminary report.

"Do you know the cause yet?"

"All indications are the fire started in the kitchen. When were you last at the house?"

"Seven a.m. yesterday." A century ago.

"The fire investigator believes it started in the kitchen, most likely on or in the stove. That's the site of the greatest damage. Could you have left something cooking on the stove?"

"No. I only had coffee. I used an automatic coffeemaker that goes off automatically."

"We'll need a statement."

"I'm in Albuquerque, but I'll get back sometime late this afternoon. I can't tell you exactly when."

"The investigator will be at the residence. I'll give you his number. Let him know when you're on your way."

"Thank you."

She hung up, feeling as if she was drowning in quicksand. The FBI wanted an interview. Now the Santa Fe Fire Department. Probably the police next.

She looked back into the eating area. Michael Gallagher was still there. His cell phone was at his right ear.

"We *might* need more help," she said to her father.

"But not until we know more about him and his employer," he said. "Betty never mentioned a cousin to me."

"But then she wouldn't have, would she?" Liz added, and immediately regretted it. It was like a knife thrust, and she knew it. Her father was beginning to learn how little trust there had been in the marriage.

"I'm sorry," she said.

"Never apologize for the truth," he said.

The words were his, but the conviction that was so much a part of him was missing.

When they reached the detention center, they were mobbed by reporters who obviously had photos of both of them. They had to fight through, ignoring comments that became more and more abusive the closer she and her father approached the entrance.

She tried to shut them out.

"Did you know your mother was a murderer?"

"What has she told you?"

"How do you feel about your mother now?"

And to her father, "How could you be married thirty-three years and not know?"

Colton Montgomery met them at the door and shielded them as they made their way to a small office. "I just heard there's an extradition hearing tomorrow. If she waives her rights, they won't need to go to a grand jury."

"You haven't talked to her?"

"We are trying to arrange something now."

"We sent her a note last night. Perhaps that might have helped."

"I'll get in to see her," he said bluntly. "She was in FBI custody yesterday, and I can always claim she was intimidated. They want a clean case on this."

A clerk called Montgomery's name. "You can go in."

He gave them an assuring smile. "I'll do my best to persuade her to accept me. I'm sure she'll be anxious to see you."

Liz nodded. But dread had congealed in the pit of her stomach. Colton's warning earlier nagged her. Could the fire have possibly been some kind of warning to her mother? If so, then her mother wouldn't say anything. Despite their differences over the years, she knew her mother would sacrifice her own life before hurting her family.

The idea was far-fetched. It was a simple fire. Nothing more. Still, the timing . . .

She looked down at her hands and noticed they were clenched together. Every second stretched endlessly.

Then the door opened, and Colton Montgomery strode over to them.

Liz's hand found her father's.

"She won't fight extradition," he said. "I've arranged a private meeting for you. You can go in now."

chapter seven

"What exactly did she say?" Liz said. Her father was at her side.

The attorney took them outside in the corridor where they wouldn't be overheard. "She plans to plead guilty," he said in a low voice.

"Has she agreed to your representation?"

"Only throughout the extradition hearing," Montgomery said. "And only because she hopes it will expedite the procedure. She wants to get it over with." He shook his head. "There are defenses. She was young, influenced by others. Her life has obviously been exemplary since then." He paused. "The FBI has indicated they would recommend a plea bargain if she would help them find the others and whatever is left of the money. It's her best chance."

Liz's legs almost buckled beneath her. In spite of the evidence, she'd held on to a glimmer of hope that there had been a monstrous mistake. Her father's face paled, but he did not look as surprised as she felt.

"Surely she's going to cooperate," she said hopefully.

"She says not," Montgomery said.

"Why not?" she asked as she caught her father's hand, her fingers tightening around his. The ground felt as if it was shifting beneath her.

"She wouldn't say," the attorney replied. "Perhaps you can convince her."

Montgomery led them back into the reception area and talked to the clerk. He then shepherded them through doors that locked behind them and into another reception area. She surrendered her purse, and her father emptied his pockets. They were then ushered into a small room apparently used for attorney meetings with their clients. The furnishings were minimalist. A table and three chairs.

A guard led her mother inside. She was handcuffed, and the female guard linked the cuffs to a ring bolted into the table. "I'll be outside," she said, looking at Montgomery. "Knock when you're ready."

Liz stood, stunned by the change in her mother. She had last seen her at supper four days ago. They were talking about her company, and her mother's eyes had blazed with enthusiasm. Now she looked decades older. She wore a shapeless jumpsuit a size too large, and her short hair was uncombed. Her face was haggard, and there was no hint of the smile Liz knew so well.

Her father went over and kissed her cheek, but her mother seemed to withdraw from him and into herself. He stood, his hands on her shoulders as if protecting her from the world.

Montgomery's voice broke the silence. "I'll be outside for ten minutes. Then we all have to talk."

Her father paid no attention as the attorney left. Instead his hand smoothed his wife's cheek. "Why didn't you talk to me about this?

"Talk about what?" her mother said in a toneless voice. "That I was involved in a murder decades ago?" Her blue eyes looked faded, hopeless.

"Mr. Montgomery said there are defenses," Liz said. "You have to help him."

Betty Connor looked up at her, her eyes softening for a moment. "I'm sorry, baby. I never thought—"

"They can't be right," Liz said, desperately trying to find an explanation. Something to hold on to.

"They *are* right. I was foolish to think I wouldn't eventually be found."

The frank admission was like a sword in Liz's heart. "You must have been forced. Mr. Montgomery . . ."

"Mr. Montgomery will do as I ask," her mother said tonelessly. "I'm guilty. I'm going to plead guilty." Her gaze went to Liz. "I want you to go on with your business, and Steve, I want a divorce. I won't see either of you after today." Her voice was brittle, and her sky-blue eyes had the glazed look of despair.

"You can't do that," Liz said, wondering why her father was so quiet.

"I *can* do it," her mother said. "I no longer have much control over my life, but I can say who I wish to see or not."

"You don't mean it. What about Sue and the kids, and—?"

"You're better off without me. I'm going to prison, and I won't have you, any of you, live your lives around prison visits."

"Mr. Montgomery said you can cooperate and—"

"I have nothing I can cooperate with," she said, a raw edge in her voice. "I don't know where the others are. If I did . . . I wouldn't betray them."

Liz felt as if the world had turned topsy-turvy. Fierce protectiveness turned to bewilderment. "You don't mean that?"

"I mean every word, Liz, and I'm asking you to respect my wishes."

"I can't do that, not if it means abandoning you."

"If you love me, if you want to help, you'll do as I ask. It's what I want."

"What happened?" Liz begged, unwilling to leave it here, to believe the unbelievable.

"I participated in a robbery in which two men were killed," her mother said. "No one was to be hurt, but I knew there was the possibility. I knew, or should have known, what I was doing. The reasons don't matter now. I'm just so sorry it's touching you and your sister now." Her voice was frighteningly calm.

Liz had expected her mother to be confused, frightened, ready to fight to correct a wrong. This calm acceptance was terrifying in itself. She shook her head. "No, we'll fight this. Together."

"Instead of fighting each other?" her mother asked, her voice thin and, Liz thought, close to tears. It was a reminder of the arguments they'd had, the estrangement after Liz had left for a year on the road.

Her father's hand was on his wife's shoulder. He looked at Liz. "Wait outside with Montgomery," he said. "Please."

Liz didn't want to go. She looked at her mother. She knew what the charges meant. Her mother could spend the rest of her life in prison. She wept inside.

"Go, Liz," her father said.

She went over to the other side of the table and hugged her mother. Liz felt the tension in her mother's shoulders, saw it in the rigid set of her body.

"I love you," she said, hearing the tears in her voice. She couldn't remember when last she had said the words. There had been too much anger.

Her mother didn't answer. Liz's legs seemed rubbery as she forced herself to leave. Her father could convince her mother to fight, to cooperate with authorities. After a knock, the door opened, and she left, looking back as she did. Pain was etched on her mother's face.

Liz hesitated, but her father mouthed the word, "Go," again.

She almost doubled over as a guard closed the door behind her. She realized she had finally accepted the fact that there was no mistake. But there must be reasons.

"The reasons don't matter." Her mother's words. But they *did* matter. Her mother had been forced into it. She hadn't known what was going to happen.

Montgomery stood outside the door. "Will she cooperate?"

"She said not, but Dad is talking to her."

"Did she say anything we can use?"

"No." Her answer was as flat as her mother's had been. "Tell me about it," she said. "What happened?"

"I can't discuss what she told me without her permission. I can tell you what the federal authorities are alleging. A group of three men and a woman stopped an armored car. Two guards were shot. One died immediately, the other several days later. Before he died, he said a young lady, her clothes torn and her face bloody, stumbled into the road as the armored car approached. Thinking she'd been attacked or hit by a car, they stopped. They shouldn't have. They should have phoned it in, but . . ."

A rock settled in her throat. "But they were Good Samaritans?"

"Yes."

"They say that young lady is my mother?"

"She admitted it."

"She didn't explain why?"

"No. She just said she wanted to plead guilty and end it. That she knew it would happen someday, and she's relieved it's over."

Her mother, the person she had loved all her life, had a dark and dangerous secret. How it must have shadowed her life.

But why wouldn't she cooperate now? *"I wouldn't betray them."* Did she care more about those people of thirty-four years ago than her family?

The traitorous thought couldn't quite be squashed. Confusion, anger, love, and pity all washed through her like waves on a beach, some gaining in power, some fading. She couldn't help but feel the woman inside the room wasn't the mother she knew. The familiar warmth had surfaced only momentarily. Mostly, she'd been remote. Sad but composed.

A shiver crept down Liz's back.

How do you accept the fact that your well-loved mother has just admitted to being part of the murder of two innocent men? Liz simply couldn't put the two women together. She looked up, aware of Montgomery's gaze on her, weighing her reaction.

Dammit, she didn't know what her reaction was.

What was her father saying inside the room? What was her mother saying?

She knew only one thing. She had to learn as much as possible about the robbery. Only then could she understand.

"Do you know a Caleb Adams?" she asked.

"He's a private detective, though I've never used him. He has something of a reputation."

"What kind of reputation?"

"He's difficult to work with. If the client is guilty, an attorney doesn't use him. He'll work as hard to find evidence to convict him as to exonerate him. Doesn't take many cases. I hear he works only when he wants to."

"He was here last night, asking about my mother. He and the FBI agent—Monroe—had an argument. It was obvious they didn't like each other."

"That's courthouse legend," he said. "Adams was working for a defense attorney and found evidence that would clear his client, evidence the FBI had withheld. Monroe was lucky to keep his job."

"That says something about both men," she said.

"Well, Adams did some illegal wiretapping, and Monroe went after him."

"And . . ."

He shrugged. "The government didn't prosecute. It's rumored that Adams found a few more embarrassing shortcuts the prosecution had taken."

"He says he used to be with the Boston Police Department and had studied the armored car robbery. He said he would like to help us."

"Did he say why?"

"He's writing a book."

"Would you like some free legal advice?" he said.

"Yes."

"Be careful. I'll have my office do a quick background check on him, but don't say anything you wouldn't like to see in print."

"I'll watch what I say, but perhaps he has information we can't find somewhere else."

"You also asked about a Michael Gallagher. He called and introduced himself. He said his law firm would do any work in Boston we might need. I have someone checking on him as well."

She looked up at him and saw empathy in his eyes. She was grateful he didn't try to talk down to her or tell her everything would be all right. She suspected nothing would be right for a very long time.

"I have to call my sister," she said.

"The extradition hearing will be Wednesday."

"What happens then?"

"Usually the defense will make arguments against extradition. She's been an exemplary citizen of this state for more than thirty years. But she won't let me do that."

"Is there any chance of bail?"

"Not for a fugitive who has eluded the federal government for three decades."

"Fugitive. I can't get used to that word in connection with my mother."

"You're going to hear it a lot. The press will come after you like locusts. There will be requests for interviews from national talk shows. You'll have to decide whether you and your family want to publicly defend her or not."

"What would you advise?"

"I'm one of the few attorneys who believe the less said the better." He paused. "I'll help you find an attorney in Boston."

She nodded.

Her father emerged from the room then. She had thought his face had aged since yesterday. Even more lines etched it now. In answer to her silent question, he shook his head. His eyes looked tired, ravaged. Raw.

"She's determined," he told both of them. "She won't answer questions. She wants to plead guilty." He hesitated, then said, "Betty—" He stopped suddenly, obviously reminding himself that the woman he knew as Betty was really Sarah Jane.

He turned to Montgomery. "What is the worst that can happen?"

"Life in prison. There is no death penalty in Massachusetts."

Liz closed her eyes in pure agony. She knew her father felt even more pain. Her mother had been more than his wife. She'd been his best friend.

No. A best friend doesn't keep secrets.

"Did she say why?"

"She said she wouldn't make excuses."

"But why protect—?"

"Maybe she doesn't know where they are."

"She said that, but then said she wouldn't give the information if she could. I don't understand that."

"We have to do it her way," he said quietly.

"I don't," Liz replied. "Are you going to call Sue, or should I?"

He looked stricken. Even more than she, Sue had been convinced it was some type of terrible mistake.

"I will," she said. "Mr. Montgomery says the extradition hearing will be Wednesday."

Her father flinched. "So soon?"

"She's not opposing it," Montgomery broke in.

Her father glanced toward the attorney as if reminded he was there.

"She'll need some fresh clothes for the hearing," Montgomery said. "Something modest, not flashy."

"I'll do that," Liz said.

Her father nodded, then he looked at her. "She asked if you and Sue are all right."

"Did you tell her about the fire?"

"No."

Montgomery turned to her then. "Have you talked to anyone from the fire department?"

"They believe the fire started in the kitchen, around the stove. They asked if I had cooked before I left home yesterday." *Was it only yesterday?* "I hadn't. Nor the night before. I'm going to drive up there this afternoon and talk to them."

"Let me know what they say," Montgomery said.

"I'm staying here," her father said.

"I thought so," Liz replied. "I'll drive you to get a rental car."

"He and I need to talk," the attorney said. "I'll take him."

Liz hesitated. She wanted to be included. And yet she had to get back to her house and see what needed to be done there. She had to stop at her business. Her new business. They might all be depending on it.

So many conflicting demands. Her heart cried at her mother's broken appearance and apathy to her fate. She hated the feeling of helplessness. She'd always prided herself in being strong, in guiding events. But now she felt consumed by what she didn't know, and the loss of control that made her rudderless.

She hugged her father. "I'll see you later." She wanted to say something hopeful, but his expression told her he wouldn't accept it. He didn't want false comfort. He was seeking answers.

She went down the steps to the parking lot. As she reached the car, she took the cell phone from her purse, along with a piece of paper with a number written on it. She hesitated, then punched the numbers.

When a voice answered, it was curt. "Adams," he said in a voice that radiated impatience.

She hesitated, then, "Mr. Adams, this is Liz Connor."

"Ms. Connor?"

"Will you tell me what you know about the armed robbery?"

"Yes."

No questions. No elaboration. "Tomorrow?"

"What about today?" he asked.

"I have to drive home. There was a fire at my house last night."

A silence. "I'll drive with you."

"How would you get back?"

"I'll find a way."

She hesitated. He'd been a disturbing presence yesterday. She remembered the smell of alcohol on him and recalled Montgomery's comments. But after talking to her mother, she was obsessed with learning more about what happened all those years ago. And if he had been a detective involved in an investigation of the robbery, or was compiling information for a book, he would have far more information than old news accounts.

"Where are you?"

"A motel several blocks from the detention center."

"I'll pick you up. Give me directions."

He did, and she remembered seeing the motel. It was not far from her own.

"Can you be ready in ten minutes?"

"Yes." He hung up.

It was the most abrupt conversation she'd ever had. It was as if he didn't want to give her an opportunity to backtrack. She wondered about the wisdom of riding with someone she didn't know. But then he was a former cop, apparently a fairly well-known private detective, and she had gone with strangers many times on various outdoor "adventures."

She went over everything she knew about him, which was very little. *"Be careful."* Montgomery's words echoed in her head.

She could do that. She was a good judge of character. She had to be to guide tourists down dangerous rapids or take them on overnight riding trips into the mountains. One troublemaker could endanger the entire group or make the trip so unpleasant, the other guests would never again return. She'd also learned diplomacy, a skill that had propelled her onto the Santa Fe City Council.

She could make her own judgment of Caleb Adams while Montgomery did a more detailed check. She would try to learn what he knew without giving away any information of her own.

She *could* do that.

Her mind turned to other worries. She had not checked with Tracy this morning. How many calls were on her answering machine at home? How many from reporters? From friends? From cranks? Did she even have an answering machine now? She forced herself not to panic at the number of questions pounding at her. She arrived at the motel and drove up to the entrance. To her surprise, he was waiting for her. He wore what looked like the same jeans but had changed shirts. His lips were in that odd little half smile she had seen yesterday.

Without so much as a greeting, he got into the passenger's side.

"You said there was a fire at your house last night."

She told him what had happened in what she hoped

was a cool, objective voice. She wasn't going to confess her fears to him.

She pulled out of the parking lot, darting a glance at him as she waited for a light to change. "Did you find out anything yesterday?" she asked instead, knowing that the fraternity of law enforcement often talked, even if they weren't supposed to.

"No more than what was in the papers."

She had skimmed over them this morning. There had been less than she already knew and more than she wanted to read. Her family's entire life histories had been exposed to the public. The fire would have been there as well, she thought, had it not happened after the paper was printed. It would make the papers tomorrow.

She sighed.

"This must be hard on you," he said.

She glanced quickly at him before returning her concentration to the road. For some reason, she didn't think he was a man who engaged in small talk. And that was exactly what the words were. There was little feeling in them.

"Harder on my mother."

"Did she tell you anything?"

"No," she said, unwilling to give him anything until he gave her a great deal. She noted he was the second man today to ask that question.

Another quick glance. He looked relaxed, but a muscle twitched in his throat. He was all intensity, and he filled the interior of the car with a raw masculinity that was unsettling. Especially now. She didn't need it. She didn't want it.

She tensed. She felt his eyes on her. Weighing her just as she was weighing him.

"You said you worked on the armored car robbery?"

"Not officially. But yes, on and off over the years."

"Why?"

"Because it was a case that was never solved. Because two men died. Because I always suspected that one of them might have been involved." He hesitated, then added, "I don't like puzzles with missing pieces. I always want to find them."

There was an odd note in his voice, and she wondered whether he'd just revealed something he hadn't meant to reveal.

"Tell me what you know," she demanded.

"I only know what one of the guards said before he died. He said they were driving from several banks with used bills to the Federal Reserve. There were two guards. There should have been three, but one became ill just before the run, and there wasn't anyone available to take his place. More than a few rules were broken that day. A woman appeared on the side of the road, stumbled, and fell. There was blood. A lot of it. It was six in the morning, and the road was empty. They stopped.

"As one of the guards leaned over her, three men wearing masks appeared, seemingly from nowhere. The men wore black half masks, but he saw they were young. Nervous. They all had guns. Someone started firing. That's all he remembered. He died three days later."

From his short, clipped words, she could see the scene. She suspected he did, as well.

"How did they suspect my mother was involved?"

"They found the murder weapon and traced the fingerprints to your mother. She'd been arrested three months earlier in a campus protest at Harvard. In addition, one guard described her before he died. Said the attackers claimed they were members of the Defenders of Liberty, and that they planned to use the money to fight against imperial warmongers."

The news sank slowly in. So did the implication. "She didn't fire the gun! She couldn't have."

Silence.

"There were no other fingerprints on the weapon," he said.

"Perhaps she was forced."

His silence signaled his disbelief.

"You said you thought one of the guards was involved."

"Could have been," he said. "At least that was a theory. Armored car drivers aren't supposed to stop for anything or anyone. They had radios in the car. They should have called the police. They certainly shouldn't have left the car."

She had read some of the details in the newspaper, but not about the principal part played by the woman.

The woman that federal authorities said was her mother.

chapter eight

Caleb looked straight ahead at the road, feeling the first not-so-gentle stirrings of conscience.

"How far along have you gone on your book?" she probed as they left Albuquerque and turned on Interstate 25.

"I've pretty much finished the research."

"Have you written anything yet?"

"Just playing with the first chapter."

"Where does it start?"

"On a bright morning in March," he said. "The security guards are leaving their homes. I know their every movement."

"I would like to read what you have."

"It's not ready for anyone to read."

It wasn't only not ready, it didn't exist. He was an accomplished liar, a necessary skill he'd acquired when he'd worked undercover. One of the hazards had been that it was too easy to slip into the lifestyle he'd been sworn to bring down. He'd never been comfortable with the idea of betrayal, even with bad guys. He'd been damned good at it, though.

He was lying again and knew he would continue to lie.

He had to find out whether Liz and her father—knowingly or not—could lead him to the others connected with the robbery.

He could have told Liz the truth. She wasn't likely to be sympathetic to his cause, though. How was he to explain

that he wanted nothing more than to see her mother prose-
cuted to the fullest extent of the law? He had to maintain
the fiction of being a budding writer.

He directed his attention back to Elizabeth Connor, who
had turned quiet after his last abrupt answer. He'd heard
her father call her Liz, but Elizabeth shored up the barrier
he had erected against her.

Her life must be crashing down around her.

*Remember. You've been wanting justice for more than
thirty years.*

He tried not to notice how attractive he found her. Her
thick auburn hair was cut in an easy style that framed her
face and swung when she walked. Her mouth was probably too wide, and her cheekbones too angular for beauty,
but her topaz-blue eyes were striking. Her personality had
been prickly at the detention center, but there was something about her that made him think that under any other
circumstances she would have an easy way about her. Her
stride was graceful, and her body athletic without being
bone thin. She was also smart. She listened and probed as
well as any investigator.

"Tell me about your mother," he said.

She was silent for a moment, as if trying to find the
right words. "She's a good person," she said simply. "It
took me a long time to realize how good."

*A good woman who'd murdered a young boy's father. A
woman's husband.*

"How so?" he asked.

"She loves well," Elizabeth said.

He was struck by that wording. He'd never heard it said
exactly that way. It reminded him of his wife. She'd loved
well, too. Damn, but he missed her and his son. He tried
not to think about them, had tried to hide in shadows so the
terrible truth couldn't find him. And then he would hear
something, a familiar expression or a child's laughter, and
the agony returned.

He hadn't really gotten justice then. He planned to get
it now. "Does she have any close longtime friends?"

"My mother has many friends," she finally said. "Some
for as long as they've lived here."

"Thirty-two years," he said. It was a question as much as a comment.

She gave him a quick glance.

"It was in the paper this morning." That was true. But he'd also done some additional research at the computer last night.

Her gaze returned to the road. "How long were you with the Boston Police Department?"

"Eighteen years."

"You're retired?"

"Not by choice. My knee was injured, and I was put on disability." Again a half truth. He had briefly taken a desk job, but he'd gone crazy after the explosion. He hadn't been able to sleep or eat. He'd become obsessed with capturing the man who'd planted the explosives and hadn't wanted to accept the fact he'd been killed in a shoot-out with officers. He kept thinking there had to be others involved.

But no one found any other connection. The perp had been arrested years earlier by Caleb and by all accounts had harbored a grudge all the years he served in prison. A simple act of vengeance.

He couldn't accept that. Nor could he accept being a desk jockey. He couldn't stand not being on the streets. He started drinking too much, and he knew how destructive that could be to his job. He finally accepted full disability retirement and a recommendation by the department shrink to leave Boston.

"Why New Mexico?" she asked, breaking into his thoughts. "It's a long way from Boston."

He hesitated. He didn't want to talk about his family. But he needed her trust. "My wife was from Albuquerque. She loved the mountains and taught me to appreciate them as well."

Was.

What a difference a verb tense could make.

She was silent for a moment, obviously weighing every word, just as he was. He waited for the questions, was surprised when they didn't come.

"I'm sorry," she finally said, and he wondered whether his voice had given away the depth of his grief.

"She died four years ago," he said. It was the first time he'd mentioned it to a stranger since he'd been in New Mexico. He certainly had not intended to tell her even that much. He didn't want her sympathy.

She glanced over at him again, and this time her gaze lingered for a second before darting back to the road.

She returned to her original subject. "Have you ever had anything published?"

"No," he said honestly. It was, he knew, too easy to check.

"But you decided to write a book? Because it's easy?"

"Actually it's the most difficult thing I have ever done," he said. "But I found myself with time on my hands, and the case always fascinated me."

"Why that one?"

"Four young people with their futures bright and beckoning?" he said. "What made them decide to get involved with something like robbery?"

"Idealism?" she tried. "Maybe they thought they were fighting for a just cause. To prevent needless slaughter."

He had a few answers now. It was obvious she knew few—if any—details, but she would defend her mother, regardless of the facts. She was already making excuses. Perhaps, he thought honestly, he would have done the same thing if he'd found himself in similar circumstances. If his father . . .

But his father never would have become involved. Something Caleb meant to prove. He'd heard the speculation that it might have been an inside job gone wrong. His mother had lived with it as well.

She was silent the rest of the drive into Santa Fe, and he didn't want to push any more at the moment. Despite the churning inside him, the urgency he felt to learn truths that had evaded him for years, he felt an odd comfort with her. Damn it, he liked her. Was even attracted to her. And that could prove disastrous.

He forced himself to sit back and consider the next step. He would have to rent a car, drive up to his cabin, and make sure Tramp was okay before returning for his car in Albuquerque. Though he'd planned a quick trip back, he'd left enough food in a dog feeder for a week and two pails of water, along with a dog door to allow Tramp entrance and exit.

Think about the next step, and the next. Not about the woman next to him. She was a means to a long-awaited end. No more.

A fire inspector's car, a television news van, and another car with a woman leaning against it were parked in front of Liz's house as she drove up.

Her neat adobe house was a mess. The door hung on hinges, windows were broken, and the smell of smoke permeated the air.

She got out of the car and went up to the door, ignoring the television crew and the local reporter who chased her up the walk. At the broken, door she turned around and gave them what she hoped was a pleasant smile.

"I'll have a statement later," she said.

"When?"

"After I talk to the fire investigator."

"Did you know about your mother's past?" a television reporter she recognized asked.

"No comment," she said.

"Surely your father knew something," Allison Main, the local reporter said.

"Something about what?" Liz said, looking squarely at the reporter. "You're assuming something that has not been proven."

"Come on, Liz," Allison said. "Give us something. An interview would be nice. You could tell us your side."

She and Allison had met for coffee several times, once after her first meeting as a council member. Allison had given her some pointers, and Liz had been grateful, even knowing that Allison would expect something in return.

Not today.

"I'm sorry. I have to talk to the fire investigator."

"Do you think the fire had anything to do with . . ."

Caleb Adams stepped up. "You heard the lady. Give her a break."

A microphone was shoved in his face. "Who are you?"

Her self-appointed protector merely ignored both the questioner and the microphone, opened the smashed door, and shoved her inside. She noticed the lock was broken.

The house stank of smoke and wet carpet. She thought her heart would break as she viewed the interior. Smoke coated the walls now streaked with water. Her handwoven Indian rug was soaked, as were the comfortable sofa and easy chair. Several paintings were damaged.

Numb, she stood there and surveyed the wreckage. She had expected damage, of course, but the reality was like being hit with a sledgehammer. She took several deep breaths as she tried to think of everything that needed to be done. How to even start?

"One step at a time," Caleb said softly.

She nodded. His presence steadied her and she was grateful. She started a mental list. Notify her landlord. Call the insurance company. Board up the windows and fix the locks. Get someone to restore the rug.

She walked into the kitchen. The windows were blown out. The walls and ceiling were scorched. Paint on the fridge and the dishwasher was bubbled. The smell of smoke was even stronger here. She recognized Dan Howell, a fire investigator, who was leaning over the melted ruins of her cabinets.

He looked up. "Ms. Connor," he said with a nod.

"How did it start?" she asked.

"I hoped you could help tell me that," he said. "It looks like a grease fire on the stove top. The knob for the burner was melted, but it looked as if it was positioned on high. You're lucky your neighbor was so quick. This could have destroyed the house. As it is, the fire damage was pretty much contained in the kitchen, though there's water damage throughout."

"There was no pan on the stove when I left yesterday," she said. "Certainly no grease. I had a bagel for breakfast."

"Coffee?"

"In an automatic coffee brewer, but I turned it off. Even if I hadn't, it turns itself off after two hours."

He looked down at a iron frying pan lying on the floor. It was her favorite, and it was obvious that something had been in it.

"The burner wasn't on when I left," she said again, her mind frantically searching for explanations. She knew she'd left the kitchen tidy, all pans put away, and certainly knew she hadn't cooked food. She went to the back door and tried it.

The lock had been broken, the door forced. Probably by the firefighters. "Do you know whether it was locked when your men arrived?" she asked.

"No, but I'll find out."

"Were reporters here yesterday?" The question came from Caleb Adams.

"Your neighbor said there were some earlier, but none at the time of the fire," Howell said.

It would have been easy for someone to come in through the back alley that ran behind the houses. There was an adobe wall in back, but someone could go over that without being seen from the front. Had someone invaded her home, arranged for a fire that would be blamed on her carelessness? She *knew* she hadn't left the pan on the stove.

She also knew she couldn't stand here, feeling overwhelmed by what had happened, not knowing which of many calls she should make. A carpet cleaner first. Perhaps someone could save the handwoven rug that was one of her most cherished possessions. Thank God she had renter's insurance, but some of her treasures could not be replaced.

"We'll need a statement," Howell said almost apologetically.

"Of course," she said, then in a lower voice. "But I can assure you there was no pan on the stove."

"We'll take a close look at it," he said.

"Can I call someone to start on the damage?"

"I want a couple of people in here to look at this before any work is done. But go ahead and call your insurance company. Have an adjuster out here. If your insurance company doesn't fix the door and windows tonight, let me know. I'll get someone out here."

"Thank you," she said.

"I was sorry to hear about your mother," he said. "She has a lot of friends. Tell her that."

"Thank you." Gratitude flooded her, and she felt her eyes sting with tears. She fought against shedding them, but she needed that moment of kindness. She felt an arm at her back, and turned.

Caleb Adams stood just to the side of her, and his arm gave her momentary comfort. She sensed his touch had been instinctive, and as her gaze met his, he stepped back. Once more, he was the onlooker. Cool. Distant.

But the touch had been enough to keep the tears from flowing. It had been a silent reinforcement. She looked at him and was startled at the empathy in eyes that before were so guarded.

She tried the phone and wasn't surprised when it didn't work. She took her cell phone from her purse and called her insurance agency. She reported the fire and arranged for a representative to be at the house within the next two hours. She then called the out-of-town owner of the house and reported the fire to him.

With those preliminary steps taken, she started for her bedroom. The sand-colored carpet whooshed as she stepped on it. She looked in the closet. Her clothes were wet and smelled of smoke. Her bedding was soaked as well.

She started to take the sheets and quilt off the bed, and again found Caleb Adams helping.

She didn't want his help.

The bed was somehow intimate. Her reaction to him too raw. He stirred feelings in her when she wanted to be numb. Even his quiet questions evoked emotions and memories that threatened to overwhelm her.

"I can do it myself," she said more curtly than she intended. He quit and moved away. No protest. No change in his face. No sign that he was offended.

Simply acquiescence.

She wanted to hit him. No, not him. Someone. Anyone.

She bent to her task, gathering up the linen sheets and quilt that served as a bedspread. The mattress would be a total loss.

Liz looked up. Caleb Adams and his disturbing presence were gone. Had he left the house? She wasn't sure she wanted that, either.

Voices came from the kitchen. Her hands full of bedclothes, she walked to the door. Adams was talking to Howell, their heads together.

"I think she would know what was in her kitchen," she heard him say. "And I've never believed in coincidences. I would wager my last dollar that this is arson."

She couldn't hear Howell's reply, but her heart beat harder.

Someone believed her.

Someone who wanted something from her.

She had to remember that.

chapter nine

Michael Gallagher was facing failure for the second time in one day. He wasn't used to it. He didn't like it. Win Maynard would like it even less.

He'd tried to arrange a meeting with Colton Montgomery, Betty Connor's attorney, but he'd been put off until the next day. He suspected Montgomery was doing a little checking of his own. His credentials would pass muster, but he didn't like the delay.

Then he'd tried to see Betty Connor and was told she couldn't see anyone but her attorney of record and her family during visiting hours. His one hope was to see the family here and try once more to convince them he *could* help.

Frustrated, he returned to his laptop computer and continued his search on the Connors. Their credit reports might tell him something. He wanted to know exactly what leverage he had.

He faced the parking lot. Not a great view, but a useful one. He knew Liz Connor drove a red jeep. It was distinctive. But there was no such vehicle in the parking lot, nor had there been all afternoon.

He'd hoped she—or her father—would call once they realized the enormity of the charges against Betty Connor and that they would accept his employer's invitation to finance the defense. They were still in shock this morning. He'd seen it in their faces. Reality would hit soon enough.

He didn't understand the husband's antipathy, unless it was resentment against a family he'd obviously known nothing about, and the resentment had transferred to him as its agent. A good attorney was a student of human nature. He knew how easy it was to transfer anger to whomever was the nearest target.

The daughter was a different story. She was suspicious. She was obviously one of those who believed the motto, "Beware of Greeks bearing gifts." In this case, beware of strangers offering assistance.

He'd known immediately he had to back away, wait for them to make the first move.

He hit the speed dial on his cell phone. It only rang once.

"Win. It's Michael. They've refused our help, at least for the moment."

"Why?"

"Pride, I think, and suspicion. They'll find out soon enough that pride doesn't buy a good defense. I understand the district attorney in Boston plans to charge her with first-degree murder. The federal government is also clamoring for jurisdiction."

"Is she cooperating?"

"Not from what I hear, but it's early."

"I want to know if she does."

"I'm acquiring sources."

"Good. What can you tell me about the Connors?" Maynard demanded.

"The husband is a high school principal. Has a great reputation. Good with kids. No unusual debts I can find. They own their house. His wife—your cousin—has never worked, and they don't live extravagantly. The oldest daughter—Elizabeth Connor—is obviously smart and, again, well-liked in the community. She was recently appointed to the city council and will stand for election for a full term. She just bought a company called Santa Fe Adventures, which will certainly strain her finances." He hesitated, then added, "There was a fire at her home early this morning."

"How bad was it?"

"A lot of interior damage. No one was hurt."

"Find out what you can about it."

"I will. Problem is I'm not representing any of the parties."

"Then bullshit your way in," Maynard said. "What do you think of the daughter?"

"Not easily used," Michael said, remembering the wary look in her eyes. "But I think she's more of a realist than her father."

"And the other daughter?"

"Married to a real estate attorney. Two kids. Apparently a stay-at-home mother. They have a good income, but he's still paying off law school debts."

"Did you get the impression that they knew anything, anything at all, about Betty Connor's past?"

"I'm certain they'd never heard the name Maynard before," Michael said. "Mr. Connor might have had some suspicion that something dark lurked in his wife's past, but I don't think he knew anything about the robbery."

"My cousin has turned into a very good liar, it seems," Maynard said. "She couldn't keep a secret when she was a girl."

"Murder changes people," Michael said. "According to all the news accounts, she's been the epitome of respectability these last thirty-two years. The only thing unusual is that she's never worked."

"Can you gain the daughter's confidence? I want to know exactly what Sarah is saying, or plans to say."

"I can try."

"Don't try. Do it. Fast."

The phone went dead. Maynard was always abrupt. But there was an intensity that he'd not heard before. Even, perhaps, a touch of fear. One thing for sure, he wasn't only concerned with the welfare and happiness of his cousin and her family.

It went far deeper.

Michael closed the phone and placed it on the desk. Perhaps if he could find some articles about Elizabeth, he would learn more about her hobbies, her likes, her dislikes. The more he knew, the easier it would be to get close to her. Not a distasteful thought at all. Though she wasn't his usual type, she held a certain appeal for him.

He looked back at the parking lot. Still no red jeep.

He turned back to the computer and this time searched for Santa Fe Adventures. He wanted to know everything there was to know about Liz Connor.

An arson investigator joined Dan at Liz's house. She went over everything with him as well while he inspected both the doors and origin of the fire.

He shook his head. "There's no doubt about the cause," he said. "It was a grease fire. The question is how the grease got into that frying pan."

Liz started to say something, but he held up his hand. "I'm not saying we don't believe you. We're going to turn the report over to the police. But we've done all we can at this point. You can go ahead and get the house cleaned," he said.

"That's not very satisfactory."

"I know. But the firemen smashed the doors. We can't determine whether they or someone else broke the locks. The fire would have destroyed any fingerprints. We will suggest that the police department check the property on a regular basis."

Frustrated, she nodded.

Once they were gone, she went back into the kitchen and surveyed the ruined kitchen, wishing the walls could talk and tell her exactly what had happened early this morning.

But there was nothing. Only the blistered fridge with a blackened door that wouldn't close, even if it had worked. The smell of smoke, rotting food, and damp upholstery permeated the house.

She felt Caleb's presence beside her. "I don't think he believed me," she said.

"I do."

"I heard you tell him that. Thank you."

"I think you're a lady who remembers whether or not she left a frying pan full of grease on a hot stove."

She swallowed hard. Even she had started to doubt her sanity.

"I'll take you to get a rental car," she said.

"Aren't you waiting for the insurance adjusters?"

"I'll leave a note. It's not as if there's much left for anyone to steal," she added dryly. "And it shouldn't take more than twenty minutes."

"You're coming back?"

She nodded. "There's so much to do."

"I don't think you should be alone in the house," he said, "and I have nowhere better to go at the moment."

Relief flooded her. She hated that. She really had dreaded being alone. His matter-of-fact competence staved off the fear and anger that threatened to overwhelm her.

Still, she protested one last time. "I'm fine."

"I don't doubt that for a moment. I can always just watch if you want."

"No way," she said.

The side of his mouth that was perpetually in a half smile turned up even further. It gave his mouth a lopsided look, but it was a strangely pleasant expression. Perhaps because it was the first hint of humor in a man who exuded privacy, even secrecy.

She suddenly wanted to know more about him, about the wife he'd mentioned, and whether he had children, but it was none of her business, and she remembered the way his lips had tightened when he mentioned her. *Four years earlier.* The pain was obviously still there.

"Are you always a Lancelot?"

"God forbid," he said. "That's the first time anyone has said that."

"What do they usually say?"

"You don't want to know."

"A rebel then?" she asked lightly.

"That's a sanitized version."

"I have rebel in me, too," she admitted.

"I thought you were the paradigm of good behavior. Your own business. City council. Good citizen committees."

She raised an eyebrow. "Paradigm?"

He gave her a smug look. "Cops read, you know."

"You've been checking up on me." It was a challenge.

She saw a muscle move in his cheek. "A writer does research, but I admit I don't know much about Elizabeth the rebel."

Their gazes met, questioned. Sexual magnetism radiated between them. Her heart jolted at the strength of it.

His breath came quicker. Hers almost stopped.

She didn't know how much was real, how much was need. How much was the vulnerability she'd never felt before.

Then he turned away. "We had better get started cleaning up what we can," he said.

She tried to tame the dizzying current racing through her body. It was the overload of emotions. Nothing else.

He was here only because of a book he wanted to write. She turned away from him, took steps toward some sodden newspapers. She was usually more careful with her heart.

Yet some emotion, attraction, connection sizzled between them. She'd never experienced anything like it before. She'd been attracted to men before, but usually after knowing them, liking them. Trusting them. She'd never felt this raw sexuality . . .

Darn it. She wasn't going to go there. Perhaps it was just wanting to avoid reality. Perhaps emotional and physical exhaustion. *Be careful.*

She should take him to get a car. Get him away from here. He muddled her thinking. He muddled her senses. Yet his presence was comforting. And she didn't want to be alone.

"Let's start with the paintings," he said, apparently reading her mind and determined not to go. She wasn't sure she liked that. She wondered if he'd read it a few seconds earlier. She certainly hoped not.

They worked together in silence. She thought the framed oil paintings would be fine, though the frames might have to be replaced. He took one down and looked at it, his hand accidently brushing hers as she helped him lift it from the wall. It was as if lightning hit her. Electricity ran through her body, and she stood there, stunned.

It was a continuation of what had started minutes ago and had magnified many times over. He lowered the painting to the floor and reached out to her. His fingers touched her face lightly, then smoothed back a wayward lock of hair.

He leaned down, and his lips brushed hers. It was a tentative touch. Tender yet crackling. Every nerve seemed to come alive. The core of her warmed, and she needed that warmth. "Wow." Clearly, he felt it, too.

He straightened and gave her a quizzical look. "This is not a good idea."

"Why?" she asked even as she knew why. She'd told herself why more than once.

He gave her that lopsided smile. "You're vulnerable."

"No," she denied.

"You said your mother loved well," he said. "I don't love well."

He moved away then, and the room suddenly seemed to chill.

"Let's look at the books," he said, his voice cool.

Her body ached. She ached for that momentary tenderness. She called herself all kinds of a fool, but simply nodded. They went through the house listing property that had been destroyed: the television set she rarely used and the often-utilized sound system.

She checked on her small office. The computer was probably destroyed from the water damage. She started to move it when she saw a crack in the casing. She checked inside. The hard drive was missing. So were her backup disks.

Was that the reason for the fire? To cover up a theft? But why? There wouldn't be anything of interest to anyone other than herself. She paid bills via the computer. She had some financial records from Santa Fe Adventures. Her address book.

She headed for the living area. She had proof now that someone else had been in her house.

Caleb Adams was on the floor going through the books one by one, making two piles. He seemed fascinated by them, and she watched as he looked in the front of each book, then ran fingers through the pages before putting them in one of the piles.

"Caleb?"

He turned. "An interesting collection," he observed. "I think most will survive, though not in the best of condition."

"The hard drive is missing from my computer," she said without preamble.

He unwound his body from the floor and stood. "What was on it?"

"Company records. Clients. Their likes and dislikes."

"Any financial information?"

"Yes."

"Personal information? Friends? Addresses?"

"Of course, but . . ."

"Do you have backups for it?"

"My disks are gone as well."

The doorbell rang then, and she went to the door. The adjustor from her landlord's insurance company entered. She took his card, but the questions Caleb had just asked kept going through her mind. So did the image of his head bent over the books, his fingers going through each book so carefully.

She braced herself for the questions she knew were coming. She led him to the kitchen and waited as he looked around.

"How did it start?"

"I think it was arson," she said.

"You think?"

"I know," she corrected herself. She told him the story, adding now the information about the missing hard drive.

"I'll get the report from the fire department," he said. She couldn't tell whether or not he believed her.

"First thing is an electrician and cleaning crew," he said. "Will someone be here tomorrow?"

"I'll have to let you know. I might have to be in Albuquerque early in the morning, but someone will be here later in the afternoon."

They finished talking about schedules. She would have

to select paint, woodwork, and flooring in each of the rooms. That, though, could wait.

"How long will it take?" she asked.

He looked around. "It'll take at least three weeks once we get started."

She thought of the broken windows. "What about the windows and doors? Anyone could get in."

He took out a cell phone and speed dialed a number. She listened as he arranged for someone to come over immediately to board the windows and put new locks on the doors.

She accompanied him to the door, then called the fire inspector and told him about the theft. He promised to put it in the report and said police officers would be contacting her.

She turned to Caleb. "You're a detective. Where would you start?"

"Intent first. What was the main purpose? The computer? Or arson? Did whoever did this really want something that was on the computer? If so, what? Or was the main goal to destroy the house in such a way it would hurt your credibility? A combination of the two? Then look for a motive."

"I can't think of anyone who would do anything like this." To her dismay, her voice broke slightly.

"Your mother, then," he said. "What would she fear more than anything else?"

She knew exactly what her mother feared more than anything else. The well-being of her family. "One of us being hurt."

Now she was beginning to realize why her mother had been so protective all those years. Suffocatingly so. It had been fear. Perhaps fear of what she herself had embraced years ago, or fear of losing what she had: her family. If Liz had known there was a powerful reason behind her mother's protectiveness, would she have rebelled so openly?

She bit her lip as she tried to decipher the riddle. "Do you think it has something to do with her? That someone is trying to send her a message of some kind?"

Before he could answer, three men drove up in a truck, followed by a locksmith. Within thirty minutes, they'd boarded the windows in the kitchen, installed a new door, and changed the locks. By the time they all left, it was almost dark.

Caleb stood up. "You need some food. So do I."

She nodded. She wasn't hungry. The sick gnawing in her stomach rejected the idea of food. But neither of them had eaten since leaving Albuquerque this morning. Nothing here was edible. "There's a good restaurant near the car rental office."

"Sounds good."

"Thanks for helping me. I don't know if I could have coped alone."

"Oh, you would have coped. You're a strong lady." The words sent a much-needed rush of pride through her. She'd felt her life spiraling out of control these past few hours. The fact that she'd admitted that to practically a stranger told her how much.

She was aware again of heat rising between them. Of an awareness that was in quick glances.

"Don't be grateful," he said with a sudden hardness. "It's to my benefit as well. I want you and your family to help with the book."

It was like a slap in the face.

"I can't speak for the others," she said, hopefully managing a cool voice.

"And you?"

"It depends on what you want to know, and what Mr. Montgomery thinks."

A suffocating sensation tightened her throat. He'd backed away as if he'd just been burned. And not for the first time. Doubts returned again. She'd allowed him to get close to her, and yet she knew practically nothing about him.

What if he wasn't who he said he was? If he had been planning to write about the robbery, why hadn't he been in Boston where it took place? How had he reached her so quickly? Her thoughts went immediately to national scandal publications. What if . . . ?

A warning voice whispered in her head. He'd been wandering over the house, alone at times when she was talking to the adjustors and others.

"I'll get some things," she said and moved away from him, her legs rubbery. She went into the bedroom and gathered some salvageable clothing. She could wash the clothes at her parents' home. She looked at the framed photos lying on top of the chest, then checked her bottom drawer where she kept photo albums.

All four were still there. Damp but intact, as far as she could see. She would take them with her. There would be workmen in the house. She didn't want anyone getting photos they could sell to some publication.

When she returned, Caleb Adams was staring out the window. The last news truck was gone, the reporter obviously finally convinced she wasn't going to get anything more.

But Liz was going to get more. She should have asked more questions earlier. Before she let him wander around her house. "What kind of investigative work do you do here?" she asked.

He shrugged. "I'm mostly employed by attorneys. I find witnesses. Interview them. Check their backgrounds and those of prospective jurors in a case."

"And when you were with the Boston Police Department?"

"I was a detective. Organized crime when I left."

"Did you like it?"

"I don't know if it's a question of liking it."

"Then why?"

"Someone has to catch the bad guys." He said it lightly, but she sensed that was only a shield against revealing a part of himself he didn't want others to see. She'd noticed he was very good at it. She was afraid she was very bad at it. He could read her so easily, and she couldn't read him at all.

Perhaps it was the quizzical half smile that was a part of his face. Or the green eyes that so rarely showed any emotion. His hair still had that rumpled look, though there was no smell of liquor today. He didn't look dangerous until she remembered his hostility yesterday toward the FBI agent. She'd known then she would not like to be his enemy.

Someone has to catch the bad guys.

She'd always been in favor of catching the bad guys. And now the law was saying her mother was one of them. Again, a sense of unreality seized her. She shivered. And Caleb Adams? There were too many questions to trust him, not until she heard from Colton Montgomery and learned a lot more about him than she knew now.

"Let's go," she said.

He nodded and turned toward the door, then stopped. "Where do you plan to spend the night?"

"My father's house."

"Alone?"

"From what I understand, there are plenty of press people there to keep me safe. I also have a handgun locked in the jeep," she said. "Dad's an avid outdoorsman. He used to take me camping and fishing and taught me target shooting. Now I like to have a gun in the mountains because of snakes or the occasional mountain lion."

"Is your sister an adventurer as well?"

"I thought you did your research," she challenged. "And I'm not an adventurer. I help people enjoy the river and mountains, but I want them to do it safely."

A trace of humor crossed his face. "I stand corrected," he said. He walked to the door. Despite the limp, there was a certain grace about his movements. She would wager her last nickle that he'd been an athlete at one time.

Just as she locked the door behind him, she saw Garry Noland, her neighbor, pull into his driveway. She walked out to meet him.

He gave her a quick hug. "Any more information about the fire?"

She told him what had happened. "I'm not sure they believed me when I told them the fire was arson. And," she added, "that it was started by someone other than myself."

"I only wish I'd seen the varmint."

"I'm glad you didn't," she said. She knew Garry. He probably would have run over to ask questions. Then . . .

His gaze moved to Caleb, who'd joined them. "Garry, this is Caleb Adams," she said. "He was helping me. Caleb, Garry Noland. He called the fire department and probably saved the house."

She saw the curiosity in Garry's eyes as he openly examined Caleb, but she couldn't explain more. Not now.

"Will you be home tomorrow?" she asked.

"For you, yes," he said.

"There should be an electrician. And a cleaning crew." She reached in her purse and handed him the second key the locksmith had given her.

"I'll let them in and watch them as if it was my own home," he said.

"Thank you."

"Where will you be?"

"I'm not sure. Dad—or Mom—might need me. Then there's the business. I'll try to get here sometime during the day."

He frowned. "I wish there was more I could do. If your mother needs a character witness . . . but what am I saying? It will never come to that."

She kissed him on the forehead. "You're a good friend."

"Go. I'll take care of the house."

Minutes later, she was in the jeep with Caleb.

She looked at the clock on the jeep. *After nine.* A meal, a trip to the car rental place, then to her father's home. She would call Tracy from there and pick up messages from her office.

Her cell phone rang. She seldom answered it while driving, but she realized she hadn't contacted Tracy today, or it might be her father. Or Montgomery. She looked at the number.

Her sister. She pulled over to the shoulder and answered it. "Sue?"

"The director of Kim's day camp called," she said. "He said that some man called today to say that he was Kim's Uncle Tony and would pick her up early . . ."

Breath caught in her throat, gagged her.

A fire. Missing disks. Her mother. Now this.

"Kim?"

"She's fine. The camp wouldn't have released her without my permission, but now I'm scared, Liz. Really scared."

She looked down at her left hand, which was still on the steering wheel. It was shaking.

"So am I," she said.

chapter ten

"Where's David?" Liz asked. "Does he know?"

"I wanted to make sure that it wasn't you before I called him."

"Call him, Sue. Someone knows the camp Kim attends. They might know where you're staying."

"Who *are* they?"

"I wish I knew," Liz said. "But I don't. I just know someone tried to burn my house and apparently took the hard drive from my computer. They might go after David's computers as well. The FBI has Mother's and Dad's."

"That doesn't make sense."

"I know it doesn't. Tell me everything that happened with Kim," Liz said, trying to calm the hysteria in her sister's voice. "What exactly did the director say?"

"He said that after the call, he tried to call me to confirm, but couldn't reach me, then was tied up in a meeting. I picked her up early because I . . . well, I was worried about what she might hear, and truthfully, I wanted her with me. The camp secretary told the director I had picked Kim up, but then he apparently started thinking about the phone call and decided to check with me."

"Surely he wouldn't have allowed Kim to go with anyone without your permission?"

"He said not, but what if he wasn't there? What if someone tried to take her from the grounds?"

Liz's heart pounded. She heard the fear in her sister's voice. Sue lived for her kids.

She couldn't make light of threat. Something evil was shadowing them. Something that had to do with her mother, and the call to the camp had been either a warning or an actual attempt to kidnap a child. *Her niece. Her blood. Her mother's granddaughter.*

Still, she reached for straws. "Could it have been David's brother? Maybe the director didn't get the name right."

"No. Mr. Waller said the caller distinctly said Uncle Tony. There is no Uncle Tony."

"Are you and the kids alone now?"

"No. I took your advice. I'm staying with Rachel, but I drove Kim to camp. If someone knew what camp she attended, maybe they followed me here." Her voice was ragged. "I can't let her go back tomorrow and I planned to be in court. David was going to be there, too. That's why he was working tonight, to catch up on some work so he could."

"Take care of the kids. That's what Mom would want," Liz said.

"I have to be there," Sue insisted. "She has to know I love her."

Liz understood that. Sue had always been very close to their mother, far more so than she'd been. Liz had been her father's daughter. And both had resented each other for the perceived favoritisms. It had taken years for her and her sister to appreciate each other.

Liz swallowed hard.

"Is there anyone you can leave them with? Maybe David can take them somewhere safe."

"I'll talk to him," Sue said.

Liz glanced at her companion. "Maybe we can find someone to protect Kim and little David," Liz said. "I'll call you back as soon as I can. Between us we should find someone." She turned off the cell phone and looked at her companion. He couldn't have avoided hearing her side of the conversation.

"Do you know a bodyguard or someone who can look

after my sister's family for a few days? Someone really trustworthy?"

"What happened?"

She told him what had happened.

A muscle tightened in his cheek.

"Will the police protect them?" she asked.

He shook his head. "Not without proof of an actual threat."

"How much do they need? My house burned, a child threatened—"

"There's a real lack of manpower, and no direct threat to you or your niece."

"Someone identifying themselves as a relative is not a threat?"

"It could have been a sick prank," he said. "People do that. They have a grudge against your father or you, and they use the accusations against your mother as an excuse to inflict fear."

She glared at him.

"I'm simply thinking like a cop. They simply can't guard someone without a damn good reason."

"A seven-year-old and four-year-old aren't damn good reasons?"

"Of course, they are," he said. "But unless there is a direct threat . . ."

Even her position on the city council wouldn't make a difference. Sue's sister-in-law, like Liz's parents, lived outside of the city limits.

"Then a bodyguard. Can you recommend anyone?"

He shook his head. "Not offhand. What about your sister's husband? Isn't he an attorney? He might know someone."

"He's exclusively real estate," she said. "He's never been involved in criminal law. He's not very useful at practical things." She hesitated, then added ruefully, "Neither am I at the moment."

His gaze drilled into her. "Overload?"

She gave him a wan smile. "Big time." It was a humiliating confession.

"I'll make some calls," he finally said. "I'll try to find someone reliable."

"Everything has happened so fast," she said. "Mom was just arrested. How could anyone have time to . . . to try to destroy my house and threaten my sister's children?"

"The investigation has obviously been under way several weeks," Caleb said. "Word might have leaked. People might have been put in place in the event the identification panned out."

Liz shivered at the thought of someone waiting like a vulture to pounce on members of her family.

"Do you want me to drive?" he asked.

"No." She started the car again and moved out into the traffic. In minutes she'd stopped at a hotel. "There's a rental car office inside and a restaurant around the corner," she said. It was a dismissal of sorts.

"Aren't you going to eat?"

She wasn't sure she could eat anything now, and even less sure that she wanted to eat with him. He was a disturbing presence at a time she needed her wits about her. But she did need to eat, whether or not her stomach was prepared for it.

She nodded. She gave him the name of the restaurant and directions. "I'll go ahead and get a table."

She watched as he went into the hotel, then drove the short distance to the restaurant. Instead of going in, she dialed Colton Montgomery.

"Mr. Montgomery, this is Liz Connor."

"It's Colton, Liz."

"Colton, then. Is there anything new with my mother?"

"No. She's quite determined to waive extradition and then plead guilty."

Her heart sank, but she knew how stubborn her mother could be when she'd decided on a course of action. "Have you had a chance to check on Caleb Adams and Michael Gallagher?"

"I've had two associates checking on them. Both are who they say they are. Gallagher is a respected attorney in Boston, and Caleb Adams was a decorated police officer." He paused, then continued. "His wife and son were killed in an explosion. He was wounded by shrapnel. His leg is pretty well bionic."

Her breath caught in her throat. *He must have seen his wife and son die.* She couldn't even imagine the agony he must have suffered.

"And now?"

"Respected by local attorneys for his skill, but he doesn't take many cases, and he can be trouble. Sometimes he finds things they don't want him to find." He paused. "We're still working on his background."

"And Michael Gallagher. Is there any more about him?"

"Poor kid from South Boston. Worked his way through college, then hooked his star to Win Maynard. He's chief corporate attorney."

"And Mr. Maynard?"

"I have someone researching him as well. He's very wealthy, very influential. He's said to be thinking about running for the U.S. Senate."

"This can't help him."

"Probably not," he said.

"There's something else." She told him about the incident at Kim's camp. "I think my sister and her kids need some protection. I asked Caleb Adams to find someone."

"If he doesn't, I will." He hesitated, then added, "Private bodyguards are expensive."

"If I have to sell my business, I will."

"Anything else?"

"Yes. You know there was a fire at my house. There's no obvious sign of arson, but I know it was no accident. Not only that, the hard drive on my computer was missing. I think someone tried to burn the house to conceal the theft. Either that or to send a message to my mother."

"I think we need to talk."

"Tomorrow morning?

"What about eight at your hotel?"

"I'll be there."

He hesitated, then, "Be careful."

"I will," she said, then hung up. She went into the restaurant and was shown a table. She knew many of those in the restaurant and stopped to speak to several but ignored the curious stares of others. She knew this was just the beginning.

Liz ordered a glass of red wine as she waited. Her stomach was beginning to growl after all, and she nibbled at the hot bread that was immediately delivered to the table.

Heads turned again as Caleb Adams entered, made his way to her table, and sat down. Her heart thumped harder as Colton's words echoed in her mind. *His wife and son were killed in an explosion.* She couldn't even imagine the pain of that. But he'd not mentioned it to her, and now she couldn't let him know she knew, that she'd been prying into something so private.

"I made a couple of calls," he said. "A man named Tom Greene is available. He's a retired secret service agent and sometimes takes a bodyguard job. You can trust him." He handed her a piece of paper with a number on it.

She called her sister on her cell phone from the table and relayed the information. "Do it," Liz said. "I can help with the cost."

Then she turned her attention back to Caleb. "Thank you."

He shrugged, but his lips tightened. "No trouble. I don't like kids being threatened."

As his son had been.

She felt bile rise in her throat and struggled to keep her voice even. "Any problems with getting a car?"

"None, though I'll miss the jeep."

"I could have driven . . ."

"You have enough to do," he interrupted.

"Where do you live?"

"North of here. Near Truchas."

A waiter interrupted then. Caleb ordered iced tea, then quickly studied the menu and ordered a steak. She ordered grilled trout.

She started again. "I've never met a Caleb before. Is it a family name?"

"Damned if I know," he said. "I think my dad just liked it."

"And your mother?"

He shrugged.

"Are they still alive?"

"No," he said shortly.

His answer, and face, told her not to probe in that direction any longer. "The robbery," she said. "Who were the others they say were with my mother?"

"Three fine young scions of Boston society." She noted the contempt in his voice, and she went cold. She shouldn't be surprised. He'd been a police detective, and his family had been killed, just as those two armored car guards had been. But it revealed how he must feel about her mother, even though he'd hidden it well until just that moment.

"And all four disappeared? No trace of any of them?"

"Not until your mother surfaced."

"Tell me about the others."

"One was on the sailing team and was destined for politics. His father was a state senator. Another had top grades in mechanical engineering. The third was brilliant but apparently aimless. And then there was your mother. She majored in government, had been a reporter on the campus newspaper before becoming involved in various antiwar groups. Then she seemed to drop out of everything."

"I still can't believe it," she said flatly.

"Has she denied it?"

"She hasn't said anything," she said. Then she bit her lip. She hadn't meant to say that.

"Not even to you?"

"Not to any of us," she said.

"Why wouldn't she?"

She played with a piece of bread. How many times had she asked herself the same question?

"She has to know who the others are and how to find them," he said.

"Maybe," she said. "I don't know."

"She would help herself by explaining exactly what happened."

"Or condemn herself."

"Only if she's guilty."

The words hung in the air between them. The bite was back in his voice, and she doubted the wisdom of talking to him at all. She'd accepted that he was trying to write a book. But there was something more personal, more . . . raw than a writer's curiosity.

"You think she fired those shots, don't you?"

"I know what the police reports say."

"But you don't know *her.*"

He shrugged, his mouth turning up in what should have been a smile but wasn't. It didn't reach his eyes.

Their food came then, and she concentrated on that.

Whatever appetite she'd had was gone now. Yet she tried to nibble at her food. It gave her an excuse not to look at her companion. It was too easy to do that, too easy to dwell on the too-old eyes and the scar, now that she knew why they were that way. She'd never been able to hide her emotions. Her mother used to say about her, "What you see is what you get." Caleb kept his hidden.

Thirty minutes later, they finished. They both grabbed for the check, but Caleb was faster. Whatever brief camaraderie they'd had earlier in the day was gone. His face was closed, and she felt a sudden chill.

"I have it," he said curtly.

"You helped me all day."

"You keep forgetting I want something from you."

His choice of words confused her. Were they a warning? Why? Why would he so openly challenge her rather than try to coax information about her family from her?

He waited for her to stand, and then they walked in silence to the door. He walked her to her jeep and waited until she got in.

"I'll be in touch," he said, then headed toward a nondescript sedan.

She didn't understand what had just happened. She only knew that she suddenly felt very, very alone.

Caleb headed north, cursing himself all the way. He'd let Elizabeth Connor get to him. He'd touched her when it should have been hands off. He'd found himself sympathetic when he wanted to be an inquisitor.

Dammit, he wanted something from her. Justice for his father. But he had never considered himself the type of man who would use an innocent woman's emotions against her.

He needed a drink. He needed one now more than ever. *Not now. Not when I'm so close.*

Elizabeth's mother had to know something about the other participants in the crime. She probably knew too much. There was no other explanation for what was happening to her family. Someone was looking for something or trying to make a point. That someone had to be one of those Caleb wanted with all his being.

He wanted to get to them before the Feds did, before they made deals that would net them only a few years in prison. He hadn't thought he would regret anything that would help him find them.

He'd been wrong. He'd used the time he had in Liz's house to do a quick search when she'd been busy with the fire inspectors and insurance adjustors, though he hadn't really expected to find anything. Perhaps old photos with family friends or phone numbers in an address book. *Anything.*

He just hadn't known how much his probing would prick his conscience. He didn't want Liz to trust him. He wanted her to be wary of him. He wanted the exchange of information to be more of a business transaction: he would give her information, and she would give him information.

He just hadn't expected the electric attraction between them or, even worse, the fact that he liked her. Too much.

I could always tell her the truth.

It was too late now. If he said anything, she would know he'd lied to her. She wouldn't trust him again. Even if she did, how would she and her family feel if they knew he intended to push for the greatest penalty possible for her mother?

What if her mother has changed?

He would never get those years back, the years he'd missed his father, the years his mother had missed a husband she adored.

His need for alcohol raged inside him. He'd used it as a crutch for years, and now it had become a part of him. But he knew he wouldn't touch another drop until he finished what he pledged to do so many years ago when he'd leaned over his father's casket. He'd made a promise and everything he had done after that was to fulfill that promise.

The drive had lessened during the eight years he'd been married, though he'd continued asking questions, probing. Something bright and beautiful had entered his life then. His wife and son had lit a world that had become little more than dark shadows.

All too quickly the light disappeared. In his mind's eye, he heard his son yelling for him to hurry. The sound of the explosion. The smell. The falling hail of heated metal.

The sound of a horn brought his attention back to the road. He was wandering over the line, and the lights of a truck nearly blinded him until he turned the wheel suddenly and barely missed a collision.

He drove over to the side of the road and stopped the car. Then he pounded on the steering wheel before doubling up with familiar agony. The man who'd killed his wife and son was dead.

His father's killers weren't.

Now he was close. Closer than he'd ever been.

And nothing was going to get in his way.

chapter eleven

Several news vans were parked in front of her parents' home. She ignored the reporters as they jumped out of their vans and approached her.

"No comment."

"Come on, Councilwoman. You're a city official. You owe the voters an explanation."

"You're on private property," she said. "Don't make me call the county sheriff."

"Where's your father?" one shouted.

She turned her key in the lock on the front door and slipped inside. She turned off the alarm system, then reset it. She'd always thought it a bother. Now she was grateful.

She walked through the house, remembering all the years she spent here. It was an easy house in which to live. Comfortable furniture, bookcases everywhere, a large kitchen flooded with sunlight during daylight hours, and windows that overlooked her mother's garden.

She went into the room her father used as an office. His computer was gone, but then he'd said the FBI had taken it. It seemed years ago. Not just yesterday.

The office was not as neat as it usually was. The desk-top was usually empty except for a tidy to-do pile. But now papers were scattered across the surface.

Restless, she went to her mother's room and picked out a navy blue suit and light blue shell, a pair of low-heeled shoes, panty hose, underwear, and a little package of makeup, though she didn't know if the latter would be permitted. She added two books, then packed all of them in a shopping bag.

Then she returned to her mother's bedroom and looked in her night table where her mother kept the address book. Gone.

She went up into the attic through a pull down ladder and the trapdoor. She wondered whether the federal authorities had been there as well, but she knew that they would have been restricted by their search warrant.

She found the boxes, but the photo albums were gone.

She returned downstairs, found a bottle of white wine, and opened it. She poured herself a glass, then continued her search, glass in hand. She didn't know what she was looking for. A hint of the past, perhaps. But someone had wanted something in her computer, or thought there might be something there. Whoever did it must believe it was information that could hurt or benefit him. Or her.

She looked through older books, then into her mother's recipe books. Her mother loved to cook and was very good at it. She was always looking for something new she could tinker with. But she found no little note, no address, no phone number. Nothing unusual.

She called her father's cell phone. "Dad, how are you?"

"Been better," he said. "How is your house?"

"Pretty much a disaster. The adjustors were there. Insurance will cover most of the damage, but I've lost some books and watercolors."

"I'm sorry, Sport."

"Not your fault," she said. "There was something strange, though."

"What?"

"Someone took the hard drive from my computer."

"Why . . . ?"

"I don't know." She explained about the grease fire. "I had thought it might be mischief. But now I think whoever did it wanted to cover up the computer robbery. He meant the house to burn. Only Garry's nocturnal habits saved it."

Her father did something she'd never heard before.

Cursed. A mild curse for most people. For him it was major.

"You have to get Mom to talk to you," she said. "A man who said he was Kim's Uncle Tony called Kim's camp today, said he would pick her up."

"Is Kim . . . ?"

"She's okay. Sue picked her up early."

"Thank God for that."

"Me. Now Sue. Mom must know why, or know something that she doesn't realize she knows."

"She won't say anything about what happened before we met," her father said. "Where are you now?"

"I'm at your house. Came by to pick up some clothes for her. I plan to spend the night here. Dad, the photo albums are gone. Did you know that?"

A sigh. "No. The FBI must have taken them."

"I'll be up there in the morning. Meet you at seven at the motel?"

"That's fine."

"Mr. Montgomery wants to meet with us at eight. Sue will join us at the courthouse. David had been planning to come as well, but after what happened at Kim's camp, he might stay with the kids."

"I wonder if all of you shouldn't go somewhere," her father said. "I really don't like you staying there alone."

"I'm not alone. The press is right outside."

"One press reporter found me. That means they'll all be over here soon. I called the operator and told them not to put through any more calls, and I'm just answering the cell phone."

"Ignore them. Try to get some sleep, Dad."

"I worry about her," he said in a weary voice.

"I know. Me, too."

"Be careful."

"I have my gun with me," she assured him. She then called Tracy to tell her she was okay.

"The lines were jammed all day with reporters and your friends," Tracy said. "The press wanted information, the friends want to know how they can help. I want to know that, too."

"You're doing it, Tracy. Just keep the business from going bust in the next few days."

"We did have a call about a rafting trip."

"From where?"

"Bishop's Lodge."

"How many?"

"Four men. They're at some kind of conference."

"Did you find out their level of expertise?"

"You bet. All said they had rafted in class-four rapids."

"When do they want to go?"

"This weekend."

She had to do it. She had a payroll now. A business. And legal bills to help with.

"I'll take it if Doug can't," she said. Doug was one of their guides, but he also worked with other adventure firms. "Book it," she said.

"I did."

"Good. Anything else?"

"I've arranged for Geordie to take the Indian site tour, and Eric says he can take the jeep trips for the next few days."

"Thank God for you," Liz said.

"Take care of yourself, boss."

Liz hesitated. "Haven't had any strange calls, have you?"

"Other than reporters, no. Nothing out of the ordinary."

"I'll be out all day tomorrow," she said. "I'll be in Albuquerque in the morning, and I have to be back at the house in the afternoon. There's so much to do."

"I'll be here."

"You're a jewel."

"I know it."

The flip answer made her smile.

"Go to bed," Liz commanded and hung up.

She looked at the clock again. Nearly eleven now, but she knew she couldn't sleep, even as weary as her body was. Too many questions. She wished for a computer, but the Feds had taken the ones here. The only available one was in her office.

Who exactly was Winstead Maynard? What had been her mother's place in that family?

She put down the glass of wine and found her keys. She would go to the office. She probably needed to go through the mail anyway, and she wanted to back up her files. She didn't want to have another computer stolen or burned, this time with the only copy of company files.

Her handgun was in her purse as she left the house. All but one van had left. She saw someone move in that one, but she quickly turned the ignition and hopefully was gone before anyone had time to react.

She arrived at the parking area in front of the office fifteen minutes later. Santa Fe Adventures shared an adobe office building with a doctor's office, dental office, and beauty salon. They were all closed now, and the building was dark.

She unlocked the door, turned on the lights, and went inside. Posters decorated the walls: tourists riding horses, trekking in the mountains, climbing the pueblos, rafting down rivers. She felt a momentary pride that this business, as of yesterday, was hers.

Tracy's desk was neat. A sofa and two chairs were arranged around a coffee table. The surface of the table was neatly covered with various outdoor publications.

Liz went by the desk she'd occupied until yesterday, and into the one large private office. The light was on. That was surprising. Tracy was usually very good about making sure everything was off.

She brushed aside a nagging feeling about it, and sat down. Ivan, the former owner and her ex-boss, had moved out the night before the sale closed. Most of the furniture, including the computer, remained, but the office looked empty with the wall art gone.

Telephone message slips lay on the desk. She glanced through them. Several were from members of the city council, including the mayor, asking her to call. Others were from friends expressing support. Two were from the fire department, but both were before her meeting with the inspector. She tossed those away. Two from Michael Gallagher, asking her to call him. She tossed those as well.

An advertising agency needed final approval on an ad to go into a local magazine, and there was a request for an ad in the local newspaper.

She took four from the pile of more than thirty messages. She would answer those tomorrow morning. The others could wait.

Then she sat down at the computer. She assumed Ivan would have deleted any personal information, leaving only the company records. She logged onto her Internet server.

Her mind went to the two messages from Michael Gallagher. He obviously wasn't used to being ignored. Colton said he had a good reputation in Boston. What about the man who employed him? She searched for Winstead Maynard, got a number of hits. She quickly isolated *the* Winstead Maynard in Boston.

Respected CEO of a large conglomerate. Member of the Opera Guild and United Appeal Board as well as several other charities. Active as a political fund-raiser and apparently considered by some a political king maker.

She stared at the photos, trying to find a resemblance between her mother and her cousin. He was about six years older than her mother.

Then she tried to find more on the Maynard family. There were dozens of articles about her mother and the continuing search for her. One story mentioned the suicide of Sarah Jane Maynard's mother a month after her disappearance. Liz felt her stomach tightening. She hadn't heard about a suicide. She couldn't even imagine how her mother had felt when she'd heard the news. Or had she? Had she ever looked to see what happened to her family?

A few days ago, she would have been sure she could predict what her mother would do and how she would react in almost any situation. No longer. Did you ever really know anyone? The demons in their lives?

According to everything she could find, her mother had no brothers or sisters. Her father, Mason Maynard, had one sibling, who had died in an automobile accident thirty-six years earlier. Mason Maynard's nephew, Winstead Maynard, apparently inherited everything and went on to transform a shipping company into a multinational conglomerate. There were rumors now of a run for the Senate.

She looked at the time on the screen. Two in the morning. She needed to try to get at least a few hours' sleep. But first she made hard copies of the information she'd just retrieved, then copied the company's client list and financial records on CDs and slipped them into her purse.

She wondered whether she was being paranoid. Her stomach churned. But her mind kept going back to the fire and that darn frying pan. Was someone trying to discredit her? Or was it something even more ominous?

Three days ago, she'd been a respected member of the community, the newest city council member. Now she was the daughter of a fugitive and a careless firebug.

Dear God, there was a council meeting in five days. Her first. It certainly should be memorable.

She turned out the light in the office and walked out to the main area. *Mine. It's mine.* But for how long, if they needed money for legal bills? She shrugged off the thought. They would do what they had to do.

She heard something in back, a noise. The tiniest little scraping sound that came from the storeroom. She hoped their infamous rat hadn't returned. He'd taken up residence a few months ago, and nothing succeeded until she'd found a little electronic gizmo guaranteed to drive varmints away. It had.

She debated about checking. She certainly didn't need a new problem. Tomorrow. She would check for signs tomorrow. She grabbed her purse and keys, turned off all the lights. She was almost to the door when she heard another noise. She turned back. Nothing looked unusual.

A shiver of panic struck her. Another firebug?

Had someone been in the back all the time she'd been sitting at her desk? Waiting for her to leave?

Dammit, she wasn't going to let them destroy this office as well as her home. But first she had to get out. Then a phone call to the police. Would they even believe her?

She hurriedly turned the key in the lock and started to open the door, even as she pulled the pistol from her pocketbook. She sensed movement behind her and started to turn back, her pistol coming up as a figure in black attacked her, knocking the gun from her hand. He grabbed her around the neck, trying to force her back inside. She fought to keep the door open, even a little. Her elbow swung back, hitting him in the gut, and he loosened his grip slightly. She screamed as loud as she could and shoved him against the half-opened door.

"Police. Stop where you are." Shouted words from the parking lot. Relief flooded her.

Her attacker swung around and slugged her. As she started to fall, she grabbed for something, anything, and her fingers found his mask, pulling it off as she went down. Before she could get a good look, the man stooped, grabbed her pistol, fired several shots in the direction of the origin of the shout, then ran.

She climbed to her feet, opened the door, and peered out. A figure was on the ground at the base of an ornamental tree at the far end of the lot. There were no police cars in the parking lot.

She ran inside and called 911. "I need an ambulance," she said and gave the address. Then she hurried back outside.

A figure was getting up from the cement. He cradled his left arm and gave her a rueful grin.

Shock ran through her as she recognized him.

Michael Gallagher.

And blood was coloring his well-tailored shirt and spilling onto the ground.

chapter twelve

Tony Woodall picked up the phone and dialed a number he knew by memory.

Maynard would not be happy to hear from him.

Maynard had been depositing money in an offshore bank account for him for years. He'd also passed on favors: a new client here, a contact there. But Maynard had kept intermediaries between them. On the rare occasions when they met at some event, Maynard was icily polite. He seldom introduced Tony to his friends. He didn't want to dirty his fingers, a fact that irritated Tony to no end.

They were in the same boat, one that had a leaky hull but had sailed forth for the past thirty-plus years. Their fates were tied together, even if Maynard was loath to admit it.

But now both their lives were at stake, and he didn't care if Maynard was annoyed.

He didn't have Maynard's private number, another fact that angered him. He left his name and number with Maynard's secretary, knowing that the man would waste no time in calling to berate him.

He was right. Eight minutes later by Tony's watch, Maynard called.

"I thought I told you—"

"I don't care what you told me," Tony interrupted. "If Sarah Jane starts talking—"

"I'm not going to talk about this on the phone."

"I suggest we meet then. I'm not going away, Win."

"I'm taking a train to New York in the morning. The nine forty."

Tony hung up. He had what he wanted.

He, too, would be on the train at nine forty.

SANTA FE

Liz knelt by Michael Gallagher. She could barely breathe as she waited for the police to come. He was bleeding profusely, and they were alone here.

"I thought I heard someone identifying themselves as police," she said.

Gallagher had started to rise but fell back. "I didn't have a weapon. I thought that might scare the hell out of him."

She didn't waste any more time. The pool of blood beneath his arm was spreading. She took his belt off and tied it around the wound, making a tourniquet.

Just as she finished, she heard sirens.

"Why are you here?" she asked.

"I wasn't getting anything accomplished in Albuquerque. I heard about the fire at your house. I thought I would drive up here, try to see you in the morning. Offer help again," he said ruefully.

"That doesn't explain—"

"No one answered at your father's house. I went by your house, and no one was there. I was looking for your business. I planned to be there in the morning, and wanted a place to stay close by. I saw the lights on and . . . decided to wait."

A logical explanation, perhaps, but . . .

A police car pulled up, followed seconds later by an ambulance and fire truck. Two officers piled out of the car and strode quickly over to them. One recognized her. "Councilwoman," the oldest one acknowledged while the other stooped at Gallagher's side. "What happened here?"

"I went into my office to do some work. I took a gun with me since it was so late, and . . . things have happened. I thought I heard noises in the back and started for the door. I took my gun out as I was leaving, but a man in a stocking mask rammed his body against me. I dropped the weapon, and he picked it up. Mr. Gallagher apparently saw the incident, yelled 'Police.' The attacker turned the gun on him and fled.

"Where's the gun now?"

"He took it with him."

"And it's registered in your name?"

"Yes."

Two paramedics were leaning over Gallagher, releasing her handmade tourniquet and putting a pressure bandage on it. One of the paramedics looked up at them. "We're taking him to the hospital."

"I'll follow you," she said.

"We have more questions," the senior officer interrupted.

"You can ask them at the hospital."

The other officer was on his radio, calling for backup for a search of the area. He took tape from the car and placed it around the door of her office and where Gallagher still sat.

Gallagher protested when a stretcher was lowered next to him. "I can walk."

"You try to walk after losing that much blood, you'll faint and make our job that much harder," the lead paramedic said.

He surrendered. Nodded.

Liz leaned down over him. "Thank you," she said.

"I didn't do anything."

"Except get shot and save me from God knows what."

"You were doing pretty well." He winced as he moved over on the stretcher. Guilt struck her as she thought of her earlier suspicions. He'd risked his life for her.

She went to her car and stepped inside, waiting a moment as emotions flooded through her. The terror as she was attacked. The sound of her gun skittering away, and then as it fired.

No one could deny now that she was a target. She had witnesses. But the price was high for Gallagher. She wasn't sure she believed his explanation, but there was no question he'd drawn the attacker's attention away from her and to himself, and he could have died as a result.

The ambulance pulled out in front of her, and she followed in her jeep. She looked at the clock in the dashboard. Nearly three a.m. She had to leave at six for Albuquerque.

Who was behind the violence that swirled around her? Why?

Caleb Adams had asked the question: who had motive and intent?

Those who'd participated in the robbery decades earlier?

To keep her mother silent?

To insure it?

Could someone have gotten to her mother already? Was that why she wasn't defending herself?

She pulled up to the hospital as the paramedics unloaded the stretcher, then found a spot in the crowded parking lot and went inside.

She felt responsible. She knew it was illogical. He shouldn't have been there. She hadn't asked him to be there.

Dammit, he might well have saved my life.

She went to the reception desk and was told Gallagher was in the third cubicle. She left for the room just as the woman behind the desk uttered something about needing information. She ignored the cry of "Miss," as she hurried down the hall.

Gallagher saw her, gave her a wan smile obviously meant to be encouraging, then, closed his eyes.

A doctor came into the cubicle, then, and asked her to leave. She left reluctantly and leaned against the wall outside. In minutes, he was being wheeled out.

She confronted the doctor. "Where are you taking him?"

"Are you a family member?"

"No," she admitted, "but we were together when he was shot."

"He's going to X ray, then surgery. A vein has to be repaired. The bullet nicked a bone, but there shouldn't be any permanent damage."

Relief flooded through her. If he had died . . .

"One of the paramedics said you used a tourniquet. You might have saved his life," the doctor said.

She didn't explain that it had probably been the other way around. She looked at her watch. She needed to be on her way. She had to go to her parents' home, pick up the items she'd put on the front table, and drive to Albuquerque. But she also really wanted to stay and make sure Michael Gallagher would be all right.

As she stood there indecisively, too tired to make any kind of rational decision, the senior officer found her. "We have a few more questions," he said.

They found an empty room, and she was asked to repeat everything again as he recorded it.

She recited what had happened, trying to make sense of it as she did. "I was working late. I'd locked the door, but when I started to leave, I heard a noise in back. He must have realized I heard something. As I reached the door, he came out of nowhere and tried to pull me back inside. I tore off his mask as he tried to get my gun," she said.

He straightened. "You didn't tell me you saw his face. Can you identify him?"

"It was so fast," she said. "I don't know. Dark hair, dark brown eyes." She shivered as she remembered them. "Cold . . . like agates, and his lips were thin." She didn't add that they had been pulled back in a snarl.

"Can you come down to the office and look through photos?"

"Later today, I think. I'm going to Albuquerque this morning."

Comprehension sprang into his eyes. They became curious. "Odd coincidence."

"Not so odd," she said, then related the events of the past few days. "A pattern, wouldn't you say?" she asked.

He didn't agree. Nor disagree. "I'll give the information

to the detectives," he said. "They'll want to talk to you as well."

"I want to talk to them, too, but now I have to leave."

She went to the nurse's reception desk and gave the clerk what information she had about Michael Gallagher. Asked about next of kin, she suggested they call Winstead Maynard in Boston. Yes, she did have the number. She dug in her purse and found the card that Gallagher had given her yesterday and handed it to the clerk, waited for the woman to take down the number, then took it back.

She held it for a moment, thinking about calling the man claiming to be her cousin. Perhaps Michael Gallagher had a wife who would be anxious, who would want to fly to his bedside.

Still, she hesitated. It was one step toward a life her mother apparently rejected.

Curiosity and a sense of responsibility toward the man who might have saved her won. She looked at her watch. It would be seven in Boston.

She punched in the numbers. Despite the early hour, the phone was answered with surprising swiftness. "Maynard," the voice said roughly.

"Mr. Maynard," she said, "I'm Liz Connor."

"Liz," the voice said, the roughness gone and his voice suddenly warm. "What is it?"

"Michael Gallagher was just shot. I didn't know who else to call. I thought you could notify whoever should be notified."

"What happened?" The question was sharp and fully awake.

"I was attacked at my office. He came to my assistance."

"How bad is he?"

"He was shot in the arm. The doctors say there shouldn't be any permanent damage."

"What hospital?"

She relayed the name. "They need personal information I don't have. He was conscious for a while, then—"

"I'll take care of everything."

"His wife?"

"There's no wife."

She was surprised. Gallagher was a good-looking man. She'd assumed he was married. She hadn't looked to see whether there was a wedding ring.

"Did Michael give you the message?"

"He did. We don't need any help."

"The offer stands," he said.

"I'll remember that. I have to go."

"Thank you for calling me," he said, and the warmth in his voice radiated over several thousand miles.

She clicked the phone off and headed for the door, Michael Gallagher's face lingering in her mind. She wasn't sure she entirely believed his story about how he happened to be at her office.

Two knights in shining armor in twenty-four hours seemed a little too good to be true. Especially since they'd been missing from her life until now.

She tried to remember the facial features of her attacker. Impressions. Little else, other than the dark eyes.

What had he wanted?

She wondered whether she would ever know.

She left the hospital just as dawn came.

The sun was a huge ball rising above the horizon. She drove to her parents' home, splashed water on her face to rejuvenate herself, then picked up the clothes she'd selected for her mother.

She started driving. Two faces were in her mind. Michael Gallagher's dark good looks. Caleb Adams's intensity. Two very attractive men appearing out of nowhere.

She'd never believed in the tooth fairy. She didn't now, either.

Both had appeared at opportune times. Or inopportune ones.

Don't think about them. Think about Mom. Dad. The days ahead.

The dog was on the porch when Caleb arrived. His tail looked like a propeller as Caleb stepped out of the rental car. It was the first time that Tramp had demonstrated any emotion at his arrival or departure.

He told himself he didn't want that. The reason he'd fed Tramp was that he was exactly that. A temporary visitor who would leave in his own time.

He hadn't wanted a living creature ever to depend on him again. He'd been responsible for the death of his wife and child. If he hadn't been a cop, they would be alive today.

Maryanne had never asked him to quit. She'd known that was who he was, which was the reason he'd loved her so much. But he'd seen the worry in her eyes. Worry for him. Not for her. Or their son.

"Don't get too dependent on me," he told the dog. Tramp sat in front of him and looked at him curiously as if he didn't quite understand.

Caleb unlocked the door and went inside. The overlarge water bowl was still full, and so was the feeder that held and slowly released something like twenty pounds of dog food.

He went into the kitchen. A bottle of scotch was on the counter. He stared at it for a moment, the need inside him raw and thirsty. Then he put it in the cabinet.

Not tonight.

He had work to do. He went to the room he'd turned into his office. All his files on the case were there. He started to go through them, one by one. Files on the suspects. Files on the backgrounds of the two guards, including his father. Except he knew more than what was in those files. Files on the investigation. The suppositions. The theories.

The big question was how four spoiled preppies could disappear so completely, so cleanly. He'd even thought for a while that they might be dead. That a fifth person had been involved and had made sure none of them would ever talk. But with the arrest of Sarah Jane Maynard / Betty Connor, he knew at least one had successfully disappeared. Then the others probably had, as well.

Why wouldn't she tell the Feds where the others were

in exchange for a lesser sentence? After thirty-four years, any loyalty should have faded away.

Unless someone—her family—was being threatened.

He wished he knew more about the woman, but she was a cardboard figure to him. Happy homemaker. Community saint. Great mother. Better wife.

He tried to equate that figure with the one he'd held in his mind for so many years. Sarah Jane Maynard. Rich. Spoiled. Reckless. Out for thrills.

He closed his eyes. He had seen her photos. He tried to see her daughter in her. Sarah Jane had dark hair and blue eyes. Liz Connor had auburn hair and deep blue, thoughtful eyes. Responsible as hell. Everything about her proclaimed that fact.

And easy to be with. She was without guile or vanity. He'd noticed that in the hours they'd spent at her house. No hysterics. No tears. Just commonsense effort. He'd found himself admiring her, even as he found minutes here and there to snoop into her life.

He couldn't get her out of his mind. Perhaps he should have stayed with her. But she'd said she was going to her parents' home, and that should be well covered by news media. He couldn't protect her from that, and he doubted there would be more attacks. Whoever had tried to destroy her home had made a point.

Anything more would be overkill.

With that thought in his mind, he went outside and looked up at the sky. Usually he was well oiled with scotch by now. But he was cold sober, and his gut burned.

Damn but there were a million stars. He wondered if his father was out there. His mother? His wife? His son?

So many.

Why am I still here?

He would never understand that.

He turned away and went inside. The next few days should prove interesting.

So why didn't he feel the satisfaction he'd expected?

chapter thirteen

As he sat on one of the courtroom benches, Caleb fingered the leather cover of his old badge. It and the press credentials he'd finagled gave him an advantage over all the other would-be spectators at the arraignment hearing.

He'd kept the former since the day he left the department. He'd buried it in the bottom of a drawer and had scrounged it up early this morning and stared at it for a long time.

The badge was the symbol of his failure. His failure to bring justice for his father. His failure to protect his family. He'd tried to be a good father, as good as his father had been. He had kissed his wife and son every time he'd left the house, and he'd tried his damnedest to be at memorable events. He'd lived every moment as if it would be the last because he'd learned as a boy it might be.

But still there had been too many times he'd been gone. His job had required it. He'd tried to compensate, but after the explosion he'd relived every moment he wished he had been with them. He'd agonized over every choice he'd made. He'd come to hate the job that had obsessed him and taken him away from those he loved most. He hated himself for exposing his family to danger because he'd been driven to find his father's killers.

Perhaps getting them would take some of the guilt away, though it would never take away the pain.

He waited as the courtroom began to fill. Elizabeth and

her father had not yet arrived. Nor had the woman who had stumbled in front of the armored car so many years ago.

He ached to see her, to confront her.

He saw other faces turn, and he twisted around. Two deputies were leading a woman in. Except for the handcuffs fastened on her wrists, she was unremarkable in a plain blue suit. Her short hair was peppered with gray and her body gently rounded. What had he expected? The mark of Cain?

He'd memorized her photos years ago. She had looked like a young rebel with long dark hair and eyes that leapt from the newspaper. The photos had been black-and-white, but he knew from others that her eyes were blue.

Elizabeth's were blue as well, but while her mother's were pale as cornflowers, her daughters were the deep warm blue of an evening sky.

He searched the older woman's face for whatever had been there that caused her to pull a trigger on a man doing his job. Her face, though pale, showed little emotion. It was as if her features had been painted on.

What was it about this killer that engendered obvious loyalty from her husband and daughters?

Then he saw her glance behind her. Elizabeth and another woman entered the room. For a moment, Sarah Jane Maynard's face changed, and her chin trembled. He saw pain in those pale blue eyes.

He didn't want to acknowledge it. Her pain was for *her* family. It was much too late for his.

Elizabeth looked tired. Dark circles shadowed her eyes. The woman with her looked more like Sarah Jane. A little plump. More makeup. Unquestionably the sister. Their hands were clenched together. Behind them came Steve Connor. He, too, looked tired, but his eyes didn't leave his wife's as her handcuffs were removed.

All three of them sat behind her.

The extradition hearing was short. Before the judge could ask how she pled, an attorney for Massachusetts and a federal prosecutor both asked to file papers for jurisdiction.

The judge sighed. "We're not having a jurisdictional dispute, are we?"

"Massachusetts claims jurisdiction," said one attorney.

"The federal government has first call," said the other.

"File your papers," the judge said. He looked to where Betty Connor and her attorney sat. "We can't go any further today, and I'm out of town for the rest of the week. I'm postponing the hearing until Monday."

Caleb watched her being led out, saw the protective expressions of her family as they gathered around Colton Montgomery. At least they could afford the best.

He tried to stoke his bitterness. It was no time to go soft. He had too much invested.

Then Elizabeth spotted him and started in his direction. She looked more vulnerable than at any time he'd seen her. Even more so than when she'd looked over so many ruined belongings in a house she'd obviously loved. Yet he saw determination in her eyes. Raw moral strength.

Gutsy.

There was no other word for her. He didn't want to admire her. He hated the jolt of the familiar physical awareness. He remembered the way her hair slipped through his fingers, the damned softness of her cheek.

He couldn't afford any of those memories nor the emotions they evoked. Her loyalty to her living family was at odds with his to his dead father.

Her gaze met his. "Something happened last night," she said.

He waited. Warned himself. *Don't care.*

"I was attacked at my office. Someone who tried to help me was shot. I've talked to Mr. Montgomery. My family— I—want to hire you as an investigator. Mr. Montgomery says you're good at what you do."

He looked at her again. His gaze followed the angle of her jaw. She'd used a heavy makeup base that couldn't quite conceal a purplish bruise.

Rage filled him. Not just against her attacker. He shouldn't have left her last night, but he hadn't anticipated that whoever tried to burn her house would strike again. "What happened?" he asked.

She told him in short sentences. He could feel her fear when she said she had tried to fight back. Alone.

And then someone had conveniently appeared. "Who helped you?"

"An attorney for my . . . cousin. Michael Gallagher. He was sent here to offer legal assistance. And money."

She'd not told him that yesterday. But then why should she? Still, he couldn't resist the question. "You didn't say anything about him."

"We weren't going to accept the offer. We didn't know anything about the Maynard family. I didn't trust him."

"And do you now?"

"He may have saved my life," she said simply.

And he might have staged the entire scenario. Would he take the risk of being shot? Probably not.

It was another oddity, though. He'd always thought that one of the fugitives might contact a family member. The BPD had taps on their phones on and off for years. He was familiar with Win Maynard, had studied him and his friends. He'd followed the man's career, particularly his interest in politics. He also knew the name of Michael Gallagher. He was said to be a legal shark.

Why would Maynard embrace the black sheep of his family now?

Why did he send the man said to be closest to him? And why was that man sneaking around Elizabeth's office in the wee hours of the morning?

And finally, why didn't Sarah Jane's family accept the help?

His hand went to her cheek, though he was careful not to touch the bruised area. "Any other injuries?" he asked.

"No, but I got a fleeting glimpse of the guy. I'm going to the police department later to go through photos, but it happened so quickly, I just had a few impressions, not a good look."

"What kind of impressions?"

"Speed. Assurance. He didn't seem to have a weapon until he picked up mine. His hair was dark. As were his eyes. I saw those through the mask. They were cold. Very cold."

"Did you have any idea of whether he wanted something in the office, or wanted to harm you?"

She shook her head.

"I should have stayed with you," he said.

She gave him a slight smile that went straight to his gut. "You can't stay with me every moment. But I do want to hire you. Mr. Montgomery said you were a good investigator. Maybe you can find out something."

"Your mother should have an idea who he was."

"She won't talk to us."

That her mother was still silent despite several attacks on her family surprised him.

He could not take her money, knowing he meant to use her. And her family. He simply couldn't do it.

"I'm not available," he said curtly. "I'm writing a book."

"You want access to my family," she countered. Her chin was set, her teeth biting her lip. It was obvious she wasn't quite sure this was a good idea but had decided it was the best of bad choices.

He *knew* it wasn't a good idea.

Yet he was being given an invitation into a family that might lead him to the others involved in his father's murder, who might know whether there had been an inside accomplice that night. He might also find the key to exactly what happened that day.

"Would your mother talk to me?"

"I don't know," she said. "Perhaps if she knew about last night, and my niece . . ."

But she didn't sound sure at all.

Why? The question pounded him. That was the million dollar question.

"Will you?" she asked again.

"I'll not take your money," he said. "But I'll do what I can on my own. Because of the book," he added.

"I want you on our side," Liz said.

"I won't be on anyone's side," Caleb said, knowing the lie as he said it. He was on his own side. And his father's.

Those incredible blue eyes didn't give an inch. They seemed to bore into him. *Dammit.*

"A bargain then," she said. "You help us, and we'll help

you. But you made me a promise earlier. You wouldn't publish anything until we read it first."

An easy promise since he didn't intend to publish anything. Still, it was, in truth, a lie, and it ate at him. Perhaps her mother deserved it. She didn't. But his gut demanded justice. It was the only thing that could give his life meaning. "You have my word."

"Mr. Montgomery says that means something."

The comment startled him. It did not particularly please him, not when he was twisting it. "And did he investigate your Mr. Gallagher as well?"

"Yes."

"And?"

"He apparently is everything he said he was. Just as you are."

"Don't be trusting," he admonished her. "Someone wants something bad enough to hurt you very badly. He probably won't stop with you."

"I know," she said. "Which is why I need help." Her gaze pierced his. "You said you *know* the case. Where do we start?"

"At the beginning."

BOSTON

Tony Woodall caught the train and worked himself through the cars until he found Maynard.

He was sitting alone, reading a newspaper.

"Is this seat taken?" he asked as he hovered above.

A curt nod gave him permission, and Tony sank defiantly into the seat.

"I thought I would relieve your mind. Sarah Jane won't be talking. But I'll need some more cash from you."

"No violence," Maynard warned.

Tony shrugged. "I'll do what I have to do. You should be damned glad that I am."

"You can only push me so far, Tony."

"I can push you as far as I want to. I need fifty thousand dollars. Write it off as a retainer."

"I don't want you on my books."

"Then do it off the books, but I need the cash tomorrow."

Maynard's lips thinned. "How do you know she won't say anything?"

"She hasn't yet, despite pressure. She knows the consequences. I made sure of that."

"I don't want any killing."

"Don't get soft on me now. If she points a finger in my direction, I'll lead them directly to you."

"Don't threaten me. I'm your golden goose, and you know it. You can only push me so far."

"The money?" Tony said.

"I'll have it delivered to your office tomorrow."

"Very good. That's more like it."

He left the train at the next station. The sight of a defeated-looking Win Maynard boosted his spirits. He had originally thought the arrest was a disaster. Now he saw it as another opportunity.

ALBUQUERQUE

Steve Connor watched his wife being marched away in handcuffs and felt as if his very foundation had just folded in upon itself.

He kept berating himself. Yes, he should have asked more questions. He knew that now. But when he'd met his wife to be, he'd known what it was to be alone. He'd been abandoned by a single mother who couldn't cope and had suffered through numerous foster families.

Everyone thought he was an extrovert. He had a memory for names and faces. Once he'd met a child, he never forgot her or him.

But that was the exterior Steve Connor, not the lonely boy who still lurked inside him. He'd mastered the facade. It had taken years to master the insecurity he felt. He'd recognized the same loneliness and fear in Betty Frazier when he had met her in that park in Boulder.

She was walking a dog, an unrecognizable mixture of breeds. He'd always liked dogs but was never allowed to have one. After he graduated, and the state no longer had an interest in him, he'd worked two jobs to get through college. He lived in the cheapest accommodations. No animals allowed.

He'd received his degree and had a teaching job in place. He'd intended to get his master's as well and had no time for romance, or even an animal, but he'd watched the pretty girl with dark hair and cornflower-blue eyes bend over the dog, give it a small assuring pat, and he had fallen in love.

He'd never believed in love at first sight. Not until that day. But there had been something in her that reached out to him. Perhaps the haunted look in her eyes, perhaps the way she glanced around the park as if terrified someone might be lurking there.

He knew fear. He'd had a taste of it in some of the foster homes.

So he had never asked. Nor had he ever shared his own experiences. It was as if they had recognized wounded souls in one another and thought it best to let the demons lie.

He knew now how wrong that had been. And how wrong his assumption that she would confide in him one day. He'd never confided in her. His past had been too painful.

But why would she not say anything now?

He'd pleaded with her. *Save yourself. Save our daughters.* But she'd turned to stone, to someone he no longer knew. Something, or someone, was more important than her family.

For the first time in his life, he doubted her. And it was an agony like none he'd ever known. It had been debilitating. He'd allowed Liz to assume responsibilities he should have taken. But he'd felt cut off at the knees. Of all the scenarios he'd ever imagined, Betty's involvement in murder was never one of them.

They'd been married thirty-three years, and now he was discovering he knew nothing about her, that she had shared nothing with him. He'd held back as well, but then he hadn't been accused of killing two men.

He loved her. He'd always loved her. Nothing would

change that, not even if the accusations now leveled against her proved to be true. But he wanted to understand.

Not even his comments about the attacks on their daughter had budged her. Betty's lips had trembled, but she merely said that she didn't know where any one of her companions from that long-ago morning were. She would not speak of anyone's part but her own.

He still saw her face across that accursed table. Except for that brief trembling, her expression had been stoic. Unreadable. He'd tried to break through to the beloved features that had changed into a hardened mask.

Even in the courtroom, she'd looked at him as if he was a stranger, almost as if she'd already divorced him. She'd said she wanted him to divorce her as soon as possible. It had shocked him as much as her failure to defend herself.

He had no intention of seeking one. Not now. Not ever.

But why wouldn't she tell him what happened thirty-four years ago? Why wouldn't she give him the ammunition to protect their daughters?

He heard the door close behind her. It was as if a coffin had slammed shut.

chapter fourteen

Start at the beginning.

Caleb's words ran through Liz's mind as she drove back to Santa Fe. What was the beginning? How could they learn anything without her mother's help?

She would meet Caleb later this afternoon at her office. She'd given him the address—and directions—though she suspected that he, like Michael Gallagher, already knew where it was. He'd glanced at the directions she'd written, then stuffed them in his pocket. He'd suggested following her, but she declined. She'd wanted to talk to her father and her mother's attorney first. Plus, she needed to make another attempt to talk to her mother.

To her dismay, her mother refused to see any of them, even after hearing about the attacks. Her mother told Montgomery she would not see anyone, that she had nothing more to say, and she wanted her family to get on with their lives.

How could Liz get on with her life? How could her father? How could any of them? Did her mother really think they could act as if Betty Connor no longer existed.

She couldn't suppress the anger that was building in her. Anger on her father's behalf. On her own. Why didn't her mother realize what she was doing to them by refusing their help and comfort and understanding? Could she possibly believe they wouldn't understand? That they wouldn't continue to love her?

She needed this time alone to cope with that anger, to try to comprehend the incomprehensible.

A truck whizzed past her, almost cutting her off. She stomped her foot on the brake. The car swerved back and forth before finding the lane again. Unsettled, she looked in the rearview mirror.

Just an impatient driver.

She was becoming paranoid.

There are reasons to be paranoid.

She made plans. She would stay at her parents' house while her own was being repaired. It wouldn't be the same without either of them there. But there was a good security system, something her mother had always insisted on.

Now she knew why. Her mother apparently had lived in fear of being discovered. By law enforcement. Maybe by someone else.

She reached the hospital at noon. Gallagher was still there, she was told, but should be released as soon as a doctor saw him.

She obtained his room number and went up to see him.

He was sitting in a chair rather than on the bed when she arrived. He wore the same bloody shirt as last night. It stretched over what must be a bulky bandage, and the pair of slacks he'd worn the night before. But he was freshly shaved, and his hair was neatly combed.

She wished she had thought about his needing a clean shirt. She'd just supposed that he would have the resources to get one. But then he was alone here.

That thought saddened her. Everyone should have someone to take care of them, of those details.

He looked up as she stood at the door. An engaging smile spread across his lips. "Hi," he said.

"Hi, yourself. How are you feeling?"

"All things considered, well," he said politely, but a devil seemed to dance in his eyes. "Thanks for calling Win Maynard."

"It was the least I could do. I wanted to stay but . . ."

"But your mother's hearing was this morning," he finished.

She nodded.

"What happened?"

"Attorneys are fighting over jurisdiction. The hearing was postponed to Monday."

"I'm sorry," he said.

"Why should you be?" she asked.

"Because I know it hurts you."

"And why should you care? You don't know me."

"No," he said. "But I know something about loss."

"Do you?"

"Doesn't everyone?" He stood, swayed for a moment, his tanned face turning pale. She leaned over and steadied him, then eased him down on the bed.

"Sorry," he said. Sweat beaded on his forehead, and she realized his earlier cavalier attitude had been a lie.

"There's a reason the hospital requires their patients to depart in a wheelchair," she said.

"To hell with that," he said.

She admitted privately that she couldn't imagine him being rolled sedately to the hospital entrance.

"Where are you planning to go?"

"Win suggested I return to Boston."

"Now?"

"Why not?"

"That means you have to go to Albuquerque. How are you going to get there?"

He shrugged. "Drive. Can I get a lift to your office? My car is there."

She looked at him. "With clothes, I hope."

He looked down at his shirt. "I didn't know I would be staying overnight. Perhaps you can suggest a store?"

She regarded him with frustration. He shouldn't be shopping and driving. Not without rest and food.

"I don't think you're up to driving."

"Oh, I'm up to a lot of things."

That statement could have too many meanings to analyze. She wasn't going to bite. But his cavalier attitude bothered her. She would never forgive herself if she allowed him to wander about without rest and food. Darn it, she felt responsible for him.

"Why don't I take you to my dad's house? You can eat

and relax. You're about his size and can borrow some clothes. I have to go to my office, but my assistant, Tracy, can drive your car to my house." She knew she could offer to take him to a hotel, but she certainly owed him something. The least she could do was make sure he was well enough to drive before he took to the road. "You can leave when you feel strong enough."

"An offer I can't refuse," he said lightly.

He had a charm that, despite her reservations, was beginning to affect her. She still wasn't sure she trusted him, but he was easy to be around. Charisma oozed from him.

Once he was in the car, she drove to her parents' house. Her passenger stretched out in the seat, glancing occasionally in the side door mirror.

"How long have you worked for Mr. Maynard?" she asked.

"Fifteen years."

"Tell me about him."

"What do you want to know?"

"Is he a good employer? Do you like him? Does he have a family?"

He looked at her with amusement. "He's a good employer. I respect him. And yes, he has a family. A wife and two daughters."

"My cousins," she mused.

"Second cousins," he said.

"Would I like them?"

"Probably."

It was a rather noncommittal reply. She decided not to comment on it. "It takes some getting used to," she said. "I never had an extended family, or didn't think I had."

"Your father?"

"He was an orphan. We thought mother was, as well. I always thought that was what drew them together, why they had such a tight bond." She hadn't meant to say that. She hadn't meant to tell him anything about her family, and certainly not about her mother.

"It's all right," he said in a soft voice. "I'm not trying to intrude. That's not why I'm here."

"I still don't understand why Maynard—after all these

years—is interested enough to send you. Is it because he plans to run for the Senate and wants to do damage control?"

"You're a cynic, Ms. Connor," he said. "But wrong. You're family, and he believes in family. He's close to his two daughters, and I understand he was close to your mother."

"I didn't used to be a cynic," she said quietly. "I'm learning fast, though."

His gaze sharpened on her. "Something has happened? Want to tell me about it?"

Was she just imagining that she heard more demand than query in his voice? In defiance of the paranoia dogging her heels, she flashed a quick, rueful smile. "I'm afraid my father's job might be in jeopardy."

"And your position on the city council?"

She shrugged. "I plan to resign. I won't have time to give it the attention it needs, and I would be a distraction."

"I'm sorry about that," he said. "Politics seem to run in Maynard blood."

"Is he serious about running for the Senate?"

"You've been doing some research."

"Haven't you? About us?"

He met her gaze. And nodded.

She appreciated the honesty. "He runs a large conglomerate. What does he plan to do with it if he runs for the Senate?"

"He's groomed some good men to take over."

"And his family?"

"His wife would enjoy the Washington scene. His two daughters are well married."

"Well married? Not happily?"

"They can be the same. Don't you believe your mother is well married as well as happily?"

"It's just an odd way to put it."

"Perhaps I don't believe in happily married," he said.

"Now who's the cynic?"

His smile spread to his eyes, and he was even more attractive than before.

"I've never had time for serious relationships," he said as if he'd read her mind.

Too many people were doing that lately. She didn't like the invasion. "Tell me about you."

He shrugged. "Not much to tell. I came from an Irish neighborhood. Not much money. My father was an alcoholic who ignored us most of the time."

His eyes turned hard and cold. Under that charm was something chilling. There was more to the story than he was telling.

His expression changed quickly into a rueful grin. "I worked my way through college, then law school. I was recruited by the law firm that was retained by your cousin. I worked on several minor matters for him, then one day he presented me with an offer I couldn't refuse. He said I was tough and hungry. And I was."

"And grateful?"

"Yes."

"Just what do you do for him?"

"I represent his various interests. When something comes up outside my specialty, I find him the very best to do what he needs."

She reached her father's house. News media trucks were still there. A group of reporters talking with each other turned and followed the car into the driveway. Cameras clicked as questions were thrown at her.

"Are the fire and the attack linked?"

"How do you feel about your mother now?"

Then Michael was out of the car and facing them. "I'm an attorney, and I believe you are on private property."

"Come on Ms. Connor. Give us something."

"There's nothing to give," she said. "Everything is in the police and court records, and my feelings are my own. I do intend to resign my post, though. I don't want to become a distraction to the city council."

"Have you informed the mayor?"

"Not yet. I'll do it shortly."

They left then, off to file their stories and send back tape. She used to like the press. Now she felt toward them like she would a plague of locusts. She tried to tell herself they were just doing their jobs, but . . .

"Let's go inside before they get their second wind," Michael said.

She went to the door and unlocked it, stepping inside to turn off the alarm.

He followed, and she pulled down the curtains and shades to shield them from cameras. Everything seemed to be the same as she left it. She turned back toward him.

She was struck again at how fine looking he was and also at how little it affected her. Would it have been the same if she was not already so fascinated by Caleb Adams? He was the one who nagged her every thought, even though she was appalled by the fact.

Despite the attraction that flickered and flamed between she and Caleb, it had been obvious that he'd wanted no part of it. And she certainly didn't need any distractions at the moment, either.

Gallagher had a bemused look as he glanced at her, but she also saw how pale he still was.

"There's a guest room down the hall," she said. "I'll make a toasted cheese sandwich, the perfect comfort food after a hospital."

"You don't have to do that."

"I might not be here were it not for you. Besides, I'm starving as well, and I definitely need comfort food."

"You talked me into it."

"There's a bath at the end of the hall. I'll get you one of Dad's shirts."

She led the way, stopping first at her father's room where she picked out a blue shirt.

"Are you sure he wouldn't mind?"

"Not after last night."

He took the shirt and disappeared into the bathroom. In minutes, she heard the sound of water running, and she returned to the kitchen.

She should have taken him to a hotel.

But then she would be racked with guilt, and she didn't need that right now. A few hours of rest and food, and he would be on his way.

She went into the kitchen and looked hopefully in the fridge. She thought she remembered seeing cheese there, and there was. She found the griddle and quickly made grilled toasted cheese sandwiches. She put two sandwiches on a plate for him, and one for her, and poured them both a glass of milk.

He appeared in the kitchen and sank down into a chair. He wolfed down the food and grinned at her. "I don't know when anything tasted so good. You're right. It *is* great comfort food."

She wasn't sure she believed anything he'd said, but she definitely was liking him more.

"I have to go," she said. "I have to see to things at my office and my home. But stay as long as you want."

"You trust me that much?"

"The FBI took everything of interest," she countered. "And I don't think you're involved in petty thievery."

"That's reassuring," he said with his wicked grin.

"We still don't want anything from Mr. Maynard."

"I understand," he replied.

"My assistant will bring your car here, but don't leave unless you feel well enough."

"I promise," he said with mock seriousness.

She nodded, not sure she should leave him alone here, but as she'd noted, there was absolutely nothing left that was of interest. And she liked the idea of someone being here while she was gone.

Once outside, she called her father on his cell phone and told him what she'd done.

He hesitated before answering, then, "If you think it's all right, then it's okay with me. I'm staying up here. I still hope I can talk to your mother."

"Let me know if you do. Or if she'll see me."

A silence.

"Dad?"

"I will, Sport."

She put the phone away, glanced around at surroundings in a way she'd never done before. Was that car supposed to be on this road? Was the van down the street really owned by a landscaping firm? Was the man in her father's house really an ally?

She closed her eyes for a moment, hoping that when she opened them again, her old world would be back. She knew it wouldn't. She had lost that sane, peaceful place.

Caleb didn't like the idea of leaving Elizabeth alone, but he had the afternoon appointment, and he didn't think there would be any danger in broad daylight. He didn't want to push too much.

Instead he found Montgomery. The attorney couldn't tell him any more than Liz had, but he was obviously frustrated at his client's refusal to help herself.

"Could she be afraid of something? Or someone?"

Montgomery had shrugged. "No one has been in to see her."

"No telephone calls?"

"I considered that as well," Montgomery said. "None."

"Does she know her family has been attacked and threatened?"

"She does."

"How did she react?"

"She didn't. Oh there were movements in her eyes. I had the feeling she's holding herself together by sheer willpower."

"The question is, why?"

"It could be as simple as what she says," Montgomery said. "That she's guilty, and she feels her family would be better off without her."

"You don't believe that?"

"No. But I don't have any other explanation."

Neither did Caleb.

Frustrated, he hopped in his car and headed toward Santa Fe. He was early and decided to drive over to Liz's parents' home. After last night he didn't want her alone.

Several news vans were parked in front of her house. He guessed he damned well didn't have to worry about her being alone. He drove down the street to a dead end, turned, and started back when he saw her jeep drive up. He stopped and watched as reporters thronged around her for several moments, then as she went up the steps with a tall, dark-haired man in a soiled shirt. His gut tightened as he watched them go inside the house.

Michael Gallagher. How many times had he seen the man in the photograph, next to Win Maynard?

The man who had assisted Elizabeth last night when he had gone to his cabin. What if Gallagher had not been there?

And why had he been there?

That was what puzzled him. Win Maynard was a charismatic figure. He was tireless in community affairs and was considered a great asset to the community. There had never been a taint of corruption around him. And yet there was something about him that bothered Caleb.

Come on, he told himself. It was only because he'd held a deep suspicion about all the families of the young conspirators. They must have been in contact or aided them in some way. How else could four spoiled young people evade the law for so long?

He'd never been able to prove it, however, and it roiled his soul that he had not.

His stomach tightened.

Not jealousy, he told himself. Concern. Gallagher's continued presence here puzzled him. Elizabeth had told him she and her father had turned down Maynard's offers. So why was Gallagher hanging about, especially in the middle of the night at her office?

It didn't make sense, and he didn't like things that didn't make sense.

She should be safe enough with him, though. People would have seen the two leave together at the hospital. He'd rescued her last night. How deep would her gratitude run? Would Elizabeth look toward Gallagher for aid rather than him?

Still, she had requested his help this morning. Not Gallagher's. He tried to relax. But too many unknown elements were at work. Why would Maynard get involved now, particularly when he was planning to run for the Senate? Who was threatening Elizabeth and her sister? And why was Sarah Jane Maynard silent when she could be helping herself? And her daughters?

He gave up speculating and drove to her office. Apparently, she'd decided to trust a man Caleb wasn't sure deserved it. But then, neither did he.

Caleb quickly found the office building. As he looked at the full parking area, he thought how lonely it must have been last night and felt a stab of guilt that he had not anticipated another attack on her. Had last night's attempt been another effort to frighten? Had she wandered into a burglary? Or had real harm been intended?

He just didn't know.

He looked at his watch. Still thirty minutes early. He didn't like the feeling he got thinking about her with Gallagher. He opened the door to the office.

A bell chimed as he entered.

No one sat at the reception desk facing the front window. He shook his head. He didn't like the idea of someone being here alone with only a bell for warning.

A young lady stepped out of an office in back. "Hi," she said. "Can I help you?"

"I have an appointment with Miss Connor in thirty minutes."

"Mr. Adams? I'm Tracy. Liz called me about you. Said she might be running a little late. Make yourself comfortable."

She looked impossibly young. Her sandy hair fell in a long braid that reached halfway down her back, and she wore blue jeans and a western-style blouse. She had a shy but contagious smile as if she really was glad to see him.

Elizabeth arrived forty minutes later, full of apologies. She asked Tracy to take a dark sedan to her house, and handed her the keys. "Take a taxi back here," she said. "Call and arrange for one."

After she left, Elizabeth turned to him. "I'm sorry I'm late. I took Michael Gallagher to my dad's house to get cleaned up."

He stood. "I hope you two don't work here alone."

"It's never been a problem before. We have good neighbors."

His eyes locked on hers. He didn't like the sense of responsibility and concern he felt. Worse, he didn't like the tension that leapt between them, filling the air with electric attraction that was becoming all too familiar. He'd hoped yesterday was an aberration. It apparently wasn't.

"How is Gallagher?" he asked.

"Walking. A little weak." Her gaze didn't waver from his. "He'll be staying at my father's house for a few hours."

He merely nodded.

"He needed some clothes."

"Have you changed your mind about accepting help from your mother's family?"

"No. But he did tell me a little about Winstead Maynard." She paused. "Now I want to know everything you do about the robbery, about the people involved. You said we should start at the beginning. Where is the beginning?"

The phone rang then.

She answered it. "Santa Fe Adventures."

He turned away, studying the posters on the wall.

"We're set for Saturday," he heard her say. "I'll pick you up in front of the Bishop's Lodge at seven."

She hung up the phone and turned all her attention to him. "The beginning," she said again. "Where do we start?"

chapter fifteen

"How much do you want to know about your mother?"

"Everything."

Caleb's eyes narrowed as if he were considering something. Then he asked, "What did Gallagher say about his employer?"

"I asked if he was offering to help financially because he was running for the Senate. He said Winstead Maynard was doing it because he felt strongly about family." She looked at him for affirmation.

He shrugged.

"How much do you know about each of the others implicated in the robbery?" she asked. He had given her a snapshot of the four young people accused of the crime. But nothing in depth.

"I know facts. I know opinions. I interviewed a lot of people who knew the four students."

"You have their statements?"

"Some of them, yes."

"I want to see them all."

"How much time do you have?"

"Tracy should be back within an hour. After that, I have the rest of the day."

"You trust Gallagher in your house?"

"There's nothing left," she said. "The FBI took everything."

Something in his green eyes flickered.

"They would," he said, then gave her a wry smile.

"You don't like them?"

"There was always a lively rivalry between us," he admitted. "They usually won."

"How long did you work on this case?" She watched him carefully. She wanted to trust him, but now she wasn't sure whether she trusted anyone.

"On and off for years," he said. "I kept going back and looking. We always believed someone would turn up."

"Four people disappearing completely," she mused. "What are the odds of that?"

"Not very high, especially as the use of computers has grown. It always puzzled me. There had to be a plan ahead of time, but none of them seemed to have the background or . . ."

"Or what?" she said.

"Abilities," he continued after a moment.

"Perhaps someone else . . ."

He turned abruptly toward the windows. She had that sense of aloneness again, a man separated from others by choice. There was something extraordinarily sensual about the way he moved. Despite his limp, the movement of his body was all athletic grace.

She ached to go over to him, to touch him, to feel that connection she'd felt yesterday when his lips had brushed hers in her house. She hadn't realized how much she needed it until now. She felt a stirring inside when he turned around and his unfathomable green eyes fastened on her.

"You shouldn't be here alone," he said.

"Tracy was here alone."

He raised an eyebrow.

Oh lord! Had she endangered Tracy? Her head throbbed as if a load of oars had been dropped on her head. When was she going to understand that her very presence put others in danger?

"I've put Tracy in danger as well?"

"Probably not," he said. "But it wouldn't hurt to have someone else here."

She counted the cost in her head. Expensive. But she

would do it tomorrow. Nothing was worth Tracy being harmed.

His gaze didn't move from her face. She wondered how eyes so green and depthless could give away so little. Had he always had that talent, or was it a skill he'd acquired? And how could he be so unapproachable and so mesmerizing at the same time?

A silence fell between them, and she wondered if it was because he felt the same expectancy, the same heat that soared through her. Her heart skipped a beat, and then he took a step away, as if trying to break that bond suddenly between them. "I tried to speak with your mother today," he said in a voice harsher than usual. "No luck."

"She won't talk to Dad or me, either," she said, hearing the break in her voice. "I don't understand. We had our differences, some I understand better now than I did then, but she always put us before anything or anyone else."

"Maybe she still is," he said.

"What do we do now?"

"I have some files at my cabin," he said. "You might learn more about your mother. If that's what you really want."

The last words sounded like a warning. "Is there something I won't like?"

"The Sarah Jane Maynard of thirty-four years ago was far different from the woman I saw in the courtroom. And the woman you and your father describe."

"I want to know, and see, everything."

"You said something about meeting people Saturday?"

She nodded. "River rafting. Group of four. My other guides are already booked."

"Do you know anything about them?"

"I have one name. Tracy said they've run rapids before."

He looked at her with exasperation.

"You don't think . . ."

"I think you have to be careful with everything you do until you find out what's going on."

You. Not we. He was distancing himself again.

"Who is it?" he asked.

She went into her office and found the name and the credit card number. "He's from Memphis."

"I'll find him," he said. He hesitated, then added, "Can you use an assistant?"

"Can you swim?"

"Yes."

"Paddle?"

"Middlingly well."

"You're hired." She felt both relief and a certain anticipation. She could handle it. She had handled these trips alone in the past, but it was far easier with a companion to help with the raft and the supplies. She hated to ask clients to do the heavy lifting.

He had a quizzical look on his face as if her decision had surprised him.

She just wished it didn't make him look so appealing. Her heart jerked. She yearned to reach out and touch him, and to share an intimacy that might chase the chill away. The intensity of that need shook her.

"Do you have other excursions planned?" he said, and her mind was yanked back to the present.

"Yes, but I already have guides to handle them."

"Do you usually book trips on short notice?"

"No, but I need the money for Mom," she said.

Something close to anger flitted across his face, but it was gone so quickly she wasn't sure exactly what it was.

"There's always Maynard," he said curtly. "And Gallagher."

It was like a splash of ice water. He was baiting her. "There's always that," she agreed, knowing that until she knew a great deal more than she did, neither she nor her father would touch a dime.

He looked disappointed at her response, then glanced at his watch.

"Have you had lunch?"

"I made some sandwiches for Mr. Gallagher. I had one as well."

"Lucky Mr. Gallagher," he said.

There was a slight bite in his voice, and she wondered why.

"Is there somewhere nearby to find something?" he asked.

"There's a café two blocks away with good Mexican food. Just turn right at the corner and go straight until you see a pink café."

He hesitated, and she wondered if he worried whether she would be safe. "There's people next door, and I'll lock the door," she promised.

His expression relaxed, and that muscle jerked in her heart again. It had been a long time since someone had taken care of her. Worried about her. She'd always shied away from anything or anyone that made her feel less independent. But now it was somehow comforting.

He left with that abrupt way of his, as if niceties were at the bottom of his list. She wanted to go with him. The space she loved so much was now cold and empty. But she had to stay here, go over advertising copy, pay bills, answer the phone, and make sure she had the equipment for Saturday.

She locked the door and started into the office, then turned back and sat at Tracy's desk where, hopefully, she could see anyone approaching. She knew she had to start thinking that way. She thought regretfully about the gun she'd lost. She would have to get a new one. Soon.

She called Garry, who was going to oversee her house repairs. "How are things coming?"

"The windows are in," he said. "They're working on the kitchen. You need to chose paint colors and carpets and sign off on some work."

She groaned. "You have good taste. Won't you do it?"

"I think you should. I'll make sure it's done right."

"I'm going to install an alarm system," she said. "Can you . . . ?"

"For you, Liz, anything. I can work at home. You worry about your mother. I'll look after the house."

Gratitude swept over her. Garry and Tracy had been pure gold. In fact, everyone in town seemed sympathetic.

She looked at the proof of an ad for a local magazine, then returned the last call for the day. *The mayor.* His administrative assistant put her through immediately.

"Liz," he said. "I wanted you to know that we are all supporting you."

She clasped the phone next to her ear. She had thought his messages would say something else. "Thank you," she said. "But I think I should resign. I . . . there's been some . . ."

"I know. I've heard. About your sister as well. I've asked the police to keep an eye on your home and business. Can't have anything happen to our newest council member."

There was a warmth she'd not felt before. She knew she'd been a compromise appointment, someone who hadn't been overtly political or allied with one of the two factions on the board.

"Thank you. But I'm resigning—"

"That's not necessary," he said, cutting her off.

"Thank you," she said again, this time heartfelt. She'd thought . . . Yet she knew she couldn't continue. "It's simply I won't have time for the next few months, perhaps longer. It's not fair to the city."

"I understand," he said after a short pause. "We hope that you'll keep involved. And of course we'll keep the police watching your home and business. The county sheriff will do the same with your father's home."

"Thanks." She felt better as she placed the phone back in its cradle. She had been uncertain as to the reaction of the community. She should have known better.

Liz looked around the office. So much fear last night. So much hope several days earlier. Now she didn't know how she felt. Too many emotions in too few days.

Tracy appeared at the door, and she went to unlock it.

"Locked?" Tracy said.

"Caleb thinks we should keep it locked during the day."

Tracy looked startled, then seemed to accept the new development without question. "Who's the hottie at your father's house?"

"Michael Gallagher?"

"You didn't tell me he looked like Mark Damon. Imagine someone like that saving you. When you told me he was an attorney, I thought he would be old. And gray. And . . ."

"Did he say when he was leaving?"

"As soon as the car came. He said to tell you he was grateful, but he couldn't impose any longer."

"How did he look to you?"

Tracy's plain, pleasant face lit. "Ah, so you care?"

"I'm simply worried about him."

"I think he decided to stay in a hotel tonight. He asked me to suggest one. I mentioned a couple. He said something about flying to Boston tomorrow."

Just then, the door opened.

Caleb leaned against the doorframe. Liz studied him. He didn't have Michael Gallagher's smooth sophistication. Instead he had a raw and untamed look about him. His worn jeans hugged a lean body, and his rolled-up shirtsleeves displayed tan, muscled arms.

"Can you do without me for the rest of the afternoon?" Liz asked Tracy. "I looked at the ad. It's ready to go."

"I'll call the ad rep." Tracy's gaze went from Liz's face to Caleb's and back again.

"If you have any questions, call me on the cell phone." Liz paused. "Don't forget about locking the door when you're here alone."

"I won't." Tracy nodded. "Sam had been trying to get me to learn to shoot. Maybe I should do that."

"Mayor Lee plans to send a patrol car by frequently, and I don't want you to stay after the other offices close."

"Sam is picking me up," she said. "I'll be fine."

Liz reluctantly went to the door. She had burdened Tracy with the business but was immensely proud at the way her assistant had assumed so much responsibility. She would never forgive herself if anything happened to her. "If you see anything, call nine-one-one," she said.

"I will."

Caleb nodded at Tracy, then opened the door. To Liz's surprise, he looked back. "Nice meeting you."

The words sounded rusty, like he hadn't used such phrases in a long time, but they also sounded sincere. His eyes were shuttered, though, as he regarded Tracy for an instant.

The door closed behind them. "She'll be okay," he said. "She's a smart kid."

How many times had he read her mind? It was uncanny.

She dismissed the notion as they moved toward his vehicle. He also had a jeep, but unlike hers it was gray and battered. A rug covered the backseat, and a half-empty water bottle sat in the corner of the passenger seat.

He turned on the engine, and for a moment she froze. What in the heck was she doing? Going up into the mountains with a man she knew little about. Especially one who made her body react in strange but compelling ways. To discover the girl her mother had once been? Did she really want to know? He'd asked her that question. She wasn't sure she wanted to know. But she *had* to know.

A Pandora's box had obviously been opened. How many more demons would be released?

Caleb drove into the yard of his cabin.

He'd built it himself in that lonely, guilt-filled year after he'd left Boston. He wanted the labor, needed to work so hard that he would fall to sleep at night. And he'd always been good with his hands, with carpentry. His father had been as well. He remembered the workshop, the way his father's hands had lovingly touched wood. His mother had kept a small jewel box his father had made for her birthday.

The memory sharpened the loss. He had never taught his own son the pleasure of turning wood into something fine.

He banished the thought as he parked the car.

Tramp was sitting on the porch and rose as he stepped out. Elizabeth had stepped out before he could go around to the passenger's side.

Tramp growled. He didn't like strangers and thought his job was to warn them away.

Instead of looking at him for reassurance or shying away, Elizabeth knelt and held out her hand to the dog.

Tramp regarded her for a moment, then stepped forward and sniffed her hand. Satisfied, he sat.

"Some watchdog," he said.

"He's yours?"

"He's not anybody's," Caleb corrected, tamping down an unexpected feeling of approval. "He's his own self. He visits."

"How long has he been visiting?"

"Two years," Caleb admitted.

She regarded the ugly hound with unconcealed delight. "He's beautiful."

Beauty must definitely be in the eye of the beholder. Tramp was many things, but beautiful was not one of them.

Caleb went up the four steps and across the porch to the door. She was behind him, and the traitorous Tramp was wagging his tail so frantically he could sweep all the dust from the small porch. Caleb was suddenly reminded that his home was not fit for company.

Too late now.

He opened the door and stood aside. The room was as he had left it. Papers were piled up on a table next to a disreputable big stuffed chair he bought at a flea market. It was unsightly but comfortable. An empty beer bottle lay on the floor next to the chair. The sofa didn't match anything else, and the dining area, if you could call it that, included only a small table and two mismatched chairs.

A large fireplace dominated the room, but its appearance was somewhat spoiled by the haphazardly stacked wood on both sides. He'd probably been drunk when he brought it in. The small, compact kitchen had several empty cups in the sink he'd used the night before, along with an empty chili can.

His cabin wasn't big, but it was well-constructed. The interior walls were logs. An Indian rug covered the plank flooring. Stairs led to a loft that served as an office for his part-time investigative work and the compilation over the years of notes and records about the burglary. A kitchen, living room, and an extra large bedroom completed his dwelling. It was all he'd wanted, all he'd needed.

Caleb watched as she looked around. He sure as hell wasn't going to apologize for its condition.

But she merely looked around with interest, then glanced out the window at the same view that both soothed and haunted him.

"What a wonderful view," she said.

He didn't have to answer. It wasn't one of those questions that required it.

"How did you find this place?" she asked, leaning down to pet Tramp and receiving a lick in gratitude. Damned dog never fussed over him like that.

"Used to come camping up here," he replied. "My . . . wife and son loved it. She lived here as a kid." The familiar stab of pain still came at the thought of Annie, but it wasn't as knee buckling as it usually was.

She was silent for a moment, though her gaze was on him. He could barely tolerate the sympathy there. Hell, every emotion she felt shone through those remarkable eyes. He wanted to reach out, touch that hair, take her in his arms, and feel the warmth of a woman again.

He turned away. Was he being unfaithful to his wife to want another woman?

"My notes are upstairs in the loft," he said abruptly. "I'll get them." He was aware that she was watching him as he mounted the stairs.

He'd sifted through four boxes of notes, clippings, and investigative reports about the armed robbery right after Cam's call. Now he chose several files containing personal information about the suspects. He removed several items, then descended the stairs to the main room. Elizabeth looked quite at home in his big chair with Tramp swooning all over himself as she rubbed his ears.

"I like your cabin," she said as he pulled up a chair from what could mockingly be called his dining room set.

"It's small."

"It's cozy," she corrected. "The view alone is worth millions."

He fought against an unexpected surge of pride.

"Was the cabin already here?"

"No."

"You had it built?"

"I built it," he said.

She stared at him for several moments. "That's why you knew what needed to be done at my house."

He didn't answer but instead held out a fat file and laid it in her lap. She let it stay there, as if reluctant to open it. He went outside to the porch. The sun was sinking behind the hills. He took a step down and sat on the steps. She needed time alone.

And so did he.

This wasn't a good idea. He'd known it. But he also knew she couldn't protect herself running blind. She had to know something about the Defenders of Liberty. But the more he became involved with her, the less effective he would be. In protecting her. In finding justice for his father.

He watched as the sun sank behind the mountain and darkness settled around him. There were no other homes around. It was difficult land for development, and he'd purchased twenty acres.

How many times had he sat here with only a bottle as company?

Part of him still ached for a drink, but the need wasn't as strong as he'd thought it would be. He had too many other things to consider.

He didn't know how much time had passed when he heard the door open.

Elizabeth sat down next to him. "Thank you."

"Did you find out what you wanted to know?" he asked.

"No. There are still too many contradictions, inconsistencies. Part of it seems to portray someone spoiled and thoughtless. Speeding tickets. A DUI that was dismissed. Mediocre grades. But she also worked at a soup kitchen. There's nothing to indicate she would ever participate in . . . what they said she did."

He didn't say anything. He knew the file by heart.

"No one ever discovered who she was dating?" she asked after a moment's silence. She obviously referred to a statement by a friend that Sarah Jane was seeing someone secretly.

"As far as I know, only one person admitted knowing

she was having an affair. And she said she didn't know who it was."

"That's when her grades started going down," she said. "When she joined that group and apparently fell . . ." Pain was in her voice.

He let her muse on her own. He had nothing to add, only suppositions, and he didn't think she would want to hear those.

"Who was that one person?" she asked. "The one who knew? Did you ever speak to her?"

"I did," he admitted.

"What did she say? It's not in the file."

"I promised her I wouldn't involve her unless necessary. She'd been sworn to secrecy by your mother, who apparently feared her father would try to end it. He'd ended her relationships before."

"Was my mother's . . . lover one of the others implicated in the burglary?"

"I don't know. My source said she didn't know the name."

"Did you believe her?"

"No," he said flatly.

"Could that be why my mother won't say anything? She's trying to protect someone?"

He shrugged. "It's a possibility."

"She loves Dad!" It was more a cry of protest than a statement.

"There's something about first love," he said.

"Was that the way it was with your wife?" she asked in a low voice.

"Yes," he said shortly.

Silence settled between them. Only Tramp's eager panting broke it.

Liz reached out and touched Caleb's hand. His fingers automatically went around hers in mutual empathy. And sorrow.

Liz leaned her head against his shoulder, and he caught the light fragrance of flowers, felt the silk of hair. His hand left hers, and he put his arm around her, and they sat there together, listening to the lonely cry of an owl.

She turned her head slightly to look at him, and their lips met.

Softly at first. Then hungrily as if they couldn't get enough of each other.

An internal voice warned him to stop.

But it was too late. As need and desire exploded inside him, he wondered whether it had always been too late.

chapter sixteen

When Caleb's lips touched hers, she responded with all the need and hurt and bewilderment that had been building inside. His kiss was not tentative, but hungry and wanting, even angry. She recognized that but didn't understand it. But need bred need. His arms locked around her as he pressured her mouth to open, even his hands kneaded her back, sending ripples of sensation through her.

The quickening in her heart became a tattoo. It pounded so hard she knew he must hear it. For a fleeting second, she worried it might give her away, but then she had probably already done that as she opened her mouth to him.

Any reservations melted in the intense heat that radiated between them. She drank in the scent of him, the feel of his fingers on the back of her neck, the taste of his kiss. Her hands burned where they touched his taut, hard body. She tasted him as his tongue explored her mouth, and tingling started deep in the core of her and snaked through the rest of her until she was helpless to do anything but mutely ask for more.

The anger was still in him. She felt it in the barely restrained touches. He didn't want to succumb to what was happening. But he, like she, was helpless against it. She felt the pressure of his hands change from angry to demanding, then to gentleness as his mouth held hers in a lazy captivity that drew her deeper and deeper into a spiral of cascading feelings. Her body quivered under the impact, and she knew he felt it as well. She felt him tremble.

He tore himself away and stared at her for a moment. In the moonlight, she saw a sudden confusion on his face. He muttered something she couldn't quite hear.

"That shouldn't have happened, Elizabeth."

"Liz," she said. "My friends call me Liz."

"Is that what we are?" A coolness had crept into his voice. It startled, then stung her. She'd had enough rejection these past few days.

She stood, wanting to flee, but her legs wouldn't move. She realized there was nothing to flee to. She had come in his car. Her first mistake. Succumbing to him was the second one.

He slowly unwound himself and stood beside her. The moonlight reflected in his sandy hair, and those usually unreadable eyes now roiling with emotion. "I'm sorry," he said.

"Why?" she asked.

"We have a business arrangement. You're vulnerable . . . I took advantage."

She had been angry this morning at her mother. Now she was livid.

She rarely got angry. When she did, it was legendary, according to her mother. The thought of her mother made her even more furious.

"You didn't take anything," she contradicted. "I offered," Liz said with as much dignity as she could muster. She felt thoroughly humiliated. "You can drive me back."

"Have you finished with the files?"

She hadn't. He knew it. She couldn't have gone through all those he'd handed to her. Her mother, yes. One other member. Then she'd been drawn outside. She'd needed fresh air. She'd needed him. Dammit.

He regarded her with that half smile that—with the scar—he had little control over.

"No. Can I take them with me?"

"No."

He wasn't giving her any choice at all. She had read her

mother's files and one other. She needed to read the other two.

"Why?"

"I don't have copies, and I don't have a copying machine. So nothing leaves here."

She didn't quite understand the change in him. He had backed away before, but this time he had taken a definite step toward her before doing that. She was thoroughly confused.

Guilt over his wife? Son?

His jaw tightened.

"I *have* to read them," she said.

His gaze lowered. "I'm sorry."

"Caleb?"

He turned his gaze back to her.

"I'll stay until I finish."

"I'm not sure that's wise."

She wasn't sure, either, but she wasn't going to leave here until she had read every word of those files. There was a clue there. There had to be.

"I'll go and get something to eat," he said. "There's nothing here."

He hesitated for a moment, then went inside the cabin. Emotionally exhausted, she waited outside. In minutes, he returned with a revolver.

He handed it to her. "It's loaded. Keep it with you."

He headed for the jeep, then turned back. "Go inside. Keep the doors locked."

Tramp looked from his master to her, then back again before trotting behind him.

He turned. "Stay, Tramp. Watch. Protect."

Tramp sat and watched as Caleb stepped into the jeep and roared off as if the devil was after him.

And maybe he was.

She stood there for a moment longer. Tramp came over to her, and she scratched his ears. He made a rumble deep in his throat. It sounded like contentment. She was envious. If only a rub behind her ears would bring her the same contentment.

She stretched and looked up at the sky. Thick purple

clouds were moving across the horizon. Had the chill portended a storm? A storm more potent than the emotional one she'd just experienced? She was still stunned by its intensity, then Caleb's sudden departure.

Why?

Fighting a sudden depression, she went inside and locked the doors. She put the gun in her purse on a table, then glanced around for photos, for anything that would give her more understanding of Caleb.

She found nothing. She didn't want to go into his bedroom. Too intimate for her turbulent feelings. Instead, she went up the steps he'd taken earlier. She didn't like snooping, but she wanted to know more about Caleb Adams. She told herself it was because she'd decided to place her trust in him, and perhaps that wasn't the wisest thing.

But it was a lie, and she tried never to lie to herself.

Once up in the loft, her gaze wandered around. Unlike the rest of the house, this area was neat. There were several newspapers on an otherwise empty desktop; she recognized the Santa Fe and Albuquerque papers. All had stories about her mother and family on the front page. There was a computer on an adjacent stand. A large but battered file cabinet filled the wall next to the desk. She tried the drawers. They were locked.

Then she tried the top drawer of his very used-looking desk. It, too, was locked.

Tramp nudged her.

"You don't think I should be up here, do you?" she said. "I probably shouldn't be." But still, she sat down and thought about turning on the computer. If he checked usage, he would know she'd turned it on. Yet she couldn't stop herself.

The screen lit, and a "You Have Mail" message blinked on and off.

She pressed the button, and it asked for a password.

She had no idea what it might be.

What were the names of his wife and son?

Don't do this. It's snooping.

But she had gone too far now, and there were too many mysteries.

She clicked on the Internet server and Googled Boston and Caleb Adams. She supposed she should have done it earlier, but she had taken Colton Montgomery's word. Now she wanted—needed—to know more.

A number of hits appeared on the screen. Surprisingly there were several Caleb Adamses. She went through them and soon found what she was looking for: "Detective's Wife, Son Die in Car Explosion." She read the news story that had appeared in the Boston newspaper. It was dated four years earlier.

An explosion yesterday killed the wife and son of Boston Detective Caleb Adams and seriously wounded him.

Maryann Adams and her seven-year-old son, Samuel, were both killed when Detective Adams's car blew up just outside their home. A police department spokesman said Detective Adams was walking to the car when it exploded. He had multiple injuries from flying shrapnel and is listed in serious condition.

The spokesman said Detective Adams arrived home in a department-issue car. His wife was in his personal car to take their son to a Little League game. He went inside to leave his weapon, and when he approached the car, Mrs. Adams turned the key in the ignition, and the car exploded.

Detective Adams has been working in organized crime and is an eighteen-year veteran of the Boston Police Department.

The story continued, but the words became blurred as she tried to read the rest of the article. She felt a dampening behind her eyes. He had told her that his wife and son had died. Montgomery had also reported that they had been killed in an explosion. But somehow reading about it had more impact. A hot tear rolled down her face.

She turned off the computer. Sam. His son has been named Sam. But why no photos? She didn't understand. If she had lost a child, she would want photos, remembrances. But then she couldn't even imagine losing a child and mate, much less witnessing it.

And if it had been meant for him, the guilt would be devastating.

She felt dirty, as if she had been prying into a very private part of a man who had chosen not to tell her.

She went down the steps to the kitchen even as pain tore at her heart, and now she understood far more than she did before. Or thought she did. She knew no one could understand a loss like he suffered.

She took a detour through the kitchen, made a cup of coffee, and looked in the fridge. It was pitiful. A quart of milk with a "do not sell" dated three weeks earlier. A package of cheese. Olives. Bacon that had dried out and curled up. About the only thing that looked edible was a jar of peanut butter, a jar of jelly, and three bottles of beer.

She continued to search. The cabinets held a limited number of glasses, plates, and bowls. A few cans of soup. Another cabinet had three bottles of scotch. Two were unopened.

Another mental snapshot of the man. The cabin made more sense now, too. He didn't care how he lived downstairs, but the business area had been meticulous. It looked as if he'd divided his life into compartments. He was disciplined when he needed to be; otherwise it looked as if he did his best to avoid life.

Stop it. Read the files. Learn about the people involved with my mother.

She took the coffee back into the living area, sat in the big chair, and took up another file. Even as she listened for the sound of an approaching car, she soon became involved in the life of Terrence Colby, son of a wealthy plastic surgeon, and who, like her mother, had just disappeared.

KANSAS CITY

Jeff Baker reluctantly pulled out of his driveway for the 500-plus-mile trip to Chicago. His wife had been surprised when he'd said he had been employed to restore an antique car in the Windy City.

He rarely left Kansas City. He'd always claimed he didn't want to leave them. This, he said, was different. "A great opportunity," he'd said. "One I can't pass up."

It was a good excuse, as good as any he could contrive. It would mean a few days or weeks away from home. Before he left, though, he'd put his affairs in as good an order as he could. He had saved every penny he could these past years, knowing that even doing something as ordinary as taking out a life insurance policy could lead to an investigation he couldn't afford. His family considered him miserly. If only they knew, it wasn't his natural instinct. He did it for them. He did not want them to be left with nothing if he were caught.

He could appeal to his relatives, of course, but his father had died, and his mother had remarried. He knew that much, though he had not contacted them since the day he'd left. It was too dangerous. And he knew his father.

Terry had disgraced the family. As a child, he'd never been forgiven by his physician father for small infractions, and his mother, he knew, had been disappointed in him. He wore glasses and didn't like sports. He liked books, but he was also a natural mechanic and loved tinkering with old cars. Both parents thought that beneath their station and winced when he would appear coated in grease. Because his conservative contemporaries disdained him, he went in the other direction, finding acceptance and even admiration in a group of antiwar activists. The robbery, he now realized, had been the ultimate rebellion against a father who never accepted him. How naive he'd been. How easily manipulated.

Tony had survived the debacle, and Terry had never understood why. The last time he'd seen Tony, the man was standing next to the armored car, fury written all over his face as Stuart Marshall drove off, and police sirens closed in.

He would never forget the horror of that day. The guilt he'd lived with every moment of his life since. He'd never wanted the money. Not until he had a family of his own.

Two boys, thirteen and fifteen, whom he loved more than life itself.

In the past thirty-four years he'd managed to save a little over a hundred thousand dollars. It was in an account no one knew about but him but could be found if anything happened to him. It had been honestly made and not subject, as far as he knew, to confiscation, even if he was arrested. But now if all went well, he could get his share of the robbery money and take his family to Mexico, where laws prevented extradition of anyone charged with a capital crime. If it didn't—if he were arrested—the money would provide an education for his sons. Not a great one, but one that would, at least, give them a chance.

He kept thinking of the money in the safe-deposit boxes.

It was blood money, but it could make a difference to his family.

If it was still there.

Had one of his companions that day found a way to reach the money on his own? It wouldn't have been Sarah Jane, he knew, but Terrell was completely capable of it. So was Tony, if he'd ever discovered where it was.

Just the thought of Tony put his nerves on edge. It had been Tony who had planned the robbery, who had said one of the guards was only too willing to participate, that it would be an easy touch, and the money would go toward their antiwar efforts.

Then, in seconds, everything had gone wrong. He still got sick inside when he thought about those moments. The shots, the one guard doubling over, and then the second falling to the ground, blood gurgling from his throat. He'd just stood there until Stuart had grabbed him and steered him toward the car. How could good intentions go so awry? How could he have allowed his passion to justify committing a felony that became murder? But he knew the answer. His father. His smug father who mocked his opinions, who had called him "useless" all his life. He'd wanted to do something. Something important.

God help him, he had done something, and like the coward his father had always called him, he had run.

And for Margaret and the kids he would keep on running.

He ate up the miles, though he was careful to stay several miles below the speed limit. Nine hours later he arrived in Chicago and chose a chain motel room. Once registered, he went out and purchased a copy of the *Chicago Tribune* and scoured the want ads.

And there he found what he was searching for.

Caleb needed to give Liz time to quietly study the files, and he needed to give himself time to get his libido in check.

He'd once considered seducing Liz as part of a plan to wangle his way into her life. Seduction was still a great thought, but for different reasons. He wanted her. He hadn't wanted a woman since his wife died. Guilt had killed desire. But now he wanted Liz Connor with every fiber of his being.

She had looked too vulnerable reading those files, so determined to discover the truth. And that, he knew, was what she intended to do. She'd looked weary but appealing as she pushed back a tendril of auburn hair while studying the files with such an intent expression. He also feared for her. She was so damned unafraid, despite all that had happened. A big mistake. He'd learned in his years as a detective there were damned few coincidences. There was a pattern. Either someone wanted something very badly, or they wanted to scare the hell out of her and her mother, or they meant even greater harm. In any case, she should be far more careful than she'd been.

He shuddered to think of her running an untamed river with men she didn't know. He'd known there was no way he was going to let that happen, and he'd also known he was getting in far too deep. He cared about her, and he hadn't meant for that to happen.

He reached the small town ten miles away and stopped at a great little store he usually patronized. He selected some bacon, eggs, milk, cheese, and homemade salsa for an omelet. He used to make them for Annie, though he hadn't taken the trouble to cook them for himself these past few years.

Take her home, the internal voice warned him.

He could relent and let her take the files back, but they *were* his only copies. He'd held onto them when he'd sold everything else. They were his lifeline. Had been ever since . . .

"Hey Mr. Adams," Joe Santana greeted him. "Your friend find you?"

"Friend?"

"Someone was asking directions to your place. Said he was a friend," Joe Santana said.

"What did he look like?"

"An Anglo. Dressed well."

"Exactly how?"

"Tie and slacks. No jeans."

"What did he want to know?"

"Whether I knew a Señor Adams. Said he was a friend. Had your address all right. I saw it. But he said he couldn't find the road."

A knot formed in his stomach. "Anything else?"

Joe shook his head.

"Did he buy anything?"

"Gas and donuts."

Donuts. The mainstay of surveillance.

Dammit. His cabin. Liz was there alone.

"Thanks," he said and paid the bill, then nearly ran to his jeep and started it.

"Señor!"

He heard the shout and looked out the window. Joe was rushing out with the bag of groceries in his arms.

Caleb took it, because he didn't want more discussion. He put the jeep in gear and roared out of the parking lot.

He shouldn't have left her.

The vision of an exploding car flashed through his head as his foot pressed even harder on the gas pedal.

Liz closed the file on Terrence Colby.

She didn't know what to think about the contents. Terrence Colby was the son of a wealthy and prominent plastic surgeon, according to people who knew him. Various family and acquaintances called him a "a shy young man," "a boy never quite accepted by his peers," and "a genius at anything mechanical." Everyone expressed disbelief that he could be involved in anything violent.

Just like her mother.

The file on one of the other participants revealed a different portrait. That student, Jacob Terrell, was reported to be an arrogant young man always at war with his parents. He'd been a member of the sailing club but apparently had flunked out of college just before the robbery. His friends had been amazed that he had become involved in a student peace group just after his expulsion.

She hadn't had time to read the last file when she heard a noise outside.

Tramp stood, barked once.

Caleb?

He had been gone more than an hour. But then grocery stores and restaurants weren't around the corner out here. She felt a flurry of apprehension tinged with anticipation. She knew, though, she had to be careful not to let him know she knew about his family, the way his wife and son had died. He wasn't the type of man who wanted sympathy. She didn't even know which Caleb Adams would return: the passionate man who had kissed her, or the cool, biting stranger that had drawn away.

Placing the file on the table, she went to the door, unlocked and opened it.

Light streamed from the house to the place Caleb had parked earlier. No jeep. She'd heard a noise. She knew she had.

Her gaze searched the outside area as she clung to the door. Tramp stood by her side, his body alert. Nothing but shadows moving with a growing breeze. It must have been an animal.

She wasn't taking chances. Not after the night at her office. She locked the door again, then went to her purse and found the gun she'd been carrying. She went to the window and peered out again.

A figure darted alongside trees to the left.

A wave of terror swept over her. *The lights. Turn off the lights.*

Even as she went to turn them off, the house went dark.

chapter seventeen

Thank God she had the gun. Liz gripped it tightly. If she'd had to find it in total darkness . . .

The power had not gone off on its own. Someone was out there.

Her heart raced.

"Come," she whispered to the dog. Would he understand? Obey? Instead, he barked and held his ground.

She wasn't going to leave him. She took him by his collar with her left hand and led him to what must be the bedroom.

The gun slipped in her sweat-slicked hands.

Get a grip. Remember all those lessons.

But those lessons had involved cardboard targets, not a human being.

Caleb will be back soon.

The sound of breaking glass reached her. Tramp barked again and lunged against her hold, freeing himself and running toward the kitchen.

Liz hesitated, then followed. She wouldn't be safe anywhere in the house. At least now she would have the element of surprise. The intruder would be distracted by Tramp.

She held the .38 in both hands as she'd learned.

A shadow loomed, big and powerful, in the kitchen area.

With a growl, Tramp leaped at him.

The gunshot echoed off the cabin's walls as Tramp fell backward.

No.

The figure turned back toward her, and she knew she was next. She aimed and fired.

The intruder stepped back. "Shit."

She had hit him, but then he turned his gun toward her. The lights came on.

She blinked in the sudden glare, and the figure in black stumbled and went to his knees as he reached for the night vision goggles that shielded his eyes and tore them off. Then he aimed again.

Liz pulled the trigger twice. He went down just as another figure appeared in the broken window, a gun in his hand. She swung her weapon around.

Caleb!

She lowered the pistol. Her gaze returned to the figure on the floor. Tramp, blood dripping from his shoulder, stood and limped toward her. Her legs buckled under her, and she fell to her knees.

Caleb went over to the fallen intruder. Blood from his wounds pooled on the floor.

Caleb took the handgun that lay next to the still figure and slid it across the floor. Then he checked the intruder's neck pulse before glancing up at her. "He's dead."

She laid her gun down on the floor. She knew her fingers wouldn't hold it another moment. "I . . . I think Tramp saved my life," she stuttered.

"Are you okay?" he asked.

"I'm fine." It was a lie. She wasn't all right at all. She wanted to be sick.

At the sound of his name, Tramp limped to Caleb's side. Caleb stooped and examined the wound. "Shoulder, but it doesn't look bad. The bullet went in and out. He'll need a trip to the vet's." He rubbed the dog's ears. "Good job," he said with a slight break in his voice. "Good job."

Tramp's tail wagged.

Liz rose and took a few steps on shaky legs. She had her own thanks to deliver. She sat down beside Caleb and very carefully put her arms around the dog, her head against his.

Tramp's tongue took a big swipe on her cheek.

"Thank you," she whispered.

Caleb touched her shoulder, and she released her hold on Tramp. She shuddered with the aftermath of what had just happened. Her hands still felt the jerk of the gun as it fired, and the acrid smell of gunpowder hung in the air. She didn't have to see the body lying nearby. It would be in her mind forever.

A sob suddenly racked her body, and Caleb pulled her into his arms and wrapped them around her.

She leaned against him, needing him. Needing that human contact.

She had just killed a man. A human being.

It didn't matter that he had probably meant to kill her or Caleb. *She* had killed *him*.

Like her mother.

Oh God!

She started to shake uncontrollably. His hand went to her hair, smoothing it. "It's all right," he whispered. "It'll be all right."

A sob tore from her throat. "Why?" It was a cry rather than a question.

"I don't know."

She put her hand against his chest. Felt his heartbeat. His warmth thawed the ice inside her. She wondered, though, if she would ever be truly warm again.

After several moments, he gently drew away, his right hand taking hers. Giving her strength. She felt it in his callused fingers, in the coiled strength of his body.

"I'm okay now," she whispered.

"No, you're not," he disagreed. "But I have to take care of a few things." He paused. "I have to call the sheriff. Are you ready?"

She nodded numbly.

He let her go, then stood. He held out his hand and boosted her to her feet, leaving his hand to touch hers for a moment, obviously unsure whether she was solidly on two feet. Then he stooped down next to the man on the floor and took off the ski mask. "Is this the man who attacked you last night?"

She'd only had a glimpse of the face then, but she remembered the eyes, and now they were wide open. She would never forget them. Never. "Yes." She shuddered. "He must have meant to kill me at the office."

"Maybe not. He could have been looking for something in your office. You surprised him. But once you saw his face, he couldn't let you identify him."

"But how would he know I'm here? You were careful driving up here."

His brows furrowed in thought. "It makes sense that he's been watching you, and I've been seen with you. Both our faces have been on television. Someone might well have seen us leave your office, and my address is on tax records."

Then both of them might have been targets. She couldn't bear the thought of death watching her, following her like a shadow, that those around her could be in danger for reasons she didn't understand. And not understanding, she could do little about it. "Why the goggles?"

"Gave him an advantage in the dark," he said. "I noticed the generator was off. I thought turning it on might distract him long enough for me to get inside."

That flash of light might well have saved her life. "Thank you," she said for the second time in two days.

"You did it, lady," he said. "Not me. And now I have to call the sheriff," he added. "It's a clear breaking and entering. There won't be any problems." He hesitated, then added, "But I'm the one who shot him."

She glanced quickly at his face. It looked grim and implacable.

"I don't understand," she said.

"You don't need this right now. I saw the darkened cabin, came in, and shot him."

"No," she said.

"Your family has enough trouble." A muscle flexed in his throat. He was a cop. Had been a cop. He would be lying to other cops. She suspected it would cost him a great deal to do what he'd just offered.

It would cost her even more. She wouldn't, couldn't, let

someone take responsibility for something she had done. Not even if it caused more pain to her family.

Like mother, like daughter. She could almost read the headlines.

She looked up at him, trying to penetrate those green eyes that were always so well-guarded. "I won't let you do that," she said. "Besides, I've watched detective shows. The residue is on my hands."

"Television is the bane of every detective," he said. "They get a lot of things wrong. I doubt if they would test here in such an obvious case. But there are ways. You can wash your hands. I can fire a bullet into his body with the gun."

"No," she said flatly. I won't let you do that. Not because of you," she added. "Because of me."

"Are you sure?"

"Yes."

He nodded then. No more protests. She liked that. He'd made an offer. An unselfish offer, and he'd accepted her rejection of it.

"Then promise me you won't say anything when the sheriff arrives other than you shot in fear of your life, and you want an attorney before you make an official statement."

"Why? You said it was a clear breaking and entering."

"It is. But you're tired, and you might say something that would get into the newspapers, or something an ambitious DA could twist."

"Won't it make me look like I'm hiding something?"

"It will make you look smart," he said. He reached out and tucked a lock of hair behind her ear. "Look, as an ex-cop, it goes against my grain to offer that advice. I wouldn't do it if it weren't important."

She recalled the games the FBI had played with her mother, moving her from place to place. "The FBI . . ."

"The FBI has no jurisdiction here, but because of their involvement in your mother's case, the locals will do everything by the book."

She nodded.

"Promise?"

"Yes. What will happen then?"

"After you make the statement, the district attorney will probably decide not to press charges."

"Probably?"

"Almost certainly. But tonight will be hell. They'll keep you overnight. Probably me as well."

"The whole week has been hell."

"I know," he said softly.

"Thank you for your offer to say you were the shooter."

He turned away. "Forget it. It was a bad idea."

Which, to her, made the offer more valuable. He didn't seem like a man who had many bad ideas. Nor sentimental ones.

He went to the telephone. It was dead. "Damn," he said. "My cell phone is still in the car."

She took a few steps to where her purse lay open, took out her cell phone, and handed it to him.

He dialed.

"You know the number," she observed.

"Yep. Know him, too. Honest cop. A good cop. He'll do what he has to do, but he'll make it as easy as possible." He took a few steps away as it rang.

She listened to his end of the conversation. "Is Miguel there?" he asked.

Then, "This is Caleb Adams. Will you call him and tell him someone broke into my cabin and shot my dog and tried to shoot my guest? The bastard's dead."

Two minutes later, the cell phone rang, and Caleb answered. She heard him repeat what he'd said earlier. He listened for a moment, then said, "I know what to do." He hung up.

"He's sending a patrol car. He's not far away and will be here in a matter of minutes."

She crossed her arms and hugged herself. She was cold. So cold.

Caleb left her and returned with a blanket, wrapping it around her. But the cold wouldn't go away. Nor would the image of the body, though she avoided looking at it.

Suddenly her stomach rebelled. She dropped the blanket and ran for the bathroom. She upchucked what little was in her stomach, aware that Caleb was next to her, holding her. Her entire body shook with both nausea and the aftermath of what had happened. She'd been numb before, even in shock, but now the events hit her like a giant jackhammer.

She was aware of him leaving her, then a wet, cold cloth rinsing her face. His touch was gentle, even tender, as he washed her face, then helped her back to her feet.

She stood on shaky legs, utterly humiliated by her weakness.

Liz walked to the window and looked out. Suddenly, she felt his hand jerking her back.

"Don't stand in front of the window."

"You don't think . . . ?"

"I don't think anyone's out there, no, but I don't know. Stay here while I bring the jeep up here so the police can get through."

She glanced down at the body still on the floor, the eyes still staring at her. "I want to go with you."

"Then Tramp will want to go, and he needs to stay quiet."

It was the one argument that worked for her, but she had one last protest. "You're bleeding."

"It's nothing. Superficial cuts from the glass. Stay here," he ordered. "Lock the door. I'll keep the cabin in sight every minute, and deputies will be here shortly." Then he was gone.

She did as she was told and stayed away from the window. In the past few days nearly everything she did had spiraled into disaster. Despite his explanation that the attacker feared she might identify him, she wondered why she was the one targeted. There had been the one threat against her niece, but no real violence.

Her gaze went down to the dead man. She had avoided him, even the thought of him, these past few moments, but now she couldn't do it any longer. His eyes stared up at her, and she shivered. When was it going to stop? But most of all, why was it happening? That question wouldn't go away.

She heard the sound of a car, disobeyed Caleb's orders,

and looked out. Caleb's jeep stopped in front of the cabin, and his tall, lanky form was silhouetted. He looked around before approaching the door and apparently saw her at the window. He waggled an admonishing finger at her, and relief flooded her. There was amused aggravation in the gesture.

She went to the door and opened it. She had never been so happy to see someone. It had been only minutes, but fear had lengthened the time. It had seemed like hours that she'd been standing in the room with a corpse who'd wanted her dead for some reason, waiting for another man she barely knew.

Her eyes questioned him.

"No one seems to be out there."

"Seems?"

"No one's out there," he corrected himself. Then he studied her. "Are you okay?"

"No.

"I'm glad you're not one of those women who lie," he said with a smile that possibly was a real smile and not the one created by the scar.

"I would be crazy to be okay," she said. "People are trying to kill me for God knows what reasons. They're taking everything important: my family, my home, my safety. And I don't know why." She felt a tear starting to trickle down her cheek, and she didn't even care. She had asked herself over and over again how her mother could have possibly killed someone. And now she herself had killed, and it felt like hell. Worse than that. She felt as if she'd lost part of her soul. Even if it had been his life or hers.

He placed the palm of his right hand on her face, then his fingers caressed her. One finger wiped away a tear.

"I'm sorry," he said.

"Have you ever killed anyone?"

"Yes."

"Do you ever forget . . . that feeling?"

He was quiet for a moment, then said in a soft voice, "No. Not entirely. You learn to live with it."

"Is that what my mother had to do?"

Silence. She saw a muscle pulse in his throat as if he

was struggling with what he wanted to say. After a long pause, he shrugged. "I don't know her, but I expect so."

He stood there watching her intently. The tension in him was palpable. She could almost taste it. Feel it. It frightened her because it took him to some place she didn't understand. There was a quality about him, an elusiveness that should scare her away but instead had the opposite effect.

And she wanted him close. She took a step forward. Tremors rocked her body, and he reached out a hand to her. The events of the past hour, the body on the floor, were seeping into her reality, displacing the shock. She'd been numb, but now reaction was overwhelming her.

His fingers kneaded the tight muscles in her neck. She leaned toward him and looked up at his face, unable to take her gaze away. Those eyes that were usually as unreadable as stone held something like raw pain, a pain so strong that she felt as though she had been ripped apart. She felt his chest quiver as he held her, saw the gaze dart away as if trying to hide what was lurking there. But it was too late. He was not nearly as indifferent to her, to life, as he tried to appear.

She stood on tiptoes, touching her lips to his. She wanted to soothe his pain. And her own. She needed a human touch, an intimacy that conveyed life. She needed his warmth, his strength, because hers was draining from her body.

His lips slipped away, and her head relaxed against his chest. She heard his soft sigh, felt his arms circling her with a gentleness she hadn't expected. But she wanted something more. Needed more. A reaffirmation of life in the face of fear and horror. She stood on tiptoes again and touched her lips to his, even as she was appalled at herself.

His lips accepted the offer, brushed hers with an exquisite tenderness that stunned her. But then the tenderness erupted into the explosiveness that had marked the earlier physical exchanges between them. Her lips sought his with both need and hunger.

He hesitated again, though she could feel the way his

body responded to her, then his kiss deepened, and the ice in her started to melt away.

Her body instinctively leaned toward him. His arms tightened around hers, and hers went around the back of his neck, drawing him closer and closer to her. She wanted to drown in him, to forget the ugliness and terror and fear of the past hour. To touch and be touched was enough at first. Her hands lost themselves in his thick, sandy hair. She lifted her gaze and saw the flames of need reflected in his usually cool eyes.

Their bodies moved toward each other, and she felt his body harden even through their clothing. He groaned, a sound that seemed to reverberate throughout his body. Knowing he felt the same urgency as she did further stoked the need in her. His hands slid down her back and pulled her closer to him as their lips met again.

The wail of a siren startled her into reality, and Caleb stepped back, a stunned expression on his face. Her legs nearly folded at his sudden movement, bringing her back to a place she didn't want to be. In a room with a dead man who had just tried to kill her. She was amazed at her own behavior and yet—

The wailing became louder. He took several steps toward the window, his body rigid. She knew he'd tried to keep a wall of reserve between them for some reason, and now she saw self-disgust in his usually unreadable face. She didn't want that.

"Thank you," she said in a small voice.

"For what?" he said roughly.

"I . . . needed that."

His fingers touched her cheek. "You're going to be fine. You're a strong lady."

But even as he touched her, she knew he was moving away from her again. The softness had left his eyes. He was in firm control of himself now, and she didn't want that. She wanted him as confused as she was.

Her gaze went to his arm again. The shirt was damp with blood.

Guilt struck her.

The sirens continued to grow in volume as she heard the cars screech to a stop. He turned to open the door.

"Caleb?"

He turned and looked at her.

"Where's the first aid kit?"

"In the bathroom down the hall. Under the sink. But don't wash your hands."

She headed for the bathroom. She needed several minutes before confronting the sheriff or anyone else. She was a mess. She swallowed hard as she closed the bathroom door behind her. From the bathroom, she heard voices. Male. Then a woman's. She couldn't hear the exact words. She found the kit, then searched her face in the mirror, looking for differences.

She'd just killed a man. There must be changes. Her eyes looked hollow, and her face pallid. She saw a comb and ran it through her hair, then surveyed herself. Her clothes were blood-splattered, mostly from Tramp. She took another deep breath, then, holding the kit, went into the main area.

A Hispanic man dressed in a tan uniform and a woman in a similar uniform stood talking in low voices to Caleb. They turned as she entered the room, both of them regarding her curiously.

"Sheriff Miguel Santos," Caleb said, introducing them first. "And his deputy, Jane Duffy. This is Liz Connor."

She held out her hand to the woman, then the sheriff, heartened by the steady handshake.

"Caleb told us a little of what happened," the sheriff said. "Now we want to hear it from you."

"I think I should tend to Caleb first," she protested.

He shrugged his consent and waited as Caleb took off his dark blue shirt, and she could barely keep an exclamation inside. He had many small cuts, a few larger ones, but what turned her heart upside down were the deep scars on his side and back. Some of them were burn marks. *From hot metal raining down on him?*

His eyes were on her, almost daring a reaction. She was determined not to give him one. Instead, she swabbed at the cuts with antiseptic, then bandaged them. "You should see a doctor, get a tetanus shot," she said.

"After Tramp," he agreed.

The sheriff glanced at Tramp, who had moved next to his master. Blood had dried on his fur.

Liz finished her ministering and sat down at the kitchen table. Sheriff Santos had waited patiently. She wanted to tell him every detail, but she looked at Caleb, and he shook his head in warning.

"He broke in," she said. "He tried to kill me. I fired in self-defense. I want an attorney."

The sheriff shot a disgusted look at Caleb. "Damn it, Caleb."

Caleb shrugged. "You know better than anyone that she needs an attorney. She's been through a hell of a bad time, and the press is likely to have a field day here."

Santos looked unhappy, but shrugged. "I'll have to take both of you in."

"I told her that."

"At least tell me if you have any idea of who he is? Why he might want to harm you?" He directed his gaze toward Liz.

"It might have been me he wanted to harm," Caleb broke in. "It's my house."

"Don't give me any BS," Santos said. His eyes narrowed. "I listen to the news, Caleb. I know about Ms. Connor's mother and the recent attacks on Ms. Connor here."

"Then you can make an educated guess," Caleb said.

Santos didn't ask anything else, but it was nearly three hours before he was finished, and she sat there while a medical examiner came and went, two men took photos, made measurements, and an ambulance arrived and departed with the body.

A deputy had found a rental car parked off a maintenance road not far away. There was a map. Rental agreements in the name of John Garth, along with a wallet under the floor mat in the front. The latter included a driver's license, one credit card—both in the name of John Garth—and nearly two thousand dollars in cash.

Santos stood. "I have to take both of you to the station,"

the sheriff said. "We'll need a statement—with her attorney."

She looked at Caleb with questioning eyes.

"The district attorney will decide to nol-pros," he said, "not to prosecute. Don't worry. It's a formality in a homicide."

She was escorted to a squad car and placed in the back, behind a mesh screen. Caleb was taken to another car, Tramp with him.

A deputy drove. She looked outside. The first rays of dawn appeared in the east, a contrast with the blue lights rotating on the remaining police cars. Another day. Another nightmare. The adrenaline that had kept her focused during the attack and the interview had faded, and she was simply exhausted. She thought about the hours ahead and knew that things would probably only get worse.

chapter eighteen

Sleep was impossible in the small jail cell. The night seemed endless.

Would Colton Montgomery arrive? Or would it be someone else? She'd left an urgent message with his answering service.

Was this how her mother felt? Liz knew she would be here only a few hours. Her mother might be imprisoned for years.

A few hours. Yet it already seemed so much longer.

She had trusted Caleb when he said she should say nothing until she had an attorney, although it went against every instinct she had. One thing she had inherited from her mother was respect for authority and an obsession about telling the truth.

But her mother *hadn't* told the truth. And at one time she *hadn't* respected authority. Was that why she'd tried to drum it into Liz's head for so long?

Her mother had always feared Liz's independence, had kept her on a tight leash. In rebellion, Liz had taken a year-long bicycle trip after high school graduation. She'd gone with two friends, and they would stop for a month and work at a restaurant or whatever they could find, then continue on. She'd loved that year. But she had also discovered how much she loved her family.

Had her mother feared Liz's rebellion would lead to the same fatal steps she had taken?

She remembered that sense of freedom she'd experienced on that trip. She had the same thrill on the adventures she conducted. Now she was trapped in the worst possible way. And, despite her growing trust in Caleb, what if something went wrong? What if the FBI wanted to hold her over her mother? They had power. She had none.

She'd been allowed to keep her own clothes, although there had been a light search. She was obviously not regarded as a threat. But even given that, fear and desolation oozed from the walls. The smell of cleaning products couldn't completely disguise other odors.

She finally gave up any attempt at sleep and sat up, her mind running over all that had happened in the past week. She tried to make sense of it. Why the burglaries? Why her? Or had her sister's and father's homes also been searched?

Never far from her mind was the still figure on the floor of Caleb's cabin, the sound of his expletive as Tramp charged him, the terror she felt as she pulled the trigger.

She didn't know how long she stayed that way before the cell door opened and Colton Montgomery walked inside.

"You came," she said. "I was afraid . . ."

He gave her a slow, reassuring smile, and she felt better. "I talked to Adams," he said. "He was in the sheriff's office. He filled me in. Now I need to hear everything from you."

She told him what happened, from the moment she'd arrived at the cabin.

"Tell me how you felt," he probed. "What were your exact feelings?"

"I was terrified," she said. "And angry."

"Leave out the anger," he said with a small smile. "Talk about the fear."

She thought about that. "Is that why Caleb didn't want me to say anything until you were here?"

"He was right," Montgomery said. "The smallest thing can create a problem when you have ambitious prosecutors or ruthless investigators."

"Will the FBI try to use this against my mother?"

"They might try," he said. "Now let's go in and give your statement. I'll stop you if I think you shouldn't answer a question."

Liz nodded.

"Did you get any sleep?"

"No."

He pulled out a comb and small toothbrush and toothpaste from his briefcase.

"Part of the service?" she asked.

"Often a necessary one."

"Did you do it for my mother?"

"The jail there supplies them. But I always keep a comb and toothbrush handy."

"Thank you."

"I'll tell them you'll be ready in about five minutes," he said.

She looked down at her mussed clothes. "I must look terrible."

"You look tired," he said. He put a hand on her shoulder. "It's a clear case of self-defense. You have a retired police detective as a witness. You'll be out of here in an hour or so. My advice is to find a motel or hotel and get some rest. Your house will be swarming with press."

She nodded.

He left, and she brushed her teeth and splashed cold water on her face, then tried to comb her hair without a mirror. She was ready when a deputy came for her.

"How did you get involved in this?" Miguel asked Caleb as he entered his office. He'd apparently told his deputy to wait there with Caleb.

"She needed help," Caleb said, wincing inside at the lie. At least a partial lie. She *had* needed help. It was just that *help* hadn't been his primary motive.

Then.

God help him if it was his motive now.

Miguel raised an eyebrow. Caleb knew that might be a bit hard for Miguel to swallow. Caleb had made it clear repeatedly that he wanted to be left alone.

Miguel knew Caleb's experience in police work and had asked him for help several times. Caleb had assisted with advice in one case but rebuffed other efforts. Now that he wanted a favor from the sheriff, he knew he'd obligated himself for the future.

Surprisingly, that thought didn't annoy him as it would have several weeks ago.

"You're working for her then?"

"Not exactly."

"What does that mean?"

Caleb didn't want to lie to Miguel. The man had been more than decent despite Caleb's often rude behavior in the past. But he was in so deep now, he couldn't pull himself out. He was more than baffled by his feelings for the daughter of the woman he'd hated all these years. He'd intended to use her to see that punishment was delivered, as well as to find the other members of the group. He still cared about that, but he also cared about Liz Connor. That scared the bloody hell out of him.

And it was far too late now to admit his true relationship to the case. Liz would never speak to him again because of all the lies, and he would lose all access to the family.

Damn but he had fallen into his own trap.

"Caleb?"

"Sorry. I'm tired. About my involvement, I'd planned to write a book about that armored car robbery. The case was still open when I was with the Boston PD, and I did some investigating and still have some files I compiled on my own time. I contacted Ms. Connor in Albuquerque, and when she was attacked, she wanted to hire me. I said I would help her if she and her family would help me."

"Appeared more than that to me," Miguel said dryly.

"Then it appeared wrong."

"If you say so," Miguel said. Then he added, "You never mentioned a book to me."

"No reason to."

"That's true enough. You haven't exactly been communicative."

Miguel had that right. Caleb had made no effort to integrate himself into the community.

"How's your dog?" Miguel asked.

"Vet said he should be fine. The bullet went through him, injured some muscle tissue. Dr. Rodgers is going to keep him there for a few days. Thanks for letting me take him. And for having the other deputy drive my jeep down here."

"More efficient for us. We won't have to take you back."

"I would like to see Ms. Connor," Caleb said. "She was in pretty bad shape."

"She'll be all right. Gutsy lady. I've told my people to take it easy."

"Still . . ."

"Caleb, you know the rules."

Caleb did, and he was thankful that Miguel had extended as much professional courtesy as he had. It had been worth a try. And perhaps Liz was getting some sleep. Sleep was often the body's natural protection after a trauma.

"What now?"

"Take a nap on my sofa. I'll wake you when someone from the DA's office arrives. I've already called. The deputy told me Ms. Connor contacted her attorney."

"There must be something I can do."

"Not unless you have anything to add to the statement you gave my deputy."

"Nothing more *to* add."

"I'm sure the DA will have something."

"Will you let me know when her attorney appears?"

"Is he your attorney as well?"

"If I need one. In the meantime, I want to help in some way."

Miguel gave him a long, level stare. "I don't want to mess this up. It's not only my reputation but your friend's future."

Caleb didn't like being sidelined. Not now. But he understood. The interference of a civilian, even an ex-cop, could taint the investigation.

"You're running the perp's fingerprints through AFIS?" he persisted.

"One of my deputies has already scanned them into the system. If your intruder is in the database, we'll know in the next few hours. I also sent a man with a blood sample to the state crime lab to see if we can get a DNA match."

Caleb knew it shouldn't take long to run the prints through the Automated Fingerprint Identification System. Hopefully the assailant had a record, but if not . . .

"Have another computer I can use?" Caleb said. "I'll try to trace this John Garth. It's probably an alias, but he might have used it before."

"Not a good idea."

"Miguel, I need to do something."

Miguel sighed. "I didn't call the FBI because this is my jurisdiction, and I had no reason to do so, but they'll probably be crawling all over here as soon as they hear about this. You're a witness and—must I remind you—a civilian, and there's no way you're going to touch this investigation. I like my job too much."

Caleb knew he was right, but it galled him to wait here without doing anything. He glanced down at his watch. It was nearly nine. "What time will someone be here?"

"As soon as I tell them Ms. Connor's attorney has arrived."

A knock interrupted them.

"Come in," Miguel said.

A deputy entered. "We picked up a match on the fingerprints," he said, and handed a file to Miguel.

Miguel opened it and studied it, then nodded. "Print several copies." The deputy left, closing the door behind him.

"Must I ask?" Caleb said.

"Your dead man is Carl Patton, a suspected hit man. Three arrests. No convictions, mainly because witnesses mysteriously died."

"Where is he from?"

"Last known sighting was in Las Vegas."

"No connection to Boston?"

"If there is, it's not in here."

Caleb was not surprised the man was a gun for hire. Every action indicated as much. "And the credit card? Is that an alias?"

"We're checking on that."

The phone on his desk rang. Miguel listened for a moment, then said, "No comment, Clem. Maybe later today I'll give you an exclusive if you keep it under your hat until then." He listened a moment, then hung up.

"That was Clementine Holt. She's editor of the local newspaper. Probably heard it from someone in the DA's office, though I couldn't guarantee it didn't come from one of my deputies."

The phone rang again. "I'll be down there. Call the DA's office." He hung up and turned back to Caleb. "Colton Montgomery is here for Ms. Connor." He regarded Caleb for a moment. "It shouldn't take long, especially now that we know who the deceased is. Once the interview is over, take her and get the hell out of here. This place is going to be crawling with the press and the Feds. I think this Patton was a pretty big fish."

"Thanks, Miguel."

"You owe me next time I need help."

"You'll have it."

"Even with no sleep, you look better than I've seen you."

"Thanks. I think."

"She's good for you. Don't mess it up."

"There's nothing to mess up."

Miguel gave him a dubious look, then shrugged. "Let's go."

A hit man.

They didn't exist in Liz's world. At least they hadn't until now.

She sat in the passenger's seat of Caleb's jeep, huddled next to the door. She'd wanted to be as far away as possible. She felt filthy.

The interview with the sheriff, a deputy, and an assistant district attorney had lasted three hours. With Montgomery's reassuring presence next to her, she'd gone over every moment in the cabin ad nauseam.

When she'd learned that the intruder had been a notorious hit man, she struggled to keep from being sick again. Because that meant someone had hired him. And now that the man was dead, they might never learn who. Or why. Nor whether whoever had hired him would now hire someone else.

The moment she'd finished, Caleb had whisked her out a back door to his jeep.

"How did you manage that?" she asked.

"Miguel had a deputy drive it down when they returned. He said it was more efficient than having someone drive us back to the cabin."

She absorbed that. She imagined things could have been a great deal worse with someone else. But she knew she would never forget those hours in jail. Now she, like her mother, faced a lifetime of knowing she had played a part in someone's death.

She knew why she did it. She wanted to know why her mother had. *If* she'd had. Perhaps now her mother would tell her.

"How's Tramp?"

"Probably being spoiled at the vet clinic. The vet thinks he's a hero, even mentioned nominating him for some award after I told him what happened."

"He'll be okay?"

"Yeah. He may not be quite as fast as before, but I think he kinda likes the role of hero."

A wry humor had crept into Caleb's voice. But there was also affection and regret. She reached over and touched his leg. He'd always seemed so distant, keeping his emotions under tight rein.

He glanced over at her for a second before his gaze moved back to the road.

She rummaged in her purse for her phone, then remembered it was still in his cabin. "I have to call my father. He might hear . . ."

"I'll stop as soon as I see a phone booth."

Twenty minutes later, Caleb stopped next to a public

phone at a convenience store. She quickly got out and dialed her father's cell phone.

He stood next to her and could hear some of the exchange, especially when Connor's voice was raised.

"Sport. Thank God. I've been trying to reach you. Montgomery said you had called him."

She told him what had happened in as few words as possible.

"I'll come up there."

"No, I'm okay. Truly, I am. I'm with Caleb Adams. I'm going to get some rest, then go to your house. I have a rafting trip Saturday."

Caleb couldn't hear her father's voice, but he could imagine what Steve Connor thought of the proposed trip.

"Caleb's going with me as another guide. Dad, I need the business, and every other guide is booked this weekend." She hesitated, then asked, "Have you seen Mom?"

"No, but by God, I will today if I have to force myself in. When she finds out what's happening to you, she'll have to talk to me."

"I don't have a phone right now, but I'll call you as soon as I can."

"Let me talk to Adams."

She handed the phone to Caleb, who had been standing several feet away. "He wants to talk to you."

Caleb listened, then simply said, "I will," and hung up.

"You will what?" she asked.

"Take care of you."

With that he turned away and headed back to the jeep, not waiting for her. When she got into the car, his eyes looked guarded and closed, as if he'd just regretted his promise.

"You really don't have to take care of me," she said. "I can do that very well. Just take me back to Santa Fe."

"If you thought the media was bad before, you haven't seen anything yet," he countered. "You need some rest first."

"Where are we going?"

"Los Alamos. Close enough to Santa Fe but far enough

I hope no one finds you. And they have a lot of visitors going in and out. I doubt anyone would look for us there."

"I have to be back Friday to write checks. And I have the raft trip Saturday."

"No second thoughts about that trip?"

"It's practically Tracy's weekly salary," she said. "I can't let someone destroy my business as well. And Carl Patton is dead."

"But not the person who hired him."

Chill bumps raised on her arms. But she couldn't let fear destroy her life, not everything she'd worked for.

They reached Los Alamos, and he pulled into the parking lot of what looked like an independent motel, registered, and returned to the car. He handed her a key and drove down the parking lot to a room and parked.

They went in together, and he inspected the locks. There were three of them, plus a peephole in the door.

Apparently satisfied, he turned back to her. "Why don't you shower? There's an outfitter down the street. I'll get both of us some clothes."

She nodded, wanting nothing more than to throw away the clothes she wore. She never wanted to see them again.

"Size ten?" he asked.

She was surprised. "Yes. How did you . . ."

"My wife wore a size ten," he said curtly. "Use all the locks when I leave. Don't open the door unless you know it's me. I'll knock three times, then two. Don't look out the window."

"Yes sir," she said obediently. She was too tired to do anything else. Now.

A slow grin spread across his face. "You *do* need some rest."

Then he was out the door. She fastened the locks, then went into the bathroom. Thankfully, it was large and well-lit.

In minutes she was under a hot shower. She washed her hair, then scrubbed every inch of her body. She stayed until she felt like a prune before reluctantly turning off the water and toweling her hair.

She wrapped a second towel around herself and stumbled more than walked into the room and stared at the double beds. She turned the sheets back and sank into the bed.

She was awakened by a knocking on the door. A little bewildered and disoriented, she needed a moment to think where she was and why.

Another three knocks, a pause, and two more.

Grabbing the fallen towel and clutching it back around her, she peered through the peephole in the door and saw Caleb, holding several packages. She let him in.

He dropped most of the packages on the bed closest to the door. With one hand urgently holding the towel together, she hurriedly went through them, seizing a large T-shirt. "Turn around," she ordered.

"Yes, ma'am."

She slipped the shirt on. It fell to just above her knees. "You can turn around now."

His eyes were inscrutable as he seemed to weigh his own choice of purchases. "A little long, perhaps."

"I like them long," she replied, feeling a bit more armored against his gaze. She looked at the other offerings. A pair of jeans. A light blue shirt, and suede big shirt. The choices were much to her taste. Had he really noticed so much?

Had he chosen for his late wife as well?

She looked up at him. "Thank you. It's perfect."

"Good. I'm out of practice."

"Did you shop for your wife?"

"Yes."

She then looked in the last package. Two cell phones. The kind you buy and throw away when you've used up the number of allotted minutes. She looked askance.

"I don't think you should use your cell phone," he said. "Even if we could retrieve it. Too easy to trace."

"But why would the FBI . . ."

"Not just the FBI has access to the technology to trace cell phones."

The reminder jerked her back to reality, that someone with resources was, for some reason, after her.

"Can I call my father and give the number to him?"

He nodded.

She did that. She told him she was safe and gave him the number. He told her that Sue and the children had gone away, to Shangri-la. It was a name she and Sue had given a friend's vacation home, a lovely getaway cabin that sat high above a clear lake. They had employed the man recommended by Caleb. Her father was now carrying a weapon and being extremely cautious.

She hung up, feeling better.

Her nose caught another odor. "Food?"

"Hamburgers. Fries. Cokes. Everything that's bad for you."

She hadn't realized how hungry she was. It was more than twenty-four hours since she'd eaten anything. "I like everything that's bad for me."

"It sure as hell doesn't show."

She sat on the bed as he handed her a burger and fries, and put a Coke on the nightstand.

"I didn't know what you liked, so I got the little packages of ketchup and mustard, onions and relish," he said, handing them to her. He looked almost tentative, as if not knowing what she liked was akin to incompetence. And, she'd noticed, he was a very competent man.

She took them all, putting ketchup and onions on her burger. She practically inhaled the burger and the fries. He handed her another burger, and she ate that, too.

When she finished, she stretched out.

"I don't think I've ever seen a woman eat that much," he said. The side of his lips twisted up a little more than usual.

She yawned. "What about you? Where's yours?"

"It's there. I just enjoyed watching you."

She saw herself in his eyes. Unconsciously, a hand went to her wet hair. It was naturally curly, and wet curls clung to her head. No makeup. She suspected her eyes had shadows around them.

"You look good," he said quietly.

He said it with such tenderness, she felt warm and safe for the first time in the last twenty-four hours.

"I'm glad you're here," she said sleepily. Unable to resist the bed any longer, she crawled under the covers. She was aware that he turned off the lights and sat in a chair near the window, but not much more than that before her eyes closed and she fell asleep.

Tony swore as he read the item on the Web site of the Albuquerque newspaper. A bulletin said that Liz Connor, the daughter of Sarah Jane Maynard, recently arrested for the robbery-murder of armored car guards, had shot an assailant who attacked her. The man was identified as Carl Patton, a suspected hired killer.

Patton was supposed to have been a professional. His employment, as well as that of a second man he'd hired, had taken most of the cash Maynard had given him. But the fool admitted he'd allowed his face to be seen and decided to go a step farther than Tony intended.

Tony wanted Sarah Jane scared. Too scared to ever mention his name. He'd used her family to terrify her. A fire to one daughter's home, a threat to the grandchild. A note smuggled into her cell by a bribed guard, explaining exactly what would happen if she said anything.

Then to find the keys. *He had to have the keys.* Then he would take the money and run. The money would take him a long way.

But Patton obviously hadn't been as good as he was said to be. And now Tony had to worry about any evidence the man might have left behind.

And Sarah Jane would wonder whether her cooperation would protect her family. He had nothing more to hold over her.

Tony picked up the phone, weighing just how much damage control he needed to do.

chapter nineteen

Caleb watched Liz sleep. The room was cold, and she was covered by blankets with only a mop of dark auburn hair showing.

She would sleep hard and long, a natural reaction to all the emotional trauma she'd endured. He wanted to climb into bed with her and simply hold her.

It would be the worst thing he could do.

He was torn by loyalties. Torn by his promise to his dead father and by so many years of seeking the truth. Compelled to complete the task that had saved his sanity after the death of his wife and son.

At what cost?

To him? To Liz Connor who'd already endured as many body blows as anyone should be asked to withstand? What if he handed her another one now?

That's a damned excuse.

It was, but he had nothing better at the moment. He wasn't ready to lose her or his contacts to the family.

He went to the window and looked out. Nothing alerted him, and he tried to relax. It was late afternoon; he hoped she would sleep through until morning. He picked up one of the disposable cell phones he'd purchased. No number to trace.

He opened the door and went outside.

He dialed the Boston PD and asked for Cam Douglas.

Cam answered immediately.

"Cam?"

"Yeah."

"Do you know anything about a hit man named Patton? Carl Patton?"

He heard a long sigh on the phone. "I know the name. A bad dude, my friend. A very bad dude."

"In what way?"

"He appeared on our radar shortly after you left. Killed a politician who wouldn't play nice with some businesses. He was caught, indicted, but the one witness disappeared. Then he disappeared. We heard he headed west. Why the questions?"

"He broke into my cabin, shot my dog, and attacked my guest."

"That guest . . . could it be a woman?"

"None of your business."

"I'm glad," Cam said, amusement in his voice. "It's about time."

"No it's not," Caleb muttered.

"What else do you want to know?"

"Any records on who he might have known?"

"I'll do some snooping."

"Thanks. Also put out some feelers on whether there's a contract out on Elizabeth Connor or her mother."

"Will do. You sound like the old Cal. It's good, pal."

Caleb hung up.

He surveyed the parking lot but saw nothing that alarmed him and went back inside to sit in his chair for a short nap. He was as sure as a cop could ever be that he hadn't been followed. Still, he never underestimated an enemy.

But who was the enemy?

A cry of terror sliced sharply through his light doze. Instantly awake, he noticed the room was darker. There was no sound other than the whimpering of the woman in the bed.

She had tossed the covers away and now seemed to be

struggling. Her body moved, and he could see the terror on her face.

He rose and took the five steps to her bed. "Liz?" He didn't touch her. She was obviously in a deep sleep, and he didn't want to startle or frighten her. God knew she'd had enough of that. "Liz?" he repeated, this time in a louder voice.

She swung at him and hit one of the recent cuts. Pain shot through him as he leaned over her.

"It's all right," he said softly, just as he had last night. She continued to flail, as if someone was after her. He shook her slightly, and her eyes opened, terror in them, before she saw his face and quieted.

"Hey there," he said.

She saw his arm. It was bleeding from one of the cuts. "What . . . ?"

"It's nothing. You had a nightmare."

"I never have nightmares."

"Probably no one tried to kill you until the past week."

"Can't say they have," she said with a touch of ironic humor. "How long have I been asleep?"

"This time? About five hours."

"What about you?"

"I don't need much sleep." He reached out and took her hand. "Do you remember the dream?"

Her hand shook slightly. "I was running. Someone was chasing me. I . . . just kept barely ahead of him, but I was getting tired . . . so tired . . ."

Her breathing was still fast, and she clutched his hand as if it were a lifeline.

"You're safe now," he said, his free hand going to her cheek still flushed with sleep and the terror so recently haunting it. Her eyes, though, were wide awake and bewildered.

She looked so incredibly vulnerable. She didn't deserve this, none of it. The ultimate innocent in some Machiavellian game neither understood at the moment. He leaned down and kissed her, lightly at first. A reassuring kiss meant to soothe, not excite or seduce.

Or so he told himself.

But her lips responded with an urgency that deepened the kiss, then she was in his arms, and the kiss, like last night, turned to pure explosive energy.

He felt every curve under the cotton of the T-shirt, felt her breasts swelling against his body. His tongue entered her mouth with long, scalding sweeps, and she met each onslaught with a hungry response of her own. Her body quivered with his touch, and his did the same.

He tore his mouth away and rained kisses up and down her face, then her neck, and finally her throat. He marveled at how fine her skin was, how it tasted. Her hands moved behind his neck and played with his hair, and every touch sent waves of heat through his body, all centering in his groin.

Years of lacerating loneliness faded as need erupted between them, like a long rumbling volcano. The heated energy had been bubbling between them since that first day when he'd helped her at her house.

His hands tangled in her hair, and he felt her body tremble. She began unbuttoning his shirt. He backed away to make it easier for her. The heat inside rose to the boiling point as her hands worked impatiently at his buttons, then the zipper of his jeans.

She shoved his shirt off, and he stood, dropping his jeans and briefs to the floor. For a moment he stood there. He had not been with a woman since his wife died. Although she'd seen some of his scars, she hadn't seen those on his legs. No woman had seen all the scars on his body, scars put there by the bomb that killed his family. They were a constant reminder of that afternoon, a brand for not protecting them as he should have done.

He was aware of her gaze on those scars as well as the bandage still on his arm. Then she touched each one, her fingers gentle, as if trying to heal them. Her gaze met his, and the compassion in her eyes almost made his knees buckle. It was as if she knew, *understood,* that the physical scars were symbols of deeper ones inside.

He had intended to comfort her, yet he found himself being comforted.

He slipped the T-shirt over her head and lowered her to

the bed, his body only too aware of the softness, the strength in every curve of her body, the unrestrained reaction of her body to his.

Their mouths met in invitation, engaging in a slow, sensuous dance, even as the friction of their bodies aroused him to near madness. He broke off the kiss, and his mouth moved to her right breast, nuzzled the nipple as her breast swelled, and her body strained toward his.

He moved them both slightly to position himself above her, and it was her hands that guided him down, and he entered her, slowly, ever so slowly, to give them both maximum pleasure.

Liz's body ignited with his touch. His movements were so seductive, so enticing, that sensations cascaded through her body. She was already dizzy from his kisses, the way he licked the sensitive skin of her breasts before reaching the taut nipple, his tongue that had ignited a string of fires that ran through her body like lightning. She put her arms around him and pulled him to her until their bodies melded. He plunged deeper inside her with a rhythm that grew in intensity and speed. They moved incautiously, frantically, fanning blazes into an inferno.

She clung to him, savoring the intimacy of such pleasure. "Caleb," she uttered, knowing it was more moan that whisper.

He stilled then, though she felt the core of her wrap even tighter around him.

His eyes opened, and she marveled at the turmoil in them, at the expressiveness of eyes that were usually expressionless. The hard lines of his face appeared deeper, and his lips more vulnerable with a kind of bittersweet resignation.

"Don't go away this time," she whispered, and she didn't mean physically. "I want you. I need you."

His body shuddered, then he probed deeper, moving in and out until she felt mad with wanting, and he thrust again and again, sweeping them into a dizzying, dazzling journey she'd never taken before. Suddenly there was warmth and power sending cascades of pure sensation through her, one after another, each growing in strength until they climaxed in one magnificent, blazing explosion.

He collapsed on top of her, his breathing coming hard and fast. Her own seemed caught in her throat as he rolled over to his side, taking her with him. His arms were still around her, and he didn't let go, even as spasms still rocked her.

He sighed. "Ah Liz. I didn't mean that to happen."

"I did," she said.

"We didn't use anything." His voice was self-condemning.

She considered that for the first time. But at the moment she didn't care. She had needed him. If there were consequences, then she would face them. She snuggled deeper into his arms, relishing the feel of his warm body against hers, the life force that gave her comfort and love.

She felt his breathing slow, relax, and she realized he had gone to sleep. He probably hadn't had any sleep in far more than twenty-four hours. He had been, instead, taking care of her.

She'd never wanted someone to take care of her. She'd always wanted to take care of herself. Believed desperately in a woman's need to do that.

But now she luxuriated in his presence, in the possessive feel of his arms around her even in sleep, and thought how warm and sheltering his body was next to hers.

Suddenly, she realized that she'd found a man she trusted.

Caleb woke to darkness. And to the softness of a woman sleeping next to him. He looked at the clock. Six a.m. They'd slept and talked most of the last twenty hours.

Friday morning. Only four days since he'd heard of the apprehension of one of the fugitives. It was a lifetime now. It seemed impossible that in that period of time, he'd grown to care so much for one person when he'd thought he could never open his heart again.

He silently cursed himself. He'd crossed a line.

Hadn't he learned anything? He was a Jonah. Worse, he'd lied to her, continued to lie when she trusted him.

A part of him curled up in a tight ball and stuck in his gut.

Dammit, he knew part of her passion had come from her terror last night, and part from the nightmare that relived that horror. It was also part survival, an urge to seize what had almost been lost. An innocence.

He hadn't been innocent since he was seven. Violence and loss had traveled with him every step. Except for those years with Annie, he'd never known happiness, and that had ended in a fiery explosion.

He suspected that until now, Liz had never known anything but love and safety. He ached for her, for the sane world she'd lost and probably would never regain, for her innocence lost.

He hadn't anticipated that. He'd thought all his feelings dead. He believed he could play this one last undercover role, then leave it all behind once he'd found all those who'd had a hand in his father's murder.

Over the past few days, his driving force had changed from finding killers to protecting the daughter of one of them. And to protect, he had to continue to lie. He had to remain close to her, and he was beginning to know her now. She prized loyalty and honesty. She wouldn't forgive the lies easily. She'd had too much betrayal in her life in the past week. Hell, he wouldn't trust someone who had won his confidence with a series of lies.

"Caleb?"

She wriggled in his arms, stretched, and immediately he was aroused again.

He swore under his breath. He wanted her, he wanted her with every part of his body. Still, he'd had a few hours' sleep and time to consider exactly what he was doing.

He didn't like the conclusion.

He resisted the temptation of turning to her, losing himself in her. But he couldn't. He couldn't tell her the truth. He *could* try to solve the secrets swirling around her and her mother.

Perhaps she was right about her mother. Perhaps her mother had been a victim as much as his father.

It was a conclusion he couldn't avoid. Someone was

trying to intimidate Sara Jane Maynard. From everything he'd learned about the woman, she was devoted to her family. She wouldn't leave them in danger without a good reason. Nor would she refuse to see them without cause, not if they could help her, and she them.

That she had refused every effort to help her—despite the jeopardy to herself and her family's desperate need to help her—told him something was very, very wrong with all his previous assumptions.

"We should get breakfast and go," he said, giving her a kiss on her nose, then sitting up. Before he could change his mind, he pulled on his briefs and jeans.

She looked disgruntled for a moment, then gave him a blinding smile. And nodded. "I really do have to go by the office and my house. Poor Tracy and Garry."

He tried not to watch as she rolled out of bed and stretched. She was naked and totally open about it. His heart lurched. It hadn't done that for a very long time.

She stood on tiptoes and kissed him lightly. "Thank you for taking care of me yesterday."

He almost broke then. "I don't think I did a very good job."

"Oh, you did."

Her eyes were full of trust, and something else. Something he didn't dare explore. "I'll run out and get some coffee," he said.

She nodded. "I'll take a shower."

He didn't want to visualize that. He didn't want to think about joining her there when that was all in the world he wanted to do.

Coffee. Think coffee. Think Santa Fe. Think anything except Liz Connor.

Hours later, Liz still felt the heat and fullness of Caleb as she sat down with contractors at her house. She found it difficult to concentrate. She kept seeing his face in her mind's eye. Continued to feel his warmth inside her.

He'd dropped her off at the office, where she spent an hour catching up on everything with Tracy and writing checks, including one to Tracy with a bonus. Then Caleb had followed her to the house before disappearing and vowing to be back later to pick her up. At first he'd been reluctant to leave, but Garry promised to stay with her. He'd been horrified at hearing what had happened. At least it hadn't hit the local news. Not yet.

The changes in her house were miraculous. She didn't know if it was the insurance company's usual policy or Garry's influence, but the electricians had restored her power. Cleaning people had been in and had cleaned the walls as best as they could. Her rug was at a carpet specialist. It should be as good as new, Garry said.

Now she had to pick out paint colors and appliances, as well as cabinets. The owner had given her carte blanche to do whatever she wanted.

Going through pages of colors seemed trite after killing someone and almost being killed. And after lovemaking that was soul shattering. But she had to have a place to live, and she owed it to the owner to get the house back in good shape.

After choosing paint colors, floor coverings, and new cabinets, she grew restless. She called her father.

"I'm at my house," she said. "Anything new with Mom?"

"Colton is trying to persuade her to see me. I told him to tell her I wouldn't even consider a divorce unless I talk with her."

"You aren't . . . ?"

"No, of course not. But maybe it will get me in there."

She was silent. She wasn't sure a ruse would help at this point. Lies never helped anything. The past few days had only reinforced her opinion about that.

She said good-bye and returned to looking over options, but now she was getting antsy. Even anxious.

Caleb returned, a bucket of chicken in his hands along with a cooler full of soft drinks. He'd changed clothes, so she knew he had gone by the cabin.

"Tramp sends his regards," he said.

"You saw him?"

"Yep. The vet says he'll be as good as new in a few

days. He's staying there, though, until the wound begins to heal, and I'll be there."

"I hope you took him a dog biscuit."

"Even better, I took him a hamburger."

He continued to mystify her. He'd seemed nonchalant about the dog when she'd first arrived at the cabin, yet now he'd driven over a hundred miles to see him. He was a loner, yet he met Garry and engaged him in a matter of moments, and she knew instantly Garry liked him. He was curt one moment, gentle the next.

He invited Garry to eat with them, which surprised her. She was even more surprised when he looked at her selections as if they really mattered to him and nodded with approval at the cleaning already done.

Workmen came and went until dark. Appointments were made for painters. Garry said he would be there if she couldn't. Tears suddenly came to her eyes. She had great friends.

Caleb put an arm around her, and she leaned against him as Garry looked on like an approving uncle, then went back to his house, leaving them alone.

"I suggest a hotel tonight again," she said. "My bed is not exactly usable. I'm not up to facing reporters, and I have that raft trip in the morning. *We* have the raft trip," she corrected herself.

She felt his hesitation. Then he nodded.

He drove to a hotel she liked. It was modern and clean and not overly expensive. She knew the manager from serving on the tourist board with him, and knew he would protect her privacy.

They went in together. She asked for the manager and explained that she was trying to avoid reporters. He nodded. "Two rooms," Caleb said. She felt momentary surprise, but then pulled out her credit card.

He shook his head. "I don't want your name on record," he said.

The manager—Don Waddell—looked from one to the other, understanding in his eyes. "I heard about the attack on you Tuesday night."

"There was another one," she said. "It'll be in the news shortly, I expect."

"The rooms are comped. Then there's no record," Don said.

"Thank you." She was doing a lot of that lately. Thanking people. She'd never known how many friends she had. She had feared people would turn away from her. Instead they were embracing her.

They went up to the adjoining rooms. He opened hers and stood aside while she went inside.

"I have a few things in the jeep," he said. "I'll be back in a minute."

She sat down in the chair and turned on the television. How soon would the news get out about the killing of a professional hit man? She didn't even want to think of the press reaction.

When he returned, his arms were full. Despite his protest two nights earlier, he had files in his hands. The files she hadn't finished reading. There was also a shirt and a bag of toiletries from the Los Alamos motel, along with several cold soft drinks.

She took one and looked at the files. There was the last one, the one she hadn't quite finished.

He popped the tab on one drink and took a long swallow. "I have some calls to make," he said, gave her that half smile of his, and left through the door.

He was running again. She was getting used to it. But she also knew he would be back.

Comforted by the fact that he was only a door away, she started reading.

BOSTON

Michael Gallagher favored his right arm as he sifted through the file on his desk.

He'd arrived after taking the red-eye from Albuquerque. He had seen no reason to stay in Santa Fe after his rental car was returned. He obviously wasn't going to get an interview with Maynard's cousin, and he'd been reluctant to pursue the daughter. He'd told himself it wasn't the time to press her. She'd been overwhelmed by events, and he'd never seen the appeal of picking wings off a fly.

He would collect on her gratitude later, when it might be more meaningful.

His phone rang, and he answered it. "My office," Win's voice boomed out. "Now."

Michael dropped the phone without replying and hurried to Win's office.

Win eyed the bulge under the sleeve of Michael's shirt. He'd left his coat jacket in the office. "What happened?"

Michael suspected he already knew and kept his explanation to a minimum. "I stumbled onto a burglary," he said. "But I suspect you already knew that."

"I did. Elizabeth Connor called me."

"She told me." He hesitated, then asked, "Did you have anything to do with that burglary?"

"No." Maynard met his gaze directly.

Michael nodded. "Good."

"Going soft on me?"

Michael knew he had overstepped the bounds of a relationship that hovered between mentor and student, and uncle and adopted nephew. He had always admired Win Maynard, his drive, even his ruthlessness. But then the ruthlessness had been usually aimed at the equally ruthless.

"No, but there's such a thing as overplaying your hand. And though I dislike clichés, it's rather true that sugar catches more flies than vinegar."

Win gave him a brief smile. "Are you comparing Elizabeth to a fly?"

"No."

"What did you think of her?"

"I like her. She has grit. And loyalty."

"Then why aren't you there?"

"She has a private investigator helping her. He seems to always be there."

Win narrowed his eyes. "I wasn't informed of that."

"Name's Caleb Adams. He's an ex-cop with the Boston PD."

Michael had been watching his employer carefully. He

didn't miss the sudden look of alarm in Win's eyes. He recognized the name. No doubt about it.

But then it was gone, that sudden emotion, replaced by the poker face that dominated the board table. "You gave up that easily? You couldn't appeal to her sympathy?"

"Adams would have been there. I knew her mother would be up here in a few days."

"And . . ."

"And I want to know about Adams. He was there almost immediately and tried to make himself indispensable. There's a reason."

"Forget it," Maynard said.

"Forget it?"

"Unless he shows up here."

"As you say." But Michael had no intention of forgetting it. His curiosity had already been stirred. Now it churned.

"Keep in touch with Elizabeth," Maynard said. "Get her up here. She'll stay with me. I don't care how you do it." He allowed a small, thin smile. "And don't step in front of any more bullets. I need you."

That was a first. Michael couldn't remember when Win had ever admitted he needed someone.

"Yes sir."

Win turned to papers on his desk, which indicated dismissal.

Michael returned to his office and pored through prepared reports plus information still flowing in. Though Michael was in-house counsel and supervised three other attorneys as well as a paralegal and legal secretary, they farmed out much of their legal work to one of Boston's finest law firms. The file in front of him was the result of one of those assignments. He'd asked for complete reports on the Connors as well as Caleb Adams.

At midnight, he'd already gone through them all, several of them twice. He felt as though he knew everything Betty Connor and her family had ever done or thought. Yet there was a year in Liz's file that intrigued him. Apparently she had just taken off. She was reported missing, but then the report was withdrawn.

He thought about her, the energy in her even when she was dead tired and worried about her family. And herself. A quirky sense of humor. And he recalled the night he had been an unexpected hero.

He'd never been a hero before and, oddly enough for a person who always looked for opportunity, he'd been unwilling to soil that happenstance by doing harm to her. It would taint one of the few truly honorable things he'd done. So he'd gotten the hell out of Dodge.

He had no intention of telling his employer that.

He wouldn't take advantage of the daughter, but he didn't have the same compunction about the mother. Win wanted something from her, and it wasn't to renew an old acquaintance.

He turned to the file on Caleb Adams. Despite his employer's advice, and he chose to consider it advice rather than an order, he had no intention of "forgetting" it.

Something about the man bothered him. He was too quickly in the right place at the right time. And there was an intensity about him that made Michael wonder whether his interest was entirely in writing a book.

According to the information in the file, Adams was apparently financially independent, if not rich. He took few investigative jobs, though he was regarded as a talented and thorough investigator when he did accept one.

His researcher had dug deep. He'd been able to obtain police files through some contact Michael didn't want to know about. Caleb Adams had earned numerous decorations, though some superiors had given him poor marks for respecting authority. He'd been undercover for five years, a job that Michael knew often changed officers. Some started identifying with the targets; others became cynical and disillusioned.

He continued reading the file. Caleb Adams had left the department four years ago on disability. But it was a mental as well as physical disability. He had served on the desk for several months after four months in the hospital and rehabilitation, but anger and frustration led to drinking, both on the job and off.

Michael continued reviewing the pages. His researcher

had interviewed several of Adams's fellow officers. All remarked on his obsession with the armored car robbery and murder three decades earlier. He spent hours and hours of his own time, going back and reviewing files and interviewing witnesses and officers.

Then he reached the last page. The researcher apparently had the same questions as he did, and went even further in Caleb's background. The police application form led back to college and high school records. Caleb Adams. A further trace of the mother found a marriage certificate in 1973 between a Carolyn Burnett Murphy and Charles Adams. An earlier one reported the marriage of Carolyn Burnett to a Samuel Murphy.

Murphy.

He knew that name. He'd studied the armored car case before heading to Albuquerque. Murphy was the name of one of the slain guards. *Sam Murphy.* Left a widow and a son. He rummaged back in his mind. The son's name was Garrett Murphy. Not Caleb Murphy.

Still, the coincidence bothered him. He made notes for the researcher. *Look for the birth certificate of Garrett Murphy. Is there a middle name? And search for possible adoption records by his stepfather for Caleb Adams.*

Then he leaned back. Had the Boston Police Department known that one of the detectives investigating the armored car robbery might have had a personal connection to it?

Just as important, did the Connor family realize that Caleb Adams might have an agenda of his own?

chapter twenty

Caleb knew he was in trouble when he checked on Liz. For a moment he panicked when she wasn't there. Then he heard a shower going.

He knew he should resist. He'd just spent the last fifteen minutes taking a cold shower himself. But he couldn't. He found himself going into her bathroom. Just to make sure she was safe.

The room was steamy.

She stuck her head out from the curtain as if she'd sensed his presence. Her face lit at seeing him. "Want to join me?"

It was like asking a man dying of thirst if he wanted water. Still, he hesitated.

"Come on," she said in a seductive voice that was irresistible.

He found himself taking off his clothes. He stepped in with her, his hands feeling the soft silkiness of her body, smelling the sweet aroma of soap on her skin.

She touched his cheek.

"I need a shave."

"I like you scratchy."

So had his wife. Annie and Liz were unalike in almost every way, and yet it was uncanny that in some ways . . .

"Hummmmm," he said.

"You look good stubbly."

"I'm an old, worn-out ex-cop."

"I'm not one to disagree with authority, but . . ."

God, she made him feel alive again.

She gave him a tremulous smile as hot water pelted down her face.

He took the washcloth and soap from her hands and lathered her back, then turned her and did the same to her breasts. They stood face-to-face, and she took the cloth and soap back and washed him in turn. Each touch was sensual. More than sensual. She took great care, lingering at the jagged scar on his leg and touching it with such poignant tenderness that waves of quiet despair washed through him. She was giving all of herself, openly, to a liar.

Tell her!

He touched her face, and she stood again, the mop of auburn hair a tangle of wet curls. Her eyes were wide, seething with something he didn't want to see.

Dammit, but he wanted her again.

Every bit of his willpower was required to reach out behind her and turn off the water, then wrap a towel around her and another around himself.

It was only a few feet to the bed then. They made it in a second.

Liz jerked awake to the sound of her cell phone ringing. Caleb, beside her, stirred as well.

She looked at the clock beside her bed. Her stomach twisted inside. A four a.m. phone call only meant one thing: trouble. She grabbed the phone and turned on Talk.

"Liz," her father said in a strained voice. "Your mother . . . she was found unconscious in her cell. She's in critical condition at the medical center. I'm on the way now."

Icy fear gripped her. "What happened?"

"I don't know. Someone from Montgomery's office called. But I knew you had that rafting trip, and I might not get you later."

"I'll cancel it," she said, her heart beating so loud she thought her father could hear it. "I'll be there as soon as I can. Hold just a minute."

She turned to Caleb. "They found my mother unconscious at the jail. They've taken her to the hospital. Dad doesn't know any more right now. I should get my own jeep and drive down—"

"I'll take you," he interrupted.

She numbly agreed, then returned her attention to the cell phone. "Caleb and I are on our way. We should be there within ninety minutes." She hesitated. "What about Susan?"

"She and the children are still at the cabin. I won't call her until I know something more. With what happened to you, I don't want to put them in danger."

"About Mom. They didn't tell you anything more?"

"No. Montgomery said they claimed it was probably a suicide attempt. Drugs of some sort."

"I don't believe it."

"I don't, either."

"Call me if you learn anything more," she said and put the phone back in her purse and stared out at an awakening day. She shivered. Just a few hours earlier, she'd felt alive. Even hopeful. Now she was plunged back into a nightmare in which every turn led to more horror.

Next, she punched Tracy's number.

A drowsy voice answered. "'Ello."

"Trace, it's Liz. I can't make the rafting trip. Something's wrong with Mom. They took her to the medical center in Albuquerque."

"Oh, Liz, I'm so sorry." The voice was suddenly awake.

"You'll have to cancel for me."

"I'll hunt around first," she replied. "Maybe a guide had a cancellation."

"Thanks. I'll keep you posted." She punched the Off button and got out of bed, quickly pulling on her slacks, bra, and shirt. "You really don't have to take me," she said.

"Of course I do. You hired me."

"No, I didn't. You wouldn't take my money."

"A small detail."

That forced a smile from her.

By the time she'd brushed her teeth and washed her face, he was ready to go. They hurried down to his jeep, and she got in. Her mother's sudden illness made her realize that the momentary safety she'd felt was fleeting.

Not for a moment did she believe her mother would commit suicide. Nor did she believe her healthy mother would suddenly fall critically ill. One man had died the night before last. If someone had gotten to her mother, they must be powerful, as well as having vast sums of money at their fingertips. How could she be harmed inside a jail?

And who would benefit?

No one she knew. Her mother had no money of her own. No wealth or trust fund. There were the other members of the antiwar group. They would have an interest in keeping her mother silent. And then there was the money from the theft.

They reached the interstate, which was nearly empty. He turned onto it as she curled herself into a ball on the seat.

"It's not your fault," he said. "You can't give up your life."

He said it so easily, she had an unreasonable need to strike back. "Didn't you?"

His jaw tightened. "I suppose I did. But the circumstances aren't the same."

She'd hit a sore spot. She knew it. Perhaps she'd even tried. Her stomach ached. She'd been making love when her mother might have been dying.

"Why are you helping me so much?"

"Do you have to ask?"

"Yes."

"I told you. At first, I needed your help with my book."

"I needed your help more than you needed mine. You already had more information than I did."

"We haven't come to the end of the story yet."

"What is the end? The end you envision?"

"Justice." His voice was flat. Hard.

"Justice for whom?"

He shrugged. "Society."

"Do you think my mother being locked up for the rest of her life, or her death, would be justice?"

"Do you think if she did everything the government charges that there shouldn't be a price to pay?"

"If it's true, I think she has probably paid for it every moment in the past three decades."

"The two men lost their lives. Their children lost a father. Their wives lost a husband. You tell me. How much payment should there be?"

She heard the tension in his voice, but that, she supposed, was a police detective's view of the world.

"Dad said the jail authorities thought it might be a suicide attempt."

"Could it have been?"

"No, not Mom. She always taught us that we are responsible for ourselves, for what we do. That there's always a price to pay for bad decisions."

"Good advice," he said.

It was. It had been. But at one time she wouldn't listen. She'd felt like she was in a cage. "I went on a trip when I finished high school," she said, remembering the battles, the angry words that could never be taken back. "She didn't want to let me go."

"For how long?" he asked.

"A year. Along with some friends. I had a little money I'd saved from babysitting and summer jobs. We'd planned to earn money along the way and really see the West. It was something I'd dreamed about."

"Why did your mother object?"

His questions were keeping her sane, whether he knew that or not. She suspected he did. It kept the fear at bay, the terrible emptiness and panic that was knotting in her stomach.

"She wanted me close by. A summer job at a restaurant. Dates. Parties. A college nearby."

"Sounds reasonable for a mother."

"Except it wasn't want I wanted."

"And your father?"

"He understood both of us, and it was hell for him." She remembered the way her mother used to retreat to the bedroom after a long argument, while her father tried desperately to be peacemaker. Her sister, Susan, was the perfect daughter, the one that never wanted to stray from the nest. Liz had always wanted to jump from it.

Her mother had never understood. *"You have a family that loves you."*

Liz never quite understood herself why that wasn't enough, but it hadn't been. Not for her, though Sue was a born caretaker and had wanted nothing more than to embrace marriage and full-time motherhood. Liz had never thought that role lesser than the one she wanted. In truth, she'd partly envied it. But she'd always marched to a different drummer. She'd always loved challenges, something her mother had never accepted.

"I wish I'd told her I loved her more often."

"I suspect she knows."

"I wish I could be sure."

"I saw the way she looked at you at the courthouse," he said. "She knows."

Comforted only slightly by that observation, she leaned back, and images danced through her mind. The hugs that she had tensed against. Her mother's attempt to understand a daughter so unlike herself.

Or had she been like her mother's younger self, and that was where the overprotectiveness had come from? Had her mother known the same sense of adventure, of rebellion? Had it destroyed part of her?

Caleb glanced at his passenger huddled in the corner, her eyes closed.

He knew she was awake.

His gut twisted as he glanced at her.

He'd wanted justice, but not like this.

She loved her mother, and, God help him, he was afraid he was beginning to care much too much for Sarah Jane Maynard's daughter.

She opened her eyes and stared out the window as the sky lightened, but he didn't think she saw anything. She clenched her hands into fists in her lap, the cell phone next to them. He wanted to reach over and touch them, but he couldn't. He'd already dishonored himself by making love to her while continuing the lie. He wanted to tell her now, but she had enough problems.

She'd given him the perfect chance to tell her the truth just moments ago, yet he'd dodged her question. If he were to be completely honest, he didn't know if he was helping her out of his own self-interest or because, for the first time in years, he was interested in something—*someone*—else besides himself. Didn't know if he wanted justice for the criminals or absolution for himself.

He remembered when he'd lost his father, then his mother. When he'd lost his wife and son. The grief was inconsolable. Solace unhelpful, at least to him. The guilt had been too great. He'd never protected those who loved him.

He knew she also felt guilt. She'd been angry at her mother. Anyone would have, knowing that a large part of their history was a lie. But that reason would fade now that her mother was so ill. And she would blame herself for harboring disloyal thoughts.

Now was not the time for a confession, and he couldn't take their relationship any further until she knew exactly how he'd come to be here.

So he kept his hands to himself as he drove her to the hospital and let her off at the entrance while he found a parking space.

In minutes, he was at her side again at the reception desk. She was directed to the waiting room for the critical care unit.

Liz headed directly toward her father, who wrapped his arms around her. Caleb stood a few feet away, watching them unite in grief. An interloper. A liar. A cheat.

Father and daughter separated. "What happened?" she asked him.

"One of the guards noticed her. She'd been restless, unable to sleep. But then she appeared unusually still. The guard checked and couldn't wake her. We were lucky."

"But what . . . ?"

"No one knows right now. They asked about a diabetic coma, but I told them she's never had diabetes. They're doing tests."

"Can we see her?"

"Not now. The doctor will be here as soon as they have anything to report."

Steve Connor looked years older than when Caleb had first seen him. His face was drawn, his eyes exhausted, his shoulders slumped. The man hugged Liz, and they clung to each other for several seconds.

Caleb forced his attention away. He went through the door, down the hall to the critical care unit. From the nurse's station, he gazed down the row of glass cubicles. Across the corridor from one, a man in uniform talked to a nurse.

His gaze went back to the occupant. A woman. Tubes ran in and out of her body. She was alone.

Caleb glanced around. One nurse was sitting and staring at several computer screens. Another was in a cubicle several doors away from that of Betty Connor. The third was talking to the officer.

He started to turn away and abruptly halted as a tall man in scrubs entered Betty Connor's cubicle. Some internal alarm went off as his gaze followed the doctor. The man was wearing black shoes, not the booties most medical personnel wore inside the critical care unit.

The doctor, or whoever he was, blocked Caleb's view, but something about his arm . . .

Caleb moved swiftly to the door. He heard a shout from a nurse, but all his attention was on the man in green, and the syringe he had inserted into the IV bag.

The man whirled around and came at Caleb with the syringe. Caleb ducked, and the intruder toppled the IV stand in his way before running out the door at a dead run.

Caleb wanted to go after him, but he had to yank out the tube from the IV needle before whatever was injected into the bag went into Betty Connor's bloodstream.

The uniformed deputy yelled and charged into the cubicle. An alarm of some kind went off.

Caleb grabbed the IV needle and pulled it out of Betty Connor's arm just as the deputy aimed his gun at him. He stilled, raising his hands, as the space filled with nurses, along with another man in scrubs who leaned over Betty.

He turned and glanced at the deputy. "Get him out of here," the doctor said.

"The man who just ran out of here injected something into the IV," Caleb shouted as they all but dragged him out.

The doctor turned around. "What did you say?"

"Someone dressed as a doctor was injecting a substance into the IV," Caleb repeated as he straightened and stopped fighting the guards.

The doctor looked at the two nurses. One shook her head, the other nodded. "I saw a man in scrubs run out of here. He almost knocked me down."

"Check it," Caleb said, as he was hustled outside. The deputy frisked him, found his wallet, and stared at his private investigator's license.

"I used to be a cop," Caleb said. "I'm working on this case for the family of the lady in there."

The activity inside the cubicle increased. Caleb heard the Code Blue warning. He was pushed down the hall by the deputy and a member of hospital security. He saw Liz's face and her father's. Frightened. Their eyes met before he was shoved into an elevator and taken down to a room on the first floor.

"Sit down," the deputy said.

"If you'd been doing your damned job, no one would have gotten in there."

The deputy made a step toward him, and the security guard stepped between them. "Wait outside," the guard said.

The deputy stood firm.

"Your job was to guard the woman upstairs," the guard said. "This is mine. If I were you, I would be trying to find how someone got into your prisoner's room."

The deputy stood there for a moment, anger obviously raging with reason, then reluctantly left, a muttered curse filtering back to them.

Caleb paced the floor as he waited for the questions that most certainly would be coming. He had questions of his own. How could someone reach her so quickly? Obviously there was more than one professional launched against the Connors.

He knew he would never forget the face of the fake doctor, but evidence? He'd noticed the gloves on the man. It had been part of the attacker's disguise but just as importantly a protection against any fingerprints being found.

Liz had kept asking him the question: why?

He was asking the same question. Why was someone spending so many assets against two women? He was beginning to think that Liz was right. There was much more to her mother's complicity than anyone realized. And someone, someone with enough money and power—and need—to hire not one but two professional hit men, was trying to silence her.

BOSTON

Michael Gallagher had received a call at five in the morning, telling him of the hospitalization of Betty Connor. She obviously would not be heading for Boston. He'd called about a flight immediately.

To add more urgency to his mission, he had information that Liz Connor and her father should have, information that should turn them against Adams and toward him.

He boarded the plane and took his seat in business class. He tried to work on contracts for the purchase of the steel company that had finally been approved by both parties, but his mind kept returning to Liz Connor. Someone had attacked her the night before last, and now her mother was in critical condition.

He hoped to God his employer had nothing to do with either circumstance, but he couldn't dismiss the possibility. Win could be totally ruthless. But as far as Michael knew, he had never resorted to violence.

Yet he knew better than anyone what was at stake. For Win and for himself.

He forced his thoughts back to the contract he'd been working on. But now the purchase of another company paled in comparison to the Connor affair. It was threatening Maynard's bid for the Senate nomination. There were whispers that he or his family had somehow helped his cousin all these years. How else could the fugitive escape detection for so long? Reporters were bedeviling Win now, and the sooner she pled guilty and media attention faded, the better for his employer.

And what was better for his employer was better for Michael.

Win had made it clear that he planned to train Michael to take his place. It was something that Michael had always wanted, always craved. Respect. Money. Power.

He'd always thought he would pay any price necessary. But as the plane headed west, he wondered exactly how steep that price would be.

chapter twenty-one

Jeff Baker went to the space where a coffee shop once existed. Now the space was occupied by a small upscale restaurant.

He ordered lunch. It cost three times what he usually paid. He glanced around, found the restroom and a hall that led to a back door.

He'd returned and tried to eat, but the food stuck in his throat.

Would the others come?

Would they feel as he did?

Had someone already acted?

He recalled all the impressions he had of his fellow cell members over and over again. Of all of them, only Tony and Sarah Jane stood out. Tony was the leader, and he had sworn them all to secrecy. They were the brightest and best, he'd said, and he'd picked each of them because of their intelligence and commitment to stopping the war.

Which of them would show up?

What would the others look like? Would they have a paunch like his? Gray and thinning hair? Would he even recognize them after so many years? Were they even alive?

He put the newspaper down on the table. The *Chicago Tribune* with the personal ad they'd all agreed on.

"*Straw Dogs* memorablia wanted."

Someone had placed it. Where were the others?

The ad was to alert everyone in the case of an arrest, if they hadn't heard it by other means. He'd subscribed to the paper all these years despite the expense he couldn't quite explain to his wife. It was also a call to meet as early as possible, before the Feds discovered them. Everyone, if captured, had pledged not to say anything for at least ten days. The others would meet immediately and make decisions about the money. If it had been anyone but Sarah Jane who'd been arrested, he probably wouldn't have come. But he trusted her, always had.

Would the others?

He picked at the half-eaten meal and finished his glass of iced tea. No beer today. He needed his wits about him. He knew how dangerous Tony could be, if he'd somehow learned about this meeting.

It was thirty minutes past the time for the meeting. He paid his bill and rose. He would return tomorrow.

He walked several blocks to the public parking lot where he kept his car, aware every moment of his surroundings, of everyone on the streets. He'd learned in the past thirty-plus years to be vigilant.

He started the car and drove slowly, keeping an eye on the rearview mirror. No one was following him. He would bet his last dollar on it.

Hell, he was doing exactly that.

He arrived at the motel twenty minutes later and left the air-conditioned car for the stifling Chicago heat. Why did it seem so much hotter here than a few hundred miles south?

Jeff unlocked the door, and the moment he entered, someone slammed the door behind him. He whirled around and stared.

"You!" he exclaimed.

And then he felt excruciating pain as he was struck in the gut, then hands went around his throat.

*   *   *

Caleb answered questions ad nauseam. He knew the routine. He knew the necessity, but still he wanted to get back to the critical care unit. He wanted to know whether he'd pulled the IV tube out in time.

It was ironic how much he wanted Betty Connor to live. After all the years he'd wanted her found, convicted, even given the death penalty, he now might well have saved her life.

He hoped to God he had. Not for her sake. For Liz's sake.

And to discover who and why someone was so determined to quiet Betty Connor and terrorize her daughter.

"What alerted you?" he was asked by a detective who'd just arrived.

Caleb had already answered the question repeatedly, but he knew the routine. "He had black street shoes. Doctors don't usually wear those on duty in critical care units."

"How do you know?"

"I've been there enough times." He shrugged.

"Can you describe him?"

"I already have."

"Again. You might remember something else."

"I'm a cop. I remembered everything. Hair was covered by one of those caps. Can't help you there. Six feet tall. Well built. Glasses. Possibly used to change his appearance. I can give your artist everything she or he needs. But if the hospital has security cameras anyplace—"

"We're checking on that," the detective said.

"Do you have an artist?"

"Yes."

"What about an hour from now?"

"I'll make sure he's there."

Caleb nodded. He didn't think he would forget the man's face, but he knew only too well how important it was to convey those impressions to an artist as soon as possible.

He was allowed to leave the security office and went hunting for more information.

The intensive care cubicle occupied by Betty Connor was now guarded by two United States marshals. The guard who'd been talking to a nurse was gone. Caleb went to one of the marshals and pulled out his identification.

"I hear we owe you one," one of the marshals said.

Caleb shrugged, uncomfortable. "Take care of her."

"Don't worry. Nothing will happen while we're here."

"Have the daughter and father been in?"

"For a few moments. We've been told she's not allowed any more visitors."

"Thank you. I'll be in the visiting room."

Caleb took one last gaze at the woman he'd hated all these years. She looked peaceful, even gentle.

He watched for a moment, wondering at the emotions that flitted around a heart he thought dead, then headed for the visitor's room. Steve Connor stood, staring blankly at a television. Liz was pacing up and down.

Liz hurried to his side. "What happened?" she asked. "They won't tell us anything. But there's police all over this floor, and I heard one nurse say there was an intruder."

"I think someone tried to kill your mother," he said. "I saw someone inject something into her IV bag. I didn't think it looked right. I entered and started to ask a question. He lunged at me, then ran. I jerked the tube from the IV. There wasn't time for anything to get into her bloodstream."

"What was it?"

"I imagine they're testing the contents of the bag as we speak."

"Why won't they tell us anything?"

"Liability for one thing. A lot of explaining as to how a killer walked in and nearly killed a patient. I think they probably want to know exactly what happened and what, if anything, was in that bag before saying much."

Steve Connor approached, listening intently. "We're grateful to you," he said as he held out his hand. "It appears you're our guardian angel."

Caleb had never felt less like a guardian angel. He was a liar and a fraud.

"I'm sorry I didn't get him."

"Mom's more important," she said. "But will she be safe now?"

.

"You can bet on it," he said. "This is a major problem for the deputies and the hospital. A fly won't be able to get in here."

But Liz didn't look comforted, and he didn't blame her. She was too smart for platitudes. She must know that her mother wasn't here by accident, that someone had been able to get to her in jail, and now in the hospital.

This attempt had been more than a little risky. Someone was desperate.

But Caleb had no doubt now that the collapse in jail was not an accident. Nor was it suicide.

Someone wanted to silence her. And whoever it was had vast resources.

Go back to who benefits?

Win Maynard had offered to pay for representation. He'd even sent an attorney to New Mexico. In Caleb's world, people didn't do that when they'd not seen the beneficiary for more than thirty years. He recalled what he knew about Maynard. He'd taken over his uncle's business and built it into an empire. But that uncle was Betty Connor's father. Had he left his daughter anything? Or had he banished and forgotten her?

It was time to return to Boston.

"What are you thinking?" Liz asked.

"Who benefits if your mother dies?" he said.

"Those who are still free, I would imagine. She must know something about them, where they are."

"Then she had to know all these years and hasn't said anything. Even now, when her life, and her family's life, are in danger, she's silent. Why?"

He watched her face as she digested what he said. She had to have thought of it herself, but he suspected that she'd never really accepted it.

"Maybe it's money," she said. "The federal agents said the payroll has never been found."

"It would be amazing if any of it still exists," he replied.

"Something must have happened to it," Steve Conner broke in. "When I met Liz's mother, she was living in a rooming house and waitressing. That would have been a little less than a year after the robbery. She certainly didn't have any money."

"Okay. She's been protecting her friends all these years, and didn't have money. What—or who—does that leave?"

"Relatives?" Liz said.

"Possible," he said.

"Apparently there's only Winstead Maynard, my mother's cousin, and his family. But he's said to have more money than Midas. What interest would he have?"

"I don't know, but I'm going to find out if he has one," Caleb said. "And it's obvious someone is looking for something," he said. "Your house was entered and the computer hard drive taken. The fire was probably meant to disguise that fact. That they were in your office meant they were looking for something there as well. They must be convinced that there is something tangible."

"But why me?"

"It may not have been just you. We might never know whether your sister's home or your father's home have been searched."

A sudden anxiety crossed her face. "I left Michael there. Alone. But he wouldn't . . . he couldn't . . ." She stopped. "He saved my life."

But her expression belied the last sentence. In less than a week, she'd discovered betrayal in unexpected places. Which made his own deception more difficult to swallow, much less to explain to her.

A nurse came in. "Mr. Connor may see his wife for ten minutes," she said.

"What about me?" Liz asked.

"I'm sorry. Only one person."

"Is she still unconscious?"

"You'll have to ask the doctor. He's with her now."

Steve Connor didn't hesitate then. "I'll be back shortly, Sport."

She nodded, and her father hurried out the door behind the nurse.

She sat down in one of the chairs. Caleb followed.

"I think we should search your parents' house."

"I already did that."

"I think we should try again."

"We?"

"Only if you want me to help."

Her gaze measured him, and he wondered whether she saw all the deception inside him.

She nodded. "As soon as my dad returns."

"Fugitive attacked in local hospital." The words, coming from a news anchor on television, intruded.

Her face blanched. "How did they find out so quickly?"

"The floor was full of people. Then there's the police. Usually the police reporter with any news agency has a police radio."

She shivered, but it wasn't cold in the room. Her eyes were red-rimmed as if she'd been crying. Her eyes were dry now, but that very determined chin quivered just enough to notice.

"I think she really will be all right," he said.

"They don't even know what's wrong."

"After what just happened they'll be looking for drugs in her system," he said. "It has to be obvious to everyone now that it wasn't suicide."

"But taking the chance of entering an area that's so open," she said. "Isn't that terribly risky?"

"Yes," he said. "It is. It also means we know of two people intent on doing your family harm. We don't know if there are more out there."

"We know this one still is."

"He's been seen," Caleb said. "He'll get the hell out of here as quickly as he can. Contract killers do that."

"Contract killers?"

He should have kept his mouth shut, yet he was convinced that was what they were facing. They were too well-equipped, too ruthless, too fast to be anything else. Someone was paying very big money for their services.

He nodded.

"The other one didn't. He just kept coming after me."

"Or me," Caleb said. "And he couldn't be sure whether you had a good look at him. Several people had a good look at this man."

"Then someone else might come."

He was silent. It was a real possibility. Unless he and Liz discovered whatever the assailants were after, and the identity of the person who hired them.

"Okay, let's look at my father's house," she agreed. "Perhaps you'll think of something I haven't."

He was getting what he wanted: access to a house, and information, that might lead him to others involved in the armored-car robbery. He was strangely reluctant to take advantage of it. "I told the police I would get together·with the artist."

"Then afterward? I'll be here." She looked at him uncertainly. "I know I've been asking a lot of you. We're not, I mean, I'm not a client. I would understand . . ."

She stopped, biting her lip.

That uncertainty was like a knife in his heart. She was so damned strong. He remembered the way she had shot the intruder, faced up to the wreckage of her apartment, defended her mother so loyally even as he knew she felt a certain betrayal.

He inwardly sighed while he swore to himself he would never lie again. How easily one got caught in the tangle.

"I'll be back," he said. "I'm going over to the police station now. Describing the attacker shouldn't take long. His image is engraved in my head."

Steve Connor returned and came over to them. "They're keeping a close watch on her," he said. "But the doctor is sure none of whatever was injected into the bag got into her bloodstream, thanks to Mr. Adams's quick action. But he's still puzzled as to what put her into a coma. They've tested for drugs and can't find anything."

"Is the doctor still there?"

"Yes."

"I'll be back in a moment."

Caleb went to the small cubicle. The guard stopped him, but he gestured to the doctor inside.

The doctor came out, raised an eyebrow.

"He's the one who stopped the attack," the guard explained.

The doctor thrust out his hand. "I'm Dr. Ames."

Caleb took it, then asked abruptly, "Could it have been insulin shock that sent her into a coma?"

The doctor looked intrigued. "Could be. We dropped the idea of insulin shock when her husband said she didn't have diabetes. But how would she have gotten insulin in the detention center?"

"How could someone inject a substance into a IV bag in a critical care unit?"

"Point taken," the doctor said grimly. "It won't happen again, you can be assured of that. No one will get in here if the nurse doesn't recognize them."

Caleb left, somewhat reassured. And now there was a plan. Action to take. The police station, first, and perhaps another lead. If they could identify the second attacker, perhaps he could find a connection.

There had to be a connection.

Then there was the Connor home. A long shot, but a shot, nonetheless. There had to be something!

Depending on what they found, or didn't find, he planned a trip to Boston.

He gave Liz a reassuring smile and wished he felt as much assurance inside, then left.

Once outside the room, he called Cam.

"Find out anything more about Patton or who might have arranged a hit?" he asked without a greeting.

"I put out word to our snitches, but nothing yet."

"What do you know about Winstead Maynard?" he asked abruptly.

"He's admired here. You're probably aware of that. On every committee known to man. No scandal other than the cousin. He's about as clean as you can get. Has to be to run for senator." He paused, then added, "I asked a few questions. I was told in no uncertain terms to leave him alone."

"He's contacted the Connor family," Caleb said. "Wants to help with the legal bills. Now why would he do that?"

"Family?"

"No contact for more than thirty-four years?" Caleb replied, letting his doubt color his voice. He *wanted* to raise questions. "Can you get a copy of his uncle's will?"

"Caleb, I've been told—"

"I know, but there's been another attack. This time on the mother in the critical care unit at the hospital. Someone is pretty desperate. I want to know who benefits if she dies."

"The other three who were never caught?"

"After all these years? Even if they are alive, they've had plenty of time to run since word broke of her arrest."

"Okay," Cam said. "I'll see if I can find the will."

"I might be up that way in the next two days."

"Stirring things up?"

"I hope so."

"Be careful."

"Have you ever known me not to be?"

"Do I have to answer that?"

Caleb ignored the question. "You'll call me?"

"I've seen photos of the daughter," Cam said. "She's very attractive." It was casually said, but there was a question in it.

One Caleb didn't intend to answer. "G'bye," he said.

He didn't want to think about Cam's reaction if he'd realized that Caleb was the son of one of the murdered guards.

Another lie. Another betrayal. He hadn't worried about that before.

His Annie had known about his father. She had been the only one he'd ever told. He also knew that while she'd understood, she also disapproved, thought he should let it go. He'd been to the point of doing just that when she was killed. He had gotten nowhere in his search for the missing link, the boyfriend that apparently had changed Betty Connor's life, the one who had never been identified.

Now that boyfriend took center stage again. He was in this mix somewhere. Caleb would bet on it.

Fear clutched Liz's stomach.

And from her father's face, it did his, as well.

Now she knew someone was intent on killing her mother. And apparently her. But why her? Because she'd seen a face she wasn't supposed to see? Or had she been a target from the beginning? Liz saw something in Caleb's eyes that sent apprehension skittering up her back. Why did it seem as if he was holding something back? Something she should know?

Liz watched Caleb leave the visiting room. He was distracted, she realized that.

Was he sorry he'd become involved? Book aside, she was sure he hadn't bargained for a shoot-out in his cabin, his dog injured, his life uprooted.

She waited with her father impatiently. The doctor had allowed her to sit with her mother for several minutes, but her mother's eyes didn't open. Liz held her hand tightly. "Wake up," she coaxed. "Tell us what happened. I know you must have good reasons."

And then, quite simply, "I love you."

A tap on the glass told her it was time to go. She leaned over and kissed her mother, praying that she knew somewhere deep inside her consciousness that she was loved and had to fight.

After returning to the visiting room, she couldn't stay still. She phoned Tracy, but only the answering machine replied. Then she accessed her own answering machine. Reporters. Producers from television talk shows. After a few moments she hung up.

She stared out the glass at the corridor. Uniformed police were all over the place, as well as the marshals standing watch over her mother's cubicle.

The doctor came into the room. "The lab has analyzed the contents of the IV pack," he said.

Her father moved next to her. "And . . ."

"Potassium chloride. It would have stopped her heart almost immediately after getting into the bloodstream. It would have looked like a heart attack."

Her father closed his eyes for a moment, and she knew he was thinking how close he'd come to losing her.

She knew because she felt the same way. Her mother's arrest had stirred, in turn, outrage, disbelief, bewilderment that nothing had explanations. Then anger again. But the past few hours—and the possibility of losing her mother—had also stirred a kind of sadness she'd never known before, a desperate grief that paralyzed her.

"Have you found out why she's in a coma?"

"No. We're still testing. But after this attack, we know to look a bit further."

"Thank you."

"I'm sorry," he said. "We're lucky your friend noticed something strange."

"Why didn't the nurses notice anything?"

"There'll be a query about that," he replied.

She wanted to retort that a query would be a little late, but decided it wouldn't do any good.

He left, saying he would keep them posted on any developments. She looked at the clock. She couldn't stand *not* doing something, but neither could she wander far. She wanted to be here when Caleb returned.

In a glimmering way, the attack gave her hope and confirmed her faith in her mother. Someone wanted to silence her. Maybe because she hadn't billed the two guards. "Dad, are you staying here?"

"Yes."

"I can get your shaving gear and clothes from the motel."

"I don't know if it's safe for you to be alone."

"The guy who was here is long gone," she replied. "He has to know that Caleb saw him." Then she remembered what happened the time she saw a face she wasn't meant to see.

Her father obviously did, too. "I'm not sure you should stay with him."

"You and I can't afford guards with us all the time."

"Are you armed?"

She shook her head. "They took the gun that killed the intruder. It was Caleb's gun. The bad guy took mine."

"Get another one. Do you have your permit with you?"

She nodded.

He folded her in his arms. "For God's sake, don't let anything happen to you. I couldn't survive it."

She leaned her head against his heart. She knew it was cracked, that he was bewildered, and yet he clung to his belief in her mother. She thought about the times she'd watched them hand in hand, and the kisses they exchanged when he'd left for the school in the morning.

She'd always wanted a love like that and had never found it. She hadn't been willing to settle for less.

But now . . .

She dismissed the thought. She and Caleb had shared the aftermath of violence. Nothing more.

She pulled away from her father.

She would fetch his shaving kit from the hotel room, then stop and purchase a weapon. She would be back before Caleb returned.

And then together they would work on the mystery of her mother.

chapter twenty-two

Michael Gallagher arrived in Albuquerque, found the hospital, and located the critical care area. He couldn't miss the presence of law enforcement officers, particularly two federal marshals guarding one glass cubicle.

He immediately saw Steve Connor in one of the chairs. His eyes were closed.

Michael looked for Elizabeth Connor but didn't see her and debated whether he should wake her father or not. He decided not to. Steve Connor had been none too friendly earlier. If her father and mother were here, she would be close by. He'd learned a lot about Elizabeth Connor these past few days.

He'd also read about her resignation from the city council and the statement from the Santa Fe mayor regretting that resignation, and he'd learned what he could about the shooting at the home of Caleb Adams. The lady had moxie.

It galled him, though, that she was at Adams's cabin. How far had the man wormed his way into her life? And her trust?

He didn't know if she would appreciate his revelation. He only knew that she had the right to know the truth.

Perhaps she already knew.

As an hour went by, he grew more and more impatient. He called Colton Montgomery, who apparently was raising hell about the lack of security at both the detention center and hospital. He'd not heard from Elizabeth Connor.

Michael was about to wake Steve Connor when the television flashed a live shot of Elizabeth Connor entering her parents' house, Caleb Adams with her.

He left Steve Connor sleeping and headed for Santa Fe. He should be there in an hour.

When Liz and Caleb arrived at her parents' home, the road was crowded with news vans. Several other cars were parked illegally along the road. News of the shooting at Caleb's cabin had been on the morning shows.

As Liz and Caleb drove up, a sheriff's car pulled in behind them.

Wishing she had the remote to open the garage door, she got out of Caleb's jeep and was instantly surrounded by reporters hollering questions at her and thrusting microphones in her face.

Tired of the invasion, she simply shook her head. "I have nothing to say."

Then a sheriff's deputy came up to them, and he and Caleb took charge, ordering the reporters off her property, and telling the illegally parked reporters to move their vehicles or they would be ticketed and their cars impounded.

"Thank you," she told the deputy as she unlocked the front door of the house to admit the two men.

"They won't be going far," Caleb grumbled.

The deputy nodded his head. "I know, but we'll keep trying."

"Did you just happen by here?" Liz asked.

"We've been checking it regularly and warning those reporters to keep off your property, Ms. Connor."

"Who asked you?" she said.

"The Santa Fe mayor made the request, but our chief knows your father. He made it real clear to us that we're to do whatever we can to make sure you're safe and your privacy is respected."

"Thank you," she said again. "We'll be here overnight."

"Okay. We'll be close by. Just call if you need any help."

Caleb showed a flyer to the deputy. "This is the man

who attacked Mrs. Connor's mother this morning. A copy should have been faxed to you, but this might get to the patrol guys quicker."

"You say he attacked Mrs. Connor? I thought—"

"She was found unconscious in her cell. When she was transferred to the hospital, this man tried to kill her," Caleb said. "I think he's a hired killer."

The deputy's brows knitted together. "We don't see much of that down here."

"I hope we won't see it again," Liz said.

"Well, I'll be dropping by often."

As he left, Liz locked the door behind him and led Caleb into the living area. Nothing appeared changed since she had searched it a few days ago. But then she'd been simply hoping to find a clue into her mother's past; now she was convinced that there was something here that someone wanted.

Caleb scanned the room with an investigator's eyes. Michael Gallagher had done the same thing a few days ago. Both of them had studied the bookcases, their glances cataloguing the room. Now she wondered whether she had been wise to leave Michael here alone.

"Did your mother use a computer?" Caleb asked suddenly.

"Yes. She had an old one of Dad's. But the FBI took it, as well as the one that belonged to Dad."

"Diaries? Address books?"

"No diary. Dad said the FBI took her address book. He didn't have time to go through everything."

"Have you looked over the house to determine if anything else is missing?

"That's what I was doing the night I was attacked at the office. But I wouldn't know what is missing. I was mainly trying to find a clue to what happened years ago. A photograph. Something like that."

"Did you find anything?"

"I found some old albums that same night. But it's all just Dad and Mom, my sister, and me, and more lately, my sister's family. There's nothing that dates back before she married Dad."

"Did you ever wonder about that?"

"No. My dad was an orphan. I thought she was, as well. I thought that was why they were drawn together." Her voice wavered. It was yet another reminder of all the lies. She wondered how her father really felt about those lies. They must hurt him far more than they did her, and that was very deep, indeed.

"I'm sorry," he said.

"She always warned us about telling lies," she said. "That was her big lecture. They always catch up to you. One small lie leads to big lies, and they're not worth the pain they inevitably cost. I've always believed that. I've always hated lies. And she lived the greatest one of all." Her voice broke at the end. "I guess she proved the truth of her own lessons."

"She could say it because she knew," he said, his gaze meeting hers. "She knew the guilt and pain they cause." A muscle moved in his cheek. His face was tight with strain.

Before she could decipher his expression, he moved away from her. But an impression remained as if he felt the guilt and pain he'd just mentioned. The kind that came from lies. Not a small one, but a big, life-altering one. The kind her mother lived.

"Does she have a desk?" he asked abruptly.

"One in the kitchen, but I've gone through it. There's nothing there. I don't know if there ever was. I don't know what the FBI took."

"There will be an inventory. Ask Montgomery to get a copy of it."

She nodded. She should have thought of that, but there were so many other things.

"Anything that had a special meaning to her? Like a painting?"

"There are several paintings she and Dad bought together. She has an eye for new artists. She's helped me find some really good new artists."

"Show them to me," he said.

She took him through the house, showing him the paintings her mother loved most. He inspected the backing of each one. Each had tears in the back. "The FBI checked them out, too," he observed.

When he'd finished checking the paintings, he turned to her. "What about hobbies? Any special interests?"

"She volunteers at the women's shelter and the animal shelter. She's involved in a lot of causes, but she also loves to garden and cook. She bakes cookies and cakes for my father's school and the local fire station, and supervises dinners at the church. She was going to cater lunches for our tours."

Caleb stopped at a copy of the *Chicago Tribune* mixed in with other papers next to the fireplace, apparently there as fuel for fires.

"Dad's been taking the paper for years," she said. "I can't remember when we didn't. He's a real news hound, though I think that might change after this. He also takes the *New York Times*. Sunday was reading day around the house."

"Your father's?"

"I suppose, though I often saw Mom flipping through them. She especially liked the Chicago paper. Said they had great food sections."

He seemed to reflect on that for a moment, then shrugged.

She followed him into the kitchen, and his gaze went immediately to a shelf loaded with cookbooks. "Let's look at her cookbooks," he said.

"I already looked, but go ahead." She watched as he flipped through them. They all seemed to be what they should be. Her mother had made notes on some recipes, changing ingredients slightly, but there was nothing odd or out of the ordinary.

She looked at her watch. She needed to go over to her house and meet with the contractors.

"I have to get over to my house. I promised Garry."

"I'll take you."

"That's not necessary. I can take my dad's car."

"You're not going anywhere alone," he said.

"I did get another weapon," she said. "It's in my purse. I really will be all right."

"I still want to go with you."

She stood and went to a cabinet to get a glass for water before leaving. She opened the door and saw her mother's hand-painted recipe box that was in its usual place in the front of the cabinet. She took it down.

Recipes were neatly catalogued in her mother's fine handwriting.

Caleb joined her as she shuffled through the recipes.

How many times had she watched her mother take a recipe from that box and create something wonderful?

She didn't know why she flipped through them now. Perhaps Caleb's interest in her mother's hobbies. A long shot. But everything was a long shot now.

Many of the recipes invoked memories. Beef Stroganoff, Oysters Rockefeller, Gourmet Beef Stew, Crab Bisque, and then the pies and cakes. Christmas Eve was always huge bowls of clam chowder.

Straw Dogs? She stopped shuffling.

She looked at the recipe. *Straw Dogs?*

She picked it up and read it. It made no sense. "A tablespoon of parsley, two of sage, a pinch of rosemary and thyme." Nothing else.

Some kind of spice mixture? But why under "Straw Dogs"? She'd never heard of such a dish.

"What is it?" Caleb asked.

"A rather strange recipe."

He peered over his shoulder. "Straw Dogs," he read. "Parsley, sage . . ."

"Rosemary and thyme." It clicked then. "Simon and Garfunkel," she exclaimed. " 'Parsley, sage, rosemary, and thyme.' It's the second line in the song, 'Scarborough Fair.' The album was called *Parsley, Sage, Rosemary and Thyme.*"

"Damn, I should have known that. It was my wife's favorite song," he explained as the all-too-familiar curtain shielded his expression again.

"What about Straw Dogs? It sounds familiar but—"

"A cult movie from the same time. About a pacifist whose wife is raped and beaten, and he goes on the attack. It's violent as hell." He was thoughtful for a moment, then added. "My partner was a real movie buff. He insisted I rent it. Said it was a classic. I can't say I liked it that much. But it does make the point that extreme violence can change people in profound ways." His voice seemed to take on a stiffness she'd not heard before.

"A message of some kind?"

"Obviously, but meaning what? And for whom?"

His cell phone rang, and she heard him say, "Cam." Then he stepped beyond her hearing. She studied the card in her hand. What did it mean? Rosemary, sage, thyme, parsley. Her mother grew herbs. Could there be something there? A clue? Anything?

She heard an exclamation and turned around to see him close the cell phone. "What's wrong?"

"I had the police send the photo to my former partner in Boston. He checked with a friend in organized crime. The guy resembles an enforcer with a Boston crime family."

"Boston seems to be a common denominator."

He nodded. "I think it might be time to visit Maynard."

She nodded and started to mention the herbs, then for some reason hesitated. It was probably a foolish idea, and if there *was* anything, she wanted to see it alone. No matter how she felt about him, was growing to feel about him, she wanted to protect her mother more. And perhaps protect herself as well.

But from what . . . or whom? Her instincts had told her to trust Caleb. She'd trusted him enough to welcome intimacy with him.

Still, he was a former detective. If there was anything, would he be honor bound to report it? Or as a writer, would he be compelled to tell the story?

She didn't think so, but she wasn't ready to take the chance.

"Why don't you get us some food?" she said. "I'll stay here and continue to look."

"I don't like leaving you."

"I think I'm safe with all those reporters outside."

"Point taken. Anything special?"

She tried to think of something that would take at least thirty or forty minutes. "A pizza."

"Delivery?"

"Not out here."

"Are you the pepperoni and anchovy type?"

"I'm the onion and sausage type."

"Half and half then."

"Sounds good."

"Where?"

She gave him a name and directions.

"Why don't you call ahead and have it waiting. When I get back we'll check on plane reservations."

He left, and she hurried toward the back of the house. Thank God thick shrubs protected the yard from the reporters outside. She was near the back door when the phone rang, stopping her. Her father knew she was here.

She let the machine pick up. There was an inordinately long period, which meant the number of messages was long. This time it was a producer of a talk show, promising to give the Connor family a fair hearing.

She erased the message, thought about calling the pizza shop, but stopped herself. She needed that time. She went out the back door, pausing long enough to take a spade and shovel from a stand that held gardening tools. Turning her attention to the garden, she studied the herb plants. Rosemary. Sage. Parsley and thyme. She recognized them all. She had always been interested in nature and had questioned her mother about the plants. Now that she thought about it, her mother usually guided her attention away from the herbs and to the flowers.

Or was she only imagining it?

They had been there as long as she could remember, popping up each spring and watered patiently in the often dry summers.

They were wilted now. Her mother would be offended that no one had looked after them. Then the irony of the thought struck her. Her mother had much more to worry about than an herb garden.

If she survived.

But she would. Liz had faith. Battered faith, perhaps, but faith nonetheless. And like her mother, the plants would survive.

"Two tablespoons of sage," she reminded herself out loud, a habit she had developed when she was alone on a hiking trip. "That was the largest amount. I'll try that first."

She wanted Caleb with her. She already missed him. His competent presence. The feeling of safety she had with him. Yet this was something she had to do herself.

She got down on her knees next to the sage plants and dug deep so as to not cut the roots, and carefully picked up the cluster of sage. Then she looked down into the hole she'd dug. Nothing. She used the shovel to dig deeper. Still nothing. Time was passing.

Discarding care, she hurriedly dug through the parsley. Still nothing.

Perhaps nothing was here. Nothing at all.

Doggedly she went to the rosemary patch. Again she dug around the plants. She was just about to give up when the spade hit something hard. Now indifferent to the plants, she dug madly. She heard the sound of metal, and that gave her added impetus. In minutes she had uncovered a small box. She lifted it out of the ground and tried to open it. It was locked.

She stood, cradling the box, and took it into the kitchen. She brushed dirt off the box as she wondered how best to open it.

If she wanted to open it at all. It could be a Pandora's box that loosed any number of evils. But then how much more evil could be out there?

The doorbell rang. She ignored it for a few moments. Probably another reporter. But it kept on ringing.

She went to the front door and looked through the glass peephole.

The bell rang again.

The persistent ringer was Michael Gallagher. He had a briefcase tucked under his arm and wore a suit despite the heat.

She didn't want to talk to him now. All she wanted was to know the contents of the box. But he had saved her life. And his look was grim as newspeople yelled out questions to him.

She tucked the box under the sink and looked at herself in a hall mirror. Dirt spotted her clothes, her face, her arms. She went into the hall bathroom and washed off as much dirt as possible and pushed her hair back before going into the living room. She unlocked the dead bolt lock and opened the door, standing aside to let him in.

Michael entered. "It looks like you've been besieged."

"Understatement."

"I heard what happened to your mother," he said. "I was at the hospital."

"Is there any news? Dad would have called, but—"

"No. She's still in a coma. It's something else." His gaze wandered over her, and she wondered which drips and drops of mud remained.

She stood and waited, not inviting him farther inside.

"I thought you had returned to Boston."

"I did, but then I learned something I thought you should know."

She raised an eyebrow. "You had to come all this way? You couldn't call?"

His eyes flickered around the area he could see. "Is Adams with you?"

"Is that any of your business?"

"Perhaps," he said.

"Why?"

"Because my employer is interested in your welfare."

"Is he now?"

He must have seen or heard her doubt. "He really is, you know."

She wanted to get back to the box. As charming as the man was, the box was more intriguing. And she didn't like his questions. "I really have to go," she said.

"Were you aware that Adams's father was one of the guards your mother is accused of killing?"

She stepped backward. The words were like a body blow. "No. You're wrong."

His expression was even grimmer than it had been when she opened the door. "The Boston Police Department apparently didn't know, either, or they wouldn't have let him within miles of the case."

"You're wrong," she repeated even as she was assailed by a terrible sense that he was not wrong at all.

"I wish I was," he said. "But I'm not."

"But the names—"

"He was adopted, and his legal name is Adams. His birth name was Garrett Caleb Murphy. His father was Sam Murphy."

Her world was spinning. Her legs felt rubbery. She wanted to deny it. She wanted to scream out that he was wrong. But she knew by looking at him that he wasn't. *Sam.* That had been the name of Caleb's son. She remembered it from her research on him.

She finally found words. "Thank you," she said.

He leaned out to touch her, but she backed away.

"Please go," she said.

"I can't help in any way?"

"No," she said flatly.

"I'll be at the La Fonda for a few days. Don't hesitate to call me if you need anything. Anything at all."

Caleb would be back here in minutes. She had to get away. Now. She couldn't bear to see him.

He can't learn about the box, and it wouldn't take him long to guess, with all the holes in the yard.

"I'll remember that," she said as she guided him to the door. She opened it and practically shoved him out. He gave her that wry, charming smile, then saluted and left.

Time. How much time did she have?

She locked the door, grabbed her purse, and took the box from under the sink. Then she slipped out the back door, locking it. She looked at the holes, regretting that she had no time to fill them before fleeing out the back gate.

She was partially numb, partially furious, and partially devastated.

He knew what her mother's lies had done to her, and he had lied and lied and lied.

She slipped through the shrubs that surrounded the backyard and ran over the wooded space that separated their property from their next-door neighbors'.

Beth Stewart answered the door immediately and took one look at her face. "My God, what's happened?"

Daisy rushed to her, barking madly. She leaned down and gave her a big hug as the dog pawed at her leg. "Sorry, girl," she said. "I can't take you home quite yet."

"Is it your mother? How is she?"

"She's in a coma. Dad's with her now."

"I heard the news. They're both in my prayers. As opposed to those vultures outside your house." Her gaze went to the metal box Liz was clutching, but thankfully she didn't ask any questions.

"Have the reporters been bothering you?" Liz asked. Normal conversation when her heart was cracking into pieces.

"They tried. I gave them a piece of my mind. You don't worry about us, Liz. You just take care of yourself and your family."

For a moment, Liz was almost blind with tears. She'd never forget the depth of the value of friends. But then she'd thought Caleb was a friend. She wondered when rage would replace the raw wound he'd inflicted.

She blinked back tears, then came straight to the point. She had little time. Caleb would be back any minute. "I need a huge favor."

"Anything in my power."

"May I borrow your car? I don't want the press following me."

"Of course." Beth plucked a pair of keys from a hook on the kitchen wall and handed them to her.

"I have to ask two more favors," Liz said. She'd always hated to ask favors. But she had to leave, had to find her own answers. And had to try to heal a heart now dripping from a dozen wounds.

"Sure," Beth said.

"Can your husband pick the car up at the office, and can you keep Daisy a while longer?"

"Yes to both. Just lock the keys in the glove compartment."

Beth walked her out to the car.

Liz got in and rolled down the window. "If anyone asks, please don't tell them about the car."

"I won't."

Liz nodded her thanks again and started the car. It was going to be a very long day and evening. And once more she hadn't any clothes with her.

Nothing but a cold metallic box.

And this time she would be alone.

But then perhaps she'd been alone for the past few days but hadn't known it.

She wondered whether she could ever trust anyone again.

And whether her heart would ever mend.

chapter twenty-three

Liz concentrated on the road ahead. If she didn't, she would probably scream.

The shock of Caleb's treachery was as much a blow as someone pushing her off a cliff.

She tried telling herself that he'd told her from the beginning that he had his own agenda. She'd accepted that he planned to write a book and believed him when he said he would let her read it before publication.

He'd lied about that. There obviously never was a book. He'd only wanted to squirm his way into their lives. For what? Vengeance? How much else had he lied about?

Dear God, but she hurt. She was aware of a tear wandering down her face. She impatiently wiped it away, but another started.

Discovering Caleb had lied to her, not once, but through omission every moment they'd been together was far worse than any physical wound he could have inflicted. She felt as if he had taken a machete and sliced through her soul. She had come to trust him completely. She had, God help her, even started to fall in love with him.

How could she possibly have been so wrong?

She should have known. He was too good to be true. He had placed himself in the right place at the right time on too many occasions. How naive she'd been.

She felt betrayal so deep, she was simply hanging onto survival.

Perhaps she should have stayed and confronted him. Told him what she thought of him. But that, she feared, would have led to tears she didn't want to shed for him, or in front of him.

She'd always trusted people. Believed in them. Sometimes, she was told, to the point of recklessness. Now that basic trust had been damaged irreplaceably, and the loss was staggering to who and what she was.

She wanted to be sick. The traffic light turned in front of her, and she rammed her foot on the brake, then glanced down at the rusted box beside her. What could be in it? A truth of some kind? Or more lies? Or perhaps nothing at all. But then why would it be buried?

She wanted to open it. She didn't want to open it.

She finally reached her office. It was closed, the door locked. But then it was Saturday.

A note propped up on her desk simply read, "Call me if you need anything. Skip Greene is taking out your group. Will tell you about it later."

Skip Greene had been one of their guides six years ago but had a bitter argument with the previous owner and quit. If he was back in the guiding business, Liz would be delighted to have him.

If she had a business left after this.

Before she left, she made a plane reservation from Albuquerque to Chicago. She locked the office and went to the back of the offices where they kept the various jeeps and took the SUV.

She looked at her watch. She had been here fifteen minutes.

Caleb would have arrived back at her parents' home. He would ring the bell. Maybe ask reporters whether they had seen her leave. He might wander into the backyard and see the holes.

He would realize that she had probably found something.

What would he think about her absence? That his little game was over?

And why did she care so terribly much?

She unlocked the door to the vehicle, put the key in the ignition, and drove out the back way.

The Albuquerque to Chicago flight was scheduled in six hours. It was as good a decoy as any. That would draw everyone away from her. Perhaps any number of people would be sitting in the airport waiting for her. Good guys. Bad guys. Gray guys. It was sadly amusing to think of them standing in the waiting room, all looking at each other as they waited for her.

By then she would be well on her way somewhere else. She had a new revolver in her purse, several credit cards she could use for cash withdrawals. She would open the box and figure out what to do next. Sue and her family were safe. Her father should be safe at the hospital and could contact her any time on her temporary cell phone.

So could Caleb.

As if the very thought summoned him, her cell phone rang. She wasn't up to speaking to him. Not now.

She let it ring and ring. When it finally stopped, she called her father in case it had been him. It hadn't been.

"Mom?"

"Breathing on her own. She's still in a coma but off the critical list."

"Call me if anything happens. If you want to reach me, though, call and hang up, then call again."

"Why?" The worry in his voice was evident.

"I'm just not sure who to trust."

"Caleb? I thought—"

"No more, Dad. He's the son of one of the guards mother supposedly killed. He lied to both of us. Don't trust him if he turns up at the hospital."

A silence, then he uttered a rare muttered curse. "Are you alone?"

"Yes, but I'm safe. I'll keep in touch."

"I don't like you being alone. Come to the hospital."

"There's something I have to do first, but I'll keep in touch. Call me if anything changes."

"Where are you?"

She told the truth such as it was. "In Santa Fe."

"What about your business?"

"Tracy is running it. And very well."

"Liz . . . please don't go off on your own."

"You've always said I can take care of myself."

"Circumstances have changed."

"I'm being very careful," she said. "You take care."

"I'll be here, and this place is well guarded now." He paused. "The guard who was watching your mother seems to have disappeared."

"What do you mean?"

"The police wanted to talk to him. No one can find him, apparently. Be careful, Sport. Don't take any chances."

"I won't," she said and clicked the End button. The conversation probably hadn't been satisfactory from her father's point of view, but she was tired of reacting. Tired of being protected. Tired of explaining herself to others.

She turned off the phone. She didn't know whether a cell phone could even be traced if someone had the number. Caleb probably had the resources to do exactly that if he wanted.

She headed north on the highway. She would have to assemble the pieces of the puzzle herself. And she would have to be smart about it. First on the list was making sure no one could find her. Not an assassin. Not Caleb.

Somewhere along the way, she would stop and find tools to break into the box resting ever so innocently at her side. And sometime in the future, she would forget the intense green-eyed man who had so intrigued and attracted her.

She would never forget.

Or forgive.

Caleb let the phone ring for a long time before giving up. He looked down at the pizza box in his jeep and wanted to stomp on it.

He'd arrived minutes earlier after a frustrating journey for pizza. Liz apparently had not phoned it in or the young man at the counter had mixed up the order. He'd had to wait twenty minutes. When he'd returned, no one answered the doorbell. He'd walked around to the back and through the shrubs into the backyard.

Holes dotted the garden. A shovel and spade lay haphazardly among plants. He walked over to them. Parsley and thyme plants were strewn over the dirt. He went to the back door. It was locked.

What in the hell happened here?

He went back to the front and questioned the people in two of the news vans still hovering there. They had seen him enter with her earlier, and he showed his private investigator's license. One woman perked up, obviously sensing a story. No, she hadn't seen Elizabeth Connor leave. There had been a visitor, though. A tall, dark-haired man. Very good-looking. Confident. They'd asked his name, but he'd just shaken his head. He'd stayed ten minutes, then left. There had been no activity since.

He tried to call her with his cell phone. No answer.

A dark-haired man. Very good looking. Confident.

He would bet his last five that it was Michael Gallagher.

He tried the doorbell once more. It would have been easy enough for her to leave by the back.

Why hadn't she waited for him?

A gathering dread filled him. Had Gallagher found out who he was? Had he said anything to Liz about it?

He swore. He'd known that every moment he hadn't told her the truth, he was risking her trust. It had just never seemed the right time.

Hell, he'd just been a coward. He hadn't wanted the light to leave those blue eyes, the trust to turn to accusation.

He tried her phone again, as a stone settled into his stomach. He gave up and drove out of the driveway, television cameras on his every move.

He drove to her office. It was locked. Then he stopped at a pay phone and looked through the phone book for hotel numbers. He started with the most luxurious hotels and found a Michael Gallagher registered in the second one.

He called Gallagher from the house phone. "I want to talk to you."

Gallagher hesitated, then agreed to meet him in the coffee shop. As they sat down together, Caleb didn't waste words. "Did you say anything to Liz Connor today?"

"I told her that you were the son of one of the guards her mother is accused of killing," the attorney retorted.

"And you didn't stay to take care of her?"

"She wanted to be alone."

"She's left," Caleb said, barely controlling his rage. Most of it was directed at himself. "Do you realize what kind of danger you put her in? Or was that your intent?"

"She was surrounded by the news media."

"Well, she's gone now. There's been least two attempts on her life. Two more on her mother's. And now she's alone."

A brief silence, then the attorney's low voice. "Any ideas where she might have gone?"

Caleb sure as hell wasn't going to tell him that she might have found something important. "No. I wondered whether she'd said anything to you."

"Nothing. She showed very little emotion and said little."

"What's Maynard's interest in all this?"

"Family."

"Do you really believe that?"

He shook his head in disgust and left the table as Gallagher remained silent. He was getting nowhere fast. His anger would only make it worse. Even when most of that anger was aimed at himself.

He knew Liz well now. What would she do?

It depends on what she found.

He tried to think as she would. She'd found something. He had no idea what it was.

Bottom line: She felt she couldn't trust anyone. She was alone. She wanted to protect her family.

Facts. How could he arrange them to find her? He'd solved puzzles before. It had never been more important than now.

Her life was at stake. Possibly her mother's. And her mother's was important to him now, because he knew how important it was to her.

He didn't know if he could save either of them. Certainly not if he couldn't find her. Icy cold fear ran down his spine as he reached his car. She was running from killers. And now she was also running from him.

More than anything he feared that in the latter, she would run right into the arms of the former.

Liz reached New Mexico's Las Vegas and stopped at a mega store to purchase a chisel, hammer, and screwdriver. She hoped that among the three she could muscle the box into obedience.

Then she went to a public park. Lots of people there, yet she could find a private space. She found exactly what she was looking for, a picnic bench away from the playground areas. Too bad there wasn't a book on picking locks. She tried everything for an hour. One time a family of four sauntered by and looked at her strangely. Once she'd been part of a family like that. A lifetime ago.

With immense sadness, she returned to work with a vengeance. The lock still stubbornly resisted intrusion. Unfortunately, she was not a locksmith.

Locksmith.

She found a public telephone and phone book and looked under locksmiths. She located one who was open and with rising dread and excitement drove to his office.

He looked at her curiously as she presented the rusted box to him.

"It has memories," she said. "I buried it as a child, and now my family is selling the house. The key is long gone."

In three minutes he had the lock open. She paid him, nodded her thanks, and took the box. Once back in the car, she lifted the top and gazed at the contents.

Four envelopes. Each had the name of an herb from "Scarborough Fair." She picked one up and opened it. A key fell out. She picked it up and fingered it. She recognized it as a safe-deposit key. It had a number, but no other identifying marks. There was also a name: Burke.

The second envelope also contained a similar key with the name Baker, and the third with the name Tanner.

The fourth, the Rosemary envelope, held only a key. It was slightly different from the others.

There was nothing else. No letter. No cryptic words. That was what she'd wanted. Explanations.

Four safe-deposit boxes. Three names: Burke, Tanner, Baker. None of them matched the names of the three charged in the armored car robbery. But then neither had her mother's maiden name. *Her false one.*

There were even more questions now than before. Where were the safe-deposit boxes? How had they been paid for all these years?

Were the keys what the thief or assassin had been looking for?

Take them to the police! To the FBI!

She knew that was what she *should* do. Yet her mother had kept this secret even if it might have helped her.

Why?

Was it something that would put her mother in an even worse position than she was now? Something that might hurt her father or her sister's family?

It has to be the money.

What else? Money alone wouldn't have kept her mother silent. Money had never meant much to her. Her mind kept filtering through possibilities.

Who wanted the keys badly enough to kill for them?

She shivered, even in the hot desert air.

She'd never felt so alone.

She went over everything she knew. Keys. Boston. The *Chicago Tribune*, which had interested Caleb, but it didn't help her much. Even if the keys were for boxes in Chicago, how could she find out which bank?

She was missing something. There had to be a thread somewhere. *If only Mom would wake.* If only there was someone she could trust.

If only Caleb was here.

He wasn't. And wouldn't be again.

There *was* Win Maynard. Her cousin. The man who'd told her he'd once been close to her mother. Perhaps he could help shed some light. But she had no intention of trusting him with what she had. What she knew.

At least one of the hit men had come from Boston.

Yet Winstead Maynard was a respected businessman and civic leader. He apparently was planning to run for the Senate. She would be safe enough.

Especially if someone knew she was going there. She could call Michael to accompany her, but after Caleb, she didn't trust Michael, either. Like Caleb, his presence had been way too convenient.

She took out her cell phone and called an airline, finding a flight out of Denver she could barely make. She learned the flight wasn't crowded so she didn't risk making a reservation.

She could leave her vehicle in the parking lot. Perhaps it would be discovered, perhaps not, but by that time she should be well on her way to Boston. If she could reach the city without anyone learning about her destination, she could surprise Maynard and judge him for herself. She could learn more about her grandfather and grandmother. Perhaps that would give her a lead to the safe-deposit boxes.

She started driving north. She would leave the pistol in the car and purchase some mace as soon as she reached Boston. The keys were another matter, altogether. Her mother had kept them hidden for decades. Liz had to protect them as well.

She drove through a small town and stopped at an old-fashioned general store with a little of everything. She bought a small sewing kit, complete with scissors; a pair of slacks, a blouse, and a decorative vest. She headed back up the road.

She drove through the night and reached the Denver airport at dawn. The flight she wanted was scheduled at eight. She attached the keys she'd discovered to her key ring and locked the revolver in the glove compartment.

She had an hour before flight time. She went inside. Very few people were there. She purchased a ticket for Boston under E. Connor and easily went through security. Then she went into a restroom, appropriated a stall, and sewed the keys into the hem on her vest. By the time she finished, it was boarding time. She grabbed a cup of coffee and a cinnamon roll, boarded the plane, and collapsed in a seat. She closed her eyes, but even here, she couldn't escape her mind's image of Caleb. The wound was just as raw as it had been hours earlier.

She tried anger to plaster over it, but she was angered out.

She just felt a terrible, terrible sadness and loss as the plane rolled down the runway.

chapter twenty-four

Caleb paced the ticket area of the Albuquerque airport, his cell phone to his ear. "Dammit, Miguel, I have to know where she's gone."

"She apparently doesn't want you to know."

"You're right. She's angry. But she's also in danger."

There had been a pause, then Miguel agreed to call the airlines and ask them to alert him if an Elizabeth Connor or E. Connor purchased a flight anywhere in the southwest. "You owe me a bunch of chips," he said.

"I realize that. I'll be yours for the asking."

"I'll hold you to that."

Caleb went to one of the coffee shops and waited impatiently. He could gamble and book a connecting flight to Boston. He was pretty sure that's where she had gone. But "pretty sure" wasn't good enough. She might well have found something that would lead her to some other place.

He was furious at himself for any number of reasons, right now for driving to Albuquerque to meet her at the airport. Damn, but he should have known it was only a ploy.

But he'd been desperate. Grasping at any clue. And when Miguel had reported she'd made a reservation from Albuquerque to Chicago, he'd grabbed at it like a drowning man grabbed a rope.

She never appeared. He'd waited until the flight closed.

She was probably trying not only to mislead him but anyone else who might have an interest in her.

He'd immediately called Miguel and asked him to continue checking. Asking the sheriff for help was becoming a very bad habit.

He tried Liz's father.

Connor was short and to the point.

"Neither my daughter nor I have any interest in talking to you." Then he hung up. His voice had been icier than a glacier. Caleb had no chance to explain. Even if he had a good explanation.

Dammit, she was a walking target, and she had little experience in eluding an experienced assassin. And that was exactly what the assailant at the hospital had been.

He figured she had found something, or she probably would have replanted the herbs and put the tools back in place. Or had she been disrupted by Gallagher before she found anything and just fled?

What was she thinking now?

One thing for sure, she wouldn't trust him again. Not about anything, and if she *had* found something, she would try to throw him off track. So she'd probably gone in the opposite direction of the airport.

He knew that was what *he* would do. Draw any potential tail to one place, while disappearing in another.

If he thought of that, who else might?

He hoped to God not many. He knew her. Knew her determination. Her loyalty to her family. She was determined to seek out answers. Where did she believe those answers were? Chicago? She'd wanted him to think that.

He kept going back to Boston. Boston was where her mother's family lived, where everything had started. He'd checked flights. There were no more flights connecting to Boston tonight.

He could be wrong. He couldn't take the chance. She seemed to be a walking target for some reason. It was his fault she was going it alone. He didn't intend to see anyone else die because of his stupidity.

He checked on the availability of flights from Albuquerque to Denver and Las Vegas in the event that Miguel found something, then checked with Miguel again. Still no word from any airline.

In desperation he decided to go by the hospital where Liz's mother was being held. There was no change in her condition, but he heard from one of the marshals guarding her that the officer who had been with her during the attack had disappeared.

Then he went in the visiting room, glancing through the windows to see Steve Connor sitting there. The principal was reading a book, or trying to read. He wasn't turning pages. He came to his feet immediately as Caleb entered.

"You're not wanted here," he said with cold eyes. "I thought I made that clear."

"You did, sir," Caleb replied. "But Liz could be in a great deal of danger."

Connor frowned at him. "Do you really give a damn?"

"Yes," he said simply.

"She doesn't believe that," Connor said.

"I don't expect she does."

"Why did you lie to her?"

"I didn't think you, and she, would give me information if I didn't," Caleb admitted.

"But you continued to lie, even as she trusted you."

Caleb had no explanation. He'd been justifying his silence to himself, but now he realized how cowardly—and damaging—it had been. He wasn't going to justify it now.

After a short silence, Steve Connor pressed on. "Exactly what are you after?"

"It was the truth."

"Now that's ironic," Connor said. "Would you recognize it if you saw it?"

It was a body blow, more so because he had every reason to say it.

Connor glared at him for a moment, then a puzzled look came into his face. "You said *was*. It *was* the truth."

"I suppose it still is," Connor said. No more lying now. "I've been trying to find it for years. But Liz is more important now. Her safety is."

"I don't like people who hurt my daughter," Connor said. "You hurt her about as badly as anyone could. You may have saved my wife, and I'm grateful for that, but I'm not going to help you find Liz." He paused, then added, "She doesn't forgive easily. She seldom gets angry, but you don't betray my Liz and get away without bruises."

"Right now all I want is to see her safe."

"I can't help you. She didn't tell me anything. Probably afraid I would try to convince her not to do whatever she's going to do."

"Would you have tried to stop her?"

"You don't stop a runaway train, and that's what Liz is when she gets an idea in her head."

"Any idea where she might go? Any special friend?"

Connor shook his head, his manner still icy.

Caleb started for the door, then turned. "I'm sorry," he said. He couldn't remember when he'd last said the words. But he meant it. He'd never meant anything more.

He found a motel near the airport. He tried to sleep, but all he knew was how lonely the bed was, how empty his arms were. And how damned scared he was for her. He also was on edge, waiting for a call from Miguel, and returned to the airport at six. He wanted to be there in case Miguel found something.

She could be headed by car to somewhere else altogether.

He suppressed the thought. Every instinct told him she was headed to Boston.

Miguel called his cell phone. "An E. Connor is booked on an eight a.m. flight out of Denver. She's going to Boston."

"Flight number?"

Miguel gave it to him. "You realize she might not get on that flight, either."

"Can you let me know if she boards?"

"I will."

Caleb found a seat on an 8:20 a.m. flight to Chicago, then Boston. He barely made it through security in time to board.

Just as he was taking a seat, Miguel called. "She's on the flight."

Caleb knew if Miguel found her, others could as well. He started praying he wouldn't be too late.

CHICAGO

Greg Tanner arrived at the Chicago airport with butterflies flitting in his stomach.

He'd been here in 1968 during the Democratic Convention when the city exploded. He'd been arrested then. He'd been a freshman, and it had been an experience that had hardened his resolve to do whatever he could to stop the war. He hadn't been alone.

He wished he could go back to those days. There had been an innocence and passion that finally made his life seem important. He'd felt he could make a difference. And Sarah Jane? He'd carried a torch for her from the day Tony had asked him to bring her to a meeting.

But the moment she'd met Tony, he'd realized he couldn't compete with Tony's charisma. He'd watched helplessly as Tony had romanced her, seduced her. Seduced them all.

It hadn't taken long after the robbery before they all realized Tony had used them.

Their lives had been ruined. Tony's hadn't. Somehow he had escaped being caught that morning. Escaped and survived and even prospered. Through the Internet, Greg had followed him these past thirty-plus years, and resentment had nearly killed him. He hated Tony as he had never hated anyone. Partially because of his own ruined life, but mostly because of what Tony had done to Sarah Jane, who'd trusted him completely. She'd been completely shattered after the robbery.

He hadn't wanted to leave her, but the majority view of their small group was that they should separate. They'd taken instruction on how to build new identities. Together they had gone to a cemetery and found graves of children who had died in infancy. Sarah Jane had cried silently through the process. It was the worse kind of theft, she said, stealing the identity of an innocent child to protect themselves. She'd wanted to turn herself in, but he and the others had convinced her it could lead to their arrests as well. And what would it do to her family?

In the end, she'd agreed.

And then there was the money.

None of them, except perhaps for Jacob, had wanted anything to do with the money. He had argued with them, said it was clean and they should split it. But three of them said no. It was blood money. And someday it might be used for bargaining purposes if any of them were caught.

Bargaining for life in prison. As opposed to the death penalty for a crime they'd never anticipated.

Greg knew no one would believe them. Antiwar protestors were not the favorite people among law enforcement.

They'd compromised. Each would take ten thousand dollars. The rest was placed in three safe-deposit boxes. They would use their new names, but Sarah Jane would keep the keys. They all trusted her more than they trusted each other.

Then if they ever needed to contact each other, they would put an advertisement in the *Chicago Tribune*. They had taken their ten thousand dollars and separated. Although they had each other's last names, they didn't discuss where they were heading. It would have been all but impossible to find each other.

Except for the newspaper.

Now someone had something to say. Greg didn't know if it was the money or simply that they all needed new identities. He did know that if Sarah Jane had talked, the Feds would soon be on their trails. It would be easy enough to find all the Tanners who'd subscribed to the *Tribune*. But the pressure on her to reveal what she knew would be tremendous.

Keep the faith. He'd made that pledge years ago. He'd kept it. He couldn't ignore the advertisement now, though he didn't want any of the money. Not now. Not ever.

He picked up a copy of the *Chicago Tribune*. The ad was still there.

"Straw Dogs memorabilia wanted!"

He wondered if anyone else would appear. At least either Terry Colby or Jacob were alive, or the ad wouldn't be there. And Sarah Jane? He ached for her, for the frightened and heartsick girl she'd been. A principal's wife now. A husband who, according to the newspapers, was standing beside her.

Good for her.

He found a taxi and asked to be taken to a hotel he'd already researched on the computer. Tonight he would walk the neighborhood that four desperate, scared kids had stayed in for three terrifying weeks. He would stake out the location where they'd all agreed to meet. He would learn soon enough if they had been betrayed.

The flight to Boston was a long one, particularly when Liz was endlessly debating with herself whether she had done a very foolish thing. She'd been able to nap on and off, but each time woke to a kind of panic.

She was fleeing. As her mother had fled three decades earlier. She didn't carry the guilt that her mother must have carried, but she did carry fear and disillusionment.

She couldn't sleep. She kept reviewing the past several days, rerunning in her mind every word Caleb had said to her, every clue she'd found. There were so few: Scarborough Fair and four safe-deposit box keys. Perhaps the *Chicago Tribune*.

Was it enough? And when she ran out of money? She winced at costs now going on the credit card. They needed money for her mother's attorneys, and she needed a reserve for the business.

She was running to the only person who knew her mother before the armed robbery had occurred. To the person who had offered help.

Would that apple be as poisoned as others had been?

Would she even know? She'd always been so sure she was a good judge of character.

Wrong! Caleb Adams proved that.

And this time it might not only be her heart that was endangered. She knew very well it might be her life.

• • •

During his layover in Chicago, Caleb called his old partner and told him what had happened. Not all of it. Not that he had slept with the daughter of the woman he'd always believed responsible for his father's death. Nor the fact that he had kept his relationship to one of the guards secret all these years.

That would be another difficult confession.

Cam picked up. "Caleb?"

Caleb didn't waste words. "The daughter of Sarah Jane Maynard is headed to Boston. There's been at least two attempts of her life, and I think she's in danger. Can you meet the plane, or hire someone you trust to do it? Just stay with her. Don't let her out of your sight."

"When will she arrive?"

"About two hours." He gave the flight number and arrival time. "She's pretty. Auburn hair that's shoulder length. Dark blue eyes. Early thirties. Slender."

"I'll have someone there. And Caleb, I located a copy of her grandfather's will."

"And?"

"Half of his fortune was left in a trust for his daughter or her heirs. The other half went to his nephew, Win Maynard."

"Who's the trustee?"

"Guess."

"Maynard?"

"Right on."

"His attorney didn't mention that to Liz."

"Maybe he didn't know. Or maybe he was waiting to see what happened with the charges." Cam was silent a moment, then added, "There's never been a breath of scandal around him. He gives away more money than what probably is in the trust. He's more than quadrupled the assets of Maynard Industries since he took over. He doesn't need the money. Certainly he wouldn't risk any scandal now he intends to run for the Senate."

"That's a definite?"

"I'm told so."

"Just make sure she's safe for the moment."

"It'll cost you to get a PI."

"Whatever it takes. If you need a retainer, I'll give it to you as soon as I arrive. I'll be about three hours behind her."

"I'll take care of it."

"And Cam? She might not like being protected."

"Is there anything else I should know?" Cam said wryly.

There was. There was a lot. But not on the phone. "Thanks," he said, and cut the connection.

He tried to connect the dots. Maynard. A trust fund. And Michael Gallagher, who always seemed to be on hand.

Who stands to gain? The question he'd been asking throughout this.

And Liz was walking right into their arms.

chapter twenty-five

Tony scratched the stubble on his face and ran his fingers through the wig he wore. They smelled of alcohol he'd spilled on clothes he purchased from a thrift shop. It wasn't a perfect disguise, but it was all he could get together in two days.

Thirty-four years. That's how long he'd waited to get his due.

He felt his cell phone vibrate in his pocket, but he resisted the temptation to answer. It wouldn't do to have anyone see a bum talking on a cell phone. A rental car—one of the cheap older cars—was parked on the street in a metered spot. He'd wandered over there several times, leaning on it as he put coins in the meter.

Who would turn up?

No one but Jacob had any idea that he knew about the ad. None of them would know he was the one who placed it.

Jacob Terrell had surfaced ten years earlier, threatening Tony with exposure. Jacob had said he was in dire need of money, that he had borrowed some money from thugs in Miami. He'd threatened to reveal Tony's part in the robbery if he didn't pay him a hundred thousand dollars.

Tony had refused, until Jacob had dropped clues about

the money. The scheme he'd described was bizarre enough
to be true.

Jacob had tantalized him over the years, dropping more
hints to get more money. Most of the money from the robbery was still intact in a bank in Chicago. He'd also said
there had been safeguards, so no one person could claim it.
Tony wasn't at all sure he believed everything, but from
what he knew of the four, the tale rang true.

There were three safe-deposit boxes, each taken out by
one of the three men in the last name they'd adopted. Sarah
Jane had the keys. She'd pledged that if anything ever happened to her, they could find the keys by looking for *Straw
Dogs* and "Scarborough Fair" where she lived.

He'd even mentioned a scheme to get the remaining
members together in the event of an emergency. An ad in
the Chicago paper. *Straw Dogs* was the key.

Tony hadn't understood the meaning of either until he
started searching shortly after the visit. *Straw Dogs* was a
violent film about a man who hated violence yet became
the epitome of violence. He liked the film. The other reference hadn't been so easy. "Scarborough Fair." There had
been far too many references, most of which involved the
song of that name, until he limited his search to Chicago.
Then he found a community called Scarborough.

He hadn't gotten any further. Jacob had, cannily
enough, withheld just enough information to keep himself
safe before disappearing once more, taking the rest of the
secret with him.

He'd tried the advertisement several times, but no one
appeared. He'd come to believe that Jacob had lied to him
about that, but after Sarah Jane's arrest, he'd tried the ad
again, and one of them appeared. He'd followed him,
killed him, and stolen his identification, including a sample of his handwriting on the driver's license. That was Jeff
Baker, once Terry Colby.

One down. Two to go. He was still in the game. It felt
good. Powerful. He had several good people searching for
those keys. He suspected Jacob might be doing the same.

He was a hell of a lot smarter than Jacob. He would get

that money and rid himself of four people who knew that he'd fired the fatal shots that March day.

He glanced to the left, and one man caught his attention. Dressed in a rumpled tweed jacket and blue jeans, he was looking around as if afraid of being watched. The face looked older than he expected, but he recognized the features, even the lanky build as the figure stared at what used to be a coffee shop. Stuart Marshall.

The street was full of lunch crowd pedestrians. He couldn't approach him here. Tony didn't move, pretended he was snoozing. He waited until Marshall walked away.

Tony rolled to his feet and stumbled to his car, no longer worried if someone might wonder how someone like him had a car. Inside, he pulled off his wig and pulled off his alcohol-sodden jacket. Then he slowly followed Marshall.

BOSTON

Win Maynard picked up his cell phone. He recognized the caller ID number.

"Maynard," he answered curtly.

"Michael," his attorney identified himself as he always did. "I thought you should know that Liz Connor is on her way to Boston. Probably to see you."

"Why?"

"I don't know. I told her about Caleb Adams. She deserved to know. She wasn't happy. In effect, she told me to go away. I thought I could follow her, but she just disappeared. A police source was able to locate her on a flight that should arrive around three this afternoon."

He paused, then added, "Adams is booked on a later one."

Win closed his eyes. Adams had been a threat for years. He'd thought, hoped, the detective's forced retirement would put an end to his persistent questions.

"She doesn't trust anyone now. And rightfully so." Michael paused, then added, "You can't risk anything happening to her in Boston."

The warning was implicit. No doubt Michael thought

he might be responsible for the mayhem in New Mexico. Unfortunately, Win couldn't enlighten him.

"Nothing will," he assured Michael.

"Good. I'll be in your office as soon as I get back."

The line clicked off. It was a warning. A warning from his protégé. From his employee.

He felt like he'd been kicked in the stomach. If Elizabeth probed very deeply, she would discover what he'd covered all these years. His reputation would be destroyed, probably along with the business. Prison was a very real possibility.

Michael was right. Nothing could happen to Elizabeth Connor while she was in Boston. But Tony, damn it, was a loose cannon. He was desperate, and a desperate man was the most dangerous kind alive.

He tried to call Tony. No one answered. Hell, he didn't even know where Tony was, and he couldn't afford to leave a message.

He swore long and hard.

CHICAGO

It had been easy. Too easy. Just as he had followed Colby two days earlier, Tony managed to keep Stuart Marshall in view all the way back to his hotel.

As Marshall parked in the large parking lot, Tony pulled on a pair of rubber gloves and purposely nicked Marshall's car. He jumped out and surprised his own disciple as he was getting out of the car, forcing him back in before hitting him in the back of his head with his gun. He then pushed Marshall to the passenger side before moving his vehicle and getting into Marshall's.

He knew exactly where he wanted to go, the same place he'd taken Colby. He'd scouted out the city when he'd arrived three days earlier. Tony knew everything there was to know about Win Maynard, had followed his business for years. One of those businesses had been an auto parts factory that soon became a casualty of outsourcing. The closing had been big news at the time.

Now Tony was consciously leading a trail to his nemesis, the man who he'd always hated, who had tried to use him, then tried, unsuccessfully, to discard him.

He'd broken the lock two days ago and replaced it with one of his own. There was no security guard, but then why should there be? The building had been stripped of anything with value, and it was too far from downtown—and food—to attract vagrants. The few businesses surrounding it were also closed, obvious casualties of the plant closing. The building itself was outdated, the windows broken and trashed by unhappy ex-employees. Tony suspected Win was waiting for a good offer for the land.

He opened the gate and drove inside, then locked it again. He then drove around to the back.

Stuart Marshall moaned, started to move.

Tony stopped the car, took a knife he'd purchased after his flight, along with the gun, and cut off a piece of Marshall's shirt, then bound his hands behind him.

He went through Marshall's pockets, taking his wallet out and flipping through it. He slipped out the driver's license. Greg Tanner. He continued his search through every slot. One credit card. An auto insurance card. He kept looking and finally found a folded piece of paper deep in one of the slots. He slid it out. A number: 3610. He then helped himself to nearly eight hundred dollars in cash.

He glanced at the man he'd known as Stuart Marshall. Blood trickled down the side of his head, and his eyes had the trapped look of a man who knew what was coming.

"You didn't really think you could run out on me, did you?" Tony asked.

"No one was to be hurt," Marshall defended himself.

"Surely you weren't that stupid," Tony said. "Where's Jacob?"

"I don't know. I haven't seen him in more than thirty years."

"But you would tell me if you had?"

"No," Marshall said defiantly.

"Your loyalty is misplaced. He told me about you. About the *Chicago Tribune*."

"You placed the ad?"

"I did."

"What do you want from me?"

"He left out a few details. Like the box numbers."

"I only know mine."

"And that is . . ."

Marshall didn't say anything.

Tony took the keys from the ignition and got out of the car. He went to the other side, opened the door, and pointed the gun at Marshall.

"Get out."

The phone in his pocket started vibrating again.

Marshall stumbled out, and Tony directed him inside through an unlocked door into the factory. He picked up a propane lantern he'd left near the door, and the beam cut the darkness.

"Keep going," he ordered. "Straight ahead."

Marshall stumbled, and Tony waited for him to regain his balance, then directed him through a cavernous room to several offices. A strong odor wafted from one of them.

Marshall turned around. Faced him.

"The bank?" he asked. "Where is the bank?"

Marshall blinked rapidly but said nothing.

Tony aimed the gun at his knee and fired.

Marshall screamed in pain and fell. "Scarborough," he screamed.

"And the bank?"

"Union Bank."

"Thank you." Tony lifted the barrel of the gun slightly and pulled the trigger. A hole appeared in Marshall's forehead as he slumped over.

Tony rolled the body into one of the offices and closed the door.

He didn't know when someone would find the bodies, but he didn't think it would be any time soon. When they did, though, Win Maynard would face questions, publicity. Perhaps enough to derail his life.

He took the bloody gloves off and put on a clean pair, left the building, and got back into the car.

Two down. Two who could link him with a murder. Two whose deaths could provide enough money to enable him to live comfortably in any number of countries.

He had two of the names, two of the signatures necessary to retrieve the stolen money. He could probably go to
the banks and claim he'd lost the keys. It would be easy
enough to doctor the driver's licenses, but having the keys
in hand would prevent any undue attention. And he wanted
the entire amount, not just two thirds of it.

He drove out onto the main road. He drove straight
back to the hotel, parked in a spot several aisles away from
his own car, and carefully wiped every spot he'd touched.

Once in his car, he checked his cell phone. One message.

He listened to it. And smiled.

Liz Connor had obviously found something. She was on
her way to Boston.

Now he had to lure her to Chicago. Jacob—alias Evan
Burke—would have to wait.

As Liz left the plane, she looked around the gate. Since
9/11, there were no greeters—relatives, friends, limousine
drivers—at the gate. She hurried down the concourse and
out the exit gates. No luggage to fetch.

She felt naked with her small duffel. Her gaze never
stopped moving as she headed toward the taxi stand. Was
there any special interest in her? Any individual that appeared more than once?

She'd already checked the address of Maynard Industries. Perhaps her cousin wasn't in the city. Or she
wouldn't be admitted. Any number of scenarios crossed
her mind, but she had come this far. She had no intention
of retreating. She needed answers.

She was going out the door when she saw a man hurrying after her. She thought she had seen him earlier, when
she first passed through the gate to the transportation area.

His gaze immediately skittered away.

She looked around, saw a policeman, and decided to
confront whoever it was in the presence of the law.

She went up to the man. Her eyes went down to hands
that carried no luggage. "Are you following me?" she challenged him.

He gave her a rueful smile. He started to deny it, then shrugged. "I'm Abe Cannon. A private investigator," he said. "Apparently not a great one, to be spotted so easily. I was hired to look out for you."

"Who hired you?"

"A police detective. It's all aboveboard," he said, taking out his wallet and showing his license. "I'm an ex-cop myself."

"That doesn't commend you," she replied sharply. "My experience with ex-cops has not been good."

"I'm sorry," he said and sounded as if he really was. "But I was told your life might be in danger."

"Who employed you?"

"Cam Douglas. He's a detective in homicide. You can call him and check."

She remembered the name. Caleb had mentioned it. She took out her cell phone. "The number?"

He looked nonplussed, then gave her a number.

She dialed the number.

"Douglas," came the crisp voice.

She hung up. "What's the number of the Boston Police Department?"

He didn't hesitate before giving it to her.

She called that number.

She received a disembodied voice from the Boston Police Department with options. She waited, then went through the steps and finally got to Detective Douglas.

She hung up again. She knew what she wanted to know. That much, at least, was true.

She glanced up at the man standing next to her. He was regarding her with a glint of admiration in his eyes.

"Since you seem determined to do your job, I'll make it easy for you. I'm going to a hotel, then to Maynard Industries in the morning," she said.

"I'll drive you."

She tried to kill him with a glance. "I'm taking a taxi."

"I'll follow."

"You do what you like. Just keep out of my way." She paused, then added, "You can tell Mr. Adams I don't need or want his help."

"I don't know a Mr. Adams, but I'll pass the word on."

She stared at him. "I can't stop you," she said. "But I won't cooperate with you."

She got into the taxi line, ignoring him as he stepped in line behind her. When her turn came, she had a five dollar bill out. She folded it into the hand of the man directing the taxi line. "The man behind me is following me. Could you delay him? Just for a moment?"

She got into the taxi and looked back. No taxi was pulling out after them, and Abe Cannon was arguing furiously with the recipient of her five dollar bill. She didn't need Abe Cannon. Nor the man who'd hired him. She was so buffeted by emotions she didn't know who to trust and who not to. She could only go on instinct, and that had already betrayed her.

She looked at her watch. It was nearly four. Sunday. She thought about calling Win Maynard at home, but she didn't want to do that. She wanted to be in a public place. In offices with dozens of people around her.

Her cousin.

A blood relation she hadn't even known existed until last week.

"Where to, miss?" the driver asked.

She asked for suggestions for a hotel close to her uncle's address, chose one, then asked him if he knew a gun shop.

"Not on Sunday. All closed. Besides, you gotta have a license," he said. "There's a waiting period."

"I know," she said. "I want to get pepper spray."

"Can't do it. Not in Boston. Need a permit for that, too."

"Then a drugstore."

"Cost ya extra."

"I understand." She settled back in her seat. It started raining. The cab was warm, steaming. She felt dirty and sweaty and very much alone. She looked back. There were a number of cabs streaming out from the airport. Was the private detective in one? Or someone else?

She wanted Caleb, darn it. *Stupid name. Caleb.*

And then she thought of a young boy waiting for his father. Hearing of his death.

Because of her mother.

A tear rolled down her face, and she wiped it away with her hand.

Ten minutes later, they arrived at a drugstore. "I'll wait out here," the taxi driver said.

She went inside and made several purchases, including a small can of hair spray. It could be as effective as pepper spray.

She asked questions as they crossed the city. Her mother had grown up here, and she tried to see it through those eyes. But she couldn't. Her emotions were too strong.

Liz heard the static of a car radio, then a query about the passenger.

"Dropped her off ten minutes ago," he said and gave the name of a hotel.

When he switched the radio off, he looked back at her. "Don't know what kind of trouble you're in, but they're not getting any help from me."

She was flooded with gratitude. "Can you get in trouble about this?"

"Not unless you tell them I lied."

He pulled up at a hotel. She saw another down the street.

"This looks fine," she said. "Thank you." She noticed it wasn't the one he mentioned.

"No problem."

She looked at the meter and gave him a big tip.

He took out a card. "You need another ride, miss, you call me."

"I'll do that," she said, and scrambled out the side of the cab. It was nearly six now, and surprisingly she was starving. She went into the hotel, out a side door, and headed toward the second hotel.

She stopped at a sandwich shop and ate, then checked into the second hotel under a false name. She'd been stranded by a canceled plane, she said, and her luggage was gone. She winced as she paid for a night's stay in cash. She was going to need more money.

Wearily she entered her room, made sure all the locks were in place, then checked her cell phone. No more calls from Caleb. Nor one from her father.

She called him, felt a familiar comfort at the sound of his voice. "Just wanted to let you know I'm okay," she said. "How's Mom?"

"Still in the coma. Where are you?"

"Boston."

Silence.

"I want to meet Mr. Maynard. He might know something."

"Dammit, Sport. He might also be involved."

"He's eminently respectable."

"I've heard of eminently respectable people committing murder."

Like her mother.

She knew he hadn't meant that, but a sudden silence made her realize he had meant it. They were both wandering in unfamiliar territory and confronted with truths that neither had entirely accepted.

She got into bed and realized suddenly how exhausted she was.

She turned on the television to a movie. It dulled the loneliness as her eyes closed.

Perhaps tomorrow she would solve a piece of the mystery.

Maynard finally reached Tony.

"Elizabeth Connor is on her way here."

"I know."

"How?"

"I have sources, too."

"I should have known. Damn it, Tony, you can ruin everything. I just wanted her scared. Now you're turning Santa Fe into a war zone. You're taking chances that affect me."

"I don't care what you want," Tony said.

Fear and anger knotted inside him. Having anything to do with Tony had been Win's first mistake. The second had been trusting him one more time to get rid of a problem. Instead, everything was much worse.

If only Michael Gallagher had been able to get to Sarah Jane before Tony had sicced his hired dogs on her.

And now Elizabeth Connor was on her way here, most likely to see him. She would want answers.

"What do I tell her?"

"Suggest she come to Chicago."

"Why?"

"Just do it. Find a way. Tell her Sarah Jane mentioned a café in the Scarborough area, a place called Sancha's."

"Why?"

"You really don't want to know, Maynard."

The phone went dead.

Caleb arrived in Boston at five p.m. and was met by his old partner at the gate.

"My guy lost her."

Caleb muttered under his breath, and Cam winced.

"You didn't tell us she was great at ducking a tail."

"How did she do it?"

"Hell if I know. My guy met her. She told him he could tell you to forget it and grabbed a cab. He thought he could find her by calling the cab company. But she wasn't at the hotel the driver said he took her to."

"You sound as if you doubt the driver."

"It took him a little too long to return to service," he said. "He said he went to eat, but he was evasive."

"People like her," Caleb said.

"They say opposites attract," Cam replied.

"Right now she's not attracted to me at all."

"Do you want to tell me why?"

"I lied to her."

"Men often lie to women."

"Look, can we skip this and try to find her?"

"Abe Cannon's looking for her."

"Sorry, my faith in him is gone."

"If we can't find her, neither can the bad guys."

Cam had a point. *Unless* someone knew what flight she was on. They could be watching at pickup, cell phone someone on the exit road to follow.

"She could be going to Maynard's home."

"As soon as Cannon realized he'd lost her, he sent someone over there to watch. If she comes or goes, we'll know about it." He hesitated. "Is there anyone she trusts now?"

"Her father, but I don't know how much he'll tell me."

"Would he talk to me?"

"I doubt it."

They walked out to where Cam had parked his car. It was dark and rainy. Steaming, really. He remembered that late summer heat.

After they were both inside, Cam turned to him. "I think it's time you tell me everything," he said.

Caleb nodded. Nothing mattered now except Liz's safety.

By the time they reached the police department, and Cam's office, his old partner was grim. "Why didn't you ever tell me?"

"Because you would be duty bound to tell the commander, and they wouldn't let me within a mile of the case."

"In other words, you didn't trust me."

"No, I just wasn't going to put you in that position."

"And she knows you're the son of one of the guards?"

"Yes. Maynard's attorney told her. She left shortly after he did. Her father wouldn't talk to me. She doesn't answer my calls."

"And you care about that?"

"There have been at least two attempts on her life, along with arson on her house. Someone wanted something, and from the way the garden was strewn about, she might have found whatever it is. Which puts her in even more danger.

"Let's find that cabdriver," Cam said, picking up the phone.

chapter twenty-six

Liz didn't pause in front of the imposing Maynard Industries Building but found a side entrance and went right in. She wanted to meet Winstead Maynard. She wanted answers to her questions.

She glanced around for any lurking figures. All she saw were people hurrying along, most of them—men and women—dressed in suits and carrying briefcases. She had washed out her clothes last night and used the hair dryer to finish the drying process, but she felt out of place in her slacks, blouse, and vest. And carrying her duffel.

But the duffel contained what little she had, and she couldn't continue to buy new clothes wherever she went. She had no intention of returning to the hotel.

Then she glimpsed Caleb, standing in the lobby, glancing in the faces of those who came through the front door.

Her heart thudded, her legs nearly buckled under her, yet she managed to duck into an elevator. She had Maynard's card, tucked in her wallet from the day that Michael Gallagher had given it to her. She pressed the button, then leaned against the wall of the elevator.

Maynard didn't know she was coming. Or perhaps he did.

She hadn't thrown off Caleb as she'd hoped. And if Caleb knew where she had gone, then others might, as well.

She might have been very foolish coming here today,

but at this moment she didn't trust anyone but herself to discover the truth. She didn't even trust herself. There was too much confusion; her judgment had been faulty on several fronts.

Who stands to benefit?

That had been Caleb's question. But was it meant to lead her to a certain conclusion? Had he been intent on proving her mother's guilt? Or on finding the others charged at the expense of her mother?

And Michael Gallagher? What interest had he in being at her office in Santa Fe in the very early hours of morning, and why did he feel it necessary to expose Caleb?

She'd always hated lies, and now she was trapped in them, like a calf wrapped in barbed wire. The more she tried to free herself, the more entangled she became.

The elevator opened to a reception area. She walked up to the receptionist, hoping that Maynard would be in. "Ms. Connor to see Mr. Maynard," she said.

"You have an appointment?"

"No, but he has asked to see me." She presented the card Michael had given her.

The young woman regarded her with skepticism but picked up the phone and punched a number. "There's a Ms. Connor to see you. She doesn't have an appointment." The woman listened, then turned back to her and nodded toward the double doors across the hall. "Mr. Maynard will see you."

Liz opened the double doors to a large reception area, and yet another woman at her desk. This one was older, probably in her late forties. She gave Liz a smile. "He'll be with you in a moment. Would you like a cup of coffee?"

"Yes, thanks." She needed something to do with her hands. "Just black, please."

The woman disappeared through a side door and returned with a large cup. Just as the cup was thrust in her hands, the door opened, and a tall man approached her, a smile on his face.

Win Maynard was a handsome man with salt-and-pepper hair, a beautifully tailored suit on what looked like a well-toned body. From her research, she knew he was sixty-one, but he looked younger and had a smile that was contagious. Her first impulse was to smile back at him.

She resisted. She didn't know his motives. Not yet.

She did offer her hand, though. He had one of those warm, firm handshakes. "I'm glad to meet you," he said simply. "I don't have that much family left." Then he led her into his office.

She was surprised. She had expected a large, masculine, wood-paneled office. Though spacious and, indeed, wood paneled, his was comfortable but modest for a CEO of a multinational company. A framed photo on his desk showed a pretty woman and two pretty young ladies. The desk was covered by neatly stacked papers, and newspapers sat on a table next to a sofa.

Instead of going to his desk, he led her to two large upholstered chairs. She knew what he was doing; she'd done it many times with potential clients: establishing an intimacy. She understood why he was being urged to run for the Senate. There was a warmth and charisma about him. But she also knew he was regarded as a tough—some said ruthless—business competitor.

"Tell me about you," he said. "How you're holding up. Michael's kept me posted. He said you're really exceptional." He paused. "I'm sorry about your mother."

"How well did you know her?"

"Very well. We were more brother and sister than cousins. She was an only child, and so was I. Both our fathers were workaholics."

"Tell me about her."

"She was lonely. We both were. Her mother drank a lot, and she hated that. I had finished Harvard and was working at a bank."

She remembered reading about that in his bio. She wondered briefly why he hadn't worked for her grandfather then, but it wasn't all that important.

"How did she get involved with that group?"

"Loneliness, I think. And she always wanted to improve things. She used to work holidays at food kitchens and volunteered at work shelters. She was active in any number of protests and even tried to go south for a demonstration. My uncle stopped that. It drove him crazy. He was conservative, a strong believer in the sanctity of government. The more he tried to stop her, the deeper she became involved. I tried to talk to her about it but . . ."

His voice trailed off.

"Did you know anything about the group responsible for the robbery?"

"Hell no," he said emphatically. "I knew she was taking part in campus protests. She was even arrested during a sit-in, which grounded her for a month. But anything violent? It just wasn't in her."

"You didn't know any others in the group, then?"

"No. But then I was working twelve hours a day. I didn't see her at all after Christmas."

She studied his face, his eyes. She wanted to find something duplicitous there. But she found only regret. Still, he was a politician and a very well-known businessman. She suspected some of the CEOs charged with defrauding their companies were equally as charismatic.

"How's your mother doing?" he asked.

"Didn't Mr. Gallagher tell you?"

"He said she was in a coma. I thought you might have an update."

"I don't."

"I'm sorry," he said.

"I don't suppose this is helping your political career."

A glint of amusement shone in his eyes. "You've inherited her forthrightness," he said. "She always spoke her mind."

She hadn't to her family. That sharp pain that hadn't gone away since she first came to believe at least part of the charges deepened.

"I suppose you know from Mr. Gallagher that there have been attacks on her, on me, on my sister's family."

He nodded.

"Do you have any idea why?"

"Only the most obvious ones. She may know where the others are, and they—one or more—want to make sure she doesn't tell the authorities."

"But why me?"

"A threat, perhaps."

"But if she told authorities, there would be no more reason to hurt me or our family."

He was silent. "I don't know, Elizabeth."

"Liz. Everyone calls me Liz."

"Liz, then. I don't know. I wish I did."

"And the money," she added. "No one seems to know what happened to the money."

"Didn't she say anything to you about that?"

"She wouldn't see us. I would have thought Mr. Gallagher told you that as well."

She didn't know why she continued to use the Mr. before his name. She'd been on a first name basis with him since he saved her at her office. But his showing up on her doorstep with the news about Caleb had bothered her. She was grateful for the knowledge, if gratitude was the word. She needed to know. Still, she suspected his motives in telling her.

"He did, but I thought . . ."

"I wanted to thank you for offering to help."

Something flickered in his eyes for only a second. "I wanted to talk to you about that. If you hadn't come, I would have flown out there. I wasn't only trying to help. Your grandfather left funds in a trust for Sara Jane. It will go to her now."

"Mr. Gallagher *didn't* tell us about that."

"That's why he gave you my card, why I wanted you to come here. I didn't want to talk about it over the phone. Michael doesn't have the details of the trust. But the help would have been there, anyway," he added.

Who would benefit?

"How much?" she asked.

"Part of it is in stock," he said. "I can't tell you exactly, but it's probably around ten million."

Her jaw dropped. "I beg your pardon."

"That's the round number. I'll have my accountant give you a complete accounting."

She blinked as her mind reeled. *Ten million?* So much money, and all she could think was how much legal help for her mother that could buy. "Who's the trustee?" she asked, her voice unsteady.

"Myself, and Harold Eakin. He's an attorney here in Boston."

"Why hasn't *he* gotten in touch with us?"

"He's been ill."

Convenient. But she wasn't ready to say as much now. She was still reeling from the news. Ten million dollars. It would buy some very good attorneys. She wondered exactly how long he was going to withhold the news.

And Michael hadn't said a word, either.

She told herself there might well be good reasons. Everything had happened so quickly. And it would have been very difficult to cover up a trust, in any event. But it added to her paranoia.

A paranoia that had every reason to exist. And flourish.

She needed to know two more things. "Did she ever go to Chicago, or have friends there?"

Again a flicker in his eyes gave him away. Chicago meant something to him.

But he shook his head. "No, not that I know of."

"What about Scarborough Fair?"

He looked completely blank. This time it seemed real.

"Thank you," she said, rising from the chair. She sensed he wouldn't give her anything else.

He rose with her. "I want to help," he said.

"I'm not sure anyone can help right now," she replied. "But thank you."

Michael walked in then. Without a knock. That told her a great deal.

"Hi," he said.

"I thought you were in Santa Fe."

"Nothing more I could do there."

"Are you following me, Mr. Gallagher?"

He looked surprised at the obvious assault. "Not deliberately. But when you left, there seemed no reason to stay."

"And how did you know I'd left?"

She didn't think she would ever see the unflappable Michael Gallagher taken by surprise, but he looked disconcerted. She looked at Maynard. "You really weren't surprised when I appeared at your door, either, were you?"

"I asked Michael to look after you. When he couldn't find you, he started checking airlines."

"I thought that was supposed to be private information." She knew it was probably easy enough for a skilled hacker to get into passenger lists, but more likely they used some kind of official pull.

It made her even angrier than she had been. She was tired of integrity being for sale, of private agendas, of deputies being killers, of no one being who they seemed to be, or who they should be.

"I was worried about you," Michael said simply.

"And trust funds."

She didn't miss the quick exchange of looks between Michael and his employer. So he had known.

She stared at him. "Damn you," she said and turned on her heel and left.

She stopped at the elevator. Caleb was probably still in the lobby. She thought about trying to avoid him, but to heck with that. She was too angry. She had ducked out before. She wouldn't give him the satisfaction of doing that again.

She punched the Down button.

Caleb had grown increasingly worried.

He hadn't seen her go into an elevator, but he felt she must be somewhere in the building. A knot formed in his gut. Cam had told him about the will, and the trust.

She might well have stepped from the frying pan into the fire. After searching faces for an hour, he found the Maynard Industries directory and went up in the elevator. He stepped out to find a receptionist.

She glanced over him, and he was glad he'd borrowed a razor from Cam. He gave her the closest thing to a smile he could imagine.

She smiled back.

"I was supposed to meet my girlfriend downstairs. She was coming up here. I'm afraid I might have missed her."

"Ms. Connor?"

He tried a wider smile and hoped he wasn't completely out of practice. "That's her."

"She's still in there."

"Thanks." He leaned over the desk. "Do me a favor. Don't tell her I was up here. She thinks I worry too much as it is."

"I wouldn't mind that," she said.

"She's an independent lady," he said. "I admire that. But a big city like Boston . . ."

"I won't say a word."

He went down to the first floor and stood against the wall opposite the elevators to wait for her. He could also keep an eye on the exit stairs.

Somehow he had to convince her to let him tail along. She had already proved she could lose him. He needed her cooperation to protect her. That was his interest now. His only interest.

But how to convince her of it?

The foot traffic slowed. Every time the elevator hit the twenty-seventh floor on the way down, he tensed.

The lights indicated it had stopped at that floor. He waited as the elevator stopped at three other floors on the way down, then spilled out its passengers on the ground floor.

Liz Connor was the first to leave. She stopped when she saw him, and he saw the fierce anger in her eyes. She didn't turn to go, though, and instead marched up to him.

"Go away," she said.

"I can't."

"Is it true?" she asked.

He didn't have to ask what she meant. "Yes," he said simply.

Her eyes were full of hurt, disillusionment, anger.

She slapped him so hard his ears rang.

Heads turned.

He just shrugged.

Averting their glances, the bystanders moved on.

"You do that very well," she said. "Shrug things off."

"I don't think I do anything very well," he admitted.

"You lie well."

God, the thrust hurt.

"I'm sorry. I didn't know you when it started and then . . . there didn't seem to be a good time."

She gave him a withering look.

Well deserved. "Look, Liz, I need to talk to you. At least let me buy you a cup of coffee. Ten minutes. No more."

"Why?"

"I want to try to explain."

"I don't want explanations. I wouldn't believe anything you said."

The elevator doors opened. She turned toward them and saw Michael Gallagher get out and stride toward them.

She closed her eyes for a moment. She looked as if she wanted to wish both of them away.

"Need help?" Gallagher said.

She opened her eyes. "No."

He didn't go away. Just stood there, looking from Caleb to her.

"Just what do you want, Mr. Gallagher?" No more Michael for her. She was too angry. "And why did you feel that Caleb was your problem?"

He glanced at Caleb. "Mr. Maynard made it clear that your interests were mine. I thought you should know."

"I would like to be alone with Mr. Adams," she said.

He glanced again at Caleb. "Are you sure I can't do anything?"

She shook her head. "I don't need anything from you, from my cousin, or from Mr. Adams," she said.

Caleb's cheek still stung from the slap, but the toneless quality in her voice caused him far more pain.

Michael Gallagher stood still for a moment, glanced at Caleb, then her. "You have my number. If you need anything . . ."

"I know. Call you. Don't wait."

He gave her that rueful grin of his and left. She turned back to Caleb.

"You lied to me."

"Yes."

"Why?"

"I want to find the others who were with your mother."

"And my mother? What about her?"

"At first, I wanted justice."

Her cheeks were red with anger, and her dark blue eyes might well have resembled a hurricane at sea. They were frothing with fury.

"Justice? Or revenge?" Every word was like an ice cube dropping in a glass.

"At first, I suppose you could call it revenge."

"At first?"

"Things changed," he said simply.

"But the lies didn't."

He didn't say anything. There was nothing to say. No defense. No justification.

"Was going to bed part of your plan?" she asked, uncaring if anyone overheard.

"God no, Liz." He took a step toward her, but she backed away.

"Don't come any closer."

He stilled.

"There was never a book," she stated as fact.

"No."

"First my mother," she said through clenched lips. "Now you. Lies and lies and lies." A sheen of tears misted her eyes.

"Go," she said. "Get out and keep away from me."

"I can't do that. You're still in danger."

Her usually warm eyes were as cold as any arctic blast. "I'll manage," she said. "I was the one who shot the intruder at the cabin."

She was right. His heart twisted into a painful knot. How many times had he argued with himself about telling her the truth? It would have been painful but nothing to the betrayal she felt now.

"I was going to tell you," he said. "I didn't know how, not after . . ."

"When? After we slept together? After you found what you wanted to find? After we opened that recipe box? After you had enough information to hurt my mother? To find the others? Is that why you tried to save her life? Not because of her or me, but because you wanted something from both of us?" Her words were bitter, her voice breaking slightly.

She turned away.

He took several steps toward her, took a resistant hand and urged her toward an exit door, leading to the stairs. And privacy. The people waiting for an elevator turned away from what must have looked like a lovers' spat.

"Please," she said.

"Just a moment."

It was obvious from her face she didn't want to go. But just as obviously, she didn't want to make more of a scene. She allowed herself to be maneuvered until the door closed behind them, then she jerked away from him.

She faced him defiantly in the dim light of the stairway.

She looked strong and beautiful and yet wounded. He'd done that.

He reached out to touch her face, and she seemed to turn to stone. He pulled her roughly to him. "Dammit, Liz. Don't do this."

"Why? Because you care about me? My mother? My father? I don't like liars. I never have. I told you that. You know how much it hurt that my mother—"

Almost desperately, he leaned down and kissed her, his mouth covering hers. He couldn't convince her with words. Perhaps—

For a moment, she didn't respond, but then that chemistry between them exploded. The kiss deepened, and her response had all the desperation of the condemned. So did his.

He hadn't completely realized how quickly she had come to mean so much to him. Everything else had faded under the impact of that attraction, of that caring. She'd awakened something long dormant in him, had made him feel alive again.

She pulled away, one tear snaking down her cheek. "That was a mistake."

"I'm sorry."

She looked up at him, her dark blue eyes swimming in

tears. "No, you're not," she said. "You're trying to manipulate me again."

"No," he replied.

"It doesn't matter anymore, anyway," she said.

But feelings were still there. He'd felt it in that momentary surrender. God, he'd felt it in the intensity of his own feelings. He wasn't in a position to press the point, though.

"What are you going to do?"

"It's no longer your concern. Stay away from me. From my father. My mother."

"I can't do that."

"I'll take out a restraining order if I must." Her chin trembled, but her eyes seared him. "I'll never trust you again. I would have understood if you had told me in the beginning. I could understand your need to find answers. Dear God, how I understand that. But you lied. Over and over again. I can't understand that."

He stood there, helpless against the onslaught. Every word was another stab in his heart. He could survive that. He was responsible. What he couldn't survive was knowing that each word was a stab in her heart as well.

In the beginning he'd been so wrapped up in his own righteousness, he hadn't thought beyond finally achieving his goal.

"I won't touch you again if that's what you want," he said. "But let me do what you wanted me to do days ago. Let me help you."

"And how will I know if you're helping me or yourself?"

"I guess you won't," he said. "Go on instinct. You have good ones."

"Right now I think my instincts are pretty bad. I trusted *you*."

He had no defense to that.

"I know it's hard to believe now," he said, "but I no longer give a damn about my so-called justice." He willed her to believe him. "I only want to keep you safe. Dammit. I couldn't keep my own family alive. But I can keep you alive. I'm going to keep you alive."

"And my family? The woman you think killed your father?"

"They matter to *you*. They matter to *me*."

"But you want to know what it was I dug up in the garden?"

Of course she would realize he knew she had found something. She'd left enough clues to alert the world. If it hadn't been for Michael Gallagher, she would have covered her tracks.

His gaze met hers. "I would be lying if I said no. It might be the key to what's happening now, why someone is after you. And your mother."

He held out a hand again. He willed her to take it. To believe in him again.

She simply stared at it.

"No," she said. "I'll discover what there is to be discovered without you."

A chilly silence surrounded them. He didn't want to go. He knew she wanted him gone. And didn't. He knew that from the agony in her eyes.

"It wasn't all a lie," he said, then turned for the door. Once there, he looked around. She stood there defiantly, her eyes fierce, and yet there was that brave vulnerability that had touched him from the very beginning.

"A bargain?" he asked. Begged, really. "I won't touch you. I won't expect you to forget, or forgive. But let me come along with you." He tried to smile. "Otherwise I'll have to find all kinds of devious ways to follow you."

"Even if I ask you not to."

"If I can find you, others can find you," he said.

She seemed to consider what he said, then refused.

"Then the only course I have is to tell the FBI what I know, that I believe you have information they want."

She glared at him. "You wouldn't."

"I would sell my soul to keep you safe."

She seemed to consider it. Then, "Only until I know what happened. And only if you swear you won't touch me again."

"Until you know what happened," he echoed in agreement. He didn't know if he could keep the last condition.

"Swear," she demanded.

He nodded.

"I won't trust you again," she warned. "Not with my heart. Not with my mind. And I'll make sure Dad and others know who I'm with."

He nodded. Knowing he couldn't hold her in his arms again, it would be pure hell accompanying her. But if he didn't swear, she might well run again.

And at least she trusted him to keep her person safe, if not her heart.

He could live with that.

Maybe.

chapter twenty-seven

CHICAGO

Liz and Caleb arrived in Chicago on the same plane but not in adjoining seats.

She'd been more than grateful to hear that there were no seats together in the crowded plane.

While she was willing to have him along for protection, she was not willing to go back to their old companionship. She'd been wounded too deeply. She was not self-destructive enough to deny that she might well need his help. A former Boston detective, he would be an asset as protection, his lack of honesty notwithstanding.

Still, she'd been unable to stop thinking of him sitting somewhere behind her, nor could she ignore him as they deplaned, and he fell into step beside her. He still made her heart race, and memories warmed intimate places deep inside her, yet when he touched her to take her bag, she involuntarily flinched. She saw emotion flicker in his eyes, but it really no longer mattered.

"Sorry," he said, his voice even.

He knew about Scarborough Fair. He knew Straw Dogs. He didn't know about the keys, which she had taken from her vest, again in a restroom before going through security, and put on a key ring. She made sure that she was in a different line than he at the inspection point, and once through she put them in her purse before he saw them.

Someone was looking for those keys. She knew Caleb was looking for whoever was looking for the keys. She knew she didn't want anyone to find—and open—the safe-deposit boxes before she discovered what was inside them.

She was, in fact, setting herself up as a tethered goat. And Caleb was the only protection she had.

She accompanied him down the long corridors of O'Hare airport, easily matching his long strides. She stopped to get a Chicago newspaper and glanced over it as Caleb rented a car. She remembered the piles of the paper. How her mother would read through them, then always flip to the want ads. It wasn't until the last few days that she had questioned that interest.

Caleb returned quickly with the rental agreement and keys. "We catch the shuttle outside," he said.

Once they reached the car, Caleb turned to her. "Where are we going?"

"To someplace where we can find a computer."

"Do you want to drive and let me direct or vice versa?"

She looked up at the face she'd cared about so much, into the green eyes that had always been so enigmatic. They were that way now. She thought she saw new lines there and for a second wanted to touch him again. But she knew where that would lead.

Not again!

He had used her. She would use him. It was that simple. She couldn't afford any more. Her emotions were already stretched to the limit, anger and disappointment and disillusionment struggling with fear and an obsession to discover the truth, to save her family, if it could be saved.

Any personal considerations took a backseat to that.

"I'll direct," she finally said, getting in the passenger side but moving as far away from him as she could. She didn't want an accidental touch. She didn't want to feel any of that intimacy that ignited like rocket fuel between them.

He pulled out into a lane that led into Chicago. "Most hotels have business centers," he said. "What did you tell Maynard, and what did he tell you?"

Silence stretched between them.

"I know you don't trust me," he finally said. "I wouldn't, if I were you. But to help, I need to know a few things."

"I'm not sure you're here to help me."

"You are, or you wouldn't be with me now," he said bluntly. "I realize I'm a last resort. But to be of any use, I have to know what Maynard knows."

"There's a trust fund," she said, watching him carefully.

His expression didn't change.

"You knew that, didn't you?" she accused him.

"Not until yesterday. I'd asked Cameron, my old partner, to check on your grandfather's will. It was in probate court records, but it had been 'misplaced.' Three months ago, your cousin asked that the trust be dissolved, that it was obvious your mother was no longer alive."

"And was it dissolved?"

"The hearing was scheduled for next week. It was canceled by Mr. Maynard three days ago."

"He didn't say anything about a hearing."

"What did he say?"

"Only that my grandfather put some of his assets in a trust for my mother and her heirs."

"Did he say how much?"

"About ten million."

He whistled. "Would she have known about it?"

"I don't know how. I doubt it. As far as I could gather, she hadn't had any communication with them since she left."

"What else did he tell you?"

"I asked him whether she had ever gone to Chicago, or had friends there. He said no, but I saw a flicker in his eyes. I decided that was where I should go. I keep remembering copies of the *Chicago Tribune*."

"Now what?"

"We look for Scarborough. It must be a community or subdivision or something."

"Give it to the police, Liz. Let them go after it."

"What if there's . . ." She stopped.

"Something that implicates her? She's already confessed, Liz. She wouldn't want you to sacrifice yourself."

"You have no say here," she said.

"I could call them."

"But you won't, will you? You owe me."

He took his eyes off the road, and his gaze caught hers for a second. "Yes, I owe you." He hesitated. "You know you might be walking into a trap?"

She did. "I can't live the rest of my life in fear. I can't let my sister worry about her children every day they go to camp or school. I don't think it will end if Mom . . . dies. I don't think it will end until we—I—find out why."

He didn't say anything else, and she was grateful. She didn't want to explain herself. She knew she was being reckless, perhaps even foolish, but she had to draw out the perpetrators of the attacks, or she and her family would never get their lives back. The police had always been an option, but whatever was in the boxes might mean the difference between life or a year or two in prison for her mother.

He drove to a hotel. She got out and went inside while he parked in the outdoor lot. She'd asked about a business center and was assured there was one.

"Adjoining rooms, please," Caleb said as he joined her. He turned toward her. "Is that okay?"

She nodded, and Caleb looked both surprised and relieved. One small—very small—victory for him. He might have a few more. But the victory in the end would be hers. It had to be.

On the way up to her room, he paused. "You gave him your credit card."

"Yes."

"You're leading them here."

"You can always leave," she said.

"You don't have a weapon yet."

"Not entirely true."

But she didn't explain, and he didn't ask.

At their rooms she used the card key to go into her room. She went inside, taking her duffel with its rather pitiful contents inside.

Minutes later she and Caleb were in the business center, seated side by side at a computer. They had only a few moments before the center closed.

She searched Chicago/Scarborough.

A hundred hits came up, but nothing that looked promising. She was still running through them when the center closed.

She would try again in the morning. In the meantime, she'd given Win Maynard information. She'd also purposely left a trail with her credit card, first on the air flight and now with the hotel. If someone truly wanted the keys, they would contact her.

And she—they—would be waiting.

Maynard recognized the number on his cell phone and flinched as he picked it up. He'd liked Liz Connor. All that youthful determination reminded him of her mother. She even had the same impulsiveness, the same recklessness that had been used so effectively against her. But that didn't matter now. Tony had him by the balls, and he wasn't going to let go.

Tony didn't bother with preliminaries. "Did you drop a hint about Chicago?"

Maynard had, in truth, tried to steer her away from Chicago. He hoped like hell she had taken him at his word. Tony was crazy.

He lied. "Yes."

"Good."

"Don't call me again," Maynard said. "I'm through."

"You'll do what I say. I still have that recording."

"Guess what, Tony? I don't give a damn." He hung up the phone and buried his face in his hands.

A knock came at the door. He didn't answer. He didn't want to see anyone. He had decisions to make.

The door opened anyway, and Michael came in.

"She's on her way to Chicago. Adams is on the same flight."

Maynard looked up at him. "I'd hoped she wouldn't do that."

"Are you going to tell me why?"

Maynard looked at him for a long time. In the past few days, he'd been coming slowly to this decision. He just hadn't been sure he could go through with it. Now he knew he had no choice. He was getting dragged deeper and deeper into murder. His main concern now was his daughters . . . and his cousins.

"Sit down, Michael," he said.

Tony found Elizabeth Connor readily enough. Too readily, perhaps.

He had friends who had police contacts. It was easy enough to track a credit card.

What concerned him was the fact that she'd seemed to avoid using them earlier. The ex-cop with her was also using his card.

He had to separate her from Adams. He thought he had gotten rid of the nosy bastard years ago.

Tony secluded himself in the economy motel he'd used for the past several days. He planned to be at Liz's hotel early in the morning. He had the advantage now. Elizabeth Connor didn't know he existed, much less how he looked. On the other hand, he knew everything about her. After this past week, he fancied he knew how she thought.

He needed sleep. Yet he also needed to move quickly. Someone—a watchman, a homeless person—might wander into the abandoned factory and find the bodies before Tony wanted them to be found. He had two days at the most. Two days to get nearly two million dollars and get out of the country. Two days before he got the last revenge.

Yet something nagged at him. Maynard's mood had been disconcerting. Perhaps he'd pressed too hard. But he knew Maynard had too much to lose to do anything too reckless. Then there was only Jacob Terrell. He was surprised that Terrell hadn't appeared before now. Tony had been sure he would already be sniffing around the money.

Perhaps he wasn't even alive. Well, he didn't need him if he could get the keys. He could figure out the rest.

He showered, washed his dark hair, and applied a reddish rinse. He would dress in a suit, change his eye color with contacts, and add a pair of glasses to change the appearance of his face.

Then he would have to find a way to separate Elizabeth Connor and Caleb Adams.

He might need some help. He knew where she was staying, but he didn't know the room number. He called a friend in Boston who gave him a name in Chicago and a phone number. In minutes, he'd made contact.

Caleb showered, first enjoying the steamy water before turning on the cold. He hadn't had any sleep in nearly forty-eight hours, and he was finding age made a difference.

He pulled on his clothes, then knocked at the door joining his room with Liz's. He wasn't sure she would open it.

She did. Apparently she had done the same as he. Her auburn hair was wet, and the bangs curled around her forehead. She wore a T-shirt just as she had in the motel after the attack at his cabin. Her eyes were luminous, her cheeks still rosy from the shower.

But the welcome that had been on her face days ago was gone.

She merely looked up at him, a question in her face, and that question had nothing to do with lust, or affection, or love.

Love. When had that become part of the equation? When the hell had it become part of his vocabulary again?

"I wondered if you want to share room service," he said.

"I've already ordered."

"We need to talk."

"We already have." Her voice was still cool, yet it wavered just slightly.

"No. Not about what happens now."

"I'm not sure I know what you mean."

"I want your promise you won't go anywhere without me."

"And why should I give you that?"

"Because I've seen too many people I care about die," he said.

She still stood in front of him, barring him from her room. Her face, usually so mobile and readable, was closed. After a slight hesitation, she nodded.

"Promise?" he persisted.

"Yes." She stood aside, admitting him to her room. "You can use my phone to call room service for yourself."

"Thank you," he said solemnly. He went over to the phone, ordered a hamburger and fries. She sat down on the bed, and he was aware of her gaze on him. That familiar heat started coiling inside. It was the worst possible thing that could happen. He couldn't be distracted. Nor could he do anything that would make her run, as she had from Santa Fe.

He sat down in one of the chairs. "After we eat," he said, "I'm going to see about getting a weapon."

Her food arrived before she could reply. He stole several French fries, then caught her gaze as she continued to watch him. Every time his gaze met hers, his heart turned over in response. He had to fight an overwhelming need to move closer to her.

When his food arrived, he concentrated on eating. At least it kept his hands from her. Then he retreated to his room. He called several people, starting with Cam and the private investigator in Boston. He was given names of two people who might help him. He struck gold on the second call, a gun dealer who agreed to meet him a few blocks from here with the weapon he wanted.

Caleb hesitated. The last thing he wanted was a weapon already used in a crime, and that was altogether too likely when dealing with shadowy dealers. But even with his status as an ex-cop, he knew he couldn't buy a weapon, much less two, without a waiting period. He would have to take the risk.

The next call was to an electronics expert who also had what he needed and was willing, for a price, to meet him at his shop if he came immediately. Caleb looked at his watch. He had just enough time to go by the shop before meeting the gun dealer.

He would have to go to an ATM as well. Maybe several. He didn't want to drag Liz along with him, especially to the meeting with the gun dealer. But he knew now it had to be her choice or their fragile truce might well end.

He knocked at her door.

"I think I've found a weapon," he said as she opened it, trying not notice how great the T-shirt looked on her. "I'll have to leave for about an hour or so. Do you want to go with me or stay here?"

He didn't want to let her out of his sight, but he felt naked and damned vulnerable without a gun.

She hesitated. She wanted to go, he saw it in her eyes. But then she backed away again. "I'll stay."

"Don't open the door to anyone," he said. "Don't even answer the phone."

She bit her bottom lip, then agreed.

"And be cautious about the cell phone. Someone might have picked up on the number. Stay on it any length of time, and they might be able to trace you."

She nodded.

"You said you had some kind of a weapon?"

"A small can of hair spray," she said. "It's as effective as pepper spray."

Neither of which were that effective against a professional with a gun unless there was an element of surprise and you were right in their face.

"Swear you won't leave the room. That you won't open it for room service, or any other reason."

She nodded. "I'll put the Do Not Disturb on the door."

"I'll do it," he said. "I don't want you to so much as poke your head out."

"I won't," she replied.

"Lock the adjoining door as well," he said. "When I get back, I'll enter through my door and knock three quick times, stop, then once more. If you hear anything else, call security."

She nodded obediently.

"I shouldn't be more than an hour and a half. If I'm not

back in two, call Cam in Boston." He handed her a card with a name and phone number scrawled across it. "He'll contact the police here and get them to move faster."

The calm in her face cracked then, and he saw what he had seen a few days earlier.

She did still care.

He wanted to touch her. Kiss her. Hug her tight.

But though she might still care, she didn't trust.

He would have to wait, to try to restore that trust.

If they both stayed alive.

She watched the door close. She wanted to go with him. She didn't want to be alone. Yet even knowing how Caleb had lied to her, she could barely breathe; he filled the room with his presence so completely. She didn't want to think about what it would do in the car. It had been hard enough earlier when her anger temporarily immunized her. Unfortunately, the immunity hadn't lasted long. Her heart thumped when he'd entered the room, and that half smile still sent jolts of awareness down her spine. She wanted nothing more than to fall into his arms again, to feel him inside her, and to believe he was all he'd seemed to be.

How had her father felt when he discovered the woman he'd loved had lied to him all these years?

He'd stayed by her side. Believed in her.

But she knew she couldn't do the same. She'd waited too long for the perfect knight. She didn't want a tarnished one. Or one that would take on the black helmet as readily as the white one.

She wanted more than that.

Maybe her father had, too.

But now it didn't seem to matter to him. Only love did.

She locked both doors, using every one of the locks, then turned on an all-news television station, mostly to pierce the loneliness she felt and to rid the room of the last remaining hiss and spit of the electricity that always arced between them.

The news was the same old, same old until she heard an update on her mother. She was still in a coma. The report included all the details of the three-decades-old crime, along with the fact that the money had never been found.

There was a certain irony that her mother was the heiress to several times the missing sum, but then from everything she knew and had heard, money had never been her mother's motivation.

Her father should know of the will as well. It would take the financial pressure off regarding legal bills. *If* he and her mother accepted it. But then she didn't know the terms of the trust.

She would ask Colton Montgomery to suggest a good independent attorney to look into it.

The phone rang. She resisted the urge to pick it up. She'd promised.

It rang and rang. Quit. Then rang again.

She'd promised.

Two hours. She would wait two hours. Then all promises were off.

chapter twenty-eight

Michael took a cab from O'Hare airport to a hotel, hoping that his employer had found the information he needed.

His stomach churned.

He'd known of Tony Woodall for years. He'd always considered him a leech that Win had tolerated for some reason. He'd warned Win several times about Tony's rumored ties to organized crime, but Win had shrugged off his concerns. "We grew up together, and attorneys represent some bad people."

Michael had ceased to worry about it. It had nothing to do with his job.

But he'd sickened at what Win had told him. Still, client-attorney relationship aside, he knew he would never use the information to hurt Maynard. His boss had been too much his mentor.

The information, though, had changed his view of his employer. He knew now that Win would never run for the Senate seat. He would be lucky to stay out of prison.

He used his cell phone in the cab. "Do you have any more information?"

"No," Win said. The usual energy was gone from his voice. He sounded defeated. "Tony Woodall seems to have disappeared."

"You'll let me know if you learn any more?"

"You'll know as soon as I do." A pause. Then, "Find them before Tony does."

• • •

Caleb drove his rental car to the electronics shop and purchased a covert tracker unit, paid by credit card, then went by three ATM machines. He used his personal bank account to withdraw the maximum allowed, then his two credit cards with which he got the maximum cash advance. He put half the cash in his pocket, the other half in his shoe, an extra precaution in dealing with someone he didn't know.

He would get more money tomorrow, after the twenty-four-hour rule expired.

The gun dealer—if you could call him that—was late. Caleb waited nearly an hour outside an adult movie theater, an area that sent all nerve endings clanging. He was just about ready to leave when a man sauntered up to him.

"Adams?" he asked.

Caleb nodded. "You're late."

"I wanted to be sure you were alone."

"I'm alone. Do you have what I need?"

"My car is over in the parking lot."

Caleb had avoided that particular lot because it was dark. But now he didn't have a lot of options and Cam's contact had vouched for the man.

He followed the dealer to the car and got in the passenger side. The dealer patted him down, then unbuttoned his shirt.

"There's no wire," he said.

"No offense intended. I don't take chances." He reached into the glove compartment, took out a revolver, and handed it to Caleb.

Caleb checked it over. It looked to be in good condition. "Is it cold?" he asked. He didn't want a weapon that had been used in a previous crime.

The dealer looked hurt. "I have a reputation to maintain. No, it isn't hot. I'm doing a favor for a friend."

"At a substantial profit."

The dealer shrugged. "I'm risking my license here, not to say a prison sentence."

"I'll take it."

"Six hundred."

"My source said three hundred."

"He said wrong. I can sell this tonight for seven. I'm doing you a favor."

Caleb had intended to buy a second one for Liz, but he didn't have enough cash with him.

He handed over six hundred.

"Good doing business with you," the dealer said.

"I bet," Caleb muttered under his breath. He looked at his watch. He had said he would be back in two hours. It was nearly that now. He prayed Liz wouldn't get impatient as he trotted to his car.

An hour crawled by. Then another thirty minutes.

Liz watched the clock as if her life depended on it. And maybe it did.

And perhaps Caleb's as well.

He would be back if he could. She knew that with every fiber of her being. He had lied to her about his motives, but he'd always been there when she'd needed him.

What if something had happened to him? Even she knew buying guns on the streets of Chicago must be a dangerous, as well as illegal, business.

The television was still on, this time turned to local news. Life was going on. Murder, mayhem, and yet a heartwarming story about a school class gathering school supplies for their counterparts in Iraq.

But even as she tried to concentrate, she kept seeing the lanky form of Caleb Adams, the permanent half smile on his face, his eyes hiding so much of himself. She'd been so angry. But she didn't want anything to happen to him, especially when he was working on her behalf.

Or was it his own?

Would she ever know?

The phone rang again. She itched to answer it. What if it was Caleb? But certainly he wouldn't use that phone when he'd told her not to answer. Who would be calling?

She looked at the clock radio again. Fifteen more minutes.

She felt like a cat on a hot tin roof. She was about to

jump out of her skin. Time had never moved so slowly. *Please God, let him return.*

She looked at the telephone. The message light was on. Surely it would be okay to pick up a message. Perhaps from him.

It's not the same thing as answering the phone.

She read the instructions, then pressed the buttons for message retrieval.

A New England accent came across. "There is a letter for Ms. Connor at the desk. Please pick it up alone and follow the instructions if you want to know about your mother."

It cut off then.

She debated about saving it. That would be the smart thing to do. A voice identification, if needed. But then perhaps Caleb would hear it and take matters into his own hands. Was his interest still principally in her mother? Or in her?

She just didn't know. She wanted to believe it was the latter. She wanted to believe more than anything. But the doubt was like a fast-growing seed.

Still, she saved it.

Two minutes later, she heard a sound from the other room, then the tap, tap, tap, silence, tap on the adjoining door. She looked at the blinking light on the telephone, then opened the door and went into his room before he could come into hers.

He'd never looked so good to her. She looked at her watch. Two hours and one minute.

He gave her a wry look. "Sorry, I'm late."

"Did you get what you wanted?"

He pulled up a pant leg, and she saw the ankle holster with a gun inside.

"Could you find one for me?"

"I tried. It was more cash than I had with me. Promises and checks don't impress these guys." His gaze searched her face.

"I was beginning to worry," she admitted.

"About me, I hope."

"About getting a gun," she corrected.

He gave her a brief nod, but something flickered in his eyes.

She wanted to step toward him. It took all her will to stay where she was. That electricity was hissing again, snapping between them, heating the air around them.

The green in his eyes darkened. "Liz?"

Her phone rang.

"It's been doing that since you left," she said.

"Answer it," he said.

She went into the room quickly and picked up the phone before he saw the red light. She wasn't sure yet whether she was going to share that information with him.

She picked it up. "Yes?" she said.

"This is the desk. We have a message downstairs for you."

"Thank you," she said.

He looked at her quizzically.

She made up her mind. There was no way she could do this alone, especially without a weapon. "There's a message downstairs for me. There was one earlier on my phone. Someone with a New England accent. He said there was a message and to come alone if I wanted more information about my mother."

His gaze told her that he realized that she'd not decided to tell him that. His lips tightened.

"He's probably down there, you know. He knows what you look like. You don't have any idea of what he looks like."

She didn't have to ask who "he" was. "He" was whoever was behind the violence that had engulfed her. "He" had tried to kill her mother, had tried to kill her, had terrorized her sister. And "he" expected her to wander out alone to meet him. Or it might be someone "he" hired.

But would he share information about her mother with a hired hand?

Was "he" as desperate as she was?

He looked at the clock. It was past midnight. The lobby would be empty.

"Give me about ten minutes," he said, "then call the desk and ask them to have someone bring it up to you."

She nodded.

"I have something for you first," he said. He took a tiny object out of his pocket and gave it to her. She looked up at him.

"It's a covert tracker. If we lose contact with each other, I can find you through this. Keep it somewhere safe."

"My bra?"

"I think it would be most appropriate," he said with the first hint of a smile she'd seen since the last day in Santa Fe. She didn't realize how much she'd missed that rare smile.

Without a word, she slipped the tiny button into her bra.

"Lock the door when I leave," he said. "When someone knocks, call down to the desk and make sure it's someone from the hotel."

Caleb took the elevator down to the ground floor and stepped out. The lobby area was nearly empty. One man was at the bell stand. Two people were behind the desk. The gift shop and restaurant were closed, but a lobby bar was still open. Three men sat at the bar, and one couple draped over each other at a table.

He saw someone at the desk answer the phone, then gesture to the man at the bell stand. He handed him an envelope, and the bellman turned toward the elevator. No one followed.

Caleb wandered into the bar area, ordered a beer, and took a very small sip as he looked over the occupants. One of the men was on a cell phone. Another was staring bleakly at what looked like a glass of scotch. He started a conversation with the man next to him, discovering there was a medical supplies conference under way.

His gaze went back to the man who had been on the cell phone. He was wearing a sports shirt and tan slacks, but he was little too alert for a tired conference attendee. "You with the convention, too?" he asked.

He nodded, but he wasn't wearing a badge, and the other two were.

A very bad feeling settled in his gut.

He stood, tossed a ten dollar bill down, and hurried toward the elevator. He had to wait several precious seconds. He used his cell phone to call her.

The phone rang and rang. He turned. The man was gone from the bar. Calling himself all kinds of an idiot, he willed the elevator to return. It finally did.

The damned elevator stopped at two floors before going on up. Someone from the workout room. Someone else apparently attending another conference. He had a plastic glass filled with what looked like champagne in his hand.

Caleb finally reached the eighth floor, ran out the door and down to his room. He opened it.

The adjoining door was closed. Locked. He used the knock he had given her. Silence.

His gut twisted.

He called downstairs for someone to unlock her door, but he knew it wouldn't make a difference. She was gone.

chapter twenty-nine

Liz heard the knock on the door, called the front desk, and was told a bellman was on his way. She unlocked all but the chain lock, peered outside, saw the uniform, the envelope in his hand. She closed the door and slid off the chain.

She opened the door. A man dressed in a bellman's jacket shoved his way inside, a gun in his hand.

He held it on her as he looked around, saw the duffel and purse. "Get them," he said. She was stunned for a second, but he gave her no time to think. "Now," he demanded.

She did as ordered, slipping the purse onto her shoulder and clutching the duffel. He pulled her to him and put the gun to her neck. "We're going down the stairs," he said. "Fast. And believe me, I won't hesitate to shoot."

Liz didn't argue. She prayed he wouldn't check her pockets and find the can of hair spray or feel her bra where she'd put the tracker. The vest with the keys was in the duffel. That was her bargaining chip. The only one she had.

Don't panic. She kept telling herself that as he pushed her to the exit door and down the stairs. As he hustled her out, she tried to get a better glance at him. Looked for weaknesses even as stark fear wrapped around her. He was older, probably in his late fifties, though his hair was reddish. Probably dyed. He wore casual clothes well, and he was smooth shaven. But he had the coldest eyes she had ever seen.

With the gun at her neck, she had few options. The end of the barrel was cold. Hard. She tried to tell herself that she had something he wanted. She was safe until he got it. She had to make sure that took as long as possible.

Caleb would find her.

They reached the bottom floor, then the exit doors leading out the back of the hotel. He'd put one arm around her neck and shoved the pistol into her back.

He had her open the passenger side of the car, and as she started to get inside, pain exploded in her head, and everything went back.

Michael was halfway through the list of hotels before he located her. It worried him that he had found it. He wondered if she knew other people were still looking for her as well. God, he hoped so. He also hoped that Adams, regardless of his motives, was as good a cop as everyone had said he was.

He knew he was walking a thin line. He had been appalled when Win had told him everything. At least, he hoped to hell it was everything. He was caught in the classic dilemma: his obligation to his client when he knew that a crime might be committed.

It was really quite clear legally. He had an obligation to stop the crime. Still, his obligation went beyond the usual. Win Maynard had his loyalty and respect as well as obligation. He'd done a lot of good in the past twenty years, and Michael owed him his career. Demanding as he'd been, Win Maynard had been more a father than his own father had been.

He would worry about the legalities and morality later. Right now he had to get to Adams and Liz and make them aware of what they were up against.

He left the Palmer House and took a cab to the hotel that listed Liz Connor as a guest. He only hoped it wasn't another feint on her part. As he arrived, he went to the house phone and asked for Liz Connor's room. As he waited for someone to answer, he saw Adams hurry out of the elevator at a near run and head for the door, urgency in every movement.

Michael dropped the phone and followed him, catching up with him at a car. "What's wrong?" he asked as he reached out a hand to stop Adams from opening the door.

Adams went into a crouch, ready to spring, but Michael had been in enough street fights as a kid to instinctively duck the fist driving at him.

"Listen to me," Michael said sharply. "I have information you need."

Adams straightened, recognized him then, and Michael realized the attempted punch had been instinctive, not necessarily against him.

"Gallagher! Did you have anything to do with Liz's disappearance?"

"She's gone?"

"Just a few minutes ago." His eyes were full of suspicion.

"I didn't know. I've been trying to find you two. There's information you should have."

Indecision hovered in Adams's eyes. Then, "Got a weapon with you?"

"No."

"Raise your arms."

Adams quickly frisked him, then said, "Get in the car."

Michael got into the passenger's side as Adams got in the driver's seat and started the engine. He handed Michael a map and a cell phone.

"Find our location on the map and follow the directions on the cell phone. They should come every two minutes."

Michael didn't ask any questions. In just a moment, he had marked their location with a pen. Then he asked, "What happened?"

"You first. You said you have information."

"The man after the Connor family is Tony Woodall."

Adams took his eyes off the road to glance at him. Surprise was in his face. "The Tony Woodall who shilled for the Italian Mafia?"

"That's the one."

"Why?"

"It's a long story. The short answer is that he planned the armed robbery all those years ago. He's the one that most likely shot the two guards."

"How do you know that?"

The cell phone beeped. Michael picked it up, wrote down something, and marked it on the map. "Turn right at the next main intersection."

Michael continued. "I have a question of my own. What are we following?"

"A covert tracking device."

"Where is it?"

"On Liz."

"You're using her as a decoy?"

"Not me. She insisted on coming here. With me or without me. The tracker was a precaution on my part."

"When did she disappear?" Michael asked.

"Minutes before you arrived. I had to get out before there were questions. I imagine there's a dead or unconscious bellman somewhere in that hotel."

"Where were *you?*"

"She received a message. I went downstairs to see if I noticed anyone lingering about waiting for her to pick it up. She wasn't to open the door without checking with the desk to see whether a bellman was on his way with it. When I got back up, she was gone. Along with her purse and duffel."

"Maybe she went on her own?"

"If she had, we wouldn't be receiving that signal. She would have ditched it. Now it's your turn. How do you know about Tony Woodall?"

"Whatever I tell you is hearsay," Michael said. "I can't testify against my client."

"Then Maynard *is* involved."

Michael hesitated, then said, "Not exactly."

The phone beeped again. Michael gave him new directions.

"Tell me more," Adams said. "If I don't like what I hear, I'm dropping you on the nearest corner."

"Maynard's father worked for his brother, the CEO of Maynard Shipping. He headed sales. Apparently he embezzled some money and was fired and disowned by his brother. The stain applied to Win Maynard as well. The old man cut off funds for Maynard's education and made it clear he wouldn't be welcomed into the business. Win's father died a few months later in a drunk driving accident.

"Win Maynard blamed his uncle for everything. He had to drop out of law school, and his mother was broken." He stopped and stared out at the nearly empty street.

"Go on," Caleb said.

"He wanted retribution. He thought his father had been falsely accused, and his mother should have at least some shares of Maynard Shipping. The best revenge, he believed, was to show the old man that his precious daughter was no better."

"And so he set her up?" Adams said.

"He knew Tony slightly. Tony had been a freshman at Harvard when Win was at Harvard Law School. Tony had his fingers into everything, even then. Stealing tests. Writing papers for students. Drugs. Through the latter he got involved in the antiwar movement. He was charismatic and soon became a leader. Maynard put Sarah Jane in his path and told Tony that he would make it worth his while if Sarah Jane was arrested and humiliated."

The cell phone rang again. More directions. Tony told him to turn right on a freeway. They were leaving downtown Chicago.

"Go on," Adams said.

Michael hesitated. Win had given him permission to say what he had said so far, but now he was going further. He needed Adams's trust. And he had to trust Adams.

"Tony did as asked. He put himself in Sarah Jane's way, courted her, flattered her for her strength of purpose, her dedication to helping end a horrible war. Apparently he could be quite charming then. He led her deeper into his private little cell. She was arrested once, and her father warned her, but that wasn't enough for Win. Not then."

He glanced at Caleb. "You should know about that kind of need."

Caleb didn't answer, but a muscle throbbed in his throat, and Michael knew he'd hit a nerve.

"So Tony came up with another plan, a more extreme one. He was thoroughly into the game by then, enjoying the manipulation of Sarah Jane and other disciples he'd gathered in his web. What Win didn't know was that Tony was taping every conversation."

The phone beeped again. Michael traced it on the map, then gave directions to Caleb. They were getting closer.

Michael continued. "Tony heard about a group of anti-war activists holding up an armored car in New York. It put ideas in his head. Win worked at a bank then and could get information about routes.

"When Win protested, Tony produced the tapes he'd made, said he would take them to Win's uncle. He knew that would be the end of any hope he would have to get any part of the family fortune, as well as involve him in a conspiracy. He gave Tony what he wanted after being assured no one would be hurt."

Caleb's jaw had tightened. "He's been blackmailing Maynard."

"Yes."

"And why are you still loyal to the son of a bitch?"

"Maynard isn't a villain. He did something stupid when he was young and bitter. He's paid for it all these years. He doesn't want anyone else dead because of him."

"A pretty defense," Adams said bitterly.

Michael glanced at Caleb. "I know your father was killed, but the robbery would have happened anyway. Perhaps Sarah Jane wouldn't have been involved, but others would have. Tony meant to keep the money for himself. All of it. He couldn't afford to let the driver, his contact, live. Nor could he allow the other guard to live."

Caleb was jolted by the statement. *"He couldn't afford to let the driver, his contact, live."* His father had not been the driver that day. At least one reputation would be repaired this day.

"Sorry, but I don't buy Maynard as a victim. Woodall never would have had the names and routes without Maynard, would he?"

Michael had no answer for that one.

"Tell me more about Tony Woodall. I was aware of him

when I was with the Boston PD. I even checked him out when I was looking into the robbery, because he was a leader in the antiwar protests, but I never found anything connecting him to Sarah Jane."

"He was careful. He's always been careful, according to Win. Always watching his back. Secrecy was probably one of the attractions for Sarah Jane. A secret, outlaw romance."

"And today?"

"Tony has never made it big. Too many skeletons. No convictions but a lot of rumors. He's on the fringes of the Mafia. They don't really trust outsiders, though he made himself useful enough to use their resources. He's lived on blackmail, but he knew just how far he could push Maynard. Nearly two million would take him a long way away from here."

"How did Sarah Jane's fingerprints get on the weapon?"

"I don't know that. Neither does Win. Only she—and the other participants—know."

"Why were you sent to Albuquerque?"

"To help Sarah Jane. Guilt has racked Win all these years."

"He also wanted to know what she knew and what she was going to say," Caleb interjected.

"That, too," Michael admitted, "until the killing continued."

"And there *is* the trust fund," Caleb said. "You conveniently left that out."

"Win didn't try to hide it. I didn't have a chance to talk to Sarah Jane about it."

"You could have told her husband or daughters. Or her attorney. Instead you appeared like Daddy Warbucks offering a handout. No wonder they were suspicious."

"He told Liz in Boston."

"Too late." Caleb's voice was harsh.

And it was. Michael knew that as well. He didn't know why Maynard hadn't asked him to mention it to the Connors immediately.

The phone beeped again. Michael read the coordinates, looked at the map. "Turn left the next exit."

"Where do you fit into all this now?" Adams asked.

"I want to fix what can be fixed," Michael said. "I want to save what I can of Maynard Industries, what will be left of his reputation."

"I won't be silent about him."

"I didn't suppose you would. Neither did Maynard."

As they turned off the interstate, Michael thought about Liz. He hadn't stopped thinking about her, but the more he'd tried to explain, the more apprehension he felt. Tony Woodall had always been a killer, but now he was a desperate one. "We should call the police," he said.

"We don't know exactly where we're going yet, and a lot of sirens might just spook him."

Michael reluctantly agreed. "How do you know he won't just kill her anyway?"

"He thinks she has something he wants. She knows that. She's smart as hell."

Michael hadn't prayed in a long time, but he did now. He prayed she was smart enough. And that Caleb Adams was right.

Liz woke to blinding pain. She tried to move, but every effort resulted in greater pain. In her arms. In her legs. Something seemed to be smothering her. *Be calm.* She forced herself to take inventory. She lay on her stomach, her hands tied behind her, as well as her feet, and a rope apparently connected the two. Every time she tried to move, the pain increased.

But her clothes were still on, as well as the device taped inside her bra.

Caleb would not be far behind. She knew that.

She also knew he would fight a band of rogues for her. Not because he wanted justice for an old wrong. Because he cared about her. Even loved her. She'd seen it in his eyes tonight.

And with that, an immense calm settled over her.

She tried not to move, because the ropes bit into her skin. Her head pounded with every bump of the car. She tried to relax her body, but it was too sore.

The ride became rougher as if tires were running over uneven pavement. The car stopped. She heard the sound of metal creaking. Then he was back in the car, and it moved a short distance. He was out again. The sound of metal again. In another minute or so, he stopped again. The back door opened, and she was pulled out. Hobbled, she fell.

Her attacker cut the ropes binding her ankles, pulled her to her feet. They didn't want to work. They were weak. Aching. She stumbled.

He stopped, waited for a moment. She took those seconds to look around. A nearly full moon illuminated a huge building just feet in front of her. It looked sad. Windows were broken. Glass lay on the ground. Weeds grew in cracks in the pavement. A tall wire fence protected the property. She didn't see the road. It meant they were parked in the back.

He pushed her forward again, through a door into the building. He turned on a flashlight then, and told her to follow the beam. Her hands were still tied tightly behind her, her legs still unsteady.

Then he stopped and gestured to a chair. She saw stains on it, and there was a smell that repulsed her. Still, she did as she was told. Obedience would buy her time. And talk. *Keep him talking.*

He wrapped the rope from her ankles around her chest, anchoring her to the chair.

"Who are you?" she asked. "What do you want?"

"I understand you might have found something in your garden," he said, flashing the beam of the light into her eyes.

How did he know? Caleb had been there. And Michael Gallagher.

"I was digging up herbs," she said.

"You came to Chicago for a reason."

"My mother subscribed to the *Chicago Tribune*. I thought there had to be a reason."

"Nothing more? Nothing like, say, keys?"

"What keys?"

He slapped her sideways against her ropes. Her ears rang, and her eyes blurred with tears.

"Don't play games with me. Tell me what I want to know, and I'll let you go."

But he wouldn't. She knew that. She saw it in his eyes. She knew it when he'd allowed her to see his face. The moment she told him what he wanted to know, she would die.

"Who are you?" she asked.

An amused look came over his face. "An old friend of your mother's."

"Terry Colby? Stuart Marshall? Jacob Terrell?"

"Did your mother tell you about them?"

"She didn't tell me anything."

"Then how do you know? That damned detective?"

She had gotten him off subject, but the menace in his voice told her Caleb meant something to him.

"Why do you think he knows anything?"

"He snooped in my business. He . . ."

Her blood chilled. "He what?" she asked, wanting to know more, wanting to keep his mind off her for a few more minutes.

"He paid big time for his interference," he said.

Shock dulled the pain. Shock and horror. "My God! You killed his wife and son."

He shrugged. "It was meant for him."

"I thought they found—"

"A patsy with a convenient grudge. Now just how much more do you know?"

"How is my mother's cousin involved?" She struggled to keep her voice steady, to keep the tremble of fear from it. He had just admitted murder to her. There was no doubt now that he intended to kill her.

When would Caleb arrive? She strained to hear the sound of sirens. But there was none. Then her ears caught a faint noise, some movement. She shuffled her feet. Coughed. Just in case . . .

Please God, please be Caleb.

Please be safe.

•   •   •

"It has to be over there," Michael said, pointing to a high fence and a stark brick building beyond it.

Caleb saw a driveway leading to a closed gate and drove up. It had a No Trespassing sign on it. Another sign, proclaiming the property as Keller Manufacturing, had been disfigured by graffiti. Caleb got out and checked the gate. It was unlocked. The ground beneath looked as if dirt had been recently scraped away.

"Keller Manufacturing," Michael said in a tight voice. "It's one of Maynard's companies. He closed the factory and moved the manufacturing overseas."

He drove inside, not bothering to close the gate, then parked the car and looked at Michael, wondering what use he might be. Or whether he might be with the bad guys after all.

He'd accepted Gallagher's help because he knew he couldn't read the coordinates and map and drive at the same time. He had listened to Gallagher's story, and his instincts told him the man was on the level. Still, a seed of doubt remained in him. And without a gun, he wouldn't be of much help.

"Call the police," he said. "Tell them you're the agent of the owner, that there seem to be trespassers. Ask them not to use sirens and to open the gate."

He waited while Michael made the call. When the attorney finished, Caleb told him to wait outside the gate. "Tell them you heard a scream and believe someone is holding a hostage inside. Make them aware there's an ex-cop in there with a gun."

"I want to go in with you."

"Without a gun, you're more danger to me—and Liz—than help." He didn't wait for an answer but got out of the car. He took the revolver from his ankle holster and walked around the building. There was an empty loading dock there, and a vast parking area. He saw a car, then a door next to the loading dock. He moved swiftly to the door, tried it slowly. Softly. Felt it give. It was unlocked.

A hard fist of fear grew in his stomach. Not for himself but for Liz. He'd been a fool to let her come to Chicago. A worse fool for leaving her alone in the hotel even for a few moments. Would he ever stop making mistakes about people he loved? Another mistake could kill her.

One woman had died because of him. He didn't intend another one to do the same. He slipped inside, only too aware he had no flashlight with him. It was completely dark inside. He stood still for a moment, letting his eyes adjust to the darkness. His ears strained to pick up any sound. There was the scurry of an animal, probably a rat. Nothing more.

After several seconds, he could see outlines. A door. He moved slowly toward it, exploring the floor with his foot before moving. The last thing he needed was to stumble or crash into something. He opened the door a crack and heard a soft voice. Her voice. It trembled slightly, but he heard her asking questions. He heard his name mentioned, and he froze as he heard the replies.

"You killed his wife and son."

"It was meant for him."

Blood roared in his ears. He wanted to hurl himself at the man who'd killed his wife and son, but he couldn't, not until he knew more. He opened the door wider and saw a beam of a light shining on Liz, sitting tied in a chair. Her captor's back was to him, and he didn't know whether the perp held a gun as well as the flashlight.

He knew she couldn't see him. The light was in her face.

He didn't dare move, not without knowing what was around his feet, nor could he shoot without knowing what was in the perp's hand. If his finger was on the trigger, he could well shoot her, even if Caleb's shot was perfect.

"You have your chance now," he said and, as expected, the perp swung around, an automatic in his hand. Caleb moved quickly to the side, forcing Woodall to turn and step away from Liz. He was aiming when the beam turned toward him, blinding him. He heard the crash of a chair against cement, then a shot.

The light went out.

He hadn't been hit. He heard a scrambling sound, another curse.

He threw himself toward the sound. His body hit muscle and flesh. He went for the throat. His adversary tried to kick him in the groin, but Caleb rolled over him.

Then he saw the gun. Caleb reached for it. Woodall took that second of distraction to loosen the hold on his throat and direct a fist at Caleb's gut. Caleb took the blow but didn't let go.

Then he heard the sound, "Police. Everyone drop your guns."

Caleb recognized Michael's voice. He didn't know whether his opponent had. He wondered where in the hell the police really were.

"I repeat. Drop your guns," came the voice again. It reverberated with authority. Woodall took one last lunge for the automatic, leaving himself open, and Caleb used his arm to strike across on his neck. Woodall went still.

Caleb searched for the flashlight. Found it. Turned it on.

He could hear the faint sound of sirens as he swept the room with the flashlight. Tony Woodall was still on the floor. Liz was tied to a chair, which had fallen sideways.

He'd realized immediately that she had thrown herself, and the chair, toward Woodall to deflect his shot. She had probably saved his life at the risk of her own.

He righted the chair and untied her. He leaned down. "You never quit, do you?"

Then he called out, "Gallagher, get in here."

Michael Gallagher appeared beside him.

"I thought I told you to wait outside."

"You did," Gallagher said. "But I thought you might need some help. Impersonating the police worked the last time I tried it."

He heard Liz giggle. It was a hysterical giggle, rightfully deserved. He loved the sound of it. Hell, he even liked Gallagher.

He helped Liz to her feet, pulling her next to him, knowing the exultation of having her there. He kept his arm around her, steadying her as the sound of the sirens grew louder.

"Didn't you tell them not to use sirens?" Caleb asked.

Michael shrugged. "I did. No one listens to an attorney."

Woodall groaned and moved.

"The bastard's alive," Caleb said.

"Not for long."

The three of them turned toward the sound of a new, unfamiliar voice coming from the darkness.

A figure emerged into the circle of light, a gun in his hand. He seemed indifferent to anyone but the man on the floor.

"I found Terry and Stuart," he said with a slight smile on his lips. "I knew I was next. I followed you here. I found their bodies. I was waiting for you to come back."

Before Caleb could move, the man pumped three shots into Tony Woodall just as police officers streamed into the room, yelling for all of them to fall to the floor. The newcomer didn't react. Shots rang out and he dropped to the floor.

The number of police officers and federal agents multiplied as morning dawned. Caleb couldn't take his hands off Liz, and Michael was proving how good an attorney he was. He answered endless questions, countered every hostile accusation, and turned Caleb and Liz into heroes.

The man who'd kidnapped Liz was dead. The one who'd suddenly appeared was badly wounded. Before an ambulance had taken him away, he'd identified the dead man as Tony Woodall. He'd also said that Woodall had been the one who killed the two guards in the robbery decades ago. And he said it before a number of witnesses.

Caleb walked Liz outside into the dawn. Three of the five involved in his father's death were dead. Jacob Terrell was critically wounded. The last one—Sarah Jane—was in a coma.

He should have felt triumph. He didn't. Instead there was an infinite sadness for lives lost. Four young people had been destroyed more than thirty years ago for a cause they thought noble and a leader who had betrayed them. They'd lived on, but in the shadow of fear.

He looked down at Liz and saw her gaze on his face.

He touched her cheek, then her hair. He thought how

fine they felt. But the true beauty was in her spirit. She'd fought like the hounds of hell for those she loved. She'd fought for her mother. Unmindful of any injury to herself, she'd thrown herself against Woodall to save him.

Caleb had never felt so small, so unworthy. He'd allowed hate to rule his life since his father died. He'd disguised it with the badge, with noble words that had meant nothing.

Her hand squeezed his.

She knows.

She knows and she loves.

She loves well. He remembered her saying that about her mother. But Liz must have learned the lesson well. And he hoped he could, too.

His cell phone rang.

He answered it.

"Steven Connor. I've been trying to reach my daughter. Do you know where she is?"

Wordlessly, he handed the phone to her, watched as worry creased her bruised face, then joy flood it.

"Thank God," she whispered. "I'll be there as soon as I can."

She gave him back the phone. "Mom's come out of the coma. She's going to be okay."

He wrapped his arms around her, sharing her joy. Betty Connor would be okay. He would fight for her, just as long and hard as he'd fought against her.

He hugged her close to him. He'd almost lost her. As he had lost others.

She looked up at him. "I knew you would come. I knew you would be there."

He wanted to kiss her. He wanted to keep her in his arms and never let go. But he couldn't. "I've always been a Jonah," he said in a ragged voice. "My father. My wife. My son."

She reached out and touched his cheek. "You aren't a Jonah," she said softly. "You've had more grief than most. But it wasn't your doing."

But the words he'd heard inside the factory said otherwise. "I was after revenge. I thought the bombing was because of my job. It wasn't. It was because I couldn't let go." The knowledge twisted inside him.

She reached up and kissed him, so tenderly. "You wanted to right a wrong. Don't ever be ashamed of that."

He was aware that she was touching his cheek as well. Wiping something from it. A tear.

He'd never cried. Not once.

Until now.

"I love you," she said.

The last walls crumbled. Another tear came down, but he didn't care. For the first time since he was seven years old, he was free.

And right in front of Michael Gallagher and numerous police officers and med techs and federal agents, he kissed her. Long and hard.

And forever.

epilogue

Two Years Later

A Welcome Home banner stretched across the wall in the living room of the home of Steven and Betty Connor.

Liz tipped her head and examined her sign with her sister as their husbands stood on ladders, waiting to tape the banner to the wall.

"They'll be here soon," Sue said nervously.

"It's okay," Liz said. "Tape it."

In seconds the ladders were down and put away, and Liz went to the window. Caleb joined her, draping an arm around her shoulders.

"It'll be good to have her back," she said nervously.

He leaned down and kissed her. "I know."

"She'll love Sarah Ann."

As if she knew her name was being mentioned, the four-month-old Sarah Ann gurgled behind them. Liz slipped around Caleb and picked her up. Blue eyes stared back, and the tiny mouth puckered into a smile.

She was Liz's miracle. Another miracle had been Caleb's suggestion that they name her Sarah, after Liz's mother. It had been his final step in letting go of the past.

The first step had been fighting for her mother in court, testifying for her and asking for probation. The Massachusetts judge hadn't been willing to go that far, but he did settle on a short sentence. Jacob Terrell had given a deathbed confession that Tony Woodall was the shooter in the armed robbery, and the others thought blanks were in their pistols. Sarah Jane's fingerprints were on the gun because Tony had handed her the gun just prior to the robbery to hold for him. Tony had been wearing gloves.

Betty Connor's unblemished reputation during the past thirty-three years helped as did the return of all but forty thousand dollars of the money taken in the robbery. So did the letter that she'd left in the fourth safe-deposit box that included a minute-by-minute account of what had happened. In case anything happened to her, she wanted to help the others.

She'd also testified in court that she hadn't said anything immediately after her arrest because of a whisper on her first night in jail by a guard, the same one who had guarded her hospital room. He had told her there would be a fire at her daughter's house, and if she said anything, anything at all, her daughters would die. It wasn't until after Tony's death that she felt she could say anything.

The two years in prison, she told Liz during one of her visits, helped ease the guilt she carried all those years, the images that had never gone away, the horror that someone she thought she loved could callously kill two human beings, the grief she'd caused her parents. She'd tried to compensate just a little by teaching reading to other inmates and starting a writing program. She intended to continue, if permitted, in New Mexico prisons.

But now she was coming home. Steve had been commuting back and forth for two years, going whenever there was a school holiday and now, finally accompanying her back.

Win Maynard had been charged as an accessory before and after the fact. He'd also admitted stealing money from Sarah Jane's trust fund to expand Maynard Industries. Although he replaced the money later, an audit would have revealed the original theft.

After a judge listened to hordes of witnesses and the fact that he had tried to prevent a murder and thereby incriminated himself, Maynard received probation, a huge fine, and a thousand hours of community service. He had to resign from his position as CEO of Maynard Industries and was replaced by men he'd trained.

Liz thought of the trust fund and smiled. Some of it was in Maynard Industries stock, and her mother hadn't wanted to touch that, afraid it might bring down company stock and hurt the thousands of people who worked for the firm.

Neither did her mother or father want any penny of a fund established in grief by her father. Instead, Betty Connor wanted some good to come from it, especially for women's shelters. She'd learned in prison the desperation of so many women caught in abusive relationships.

Any dividends from Maynard Industries would go with the remainder of the estate into a charitable trust fund. Michael Gallagher, who had gone into private practice, had visited her mother regularly and had been instrumental in establishing the trust. He'd become almost a member of the family in the months following the shooting in Chicago and the ensuing legalities.

"Liz?"

Still holding little Sarah, she went to the window as her father's car turned into the driveway. Caleb put his arm around her, and she leaned back against him, secure in his love. He'd expanded the cabin, and she lived there with him, even as she had commuted to Santa Fe Adventures until Sarah was born. Now she left most of it to Tracy, though she went in a few days a week, Sarah in tow. The business was thriving. Tracy had married one of the guides, and together they ran the company as well as she could.

Her mother stepped out of the car. Her hair was short and far grayer than it had been. She weighed less, but her smile was huge as she clutched her husband's hand.

Sue opened the door and hugged their mother, and then she was swamped by Sue's two children and David. Her mother's gaze, though, kept going to her new granddaughter.

Liz handed Sarah to her. Her mother gazed down at her namesake, hugged her tenderly, then looked up at Caleb. "Thank you," she said with tears in her eyes.

Caleb simply nodded in reply. He was still a man of few words.

Liz turned around, stood on tiptoes, and kissed him.

The lines were still there, but his eyes were no longer shuttered. He'd learned to love again, and there was joy in the loving, not fear. He would, she knew, always be protective, always a little afraid for her, but it wasn't the terrible black hole it had once been.

His arms went around her, and he hugged her tightly.

"Yes," she whispered into his ear, "thank you."

His eyes softened. Glowed with love. "Ah no, Sport," he said, having adopted her father's nickname for her. "None of that."

"Okay," she replied with a seductive smile. "Still, I would like to express it. Later?"

He didn't have to ask what she meant. But the green in his eyes deepened. "You're on."

She grinned, then the two clasped hands and joined the celebration.

Of love, of life, of forgiveness.

Historical romance from
USA Today bestselling author

PATRICIA
POTTER

Beloved Impostor
0-425-198014

Dancing With a Rogue
0-425-19100-1

The Scottish Trilogy:
The Black Knave
0-515-12864-3

The Heart Queen
0-515-13098-2

The Diamond King
0-515-13332-9

**Available wherever books are sold or at
www.penguin.com**